White Crane Wisdom Series

White Crane Institute's guiding principle: "fostering the gathering and dissemination of information about the critical role sexuality and gender has played and continues to play in the development of cultural, spiritual and religious traditions and to provide a nurturing environment for the continuation and expansion of those explorations for the greater good of all society."

As Gay people we bear wisdom. As Gay people we create culture. White Crane is proud to present these valuable treasures through our Gay Wisdom Series. Our aim is to provide you with fine books of insight, discernment and spiritual discovery.

Also by Toby Johnson

The Myth of the Great Secret
In Search of God in the Sexual Underworld
Plague: A Novel About Healing
Getting Life in Perspective
An Appreciation of Joseph Campbell
Gay Spirituality
Gay Perspective
Secret Matter
Two Spirits (with Walter L. Williams)

Also by Steve Berman

Trysts
Vintage: A Ghost Story

Charmed Lives
Gay Spirit in Storytelling

edited by

Toby Johnson & Steve Berman

white crane institute

Printed in the United States of America
Cover photo by Kip Dollar
Cover design copyright © 2006 by Sou MacMillan

Published as a trade paperback original
by Lethe Press, 102 Heritage Avenue, Maple Shade, NJ 08052
lethepress@aol.com
www.lethepressbooks.com

First U.S. edition, 2006

Library of Congress Cataloging-in-Publication Data

Charmed lives : gay spirit in storytelling / edited by Toby Johnson & Steve Berman. -- 1st U.S. ed.
     p. cm. -- (White crane wisdom series)
   ISBN 1-59021-016-6 (alk. paper)
   1. Gay men--Fiction. 2. Gay men--Literary collections. 3. Gay men's writings, American. I. Johnson, Edwin Clark. II. Berman, Steve.
   PS648.H57C5 2006
   813'.0108358'086642--dc22
                                        2006036383

White Crane Institute is a 501(c)(3) education corporation, committed to the certainty that gay consciousness plays a special and important role in the evolution of life on Earth. White Crane Institute publishes White Crane, the Journal of Gay Wisdom & Culture. Your contributions and support are tax-deductible to the fullest extent of the law. White Crane Institute, 172 Fifth Avenue, Suite 69, Brooklyn NY 11217.

Table of Contents

more...

Charmed Lives

Introduction
Straw into Gold: Storytelling as Self-fulfilling Prophecy

Toby Johnson

"Let me tell you a story…" These are words as potent as the creative declaration in Genesis: "Let there be light." For in just the same way that from the light (of the Big Bang) flowed all that now exists materially, so from the stories told through the ages, the world of human experience has been created.

Everything we know we learned from "stories" others told us: about experience, about life, about meaning, about love and sex, about God and the whole of the cosmos.

Some stories scared us—like those about "the boogeyman" or about "the Terrorists" or, too often, about "the sexual perverts." Some of the stories literally produced our personalities—like the stories of The Little Engine That Could or The Three Pigs and the Big Bad Wolf or Goldilocks and the Three Bears. If we're tenacious, provident and temperate as adults, it's in great part because we took to the heart the lessons of those stories. Telling stories can be powerful. Stories set up "self-fulfilling prophecies."

~⁚⁓

The goal of this collection of stories and personal anecdotes is to offer alternative stories to the ones the culture is telling about what it means to be gay. The stories we tell ourselves and share with one another are the way we alter our attitude of mind.

Some of the entries in this collection are personal anecdotes and accounts of real experiences. Some are delightfully whimsical, some profoundly religious. Most are fictional short stories in the vein of the TV show *The Twilight Zone*, that is, tales with imaginative fantastical elements and neat and surprising—and meaningful—twists. Gay consciousness seems to naturally see life with a twist—sometimes ironic, or sardonic or campy, sometimes sweet and sensitive. The point of telling stories with a touch of the Twilight Zone is to move them into the realm of myth and metaphor. That is, after all, how the stories of religion have come down to us: adding mystical, magical, miraculous details to a story gives the insight or spiritual/moral wisdom eternal verity. Such stories are not literally "true," but, and more importantly, they're memorable and richly meaningful.

Such stories achieve mythic stature because they transcend ordinary reality to hint at something beyond. Dealing with death and afterlife is one of the most familiar ways stories achieve this mythic stature. A number of the stories in this collection are like that. Death signifies transcending ego, going beyond self into a greater—and mysterious—reality. In that sense, death is a metaphor for eternity.

The gay community has become sensitive to death in the last decades because of the mysterious happenstance of a new and virulent virus showing up among our numbers as the clue to a threat to planetary survival. So many deaths around us spurred gay spiritual awareness. Being in the presence of death tends to "focus the mind"—to cite the famous quotation from Samuel Johnson about the threat of being hanged—and to make one look at life from the larger perspective. Indeed, to cite another popular chestnut that's come to be part of modern mythology, when you're in the presence of somebody who is dying and the portal to the metaphorical "tunnel of light" opens for them, you yourself can sometimes see the radiance shining out, and it changes you.

That light is part of the story we tell ourselves about the larger universe referred to as supernatural. The supernatural is the realm of God, Jesus and the Saints of religion; it is also the world of vampires, ghosts and paranormal powers. The supernatural is what's invisible to the eye.

"L'essentiel est invisible pour les yeux," according to the sexually ambiguous French aviator / storyteller / *puer aeternis* Antoine de Saint-Exupéry's Little Prince: "It is only with the heart that one can see rightly; what is essential is invisible to the eye."

And what's invisible to all of us is other people's consciousness—their thoughts and experience of being aware. So reference to the supernatural and the mysterious is reference to the larger consciousness of which we are somehow a part, but don't immediately realize—all of us like neurons in the planetary mind of the sun as it has evolved on Planet Earth. The way we actually *do* experience other people's consciousness is through being compassionate. That is why all stories about the supernatural realm are lessons about feeling others' pain and others' joys.

The aim of this collection is to offer new stories, new ways of thinking about gay experience. Mark Abramson's story, "Ella, Kelly and Me..." reminds us of the camaraderie and opportunity gay life offers—and of the enduring quality of love. Joseph de Marco's "Great Uncle Ned" will likely bring tears to your eyes, and remind you to get over personal biases. After reading Martin K. Smith's story, "Free Speech," you and your lover might find the reference to "kalpataru tea" can be the code word to allow you to speak what's really on your mind; it could change your life. Truthtelling, after all, is at the heart of coming out. Mark Thompson and Malcolm Boyd's account of their real life journey together gives hope and humor. And Don Clark's recounting his spirit guides might suggest you too can see your life magically and spiritually guided. And that's only mentioning a handful of the more than thirty stories that follow!

This is the work of religion—but in the modern culture religion has fallen behind. They're not telling new stories. *We* need new stories: the old ones haven't worked as they should. And gay people's experience is a sign of that. We—of all people—are motivated to change the stories people tell about homosexuality, about deviance, about the meaning of incarnation in flesh.

Science and human discovery has been about dropping old stories and learning new and better ones. The story about the stork bringing babies is replaced by the story of sexuality, just as the story about God creating the animals in the Garden of Eden has been replaced by the story of the origin and evolution of species on earth. The whole universe is changing because we're coming to understand just how arbitrary some of these stories are. What's peculiar to modern human consciousness is that now we, unlike most human beings before us, can be aware of the nature and power of stories, yet can also stand outside them and see their metaphorical/mythical character. And we can contrive how to change them.

Changing stories is an act of transformation. And transformation is one of the great thoughts of the planet. We all resonate with it. This is the underlying meaning behind the great myths from Jesus and the Resurrection to Persephone and the seasons to Rumpelstiltskin and the secret for turning straw into gold. And indeed our current awareness of the nature of myth as metaphor, not history, is transforming how the content of the myths and stories is understood.

In traditional mythology, knowing the name of something—a god, a beast of prey or predation, a monster, a Beloved—was believed to give power over that thing. It bestowed the talent of summoning it. Hence the Biblical God had an unpronounceable name (just four consonants without vowels so it couldn't be spoken, except once a year by the High Priest to whom had been revealed the vowels as a secret initiation). One of the powers that came with name-giving was transformation. Naming something transforms it.

Transformation is a power of gay people. In the most mundane way, "coming out" itself is an experience of transformation. The meaning and significance and feeling tone of homosexuality changes dramatically in this experience that people necessarily go through to be gay. You have to realize that almost everything everybody (including YHWH) says about sex, gender and love is wrong—at least for you. You have to look within to find your own truth instead of listening to parents and authorities. You have to transform your world.

And the traits that are associated with homosexuality—in particular, with gay men—are those of transformation. Rearranging the furniture, remodeling a house, making up a floral arrangement, doing another person's hair, or soothing a patient's pain, teaching a child, writing a book, composing a symphony—all are forms of transformation. And these require "talent." Talents are what are spoken about in the myths as "powers." And the people in the myths with powers—fairies, witch-crones, warlocks, blind seers, berdache two-spirits—are frequently gender variant.

The secret of turning straw into gold in the fairy tale was tied to knowing the name of the elf/demon/daimon who performed the transformation. Knowing the name gave power. Remember the story was that a boastful merchant exaggerated the skills of his seamstress daughter and proclaimed she could virtually spin gold out of straw. When this exaggeration got reported to the King, it was taken seriously and a royal order went out that, under threat of beheading if she failed, the girl should transform a barnful of straw into gold for the kingdom's treasury.

There was no way, of course, for the merchant's daughter to accomplish this task. But then out of nowhere appeared an elf who said he could and agreed to perform the transformation on condition the girl give him a gift of her necklace. She did so and he spun the whole barnful into gold. The King was so pleased he ordered her to work another night at her spinning wheel. Again the elf appeared and agreed to perform, this time asking for her ring. And again the King wanted more gold and sent her back to work. On the third night the gift the elf asked for was the girl's first son when the baby would be born. In fear of losing her head, the girl agreed.

The greedy King was so impressed he married the merchant's daughter himself, and a year later she gave birth to a prince. Soon the elf returned to claim his final payment. The young mother begged and begged, offering all the wealth in the kingdom, but he was adamant. They had an agreement; he wanted the infant. But he agreed to drop his claim if in three days she could guess his name (i.e., identify the power by which transformation occurs).

The Queen sent messengers out to investigate the background of this magical creature. One of them happened to discover the elf out in the woods being elf-like, celebrating his power, dancing around a fire, singing: "Nobody can guess my name is Rumpelstiltskin." On the third night, then, the Queen was able to confront the elf with his secret name and void the agreement and keep her son.

The secret of turning straw/dross into gold—the secret sought by the alchemists, in a complex metaphor for transforming human consciousness into divine consciousness—is linked to knowing the potent name. The name is a key to power. (Rumpelstiltskin, by the way, is a German name of a kind of poltergeist that shakes ["rumples"] the stilts of raised houses—not so terribly secret.)

In a surprisingly similar way, one of the healing powers of psychotherapy and medicine is giving a name to troubling symptoms. We've all likely had an experience of the power of medical diagnosis. Just having a doctor look at some condition and giving it a name can result in the symptoms disappearing. This is an aspect of what's called the placebo effect, and it is especially so in mental health services.

A major way that psychotherapy works is by giving the patient a name—a handle—for their problem and / or assuring them the problem is "normal." Of course, knowing the diagnosis Broken Arm isn't going to make bone knit back together automatically, but seeing the doctor and getting X-rays can make the pain diminish immediately, if only because uncertainty and anxiety are assuaged. And being told you're just having a predictable mid-life crisis does make your craziness seem more manageable—and the shaking of the stilts of your life less threatening.

People tell themselves stories in their mind. They repeat over and over comments made by parents or teachers or ex-boyfriends or girlfriends; in serious schizophrenia these are experienced as hearing voices. Such self-talk becomes self-fulfilling prophecy. How we experience our lives is mediated by the stories we were told and the stories we are still telling ourselves. Some of these stories have contributed greatly to our lives; some have resulted in torment and guilt. Psychological maturity—the aim of psychotherapy and psychoanalysis—includes being aware of the stories and taking responsibility for continuing to honor or believe them or deciding not to. Sometimes maturity and mental health comes from *not* listening to the stories anymore or beginning to tell oneself new stories.

People become what they think they are. They become the labels they use for themselves. If you think of yourself as a "miserable sinner" and continually berate yourself for failing to succeed at anything you try because, after all, you're a miserable sinner, you'll make yourself unhappy and feckless.

Cognitive styles of psychotherapy seek to change people's behavior and self-experience by getting them to recognize the terms of their self-talk and then to change them. Thinking of yourself as a vital, loving person instead of a miserable sinner is sure more likely to enliven your life and attract other loving persons to you.

New Age Religious Science and Western esoteric tradition calls this phenomenon The Law of Attraction. We become what we think we are and we attract into our lives what we think about. The stories we tell ourselves become true, sometimes through what seem like coincidences or, even, miracles. This is the dynamic of self-fulfilling prophecy and it operates even at the level of karma and luck: what we expect to happen comes true because we—consciously or unconsciously and maybe mystically—set it up to happen.

⸱⸱⊃

Homosexual liberation comes from being able to name the experience of inexplicable and taboo feelings of sexual attraction for members of one's own sex. The first step of coming out is being able to say to oneself "I'm not like everybody else. I'm a homosexual." And because the word homosexual has been given such negative connotations, the gay population over the years has given more felicitous, self-chosen names for this experience of sexuality.

Naming our aberrant sexual orientation has been an ongoing theme. Each generation and wave of political and cultural organizing has sought to rename itself to give a new and different tenor to homosexual consciousness and set up different self-fulfilling prophecies in order to transform and improve gay people's lives.

"Gay" is, indeed, the word that's been in use for at least the last century, though organized groups of homosexuals and individuals have called for other self-identifiers to suggest other connotations: uranian, intermediate type, urning, third sex, homophile, gay, lesbian, bisexual, faggot and dyke, queer, same-sex, men who love men and women who love women, LGBTQ, even "I-don't-want-to-be-labeled." Each of these names suggests certain qualities of sexual orientation—either of innocuousness or of threat, depending on context and political or personal vicissitudes for which the identification is proclaimed.

If you think about your homosexuality as creating a psychiatric condition, a cause of sin and a perverse abnormality (the way the anti-gay forces teach), something to keep secret, you're likely to become a miserable sinner. If you think of your homosexuality as revealing Rumpelstiltskin's secret for producing gold, you're much more likely to find happiness, love and fulfillment. The transformation comes from relaxing resistance to the way things are. So listen to your heart, and be what and who you really are.

Twisting the straw metaphor, you might say life is like the game of drawing straws: sometimes you win, sometimes you lose, most of the time it's all a matter of chance. If you think you have won the game, you're ahead. The way to change your fortune is to conceive of your life as having pulled the long straw in this lifetime. And being gay *is* one of the long straws in the game of karmic straw pull—indeed, a gold one.

There's a charm in gay life, a bit of magic, of specialness, a secret the others don't know, a talent in how to live well—*joie d'vivre*—and how to see and tell the truth. There's an allure to gay life, a golden glimmer—at least for those of us who see it—that our gay consciousness, born of seeing from a different perspective and through different filters, gives us insight into eternal, spiritual truth. The charm makes us lovable people, makes our lives interesting and helps make the world around us richer and neater for everybody. We perform an act of transformation when we claim and live our charm.

That has been the long-term goal of all the various manifestations of the homosexual rights/gay liberation movements. When homosexually-oriented people think positively and felicitously about homosexuality and tell themselves and others positive stories about their sexual experiences and affections, they—and everyone around them—are going to be happier, more fulfilled, more productive, and more contributing to society.

That's why positive and charming stories about homosexual experience—and positively charged names for these experiences—are an important part of improving gay people's lives.

New stories change how we see the world.

And, lo and behold, the world will change to fit the better stories. This is how we change the world. This is how we save the world. Metaphorically, this is how we create gold out of straw.

Introduction:
Straw Is Neither Dross or Gold

Steve Berman

So I wonder who taught Rumpel-stiltskin how to spin straw into gold. Certainly it's a useful talent. Yet, by the end of the fairy tale, this magical skill fails to obtain the stunted faery's deepest desire: companionship (why else would he want the child?). Rumpelstiltskin is not interested in the maiden's hand; rather, he seeks to circumvent what society often considers the proper mode of family life—taking a wife—for an entirely male household.

As a writer, a fantasist by nature, I have always wondered about Rumpelstiltskin. He seems symbolic of so many gay men. Capering and mischievous, forced to the edges of the general public, reviled yet sought after for his gifts. We are as fey as he is. And, like Rumpelstiltskin, we often try to transform the world from something lackluster into enchanting.

But what is wrong with straw? Or our lives? These amber stalks have been our bedding and roofs, and have been woven to carry our every belonging. Sheaves of wheat will not really turn to pieces of gold in our hands, and the majority of us lead very ordinary lives without the adventures of fairy tales.

Perhaps that is for the best. For when we only see the dross, the less-than-perfect aspects of our own existence, then the simple pleasures become meaningless. In those old stories, the simpleton son is often the happiest of his brothers, understanding that life may not be fair, but it can still be enjoyed. By not chasing after fool's gold, the simpleton emerges the victor and lauded by his kin and neighbors for actually being the wisest of them all.

I'm not saying gay men should avoid daydreaming or hoping for a better life. To strive for more is human. But we need to take some time and notice the golden aspects of our present. The warmth of a lover's hand, the encouragement in a sibling's smile, remembering all the leaps forward.

Rumpelstiltskin was alone. Many gay men feel that way too often in life. In the stories that follow, loneliness and despair are the real villains and hope comes in knowing that such conditions are temporary. Much like the pitfalls in a fairy tale. Perhaps the best transformation is not straw into gold, but gilding the heart and spirit.

Oh, if you happen one evening to be out for a late walk and happen upon a bitter little man complaining of the selfishness of princesses, do tell him your story, spend some time with him, become friends. It may end up magical for both of you.

Ella, Kelly and Me

Mark Abramson

"There is no greater agony than bearing
an untold story inside you."
Maya Angelou

I was sweeping out the dressing rooms of the Victoria Theatre in San Francisco's Mission District after our first annual AIDS benefit, *Men Behind Bars: the bartenders' folly*, when I found an unmarked audio cassette. I figured that a cast member had been using it to practice dance steps and now that the show was closed, had left the tape behind. It found its way into my pocket and came home with me. I didn't know who the singer was, but the music was soothing and uplifting.

I worked as a bartender on Castro Street in those days. After college and some graduate school, I was at an age when I knew everything except what I wanted to do with my life, so it was the perfect choice at the time. It wasn't a bar I frequented before I took the job. It was the sort of place that regulars came in to visit old friends more than to meet someone new.

That bar on Castro Street was just a neighborhood watering hole on one of the gayest blocks in the world and some of the customers had moved to San Francisco before I was born. Other than tourists, most of the guys my age didn't show up at the bar until they got off work, so I grew to appreciate the old-timers, as I first thought of them.

They had a vast knowledge of history, books and music, Hollywood trivia, politics and just about everything else.

One day at work I played the tape I'd found. "That last song was Ella Fitzgerald singing *Blue Skies* from the Irving Berlin Songbook on the Verve label in 1958," a guy named Woody said. Whenever they asked for dice in order to play 5,000, Woody reached for the pen and pad. He didn't mind keeping score—in Roman numerals.

"And this one's *Bewitched, Bothered and Bewildered* by Rogers and Hart," another customer growled. His name was Bill, but everyone called him Juanita, even though he stood well over six feet tall and had a deep thundering voice. His demeanor was imposing, but he was a sweetheart. "Someone put a tape together from different songbooks, but it's all Ella Fitzgerald. Nice stuff."

I'd never heard the uncensored lyrics to that song before, but she sang them all: *worship the trousers that cling to him* and *horizontally speaking, he's at his very best.* Hers was also the most amazing voice I'd ever heard, once I stopped to really listen. Now I wanted to hear more. I'd heard of Ella Fitzgerald, I suppose, but where I grew up the radio played twangy country music that poured through the windows of dusty pick-up trucks on gravel roads. Even back then, something told me there were better things.

I bought a couple of dozen Ella Fitzgerald albums before I realized she'd recorded nearly a hundred by then. I bought a lot of other albums, too. The boss kidded me about my new passion. When a ballad came on, he'd make wrist-slashing motions and say, "Those dead black women are depressing, but your customers seem to like them."

"Billie Holiday and Dinah Washington may be dead, but Nancy Wilson and Etta James and Ella Fitzgerald are still very much alive," I told him.

One day I came home from work, opened my mailbox and found a glossy brochure from the Paul Masson Mountain Winery advertising a series of summer concerts. There was Ella Fitzgerald on a Sunday afternoon. I immediately wrote a check and walked it to the mailbox. By the time that Sunday came, I had talked my friend Doug into driving. I held the map as we headed south from the city with the sun climbing the morning sky. We parked halfway up the mountain and walked a narrow one-lane road the rest of the way to the concert site while a limousine crept past us on a single-lane road. There was no one else in sight besides Doug and the driver and me on that whole mountaintop until an old woman popped out of the back seat with her arms full of sheet music. She spoke in a cheerful little girl's voice, "Hiya, Fellas!"

Doug said, "Good morning, Miss Fitzgerald." He wasn't star-struck like I was. He could have taken a picture of her or of the two of us or asked for her autograph or he could have done anything besides watching me back into a tree.

Ella Fitzgerald looked right at me. "Are you okay?" she asked, as if I weren't stupefied. I tried to nod and smile and she went on, "Did you boys drive all the way down from San Francisco? That sure is a pretty town. Thanks for coming to see me. You got here plenty early. Well, I hope you get some good seats and enjoy yourselves on such a beautiful day." She was talking directly to Doug and me and I couldn't even speak.

A man in a suit finally appeared and led her away, but we had a couple of hours to kill, so we drank some wine, ate lunch and were first in line. A trio came out to set the tone and then Ella Fitzgerald appeared in a long sparkling dress. Everyone leapt to their feet and cheered as she neared the microphone, "Babies, babies, sit down. It's too hot for all that! You haven't even heard me sing yet. See if you still feel that way later. There'll be time. Maybe it will even cool off a bit. Sit down now and relax."

She sang.

It wasn't exactly like the albums. She didn't pack the power of her younger recordings. When she forgot some of the lyrics, she made up her own. Still, there was an effervescent glow that radiated from her like the sweltering heat that afternoon as she projected such joyful love of the music and the rhythm! And a couple of times she ended on a note so pure and round I could almost see it soar on a breeze across the Saratoga Valley to the next mountain top, miles away.

Ella Fitzgerald was a far cry from what most of my friends were listening to in those days. I like to think of gay men as successive generations of a tribe. For my peers, most of the music and the dance were steeped in the sweat of young men on the disco floor under strobe lights and fog machines. Still I was grateful to learn the value of the elders as they passed down their lessons like secret family recipes from one generation to the next.

When I was very young, an older man once warned me, "Never date a bartender." Tending bar on Castro Street, I finally understood what he must have meant. The hours can be lonely, tips are quickly earned and spent and innocent flirtations can cause jealousy. Even in those years during the worst of the scourge of AIDS, I met incredible people from all over the world. I altered the rule to *never date a bartender unless you ARE one.* Other bartenders understood.

Sometimes I worked nights. Tips were even better and I met more guys my age, but I still enjoyed the daytime crowd, the men who had been here before me. I learned how they'd banded together in the face of hostile persecution. A neighborhood bar was their sanctuary, an extension of their living rooms, if not their bedrooms. In some ways it reminded me of the small-town church where my family belonged. The bar was where they celebrated their victories and mourned their losses and where they kindly took me under their wing.

I loved to listen to their stories. One guy named Bob had once met Ethel Merman at a cocktail party on Long Island and could still recite every word of their conversation. Jim had danced with her in the chorus of a Broadway show. Back in 1963 when Judy Garland performed here for the last time, Bill knew an usher who snuck him into her dressing room and they shared a bottle of scotch. That same year, Dan went to hear a young new singer at the Hungry i in North Beach. Afterward, they went to the Black Cat in time for last call and the cops raided the place. Dan said he rode knee-to-knee in the paddy wagon with Barbra Streisand all the way downtown.

They called one of the guys Granddad. He remembered before there were gay bars all over San Francisco. People had cocktail parties at home or met at a certain bar in the Fairmont every other Tuesday or every third Monday at the St. Francis. I was playing my Ella Fitzgerald tape one day when Woody said, *"From This Moment On…* Cole Porter Songbook, 1956,"…and that was Granddad's cue to tell us about when Cole Porter came to town. It was one of my favorite stories.

Granddad had been about the youngest guest at a party to meet the famous composer. Bouquets of roses filled the Nob Hill apartment and it was a perfect night for the view. A butler greeted each guest, took his topcoat and served him cocktails. An hour went by before people asked, "Where is he? Isn't he coming?" Everyone knew everyone else except the butler, who turned out to be Cole Porter. It had been his idea to find out how San Franciscans treated their servants and they passed his test. There were stories about other famous men, too, especially Liberace. Several had encountered Nureyev at the Ritch Street baths and everybody had a Rock Hudson tale.

2

Having been a bartender for a while, I recognized most of the faces in each week's obituaries in the B.A.R. With so many deaths in such a short time they became surreal, an endless swirl of bad dreams descending like a cold dark fog from Twin Peaks after a sunny day. San Francisco had survived earthquakes and fires, the Zodiac killer, mass suicides in Jonestown, assassinations in city hall and potholes, so I always believed that the spirit of the Barbary Coast would come alive again whenever creative people came here looking for it. But AIDS had become an even greater part of our daily lives. I was sure I would join its victims soon and grateful to have experienced what I did.

One of those experiences was Kelly. The night we met we were still talking in my bed as the sun rose. I couldn't imagine why we'd never met before. He was a bartender at the Pendulum, around the corner from where I worked and he only lived a couple of blocks away from me. I remember telling him, "My grandparents came from Sweden, but I grew up in Minnesota. Where are you from?"

"North Carolina, but I grew up in Florida and Harlem. Kelly is my last name. My great-grandfather was obviously an Irishman who raped one of his slaves. I've never had a good look at the family tree, to tell you the truth. I'm part Cherokee and part Jamaican, but I consider myself black. When I was a model in New York I wasn't black enough for some gigs. What did that mean? I remember the drinking fountains in Florida—*White Only*. There wasn't a fountain for *Not Black Enough*."

All I could say was, "Wow." We didn't exchange numbers, but I knew where he worked. After he left I found a silver ring with three onyx stones on my bathroom sink. I wore that ring until the following

Christmas, when he gave me one to replace it. I still have that ring in Kelly's old jewelry box, but one of the stones has fallen out.

We soon reached that corny stage of leaving each other little notes and surprises of cards and gifts. For Valentine's Day he bought me a huge framed photograph of Ella Fitzgerald. For his birthday I made dinner and gave him one of Billie Holiday. He wouldn't take it home, though. He said they'd look great together in *our* apartment someday. Kelly wanted to move into a place together, but I had another rule besides the one about dating bartenders: "Don't give up your apartment in the first year."

Two months after we met, an electrical fire started in my kitchen in the middle of the night. We were in the front bedroom. By the time the alarm went off, there was thick smoke coming down the hallway and flames from floor to ceiling in the back. I tried to wake the neighbors while Kelly ran toward the kitchen with a towel. The fire department came, six trucks with nearly thirty firefighters who quickly doused the fire, but everything beyond the bathroom was destroyed. Kelly came to the front door coughing and covered with soot. Once we got out in the fresh air on the sidewalk I told him, "I think you're definitely black enough, now."

He didn't laugh, but said, "I think it's time to get over your 'one year' rule. How about coming to my place? We can get cleaned up and decide on what to do with the rest of our lives."

I put my arms around him and said, "Sure." I didn't care where we lived any more. We were crowded but happy in his studio apartment near the Mint until we found a larger place on Castro Street. Both the framed photographs of Billie Holiday and Ella Fitzgerald had survived the fire.

Kelly said he couldn't cook, but he lied. I'd come home to find him stirring something on the stove with a coconut cake in the oven. Another day he was making fried chicken and biscuits. The crock-pot was full of beans and ham hocks. A cherry pie was cooling on the table. I'd been at work and missed the preparations, but it was one of the best meals ever. He had a little gold box full of recipes he always hid from me. If I tried to look inside, he would snatch it away.

When I asked about the chicken, he teased, "I learned to fry a chicken at my grandmother's knee and she made me swear never to tell her secrets to a white person. Go on now, before you get splattered."

After Kelly went to bed, I poked through the trashcan for some secret ingredients, but I never discovered any and I gave up on finding that gold box while he was still alive.

Kelly and I each had our own histories and our own photo albums. As we showed each other pictures, they would fall out and get jumbled. My Swedish family members ended up among his more exotic ones. Old friends of his and mine were mixed together as if they'd always known each other. We knew we would never have to sort them out and I suppose we tried in this way to claim parts of each other's pasts as well as whatever future we had.

We worked at our respective bars the first Sunday in October, the day of the Castro Street Fair. When we finally got home off our sore feet and started counting tips, Kelly shouted, "Let's take a trip to New York!" I was almost too tired to think straight, but I was game.

I have always loved to visit New York. You can feel its beat through your shoes as if the long fingers of a bass player were plucking the city's heartstrings from somewhere up in Harlem. Taxi horns are trumpets on the doo-wops and scattered bits of melodies are all around. The rhythm depends on the time of day or night and your frame of mind. I hadn't been there in years and I knew it would be fun to go with Kelly. During his high school years, he had lived with his Aunt Claire on Riverside Drive in Harlem.

Claire Leyba was the actress who played Blanche in the all-black version of *Anna Lucasta* in the New York play, for a long run on the London stage and in the movie version with Eartha Kitt and Sammy Davis, Jr. Also, for the past forty-odd years, Aunt Claire had been the lover of the great jazz singer, Carmen McRae. Claire wasn't about to give up her rent-controlled apartment to live with Carmen full time, so they were constantly back and forth between New York and Los Angeles.

Kelly warned me, "We'll check into our hotel before she even knows we're in town. She'll want us to come by, but we'll already have plans for every minute. If we go to her place, she'll try to feed us. Avoid eating anything Claire serves! It could be tragic. Trust me."

During the flight Kelly told me more about life with Aunt Claire. "The toast of Harlem," he called her. "No one would dare to plan anything important without inviting her first. Then, if she couldn't make it, they'd have to change the date, even for a wedding or a funeral." Now he was pulling my leg, I was sure.

We crawled into a taxi at JFK. The back seat's plastic cover crackled with the cold and the driver blared Christmas music on tinny rear speakers on this, the first weekend in November. A forest of cardboard pine-tree air fresheners made breathing painful. By the time we finally got to our hotel I felt sick. "That ride was horrible!" I complained.

Kelly frowned and pressed his hand to my forehead. "You're burning up. I packed some aspirin. I'll go get it." I promised Kelly I'd feel better in the morning, but spent most of the weekend in a daze of fever which varied by the time of day and how much aspirin I could stomach.

Saturday we walked and shopped for gifts and souvenirs. I've always had a few rituals about travel and especially visiting New York. I like to look at the view from the tallest place I can find. Rituals seemed especially important during those years in the heart of the AIDS crisis. I dragged Kelly along to the top of the World Trade Center. He took me to Radio City Music Hall, where he had once been a tour guide and could still rattle off his spiel. I thought my fever must have come up again since I was getting excited hearing about the animals they use in the Christmas show.

Aunt Claire arrived at our hotel that evening wearing a floor-length coat and fur hat that covered every inch of her except her face. She wailed, "Kelly! My Baby! Let me look at you!" When he hugged her, his chin just touched the top of her hat. He had to bend down to kiss her cheek.

"And *you* are Mark! Her voice sounded much deeper than in the movies, especially when it was directed at me. I'd finally seen *Anna Lucasta* by this time, but that was made over thirty years ago. "I am delighted to make your acquaintance. You really *dig* my Kelly, don't you?"

This was not a question, but I answered, "You know I do."

"I can tell… whenever he calls me, which isn't nearly often enough. It's about time you both settled down and made each other happy," she said. Kelly had insisted that we be dressed in suits and ties so we could take photographs. Now we put on our winter coats and hats and gloves to walk the few blocks to the Algonquin Hotel for another New York ritual of mine: a Martini to Dorothy Parker's memory.

Aunt Claire said she had to be uptown a little later because a friend of hers was doing a reading and she'd promised to come, but she and Kelly had a lot of catching up to do first. She talked about her recent stay with Carmen, but how she still didn't like L.A. very much. In spite of what Kelly had said, his eyes sparkled as he basked in her attention. Maybe he warned me about her to keep me from being let down, but he should have known better. She glanced at her watch after while and said, "My name is at the door. I can get us into my friend's reading for free and we'll all go out for a drink with her afterward. Think about it…" She asked a waiter for directions to the powder room.

I turned to Kelly and said, "I'm sorry, but I think my fever's coming back."

"Don't worry. I didn't want to go to some poetry reading anyway…"

"But now we've made her late…"

"Oh, you *sure* don't want to worry about that! She wouldn't have it any other way. Claire loves to make an entrance! "

There was a cold rain falling gently through the street-lamps as we left. Aunt Claire kissed Kelly goodnight as I flagged a cab for her. I said, "I loved meeting you. Take this… for the cab fare," I slipped a five and a ten into her coat pocket.

"Oh, Mark. Sweetheart, that isn't necessary. You boys call me tomorrow. And take good care of each other. G'Night."

As the cab splashed off in the thickening rain, Kelly said, "That was very sweet of you, but I know my Aunt Claire. She'll have that cab driver drop her off at the nearest subway station, tip him a quarter and pocket that money for later." We both laughed and walked back to our hotel. Even with a fever, I loved being in New York.

On Sunday morning we went uptown for brunch and then walked through the Guggenheim and Central Park. We were talking about his teenage years again when I asked, "Kelly, will you take me to Harlem?"

He said, "I thought you'd never ask."

While Kelly paid the cab driver, I noticed the Marquee of the Apollo Theatre just up the street. "Kelly… Look!" I shouted at him. I knew that Ella Fitzgerald had won their famous *Amateur Night* as a teenager.

I'd watched *Showtime at the Apollo* on television and wondered what it really looked like. Now here I was within a block of the place.

"Sure, we can go by there later," he said, "but c'mon... I haven't been in this old gay bar in ages."

It was a dark narrow room. The only patrons were half a dozen elderly black women down the bar. They were all dressed up in big hats and matching gloves. It seemed like a place you might end up after going somewhere else, but never a destination. We sat at two stools near the front door and I asked Kelly, "Are you sure this is a gay bar?"

"Of course it is."

"But those ladies are so dressed up. They don't look like lesbians to me."

Kelly laughed and asked, "Does Aunt Claire?" I could see his point. "And besides, it's Sunday. They all came from church."

"Do you think they're friends of Claire?"

"I'm sure they know her, anyway. Everybody does. That reminds me I promised to call."

The bartender ambled toward us. "I'll bet you fellas are here to see Miss Lynne's show up at the Apollo," he drawled as he glanced at his wristwatch. "You got plenty of time for a drink or two."

Kelly said, "We sure are," and placed a pair of tickets on the bar in front of me.

I read the tickets: *The Apollo Theater presents...Arthur Prysock, Gloria Lynn, and Lionel Hampton.* How did he score them without me knowing?

When Kelly came back from the phone, I said, "You just made my whole trip, you know. This couldn't be more perfect... how's Aunt Claire?"

"I think she has a hangover, but she was crazy about meeting you last night."

"I loved her, too. How was the reading? Did we miss anything?"

"Oh yeah, Claire said Maya sends her love, too. They went out afterward and Claire told her all about seeing me... and about you, of course."

"Who's Maya, some new girlfriend of hers?"

"Hardly... Maya Angelou... Claire's friend. The reading, remember?"

"Maya Angelou!" I shouted. "You mean I missed out on a chance to see and maybe even *meet* Maya Angelou… in person?"

"I thought you knew… besides, you were sick."

"I didn't know *who* was reading! Did you?"

"Yeah, Claire said… maybe when you went to the bathroom at the Algonquin."

"I didn't go to the bathroom at the Algonquin, Kelly."

"Maybe it was earlier at the hotel, or when I phoned Claire about meeting us. Geez, I'm sorry. I didn't realize you'd even know Maya Angelou."

"She's only the Ella Fitzgerald of writers." I nearly shouted before I looked down at the tickets again and sighed. "Kelly, I'm sorry. You didn't know… and I *was* sick. If I'd stayed out I wouldn't have been able to come here today. Come on. Come and show me where Ella got started."

The bartender said, "Now you fellas stop back in after the show, y'hear? Miss Lynne will be in to hold court between the matinee and the evening."

"Does everyone know everyone else in Harlem?" I asked Kelly, but he just smiled.

The entrance hallway's crystal chandeliers lit caricatures of every black entertainer from a young Michael Jackson to Gladys Knight to dozens more I wouldn't have recognized without Kelly there to name them. The building held the magical smells of an old theater, that mixture of make-up and sweat, dusty curtains and pulleys and greasy ropes. I wasn't sure I knew the first two performers until I heard them sing and I recognized their hits. Lionel Hampton went on far too long, but still it was great just to be there. Outside, the rain was pouring down. "Where's the nearest subway?"

"It's a ways," Kelly said. "We can take a cab there."

"How will we ever catch…?" I started to ask, but before I could finish, there was an unmarked car at the curb and we were inside. Later, on the subway, Kelly explained to me about gypsy cabs and I asked, "Aren't they dangerous? How do you recognize one? Don't they take business from licensed drivers who pay taxes? How do you know they aren't ripping you off?"

"Listen!" he said. "When you're a 6'3" black man, it doesn't matter if you pay your taxes, how well dressed you are or where your mother buys her diamonds. You watch fifty cabs pass you by to pick up some white guy who's drunk and cheats on his wife *and* his taxes. You do that a few times and you start to feel invisible or worse... and you find other ways to get by in the world... and that's something you'll never need to worry about. Enough said. "

I had wanted to see New York through Kelly's eyes, but this weekend was more than I could have imagined. God, I loved that man.

3

One morning in June, I realized it had been nearly ten months since Kelly died and I still wasn't used to sleeping alone. I looked out the bedroom window at the giant rainbow flag above Castro Street and wondered if the fog would burn off the hills that day. I groped my empty bed for the TV remote and the first words I heard were that Ella Fitzgerald had died. I wanted to pretend it was only another dark dream, crawl back under the covers and shut the world out again. Instead, I clicked through the channels to see what they said about her, mostly brief snippets of old guest spots to tell of a great woman's life. There were clips of duets with Frank Sinatra, Nat King Cole and Judy Garland. Friends of mine in Europe said the news of her death was enormous there. Radio stations played nothing but Ella Fitzgerald's music around the clock. The tributes I heard here seemed inadequate for the "First Lady of Song." What did I expect? We always seem to be looking for the newest craze, but never toward the past.

Kelly and I had called his Aunt Claire more often after our visit to New York and I kept it up after he died. She and I had only met once, but she was a comfort to me through those times and I hoped I was for her too. That Saturday morning in June I picked up the phone and called New York as I poured a cup of coffee. Aunt Claire recognized my voice right away. "Mark, I'm so glad you called today. I was feeling kind of blue, you know?"

"Yeah... me too," I said, "I guess you've heard about Ella."

"Yeah, Baby, I heard. I got a phone call first thing this morning from L.A.... that sweet brown-skinned girl."

"You know, Claire... I loved Ella's music even before I met Kelly. I even got to meet her once... sort of. I went to see her every chance I got, but Kelly and I only saw her once together down at the Circle Star Theater."

"I think I saw Sinatra there," Claire said.

"Really?" I asked. "Claire, I was thinking how sorry I am that we didn't call you when Carmen died. Kelly was so sick by then and I was in a daze, taking care of him. We were thinking of you so much, but if we'd called, you would have worried about him... hearing his voice and how weak he was. I think we wrote to you. I meant to. "

She said, "I know, Baby. I understand. Yes, you boys sent me a beautiful card. I have it right here in my hand. Sweet Kelly, sweet Carmen, sweet Ella. They're singing with the angels now and I don't know why I'm here. You and I must still have some work to do here on this earth, I guess... don't we, Baby?"

I went on, "Claire, I just wondered if you knew her... Ella, I mean. It seems like you and I have talked about so many things since Kelly died, but we've never talked about Ella Fitzgerald."

Claire started to laugh and then she grew quiet. I imagined her thinking back over her life. She finally said, "Oh, Baby, I knew Miss Ella and I loved her like nobody's business. Carmen and I would always be in the front row when Ella sang... whichever city we were all in at the same time, you know? There are so many years... so many memories."

"Uh-huh?"

"And if Ella was in town when Carmen was on that stage, Ella and I would be right there sitting together in the front row at the center table."

I longed to have been there. I could almost picture myself, maybe a miniature self, about three inches tall, hardly big enough to notice. My tiny clone could recline in the ashtray on the table between them with my hands clasped behind my head and my feet up. Ella Fitzgerald in one chair and Aunt Claire in the other and Carmen McRae in a spotlight just a few feet away, leaning into the curve of a grand piano and singing *Summertime*.

"And after the show, the three of us would go out and paint the town red! Carmen used to get jealous with me for having such a good time with Ella like I did. She'd say, 'Claire, I think you love Ella better than you love me.' But I'd just laugh and I'd say, 'Carmen, you're so crazy. I love Ella, but you know I love you too, Baby. And you know Ella don't go that way. Ella's into *men*!' "

Claire laughed and I laughed along with her. If I ever dreamed while I was growing up on a farm in Minnesota that their world even existed, I never would have believed I'd be nearly able to touch it one day. "You know, Mark, I've had some little mini-strokes lately and sometimes I don't remember things like I used to, but I'll never forget Ella Fitzgerald," Claire was saying all of this to me on the phone while Ella's face flashed across my television screen.

"I'm so glad you called to lift my spirits today. How are you doing, Baby?" she asked.

"Okay, I guess." After Kelly died I counted each Wednesday as another week I'd survived. They were starting to get mixed up in my head, so that was probably a good sign. "I miss Kelly, but I get by day to day. I have a lot of friends here in San Francisco. Not as many as I used to, but I'm good at meeting people... friends, I mean. No romance. I'm far from there, yet."

"Now Baby, you know Kelly's up there watching out for you. He's right beside you whenever you need him. I have to confess I still have the ashes you sent me. I haven't been able to bring myself to part with them yet, but I promise to do what you asked... at the Apollo Theatre... before I die."

"You can keep them as long as you want if they're a comfort to you," I told her. "We talked about so many places and it will take time. Friends of ours sprinkled some of Kelly's ashes off the Eiffel Tower last week. I took some to the Russian River and a flower bed in Seattle. Most of him is up on the red rock hill above Castro Street. He could see that hill from the bedroom window and he used to look out at it for hours. There's no hurry. Kelly has all the time in the world now."

"Thank you, Mark," she said, "I need to hold on to him for a while. You know, I pray to J.C. every day out my window and I talk to Kelly too. J.C. is taking good care of Kelly and Carmen and now Ella too. What a heavenly choir up there these days! You be good to yourself,

Mark, and thanks again for reaching out to me from so far away. I love you."

"I love you, too, Aunt Claire," I said. "Good-bye."

Ella was singing with the angels, now. Maybe she would have run into Kelly on the other side and he would have told her how much I loved her music.

I called Claire every few weeks to see how she was doing. Then there was one Saturday morning when I knew that our ritual had changed. She seemed fine at first, but then she'd stop and say, "Baby, it's so nice of you to reach out to me… and your name was?"

"Mark."

"Yes, Mark… I'm sorry… and you were married to one of my relatives? Do you have children?"

"No Claire, just the dog…"

"Oh, I know how much comfort a pet can be. My pussycat is a real whore; she just lies on her back with her legs in the air…" She laughed and then there was another long pause before she asked, "Have you and I ever met?"

"Yes Claire, when Kelly and I were in New York we went to the Algonquin and drank Martinis."

"Oh, I still like to have my little vodka now and then, but I had to give up the reefer, you know? It makes me confused," she said.

"Do you get outside much, Claire?" I asked.

"No, I used to love my walks along Riverside Drive, but I mostly just look out the window now and say my prayers to J.C. I don't know why he's kept me here on this earth for so long, but the power of prayer is mighty important to me now, you know… I'm sorry… I lost your name, again."

"It's Mark," I said. "That's okay, Claire."

"Oh yes… Mark… of course. I met a fella named Mark once, a gentleman from Minnesota. I've never been there, but they must have some nice people. He was a long ways from Minnesota, but he'd found himself some real lovin' in this life and that's just like being home, isn't it?"

"Yes, Claire, it sure is," I answered.

"San Francisco, did you say? I can't thank you enough for reaching out to me from such a long ways away. I've been there lots of times. That's a real pretty town," she used the same words with which Ella Fitzgerald had described San Francisco on that mountaintop on the morning when I backed into the tree. "Oh, did you hear the buzzer? That must be the young man who does some shopping for me."

"Yes, Claire. I can hear it. I'll let you go. Good-bye."

"Good-bye. Thank you so much for brightening my day. God bless you." I stared at the phone as if the mechanics of it had failed me.

I needed to go outside after that. I walked down Castro Street, remembering some of the many people who had passed through since Kelly and I were neighborhood bartenders here—Bob and Jim and Juanita and Granddad. As I have witnessed new arrivals to the city over the years, I've hoped that some of them might also grow to recognize each other as generations of a larger family.

Doug was still here. I ran into him and some other friends at the Edge, but it was hard to transport myself back from Claire's voice on the phone that morning to focus on the routine of a normal day.

I don't know if Aunt Claire ever figured out who was calling that morning. I never called again. It was time to stop straining her memories. After all, there was more of Kelly right here than anywhere else. There was more of him locked in my heart than anyone else could give me, even his Aunt Claire who loved him.

One Saturday morning when the sun broke through after a week of rain, I played that old Ella Fitzgerald tape again. It was perfect for spring-cleaning. I listened to those uncensored lyrics to *Bewitched, Bothered and Bewildered* and laughed and thought about those guys in the bar, so long ago. *My Funny Valentine* came next. I laughed some more, then finally cried.

That was the day I found the gold box Kelly had kept hidden from me all those years. It was under the kitchen sink among some brown paper bags and old cans of paint. I was finally about to discover the secrets he'd learned at his grandmother's knee. There were 3" X 5" recipe cards and yellowed clippings from newspapers and magazines, but not one word about how to fry a chicken.

Beneath the recipes, I found another stack of papers. Kelly had saved all the notes and cards we'd given each other. They started from before the fire that forced me to stay with him in his tiny studio apartment. One of the cards fell into my lap. I had forgotten that Kelly gave it to me when we moved into our place together on Castro Street. On the front was a quote by Aunt Claire's old friend Maya Angelou: *I long, as does every human being, to be at home wherever I find myself.*

Inside, Kelly had written, *"Sorry about your one-year rule, but welcome to OUR home at last! ... Love, Kelly"*

Lining the bottom of the box there was another card I remembered much better. It was the first Valentine he gave me. On the front was a chain of red hearts amid a swirling pattern that looked like notes of music on a staff. Inside Kelly had written: *No matter what else happens, I will always be with you... always.*

And he is.

The Story Behind the Story

Perry Brass

As a novelist who writes about the lives of gay men, I realize that most of the stories I tell at some point concern how men meet. In fact, two stories are going on simultaneously. The outside story (which seems like the primary story but isn't) is how the meeting takes place, the nuts and bolts. But the inside story, which animates fiction as well as our own lives, I call the story of *imaginative possibilities.*

We (or the characters in our story) must believe that we can meet, that it is within the larger scope of our own feelings and natures, as well as how we see ourselves and are able to expand ourselves to bring others toward us to meet, and that by opening ourselves up to the possibilities—and allowing actual feelings to prevail—something of consequence to our own happiness can result.

Therefore the real meeting is a result of some story we are "writing" inside our heads. This "story" may hardly be apparent, but it's part of an *imaginative process* going on inside us, a form of creative thinking that makes us believe in our intended future, that says, "This meeting can take place."

That kind of underlying imaginative process is lovely in books. It's probably why people read them. Imaginative processes open up the story to allow genuine feelings in, producing the kind of complications, depth, and satisfactions that make life rewarding.

Christopher Isherwood, the wonderful gay writer, said that it was "miraculous" when the "impossible, wished for thing—love" happens.

But the real miracle is writing your own story so it's full of love, so you create for yourself the wished-for-thing. It's not impossible—because you imagined it and believed in it, and once that imagining takes place, and you find yourself enlarged with your own possibilities, it is not simply amazing how meetings do happen, but strangely inevitable. You are now the "hero," the active agent, of your own story, and all it takes is one other person to come into your life, and open himself up enough to share this feeling with you.

An Angel on the Threshold

Eric Andrews-Katz

The second lap around the inside perimeter of the nightclub proved as fruitless as the first. Daniel leaned against the railing, two steps above the sunken dance-floor, feeling the club's pulsing bass. He raised his vodka-cranberry draining the glass, tipping it until the barely melted ice-chunks knocked against his teeth. He debated re-entering the growing line at the serving bar, but he had just left it. Glancing around the club, he decided on trying his luck at the bar in the adjoining room. He hoped that different luck would be found from a different view.

As his frustration grew, so did his desire just to go home and call it a night. If he could make it through the stagnant crowd filling the walkway and hugging the walls of the club, he could continue out the door. He sighed into submission, readjusted his glasses and tried to take a few more steps further through the crowd, hoping the club's music would rage so loud, it would drown out his inner voice.

His bad mood was partly from the earlier sighting of Andrew, his ex of a nearly twenty-month relationship. Against the backdrop of the club's soundstage, he replayed in his mind the break-up scene from three months earlier. Andrew had dropped the bomb on Daniel without warning.

"You've been such an incredible help," Daniel heard again Andrew's assuring—and infuriating—parting words. "I love you for that."

"Shut up," Daniel said aloud. The voices in his mind silenced.

"I'm sorry?"

Daniel looked to his right. A handsome man seemed to have materialized from the wall and reached out, touching his arm. The stranger stood a hand-span shorter than himself, an average five foot-ten inches, and his eyes sparkled out from a round face, capped with jet-black hair. He smiled widely allowing his teeth to shine brightly from behind thin, impishly curled lips.

"Usually people say 'Hello' when hitting on someone," the stranger said.

Daniel heard him despite the music. He took a deep breath, defensively raising his shoulders, ready to retaliate with some snide remark but decided against it. The day's pattern had to be broken somehow and this was as good as any other remaining chance.

Daniel scoffed at the audacity. "I wasn't hitting on you. Sorry. Bad night." He felt a slight shove from the one of the people lined up behind him. He concluded their meeting with a nod to the handsome man and allowed himself to be carried away in the stream of people. As the surge pushed him towards the front door, Daniel took his exit.

Seattle's early spring night quickly chilled Daniel's skin. It felt good from the heat that burned inside the club. He walked, ignoring the odd glances from the small groups of approaching men. He made it to the end of the alley and stopped, trying to decide what to do next. There was always another club but one was so much like any other. There was little point with his mood the way it currently was and he didn't want to subject anyone else to it. Daniel turned towards his apartment deciding that the devil he knew was better than the devil he didn't.

"Hey!" Came the voice. "Hey! Wait up!"

Daniel ignored the words, convinced they were not meant for him. He put his hands in his pockets and lowered his eyes to watch the pavement. Curiosity slowed his pace at the third calling and he stopped, raising his head. He was about to turn around when someone stomped passed him.

"I've never seen anyone walk away so fast!" The stranger from the club turned and slowed down to keep pace with him. "What are you running from?"

Daniel stopped, keeping his hands safely in his pockets. He lowered his shoulders and looked the man directly in the eye. He forgot what he was prepared to say, distracted by the reflective lights in the man's dark and shining eyes.

"Look, no offense but I really wasn't trying to pick you up. I was just having a bad day and you caught me at a wrong moment."

"That's ok. It wasn't my intention to get picked up."

Daniel didn't understand the man's comfortable audacity.

"Well, no harm, no foul. Good night." Daniel took a step away when he felt someone grab hold of his arm pulling it free from his pocket. "Is there a problem?"

"That depends," the stranger flashed a smile. "What's your name?"

"Why?"

"Why so defensive? I just asked your name?"

"I already told you, I wasn't trying to pick you up." Daniel tried to continue his walk home.

"I just asked your name."

Daniel stopped and clenched his jaw. Slowly, he turned around to face the handsome man standing before him. Daniel stared studiously through narrowed eyes. His lips were pulled into a tight pout and he fought the urge to grind his back molars.

"Daniel. Now are we done?"

"The pleasure's mine. I'm Gabriel."

"Now that we've gotten that out of the way, good night Gabriel." He made another attempt to walk away.

"I'm not a bad guy, if you give me a chance." Gabriel called out after him. "What's the problem?"

Daniel stopped walking and spun around. The light from a streetlamp created a golden glow about Gabriel's face and Daniel could see an amused look worn across his lips.

"Not a bad guy? Well, Mr. Not a Bad Guy, let me tell you what the problem is. The problem is that I was with a man I loved for almost two years. I thought we had a great life; different interests maybe but still—a good life together. He finally gets over his fear of commitment and tells me he met someone else. They're moving in together. He also told me he was 'not a bad guy', so excuse me if I don't fall for another hot jock-type that says he's 'not a bad guy'."

Daniel turned to leave. He walked across the street and onto the main strip. The storefronts were all closed and dark except for a single, low-wattage lamp lit somewhere in the back of each store. He got three steps away before he heard the voice. It was the sheer innocence and charmed tone that halted him.

"You think I'm hot?"

Daniel turned slowly as if in a melodrama. Gabriel stood still, weight leaning on his right hip. He looked posed under a street-lamp hovering on the edge of the projected conical light. His smile glowed Cheshire in the darkness and his eyes sparkled.

Daniel's mouth twisted into a shocked grimace.

"Are you kidding me?" He lowered his voice and approached Gabriel. "You're hot and what's more, you know it. You're standing there in faded jeans that are hugging your hips just enough to draw some attention. You're wearing a tank top that shows off your chest and goes right down the center of your back and highlights all the work you've done at the gym." He took hold of Gabriel's shoulders and twisted him around, tracing the shirt over the skin. He scoffed, "Look at your shoulders." Gabriel turned around wearing the look of amusement. It fueled Daniel's fire. "You can't look me in the eye and tell me you don't think yourself handsome. You have the whole exotic, South-Sea-Islander skin tone going for you."

Gabriel's expression was pure enchantment. His grin crept up the sides of his face and his eyes captured brief sparks of light. He searched Daniel's face and slowly let his front teeth show.

"I play baseball; I don't work out."

Daniel rolled his eyes and pushed Gabriel away by the shoulder.

"Whatever!" He started off again but was stopped by Gabriel's playful apologies. He ran past Daniel, standing in his way.

"I just mean I'm not the stereotype you think I am. I enjoy playing baseball. I don't like working out. Besides, we're not talking about me; we're talking about you. Don't you think you're a good looking man?"

Daniel's face transformed from mild irritation to total confusion.

"Are you kidding me? Look at me! I work on computers all day and I get sunburned from Christmas lights. I'm a little overweight and hate working out. I keep my hair brushed down over my forehead to hide the receding line. I might as well be the poster boy for 'Geeks-R-Us'!"

"Beauty is in the eyes of the beholder."

"Nice cliché."

"I just mean that you of all people should not judge others by their stereotypical looks." Gabriel watched Daniel internally struggle for an argument.

Daniel spoke softly. "Look at our shadows." He stood next to Gabriel, letting the streetlamp cast their shadows in front of them. "If I stand in front of you, you can't even be seen." He moved himself into position to prove his point.

Gabriel looked up from the darkened forms before them. He faced Daniel and his eyes saddened. He reached out and touched Daniel's shoulders. They stiffened before slowly melting under the touch. Gabriel repositioned their bodies until they faced the darkened glass of the storefront. He stepped back allowing the lamp to cast a dim reflection in the glass.

"Why look at shadows when you can see the light?" He reached over Daniel's shoulder, pointing at the two faces that stared back. "Do you know what I see? I see someone who is handsome. He's smart and that is the most attractive thing in a man. Marilyn Monroe once said that she thought Albert Einstein was the sexiest man alive."

"Yeah? Well, look what happened to her."

"You even have a sense of humor. That's a very attractive quality, believe me."

Daniel became lost in the reflection. His sight went from the smoky image of himself to the dimly lit, persuasive expression of the man looking over his shoulder.

He spoke to the glass before them. "Why should I believe you?"

"Because I'm a shallow jock-type and I wouldn't waste my time talking to the poster boy for Geeks-R-Us?"

Daniel snapped around to face Gabriel. He opened his mouth to protest but closed it again, after noticing the friendly grin.

"What do you want from me?"

Gabriel studied Daniel's face, finding an attractive vulnerability in his bewilderment. "How about letting me walk you home?"

"Look, I'm flattered, but I've had a bad night and I've already told you..."

"I know." Gabriel put his palms outward between them. "I'm not looking for that." He let his grin close to a sly smile.

"Then why? Why did you follow me out of the club?"

"You looked so… I don't know. You seemed to need a friend, or at least someone to talk to."

"Thanks, but I don't need a pity escort."

"It's not like that. If you talk to me for a moment instead of running away, maybe you'd know that by now."

"I can't talk to you! You're one of them." Gabriel laughed at his accusation. "You're one of the 'Pretty People.' I'm not. Gay society doesn't allow my type to talk to your type. You're baseball and I'm softball and that makes you in a completely different league."

"We're both in the same ball club. I'm easy to talk to."

"Yeah, right. Thanks for trying to be an angel, but I've fallen and you've failed." Daniel walked away. He replaced his hands into his pockets and lowered his head to study the pavement. Gabriel stepped next to him, keeping in line.

"An angel is only someone that delivers a message that changes your of life."

"And what is your message, Angel Gabriel?"

"You need to get over this low self-image. You can talk to anyone and have them be just as impressed as I am. There are angels all around ready to give you messages if you'd just stop and listen instead of to the worthless chatter of peer pressure."

Daniel shot a sideways, disapproving glance. They turned off the main street onto a more residential area.

Gabriel continued. "There's an old story of a student that came upon his teacher standing on a cliff, in the howling wind. He asked his teacher why and the answer was that he was listening to the messages of the angels. He asked the teacher, 'What is it like to stand in the wind?' and the answer was: 'It's like listening to the words of anyone.' The student was confused and asked: 'What is it like to listen to the words of the angels?' and the teacher's answer was: 'It's like standing in the wind.' You're so busy hearing the wind that you're not listening to the message. No one is on any kind of pedestal until you put him on it; and then you can always take him off. Stop being hung up on the ex and look towards the future.

"Easier said then done."

"Not if you don't make it that way. I'm pretty easy to talk to and you're not that difficult."

Daniel gave in to a small smile. "It might be easier if I looked like you." He stopped walking and let his shoulders roll forward. "I'm tired of the game."

"Then why let anyone else make the rules?"

"Please. People look at you and see an advertisement for fun, sex and all sorts of possibilities. They look at me and see someone they assume is safe; someone who doesn't go out much, who'd never cheat on anyone or do anything risky, and that's fine. I don't mind using what life has given me. But I get tired of always being the one to trade my heart for someone else's security. I'm a doorkeeper for them. They see in me something that they need and once they get their sense of security, they walk out leaving me holding the door open. I'm tired of being the one getting as much notice as a hotel doorman."

"Maybe you need to look for a better class of men. You've told me what you think they see in you, what do you see in them? What was it that made this guy anything special?'

Daniel raised his voice in exasperation: "Andrew was *gorgeous!*"

Gabriel stared back stoically. He waited until the echo of Daniel's yell faded off the deserted streets before quietly asking, "And?" Daniel gave him an incredulous look and spun around to leave. Gabriel grabbed onto his arm. "You've just finished telling me how you feel that gorgeous men are nothing but trouble and yet that's the first trait you focus on and the only one you mention. If that was the only thing he had to offer you, why are you so upset about losing him?"

"I don't expect someone like you to understand."

"I understand more than you think. You've shown a sense of humor and the capability of caring, so believe me when I tell you you're attractive. We've already established that I'm a shallow jock-type, remember?"

"So, you're saying that you'd go out with me?"

The momentary silence fell heavily.

"If I lived here, I would."

Daniel stopped, turning to face Gabriel with an incredulous expression. "Are you fucking kidding me? You've been flirting with me, walking with me and hitting on me only to lead me on?" He scoffed and started off.

"I've not been trying to lead you on and I told you I wasn't trying to pick you up." Gabriel snapped forward to catch up with Daniel. "I do think you're attractive and I would go out with you if I lived here."

"Thank you for your pity walk home." Daniel called over his shoulder, quickening his pace. "You've done your good deed and I thank you, but now you can go home and play in your own league. Go ahead; Blow, Gabriel blow."

"Daniel!" The call was echoed down the street causing him to stop. Gabriel caught up quickly. "You could have come up with something more original that that." He flashed a quick grin. Daniel pulled away and started off. Gabriel quickly followed, again stopping him. "If someone walked out on you, it's their problem, not yours." He reached out running his fingers down Daniel's arm, taking hold of his hand. "If I didn't believe that, why would I walk around with you, in a strange city for over fifteen minutes?" Gabriel's warm smile began to melt Daniel's iced-over expression. "I assure you that the only reason I'm resisting this temptation is not because I don't want to give in, it's just that right now, I can't give in. I'm flying home shortly and need to go. If I didn't, I promise, we wouldn't be here just talking."

The men faced each other, matching stares. Daniel's vision bounced from one of Gabriel's eyes to the other, trying to find even the slightest shred of entrapment and failed. He took a deep breath and let his shoulders and defenses drop with a long exhale, nodding slowly.

Holding hands, they walked without words. The echoes of their feet on the sidewalks were the only traces of sound as a breeze blew passed them. Shadows danced as the broken moon playfully peeked out from between Seattle clouds. Continuing to the end of the street, they crossed under another streetlamp before Daniel stopped in front of his apartment building.

"This is me," Daniel said with a nod towards the building. He flashed an awkward smile, stifling a nervous chuckle. He studied Gabriel's face, finding comfort in the reflection of himself in the dark shining eyes. Their warmth embraced him, consoling, easing his anger.

Daniel leaned in to kiss Gabriel, the gesture surprising him as much as his delight in the action. Their lips touched softly and connected. Neither opened their mouths fully and they both enjoyed the subtle passions of the kiss's innocence. It was broken with the ease of its beginning and Daniel moved his head to rest his chin on Gabriel's shoulders.

He felt Gabriel's arms move around his back and give a firm hug. He felt the strength and the power the muscled arms transferred as they wrapped themselves under his arms and tightened across his back. Daniel felt his own body heat beginning to rise and the familiar stirrings of desire and knew it was time to step back.

"Thanks," Daniel said. He found himself sincere.

Removing his keys, he opened the building's door using his foot to keep it open. Without warning, he leaned it and gave Gabriel a sharp peck on the lips. He pulled open the door far enough to bolt past without allowing anyone else to follow.

Walking up the stairs, he refused to look back somehow knowing that Gabriel was watching from below. Hesitating at another inner door, Daniel debated on whether or not to invite Gabriel up and offer to drive him to the airport later. He dismissed the idea wanting to enjoy the newfound feeling of empowerment, and disappeared behind the door without a look backwards.

Daniel entered his studio apartment and crept over to the one window. Sitting on the edge of the bed, he cautiously slipped back the curtain. Slowly he leaned inwards peering down to the street.

Gabriel was walking away. He waited for a lone car to pass by before crossing the street and kept his eyes focused in front of him. As he crossed under the streetlamp, the yellowish bulb lit up his jet-black hair, momentarily banishing his shadow.

Daniel watched the figure move out of the lit circle. The dim light reflected off his golden skin, catching the material from the tank top. The light briefly reflected off of Gabriel's exposed, muscular shoulder blades and made them resemble wings. He quickened his step, darting past the streetlamp and disappearing into the dark.

Shades

Bill Goodman

It was a lovely afternoon—the kind we get for three weeks every spring and three weeks every fall. Cool, clear, breezy. Birds singing. We were outside on the deck for lunch, as we loved to do. We were talking about where to go for our twenty-fifth anniversary. Fly to Sydney? Take a cruise? Check out Palm Springs? At one point Bob said, "Okay, I've gotta go. Gotta get downtown to the Bank, file some things at the courthouse, pick up the mail." I said, "What's the rush? Let's sit for a while and enjoy the pretty day. The phone's not ringing, there's not much going on in the office. Let's take another ten minutes."

"Nope," he said. "Gotta go. Gotta do my run." All right, I thought. I'll let you go. Since our relationship was nearly perfect anyway, I could give up the extra ten minutes. We lived and worked together, twenty-four/seven, at our law office/home. I was the attorney. Bob was everything else. Bookkeeper, typist, receptionist. Banker, notary, courier. Baker, gardener, lover. "Okay," I said. "You can go. Be careful." That was Monday, about one-thirty.

At two-fifteen I got the call. "Bill, this is Susan at the Bank. You better get down here quick. Bob stopped breathing. We called EMS. I think you should get down here right away. Be careful." I'd gotten a call like that before. The time my Dad died. The caller didn't want to tell me that Dad had died suddenly, at the poker table, surrounded by his buddies, doing what he loved to do. All he said was that they'd taken him to the hospital and that I'd better get over there right away.

Those calls just have a certain ring about them. I sensed that Bob had died, and that Susan just didn't want to tell me. I felt it in her voice. I rushed downtown, my heart racing, my whole life flashing before me. There was a chance it wasn't true, but I started making plans anyway. Call the mortuary. Call the family. By the time I got to the Bank, the technicians had Bob in the ambulance, ready to take off for the hospital. I followed them over there in my car.

I parked in front of the hospital and went inside. I was running down the hall to the emergency room when I saw a little shadow of a man coming through the swinging doors toward me. He was wearing a black suit and a white collar. I figured he was a priest. "Father?" I said.

"Yes," he replied.

"Are you Catholic?"

"Well, yes I am," he said in a thick brogue.

"Are you the Chaplain?"

"Well, I'm the Chaplain on Mondays."

"Okay, " I said. "It's Monday."

"So it is. How can I help ya'?"

"Well, I have a friend who's on the way to the E.R., and I thought you might give him last rites."

"What ya' say?" he asked, holding his hand to his ear.

"I said I have a friend coming to the emergency room, and I'd like you to give him last rites."

"Say it again?"

"Rites."

He looked puzzled and said, "What would he be needing with *rice?*"

"*Not rice,*" I said. "*RITES!*" I made the sign of the cross on my forehead with my thumb.

"Oh," he said. "Well yes, I can help with that. What would be his name?"

I gave him Bob's name, he wrote it down on a little pad, and then he toddled off back through the swinging doors into the E.R.

About an hour later, after things had settled down, the doctor came out and gave us the official word—Bob had died of a sudden heart attack. I was standing in the hallway with Bob's sisters, my mother, the rabbi, and the nurse. About that time, the little priest came toddling back down the hall. "Oh Father," I said, "I want you to meet Bob's sisters."

He came over to offer condolences. "I'm very sorry for your loss. I'm sure Bob was a good man, and that you'll miss him sorely. It may seem like a sad day for ya', but actually, it's a happy day, because Bob has gone to his reward, and he's resting peacefully in the arms of the Lord.

"And you know," he continued rapidly, "someday when you're sad, you're going to need something happy to think about, so I'm going to tell you a little joke. About an hour ago I met this gentleman in the hallway, and he came up to me and asked if I could give his friend last rites, and I thought he said rice, and I asked what he needed with rice, then I figured out he meant rites, so I want in and gave him rites, and it's all okay now and everything's taken care of. And so someday when you're sad you can look back on this and have a laugh. Just remember this little joke and be happy."

With that he was gone. *Vanished.* I think he may have been a leprechaun.

Bob's sisters looked astonished. I didn't have a chance to tell them about this in advance, so they had no clue what the little man was talking about. I tried to explain, but everything was a blur back then.

Anyway, the Father was right. The joke has come in handy. I've told his little story many times. It always brings a hearty laugh, and a happy thought.

At the funeral, the overriding theme was how friendly and cheerful Bob had been, how loving. Always happy, always smiling, always giving the kind word of encouragement. It was in some ways fitting that Bob died at the Bank. He loved that place. He worked there fourteen years before changing jobs and retiring to help me in the office. Of all his daily errands, going to the Bank was his favorite. He loved the people there. It was like his second home. In that respect, Bob was blessed—he died at home, among friends.

The day before he died, our picture was in the Sunday paper. A big picture, the top half of a page in the Metro section, in color. It showed us standing together in the sanctuary at the Temple. I'm Jewish. Bob was Catholic. As my partner, Bob was considered a full-fledged member of the Temple congregation, even though he had not converted, and didn't intend to. But Bob was steadfast in his Catholic faith, and he hadn't missed a mass on Sunday or Holy Day of Obligation since we'd gone to Rome five years earlier. That was the point of the newspaper article. It told about gay people who've managed to keep their respective faiths, despite relentless challenges from the Religious Right. We had just fought a long, hard, losing battle to defeat a same-sex marriage amendment to the Texas Constitution. We were exhausted, dejected, pissed off at the whole thing. And now our picture was in the Sunday paper for all to see, big as life, in living color. The perfect couple. Role models!

I was thrilled. Bob was nervous. He'd said some pretty strong things about the Church, and for once, the paper got the quotes right. The phone started ringing. "Hey guys, what a great photo! Way to go!" But one friend called and said, "Be careful now. People are going to recognize you. Did you hear that somebody got beat up at the bar a few nights ago? You better watch your backs." That kind of stuff doesn't bother me, but I think it really got to Bob. We went to a car wash later that day. Customers were reading the Sunday paper in the waiting room. Bob said, "Let's go outside. Someone might recognize us." So we went outside and sat in the shade.

Anyway, I began to think that Bob's nervousness about the newspaper article might have caused his heart attack. He had just gone to the doctor a few weeks before, and got a glowing report. "Best shape you've been in for a long time," the doctor said. Bob had open-heart surgery fifteen years earlier. Triple bypass. But those things don't last forever, and the newspaper publicity seemed to really stress him out. I had to know if the article was on his mind the moment he died. I had to ask the bank teller what they were talking about when Bob checked out.

The teller, Naomi, had been a shy, sullen, withdrawn kind of person. Not much to say. "Hi" and "Thanks" seemed to be the extent of her vocabulary. She had limp hair, didn't wear much makeup. Bob and I were always nice to her. We were nice to everybody, of course. But I was worried about seeing Naomi again after Bob died. I could only imagine it must have been an awful experience for her. She always seemed to be on the brink of despair, so I figured this might have thrown her over the abyss. After about a week, I went down to the Bank to see Naomi. I was apprehensive.

When Naomi saw me walk into the lobby, she came out from behind the counter, gave me a big hug, and asked me how I was doing. She was smiling, vibrant, talkative, upbeat. She took the deposit slip from my hand and walked back around the counter to process it and stamp my parking ticket. I noticed that her hair was all done up, and her makeup looked great. After a minute or two, I told her I had to ask some difficult questions. "What were you talking about with Bob when he died? Did he mention the newspaper article? How did it happen exactly?"

"Well," she said, "we were talking about Thanksgiving. What I was fixing, what he was going to take to his sister's on Thursday." Yes, they had talked about the newspaper article, but that was not the focus. He was excited about the holiday and seeing everyone. "Suddenly, he just sort of choked, caught his breath, and started to fall backward. I tried reaching across the counter to catch him, but I couldn't. He fell to the ground, and the man standing in line behind him gave him CPR until the emergency crew arrived." So perhaps it wasn't the newspaper article.

I said to Naomi, "I'm glad I you've told me these things. I needed to know what was on Bob's mind. I feel better now. It's a great relief to me. Actually, *I feel good right now.* It feels good just standing here talking with you."

At that, Naomi's eyes went wide, and she looked at the teller to her left. The other teller heard what I said and looked surprised too. Naomi said, "That's so strange. A customer was in here a few days ago, standing exactly where you are, and said exactly the same thing— that he felt good standing there. He told me he sensed a 'good spirit' abiding there, and that something special must have happened."

"Gosh," I said. "That's just how I feel. It's not exactly light, or warmth, but it's definitely a good feeling of some kind. It's wonderful to stand here and talk with you, to see how well you're doing, and how happy you are."

Looking back on it, I came to believe that there was a special spot there. Something like those pools of light that Jimmy Durante walked through at the end of his television show, when he said "Good night, Miss Calabash, wherever you are." I think there was a portal of some kind in front of Naomi's counter, where Bob beamed up, directly to Heaven. The ambulance, the emergency room, the funny little priest at the hospital—all that was after the fact. Bob died and shot up instantly, right from that spot. And it felt good to be standing there.

I told Bob's sisters about it. They said they wanted to go down to the Bank someday and stand on the spot to see what it feels like. But it's too late now. The building was sold to a hotel chain. The teller lines are gone. The bank lobby is a hotel lobby now. I wonder if the spot is still there.

The bank office was moved to a small corner of the building. Naomi remained cheerful and happy, a bright spot in anyone's day. A while back, I was telling a friend this whole story. How Naomi had so completely changed. How outgoing she had become. How smiling and friendly. How she was utterly transformed.

My friend said, "Bill. Don't you realize? *That's Bob's personality!*"

As mentioned, a few weeks before he died, Bob and I were talking about where to go to celebrate our anniversary. "Let's go somewhere special," I said. "Let's take a cruise, we've never been on a cruise. Let's go somewhere far away. Let's go to Sydney."

"No, that's too far," he said. "I don't want to be on a plane that long." I realize now, looking back, that Bob probably hadn't been feeling well, and just wasn't telling me. Bob was like that. He didn't want to complain, least of all about his health, because he knew my Florence Nightingale tendencies would kick in. He didn't want me hovering over him, or worrying.

Anyway, it got to be kind of a joke. Friends kept asking how we were going to celebrate our anniversary. Bob would say, "Bill wants to go to Sydney. But that's too far. No way we're going to Australia." After a while, I got tired of hearing about it, so one day I said:

"Okay, dear. I understand. We're not going to Sydney. Let's go somewhere else. Palm Springs, maybe. *We'll be dead before we get to Sydney.*"

The second I said that, I regretted it. It didn't come out the way I meant it. I meant to say that taking a long trip wasn't that important to me, that it was okay to stay close by, that I would give that up for him. I've always said that a relationship isn't fifty/fifty, it's a hundred/hundred. You have to put your entire self into it to make it work; you can't just go half way. Bob and I had been growing closer over the last few months, thinking about our anniversary, and I figure we were at about ninety-seven/ninety-seven. I was giving up another point or two.

But it obviously hit Bob another way. The instant those words were out of my mouth, a dreadful look came over him. I swear, it seemed like a shade came down across his face. He looked gray. It was as if a theatrical scrim had descended in front of him. You could see through it, but dimly. I didn't know what to make of it, or what to say. Bob looked rejected, disappointed, and oddly horrified. I apologized, of course, but continued to feel terrible about it.

Eventually, we made plans to host an anniversary party at home, and go to Palm Springs right after. We'd never been to Palm Springs, and were looking forward to a few quiet days at an upscale bed and breakfast.

Bob died a few weeks later. We never made it to Palm Springs.

A few months later, I was telling my sister-in-law Barbara the story about the shade coming down across Bob's face. We were at a family dinner in a nice restaurant in far north Dallas. I noticed the roll-down window shades around the perimeter of the room. It was late afternoon, and you could see daylight coming through the screens, but dimly. I told Barbara that the effect had been the same on Bob. He looked a dim shade of gray.

Then Barbara recalled the day Bob had his heart surgery. We all knew that the procedure had not gone well. The doctors later told us that they actually lost him on the table. He essentially died, but they brought him back. I had known this for a long time, and felt that each day he lived was an extra gift.

But then Barbara told me something I had never heard before. She said Bob told her, more than once, about his memory of the operation. As is often heard from near-death patients, he said he saw a bright white light and was walking down a tunnel toward the light. He said he saw his mother and other departed relatives urging him onward. But he felt something pulling on him, pulling him back, bringing him back to this world. He woke up, and went on living.

"Bob never told me that," I said. "He never once mentioned it to me."

"Really? He told me about it several times," Barbara said. "And you know what? He thought the force pulling him back was *you*, Bill."

I was astounded, dumbfounded. Ungrounded. I felt a sinking feeling come over me, and remorse. As I pondered this stunning news, I came to another realization. If I were indeed the force pulling Bob back, keeping him alive for all these years, then I understood what happened the day I gave up on the trip to Sydney. It was like I had stopped pulling, turned loose of the rope, let go of my belief in Bob, let go of my need for him. When I said those awful words, it was as if the life force in Bob had come unchained. A shade came down across his face, he began to fade, and soon he was gone.

I expressed that thought to Barbara and the other guests around the table. It put us all in a somber mood. A moment passed. Then a low whirring sound welled up across the restaurant. Suddenly, all at once, the window shades around the room began to rise. Automatically, in unison, they disappeared into the ceiling. The gentle light of evening poured in. A rosy golden sunset light. It was an awesome moment. The shades—the shade—had lifted.

Then I knew that everything would be all right.

The Canals of Mars

Victor J. Banis

Beauty may be in the eye of the beholder, but ugly is there for everyone to see. I can afford to speak so flippantly on the subject, since I was, and I say it in all modesty, beautiful indeed.

The operative word there, of course, is, was. Was, before a vial exploded in the lab, and turned that beautiful face into a road map of Mars. In the novels, in the movies, this is where the handsome plastic surgeon rushes to the rescue, and by the next chapter-reel, I am Joan Crawford all over again, and on my way to becoming Mrs. Surgeon. Or, in my gay instance, Mister and Mister Surgeon.

Cut. First off, he was older than the hills and singularly unattractive. And, he was already married and blatantly heterosexual. Don't get me wrong: I have no objections to heterosexuals, so long as they aren't too obvious. And, hell, if he had been able to make me lovely again, I'd have murdered her, had the change, and gone after the old codger regardless.

Three operations later, however, the mirror still showed me the surface of Mars. The craters had shrunk somewhat, and the canals had shifted, but it was still Mars. I balked at going under the knife a fourth time.

"No, it won't be a dramatic improvement," he said when I questioned him.

"In other words, I'm still going to look like something brought back up half eaten," I asked, and the tone in which he assured me that

I would look better told me that "better" still was not going to be very
good.

Which was where we left it. Notwithstanding the pleasure of lying
abed in a hospital—there is nothing quite like the personal touch of
your own bedpan, is there—and all that delicious food, I promised I
would get back to him, without specifying in which life.

When you are damaged, as I was, they give you lots of money, as if
that would compensate for what I had lost. I was grateful, though, that
I did not have to work. Not because I am all that fond of lying about
vegetating, but because I did not have to face all those slipping-away
eyes that I was sure to encounter.

There were not many places one could go, however, without the
same problem. Jason threw in the towel and was gone. Jason who loved
"the soul of me," who loved me "through and through," was through.
I told myself, "good riddance," he was too shallow to be of much use
as a lover, and I tried to not to think that I had mostly been just about
as shallow most of my life. I definitely tried not to remember that I
loved the bastard.

I am fortunate that I am comfortable with my own company, as
many are not, and there is a certain bitter comfort in wallowing in self-
pity. That wears thin, though, after a while, and the walls of my little
apartment seemed to shrink inward with each passing day. So, when
Douglas called me, to say he was going to spend a month or two at his
cottage on the shore, and would I like to come along, I jumped at the
chance. I might not have in the past. I had always understood that
Douglas was in love with me—whatever that meant. Jason had been
in love with me, too, he said, and what had that amounted to? Who
knew what "love" was? I didn't.

In the past, I might have wondered at Douglas' intentions, getting
me all alone in that little cottage of his. He was Jason's friend. I liked
him well enough on the few occasions when I had met him, and he
was a lovely person—just not my type. Not as old as that surgeon,
probably, but, really, too old for my tastes, sixty if he was a day, maybe
more. I didn't really know. Anyway, what difference does a number
make? There comes a point—doesn't there?—when you're just old.
Though I have to admit, if you weren't hung up on age, he was a
youthful looking sixty whatever.

They say it's an ill wind, however. With the face I now had, I did not have to worry about whether it was only my beauty that men were after.

I will give him credit. He was one of the few, the first, maybe, since the accident, who did not flinch when he saw me. He even managed to look me straight in the face, and not quickly avert his eyes.

"Pretty awful, isn't it?" I said. He had come out to help me bring my bags in.

He smiled. "I've seen worse," he said. "I used to work in a burn center."

"I hope that wasn't meant to make me feel all warm and fuzzy inside," I said, following him up the wide, shallow steps to the front door.

"No, I've got martinis waiting. That's their job."

They failed, however. All they did was lower the barriers I had so carefully raised. The martinis, and Douglas. He was an elegant man, suave and distinguished. He was also thoughtful and gentle; I hadn't known that about him before. Of course, I had never been alone at his beach cottage with him. Never, really, been alone with him at all.

He talked of all sorts of things, movies and people we both knew and recipes and the shore and the weather and, when I could bear it no longer and the tears began to stream down my cheeks, he stopped talking and just held me. He didn't try to tell me it would be okay. He didn't try to tell me that I was still beautiful. He did not swear it would all get better, or somehow magically go away, or any of the stupid, insensitive things that others had said that had only made me feel worse. He didn't even chide me when I blubbered about the canals of Mars.

He just held me and gently kissed my cheek; not even the good one. He kissed the one that was scarred, kissed Mars' canals as if they were the most natural things on this planet. He was the first person since the accident with the courage to put his lips to my flesh; the first, even, to put his arms around me. Jason had tried, and had paled and turned away before his lips touched me, and said with a sob, as if it were his heart breaking, "I can't, I just can't." Then he left.

Douglas only held me and kissed my cheek, and when the tears stopped at last, he took me upstairs and tucked me into my bed like a little child, and brought me a cup of hot chocolate, and made me drink it, and sat and held my hand until I fell asleep.

"How long are you here for?" I asked him the next day. We were sitting on the little terrace. It was early in the season, the air still cool, but the sun warm, the ocean close enough for us to smell the brine and the seaweed. Too early for the tourists; too early, if only just, for the summer crowd.

"Till you're better," he said.

"Douglas, really, I'm all right," I said. He gave me a mocking smile. "I will be, anyway. All right, I mean. You don't have to look after me."

"I don't have to do anything," he said with a snort. He got up from his chaise lounge and offered me a hand. "Let's go for a dip, why don't we?"

"I'm sure the water's icy," I said.

"No doubt." He gave me a look that said he knew perfectly well that was not my reason for declining. "There's nobody else around," he said. "If anybody comes, we'll see them miles off."

Well, say I'm a freak if you will, but don't call me a coward. I got up without a word and set my drink aside, and started for the beach. He fell into step beside me, whistling tunelessly.

I had planned to maintain my longsuffering attitude, to punish him—for what, I wasn't quite clear, but surely no good deed should go unpunished. The water, however, wasn't nearly so cold as I had expected, and the sun got warmer as it rose in the sky, and a warm breeze ruffled my hair. The gulls jeered at me and when Douglas got tired of my standing stiffly in knee deep water, toes firmly planted in the squish of sand, he splashed me, and I yelped and kicked water in his face and before I knew it, we were horsing around like a pair of kids, laughing and ducking one another, and I actually forgot that he was an old fart and I was a horror to gaze upon.

Until he said, "Shit," loudly, and I followed his gaze, and saw a couple clambering over the rocks, heading in our direction.

I ran out of the water, and grabbed my towel off the beach and started back toward the cottage, not wanting to be seen, knowing what would happen to their faces when they got close enough to see mine; and Douglas made a point of switching sides with me, so that he was between the scarred side of my face and the approaching strangers. They were probably not close enough to see, but I was grateful anyway. The canals were mine alone.

Well, of course Douglas was stuck with them too, but he seemed not to mind them. He did not pretend not to see them; he just didn't seem to mind.

Except for that intrusion, though, we were alone. His little section of rocky beach sat in a cove, so it was mostly private even as the season got on and other cottages up and down the shore were occupied. That couple, they must have been day-trippers, were the only persons we saw the whole time we were there. The only ones I saw, at any rate; he went into town every couple of days for supplies, walking the five miles or so in and out, and came back to update me: "The Jeffersons are here, they're the second cottage down," or "The Wilsons are early this year." No one came by, though. I had been here for a weekend once before, with Jason. There had been lots of neighbors dropping in, and we had made the rounds as well. Maybe he warned them off.

We swam nearly every day. I had used to swim a lot, and loved it, but I was out of practice, and out of shape. It was good exercise, and a good way to work off my frustrations and my anger. I swam sometimes for two hours with only the occasional pause for rest. He didn't swim that long, of course. He was old. When he began to tire and grow short of breath, he would go sit on the beach.

"And enjoy the view," he said. He looked my still handsome body up and down and gave me a wolfish leer. What he really did, of course, was stand guard, in case anyone should approach. I stopped watching for them myself, and trusted him. But they didn't come.

Evenings, he fixed us martinis and I got into the habit of preparing dinner. I had cooked in the past, but I had gotten away from it. I found now that I enjoyed it. I took unexpected pleasure in fixing the things he liked, the way he liked them. Nothing too fancy: steaks or lobster or burgers on the grill, and when it turned out we both loved it, the tuna casserole that Jason had always turned his nose up at. The one with potato chips. I caught Douglas licking the salt off the chips and smacked his hand with the spatula. Later, though, I tried it myself when he wasn't looking, and he caught me at it and smacked my hand.

"I was in the hospital for eight weeks," I told him petulantly. "You're not supposed to hit someone when they're recovering from surgery."

"Bullshit," he said, and offered me a chip to lick. He wasn't always elegant.

We ate sometimes on the terrace when it was warm enough, and at the kitchen table when it wasn't, and some evenings it was cool enough for a fire in the fireplace and we ate in front of it. There was no television, but he had a radio and a stereo, and somehow he had managed to stock a shelf with most of my favorite music. Sometimes he sat beside me, and he would shyly put his arm around me, and I would lean against him and put my head on his shoulder while we listened to music together, and watched the fire. We didn't talk much, but the silence was comfortable. Always, when he said good night, he kissed my cheek. The bad one.

After a week, when he started to turn away from me at my bedroom door, I said, "You don't have to go to your own room."

It took him a moment to realize what I meant. "Are you sure?" he said, uncertain and hopeful all at the same time.

"I'm sure."

I would have turned the lights out, but he wouldn't have it. "Do you have any idea how long I've dreamed of seeing you like this?" he asked. "I never thought I'd be so lucky."

I was naked by this time. He looked me up and down with undisguised pleasure while he undressed. That part of me, at least, was still fine. I was glad, for his sake as well as my own. He deserved beauty. I turned the bad cheek away.

He was naked too now, seemingly unembarrassed by his old man's body. He dropped on to the bed beside me. He looked better dressed than undressed. Old men do, don't they? I tried not to notice the spare tire, or the way his chest looked caved in, or the droop of his buns. That was just who he was. It couldn't be helped.

"That was when I was beautiful," I said. "And please don't say, 'you still are.'"

"You still are," he said.

Without thinking, I put a hand to my face. "The canals of Mars?"

"Where I shall swim in ecstasy," he said and kissed the scars. I watched and listened and felt carefully with all my senses for some hint of reluctance, of disgust or even discomfort, but if he felt any, he disguised it completely.

He took hold of my hand and rubbed it across the pouch of his belly, where he had thickened about the waist. "If you'll overlook this," he said, and leaned over to kiss my lips.

It was good sex. Not great, but good. Of course, sex had been a solitary pastime for me since the accident. Jack off and think of Jason, think of Jason and jack off. Maybe at this point in time, anybody would have made it seem good. I don't know. I don't think so. I suppose that is one of the advantages of age, though: practice makes you, if not perfect, pretty adept. He was. He made love to me. I had never experienced that before. Lots of sex, none hotter than with Jason, but no one had ever made love to me. It was nice. I kissed him when it was over, and kissing him, actually forgot about how I looked. He stayed the night in my bed. I slept comfortably in the crook of his arm.

I realized when I woke in the morning that I had forgotten, too, how old he was.

After that, we slept together every night. He could not have been more tender, more loving, and I stirred myself to be as good as I could be for him as well. It got better, our sex. I wanted it to, and it did, it got very much better. I stopped jacking off remembering Jason. I didn't stop remembering Jason, but I stopped jacking off, remembering him. Stopped jacking off altogether, to tell the truth. Who had anything left to shoot, the way we were going at it? He was insatiable. The old goat. It was flattering. Exhausting, but flattering.

One night when we finished, he rolled on his back with a gasp and said, "If you keep it up like that, you're going to kill me. I'm an old man, remember?"

"You're not so old," I said. And, to my surprise, I meant it. I'd been to bed with men forty years his junior who weren't the lover he was. Or, maybe they were. What I really mean is, that I hadn't gotten the pleasure, the same kind of pleasure, from them that I did from him. Maybe that was in part the pleasure that I was giving. I had never thought of it like that before: taking pleasure in giving it. I wanted to make him happy. I wanted to please him. When I did, and he made it quite obvious that I did, it made me happy too.

That was a new one for me.

We divided up the housecleaning. The one who scrubbed the bathroom got to pick the music. Since that was not one of my favorite chores, we listened to a lot of Sarah Vaughn and Dinah Washington, both new to me, but I quickly fell in love. It would no doubt have looked a little funny to someone else, him scrubbing the tub and me mopping the kitchen, and both of us bellowing "All of Me," along with Dinah. His lack of pitch didn't seem all that important. It was a while before I realized: I hadn't sung in years. Even before the scars. Where, I wondered, had the music gone?

I learned that he liked to read aloud. I'd never had anyone do that for me, but I found that I enjoyed that too. He had a lovely reading voice, multi-colored and far more musical than his singing voice. He read Vanity Fair, a chapter an evening. Listening to him, watching the fire, it was easy to sink into the story. Becky Sharp winked at me from the flames. I liked her.

I liked the beach at night, too, maybe because I didn't have to think about anybody seeing me. Anybody but Douglas. I would sit and watch the surf, and he would lie on his back and gaze up at the stars.

"I wonder," he said one night, "When we look at them, is it the stars twinkling, or our eyes?"

"My eyes don't twinkle," I told him.

"Oh, but they do," he said, sitting up with a grin and looking into them. "They get like Christmas lights when you're about to come."

"That is so ridiculous," I said. "You are so full of shit."

We made love in the warm sand, the murmur of the waves like muted strings to our dissonant chorus of sighs and moans. He went down on me, and just as I was about to go off, he jumped up over me and said, "There, they're sparkling like crazy."

I couldn't help laughing, and he laughed with me, and hugged me. I had almost forgotten how to laugh.

After a while, I lifted my head and looked down at myself. "Were you planning on finishing that?" I asked.

"Try to stop me," he said, sliding down in the sand.

Sometimes, after swimming, his hips bothered him. "A touch of arthritis," he said and I quickly got into the habit of massaging them for him.

"Are you going to massage me all over?" he asked with a naughty grin when I told him to strip and lie down on the floor.

"I'm going to work on the parts that are sore."

"Oh, have I got an ache here," he said with a laugh, and cupped his balls in his hand. I slapped his butt hard.

"Now you've got one there, too," I said. But I kept my word, and massaged that for him as well. Everywhere he said he ached.

He kept finding new places.

He was getting ready to walk into town one day—it was a month or more after I had arrived there, though the time had passed with astonishing rapidity—when he asked with a sly expression if I wanted to go along.

"Don't be fucking stupid," I snapped, angry out of all proportion. "Did you plan to sell tickets?"

"Come here," he said. He took my hand and brought me into his bedroom. There was a large mirror over his dresser. Mine had none. This one, and the little one on the medicine cabinet were the only ones in the cottage. I could shave in the medicine cabinet mirror without looking at the scars. The whiskers didn't grow on that side. There were advantages to having your skin burned off. Think about it, if you don't like shaving.

When I saw where he was leading me, I held back. "Don't," I said. "Don't be cruel. You know I don't want to see."

"But you do," he said, and would not let go of me, and all but dragged me to the mirror. "Look." I automatically turned the bad side away from the glass, but he put a hand on my chin and stubbornly turned my face.

It would be dramatic and exciting to say that the scars had disappeared. They hadn't; but even I could see that they had faded considerably. I still looked like the surface of Mars, but viewed through an out of focus telescope. Someone—not everyone, but probably one or two here or there—could look at it and not want to vomit.

I put a hand up and ran my fingers over my cheek, as if to confirm that it really was my face, my present face, and not some photograph he had taped up to fool me. I couldn't think what to say. I shook my head, bewildered.

He grinned and kissed my cheek, the bad side—the not-quite-so-bad-side-now—and said, "I'll be back in an hour or so. Anything you want?"

It was maybe a week after that, the day he went down to the beach alone. The weather had turned cool, and I decided to stay on the terrace and read. I read and dozed, and thought about what had happened to my face. I had only looked once since that first day, afraid that I would realize I was merely a victim of wishful thinking. It wasn't that, though. The scars were still there, but the ugly raw-liver red of the canals had faded to patches of dusty rose. I couldn't understand it. I wanted to think about it. The doctor had given me a special salve. I hadn't bothered using it, thinking there was little chance of significant improvement. Now I applied it assiduously morning and night, not minding the rotten-potato stink. If Douglas minded it, he never said.

Still, I was afraid to look, afraid to jinx whatever was happening.

Douglas shouted something from the beach, interrupting my reverie. I sat up and looked. He was holding a starfish aloft, waving it for me like a flag. I laughed and waved back, and he tossed it into the water again. Some would have kept it for a trophy, letting the living thing within the shell die. He wouldn't. He was too good a man. I had never known a better one, my whole life, or one—it surprised me to realize this—whose company pleased me more. Our days had flown by. How could I have thought him a bore, in the past? How could I have been so vacuous?

He began to climb up the rocks, coming back. I watched him and it occurred to me all at once that he looked different. His waist was trimmer, and that little paunch had shrunk away. Seeing him like this, at the distance, he might have passed for a man in his forties. His early forties. All that swimming, I thought; all those hikes into town and back.

Or, something.

"Something is happening to us," I said.

He smiled; I don't think I had ever actually noticed what a sweet smile he had. "What do you mean?" he asked.

"Well, look at us. Look at you. You look fifteen years younger than you did when we came here. Twenty years, maybe."

He lifted his head to look down at his naked body. "I've lost some weight. That's your cooking. I lived on pizza in town."

"But it's not just your weight," I said. I rolled onto my side and ran a hand across the surface of his belly, the way I had done our first night in bed. "Look, it's hard as a rock."

"That's not the only thing, in case you hadn't noticed," he said. He took my hand and put it on his erection.

"Okay, case in point," I said, but I did not take my hand away. "We just fucked, not even ten minutes ago. When was the last time you were raring to go so soon afterward?"

"The last time? Probably I was jacking off thinking about you," he said. He rolled over to face me, and took me in his arms, and kissed me, and for a while, we had no more conversation.

Really, he was insatiable. The old goat. Damned good, now, but insatiable.

But he wasn't an old goat anymore, either. I couldn't stop thinking about it. I couldn't stop looking at him. Before, at the beginning, I had mostly averted my eyes when he was naked, embarrassed for him, turned off for myself.

It wasn't just curiosity that had me staring at him whenever I could now, though I was fascinated by the changes in him; it almost seemed as if I could see them happening. I looked because he was terrific to look at. It wasn't only his body. He might have had the world's most successful face-lift. The jowls were gone, the laugh lines, the furrows on his brow. His thin hair was thicker, and lustrous. He had always been handsome in an old man way, handsome-distinguished. Now, he was just plain hot. Had he always been? Had I always been blind?

"Is this still sore?" I asked him, massaging one hip.

"Not since you started working on it," he said. "You've got magic in your hands."

I stared at him. At his round, hard butt. I still would not look at my scarred face. I was too afraid of what I would see. Or not see. But his butt was lovely to look at. I looked every chance I got. Both of us enjoyed the massages.

Of course, he wasn't going to let me avoid that other sight.

"Look," he said, holding the mirror up in front of me.

I turned away from it, like a vampire afraid that he will see no reflection. "No, I don't want to," I said sharply. "I'm afraid."

"Look," he said insistently and again put the mirror in front of my face. I had no choice but to look into it.

"What do you see?" he asked.

"I see…." I hesitated. Did I really see what I thought I saw? It was almost—not quite, but very close, to what I had used to see, in the past; before the accident. My face. Not that hideous thing that had been foisted on me, but the beautifully sculpted cheekbones, the mouth that Jason had always called "too kissable," the little rounded chin.

The smooth, porcelain skin. "It's me," I said, in wonder. "The canals. They're gone." Nearly, at any rate. I had to lean toward the glass, peer closely, to see their faint vestiges.

"Yes. I wanted to say something sooner, but I wanted to be sure," he said.

"I'm beautiful," I said. I put my hand up to touch my face, still not able to comprehend.

"You always have been," he said. "To me. It's just the surface stuff that's changing. That's really not all that important. There never really were any canals, you know." I looked my puzzlement at him. "On Mars, I mean," he said. "It was a bum lens in somebody's telescope, badly focused, the way I understand it, and somebody mistranslated the word 'channels,' so it was all a misunderstanding. Later, when they could see it better, could look at it through a proper lens, and somebody corrected the translation, they realized there weren't any canals. Never had been."

"But mine were. And now they're gone." I looked at him, kneeling over the bed, at his firm, youthful body. "We've both changed. You look entirely different as well. What can it mean?"

"Maybe," he said, putting the mirror aside, "We were just looking through the wrong lens. Maybe we're just seeing one another now through the eyes of love. Maybe we had the word wrong, too. Maybe what we thought that was, was something else."

Love. I thought about that for a while. Was that what this was? It wasn't like anything I had felt before, nothing like what I had thought love was. Nothing, for instance, compared to what I had felt in the past, for Jason. And yet, it felt good, in a way I had never felt for anyone before. It felt good knowing he loved me. Whatever it was I felt for him, that felt good too. I was afraid to call it love, though. What I had called love in the past had gone from me in a twinkling, had drowned in those canals on Mars. Before they got the telescope straightened out.

He saw my expression. "What?" he asked.

"I was just thinking."

"About?"

I looked directly at him. "About Jason," I said.

I could see that it had hurt him. His eyes, so bright a moment before, went dull, although he managed to keep a faint smile on his lips. "Still hurt, does it?"

I sighed. I couldn't lie to him. Maybe that was love, when you can't lie to someone. How would I know? About love? "Yes."

"You're thinking, if he saw you now, just like you used to be, that he would fall in love with you all over again."

Was that what I wanted? I wasn't sure. I couldn't say the idea wasn't tempting. I remembered the last time, the regret and the shame on Jason's face. What would it be worth, to see his expression change to something else? What was I willing to pay for that satisfaction? I said nothing, and after a moment, he read my silence, and sighed also.

"Well, there's only one way to know, isn't there?" he said. He sat up, and reached for his clothes where he had tossed them on the floor when we had undressed so hurriedly. I looked at his back, so firm, the muscles rippling the way a young man's muscles did, his cheeks, when he raised them to slip his boxers on, round and firm and pale, as if they were carved of alabaster. I thought of how sleek they felt when I ran my hand over them, massaging him. I almost reached out to touch him.

Almost.

We drove into the city that same day, hardly talking. We left my car at the beach. "I can bring it in for you later," he said. He never stopped thinking of ways to make things easier for me. Even now. Even taking me back to Jason.

He stopped at the curb in front of my apartment. I sat, looking for a moment up at the window on the third floor. Jason had promised to look after things, but I could see that the geranium in the window was dead.

I glanced sideways at Douglas. He was trying to smile, but the droop of his jowls and the furrows on his brow turned his smile sad. In the afternoon light, the pouches under his eyes looked like wet teabags.

"It's all right," he said, and put his hand atop mine. "Really, I mean it. You can't know how happy you've made me these last couple of months. Whatever you decide now, it won't take anything away from that. It won't make me love you any less."

I looked down at his old man's hand, knobby and wrinkled. I started to reach for the mirror over the visor, and changed my mind. I didn't need to look. I didn't need to see Jason, either. I already knew what he was. And wasn't.

"Take me home," I said.

"Home?" He glanced past me, at the apartment building, wanting to be certain, not daring to misunderstand.

"The cottage. Our cottage. Please."

He was silent for a moment. "You're sure?" he asked.

"Yes," I said. I had never in my life been more sure of anything.

He looked at me long and hard. I looked back, full face, not turning my cheek away as I had gotten into the habit of doing. I didn't need to now. I knew that.

Finally, he leaned across the seat and touched my cheek, the scarred one, with his lips, and I turned my face and found his lips with mine, and kissed him.

He put the car in gear, and drove away from the curb. About halfway to the cottage, he began to sing, "All of Me."

"You know, you never do get on pitch," I said with some asperity.

"Well, then, you sing it," he said.

I did. We sang it together at the tops of our lungs. People in the cars we passed stared. Some of them smiled. Some of them saw into the car, and looked away. Douglas grinned sideways at me, a boyish, devilish grin, and took my hand and put it on his lap.

"Guess what I want to do when we get home," he said.

"You old goat," I said, but I did not take my hand away.

What Queer Spirit Sees

Jeffery Beam

Before I had heard of reincarnation, spiritual evolution, the One-in-All, I already knew about them. My life has been a process of remembering them. The soul, before coming into this life, chooses its circumstances. Transcendence comes with the Queer territory. In any case, my daemon brings me face to face with who I can become, my utmost possibility. I have found my religious self an ally in understanding why I am Queer. I use the word "Queer" because of its ritual connotations. Making something sacred from something intended to oppress and shame. I trust it encompasses, not just homosexuality, but all free sexualities as William Blake praised them: free from Society's imposed sanctions against the body's divinity.

The Celts, even as the early Christians, and as common in many pagan societies, were Pantheists, believing the Divine permeates all things. Children are too, until we fill them with myths of power, dominance, and shame. We are *integral* to the Sacred; participant in it, of it. Grace births from the regions of the Self where Good and Evil sit at the same table, drink the same wine, have the same desires. People, unable to discern Good from Evil, make laws in hopes of doing so. But it is the Law's spirit we must honor, not just the letter. And trust Goodness will find us.

Some might say this Queer Desire Self looms so large because Society represses Desire, a material understanding perhaps adequate for political discussion. Lost, then, a broader spiritual view. Being Queer in Western society in this new millennium faces this Desire Self head-on. To couple with Death and Creativity as evolutionary forces—personal, but also human. The repression which feeds this Self is as essential to human progress as rebellion is, just as the Grim Reaper suspended above gay culture has also had its purpose.

I have found a species of mysticism, practical and ecstatic, Queer, defined by Poetry, Pantheism, Gnosticism (wisdom in process, not just believed): The Bhakti Path. The Path of Love. A poet's way, inhabited already by Whitman, Dickinson, Kabir, Mirabai, St. John of the Cross, and Rilke and so many more. I was born outside the city gates desiring the love of men, and born a poet—one with a mystical bent at that. The outsider sees with an eye washed clean of allegiances. I learned to fend for myself—the dominant law becoming revealed as arbitrary and relative. The outsider must work harder to define him or herself. Being Queer, I was either to go under, or find voices in religion and the arts that could reaffirm the One-in-All, the Body as Temple. I had finally to realize that on my own I could only do so much. A surrender of sorts had to take place before I could truly know myself. In the Divine I found a source of strength against oppression, and an understanding as to why suffering exists. This is an ongoing process. One in which I am still learning to participate. Poet James Broughton once declared, "God is my Beloved / God and I are lovers / He lifts me in tidal embraces / that turn the world on end."

Grace resides within each of us, whomever we love. I don't require that you become as I am. But if you require, as the great teachers have, that I "know myself," you must accept who I know I am. Allen Ginsberg advised, "Let the straight flower bespeak its purpose in straightness, which is to seek the light, and let the crooked flower bespeak its purpose in crookedness, which is to seek the light."

Trying to know myself, and accepting the person I find, has taught me I am Divinity itself. It has given me access to compassion for others partly because I have needed so much myself. If sin exists, then the lies that society forces homosexuals to make and seek are cardinal. Our society calls itself Christian. How difficult it is for victims of society's misplaced morality to place themselves comfortably in it. How confusing to read these words in the Sermon on the Mount: "poor in spirit," "they that mourn," "the meek," "they which hunger and thirst after righteousness," "the merciful," "pure in heart," "the peacemakers," "persecuted for righteousness sake," "men shall revile you, and persecute you, and say all manner of evil against you falsely," and "rejoice, and be exceeding glad." I remember hearing these words, and not defiling them, as some might think, by comparing myself to one of Christ's poor, but only thinking "all this happens to me, too, as a homosexual person, as a human being. Jesus must love me."

When I make love to a man, I make love to the Divine. I am your brother, just as I am brother to the stars. And the stones. If you burn me, this body dies. If you burn me, this body lives. A Queer poet, child-like, saintly, sees the Kingdom of Heaven in every leaf, every drop of blood spilled, every meal, every automobile, every homeless person's cardboard box, every bright mansion, every bird song. The Queer Spirit sees All-in-All in every act of love.

After Edward

Michael Gouda

I miss him. Of course I do. But life, as they say, must go on for the rest of us so I don't talk about him much, and my friends don't either, not after the first few terrible months. I think about him though, and I'm pretty sure he thinks of me. I have no proof of this, of course, and I don't have any religious convictions, except one and that is I don't think there's a god—well, if there is, he isn't a loving, caring one who looks after the good and innocent and punishes the guilty. The world, and the state it's in, and the way people behave in it, is surely adequate proof of that.

But there is a part of me that thinks that surely Edward and all that he was hasn't completely disappeared. Is he just there solely in the memories of his relatives and his friends and his lover—me? I suppose you could say that his influences on others, what he did and said and wrote in the world lingers on. Perhaps he changed the lives of some people, certainly he did mine and so that is passed on through me or through anyone else he touched and that I, and they, will do the same. So no one ever completely disappears though they may be forgotten.

Can there be more?

I would have said no but...

Well, this is what happened. Judge for yourself.

⁓⁚⁔

A couple of months after Edward died, I got a phone call from his mother. Now I must tell you that Edward's parents seemed to have no problem with the fact that he was gay. Actually mine said they didn't either. The thing was they (that's *my* parents) preferred not to be reminded of it, so we didn't really talk about my life, my gay life, that is. On the other hand Edward's Mum and Dad were apparently always ready to hear gay anecdotes, the stories, whether true or exaggerated, that gay people tell either against themselves or to boost their self-confidence as regards sexual conquests. Of course he didn't go into explicit details, but was quite prepared to talk of the gay life, its ups and downs.

"Hello, dear," she said (I'm back with the telephone call now), "Leonora here." And then, as I didn't immediately respond because she was the last person I expected to hear from, she added, "Edward's mother."

"Of course," I said, "it was just that I didn't expect you. How are you?"

"Bearing up," she said, and then in a lower, more caring tone, "and what about you, Mark. How are you coping?"

As always I didn't really want to talk about it, because thinking about Edward always made me tearful, but I had to say something. "It's difficult. I keep expecting him to appear, round the corner in the street, you know, sitting in his chair in the front room. And then when he isn't or it turns out to be someone else, I feel the loss more than ever." Strangely I felt better after that little outburst. From outside the window came the sound of traffic—life getting on, as normal.

Leonora said, "I rang, because I wondered if you'd like some of his things, things he left here, but perhaps it wouldn't be a good thing…" Her voice trailed away. "Perhaps it would remind you too much."

I've got things that were Edward's. Heaven knows the whole flat is full of things that were his, or his and mine, things we'd bought together. I didn't want any more. But then I thought that I hadn't got anything of his that he'd had before I knew him, things that were pre our life together.

"What sort of things?" I asked.

But Leonora became almost secretive, obviously considering that the idea had been a bad one. "No, Mark," she said. "It was stupid of me. It wouldn't help at all. It was just that Jack thought we should get rid of them, and I didn't like the idea of just throwing them out or giving them to the thrift shop. Forget I asked."

But, if anything, her trying to back out of the offer, made me all the more determined to have them, or at least to look at them and see if there were any that I'd like to have.

"I'll come round," I said, "have a look. It's ages since we saw each other anyway."

Not since the funeral was the unspoken thought that I'm sure both of us had though neither of us said it.

"Come to dinner," she said. "Make an evening of it. Jack will be pleased to see you."

We compared calendars—mine was as good as empty but hers apparently was quite crowded. Eventually we decided on a date about two weeks in the future. She rang off and I was left alone with my thoughts.

Now you mustn't think that I'd been deserted by my (that is, 'our') friends. After the funeral (to which so many of them had come) they'd come round and asked me out all the time, invited me to their houses for quiet meals, accompany them to clubs for more noisy entertainments, theatres, cinemas, trips to the country, holidays abroad but I'd excused myself from all of them and gradually the invitations had understandably dropped off. I don't blame them. It was all my fault and this dinner with Leonora and Jack would be the first time I had gone out since Edward died.

Work and home was my life and my activities at work weren't that successful. In fact I could have lost my job except that my boss was sympathetic but even he was beginning to get impatient. There were conversations which started, "Come on, Mark, you'll have to pull yourself together soon…" or "Don't you think you should put a bit of effort into…" etc. I couldn't cope though and didn't even try.

The fortnight passed slowly. I refused an invitation to drinks at a guy called Ross's place. He got quite edgy with me in fact. "You'll have to start getting out and about," he said. "This hermit-like existence isn't doing any good for you at all." Then he mentioned 'the' name. "I'm sure Edward wouldn't have wanted you to behave like this."

At which I lost my temper. "How the fuck would YOU know what Edward would or wouldn't have wanted me to do?" I blazed and slammed down the receiver. Well, that was one friend I guess I wouldn't be hearing from again.

After a while I realized that I'd behaved like an hysterical queen and rang him up to apologize. He wasn't in, or at least he didn't answer the phone so I left a message on his answering machine, hoping I sounded suitably contrite, but he didn't ring back.

Leonora and Jack welcomed me with open arms. I knew we'd be talking about Edward so had prepared myself for it. Even so, at the first mention I felt a jolt go through me like a dose of adrenaline.

"Do you want to look at Edward's things first or have some drinks and the food?" Leonora asked.

I mumbled that I'd take a look and they took me up to his old bedroom. I'd been there before, of course. In fact it was in that room that we'd first made love—no, to be accurate, had sex because he'd trolled me back from a club while his parents were on holiday in the Algarve or somewhere.

It wasn't until a good bit later that I realized I was in love with him—and he with me.

The room was smaller than I remembered it. All the pictures (copies of Cocteau ink drawings) had been taken down, the walls repainted; and the bed was unmade—just a bare mattress with, I noticed, some rather dubious stains on it which I and the parents studiously ignored.

"We're clearing it out completely," said Jack, "and turning it into an office for me. I work from home now, you know."

I didn't but I nodded anyway.

It crossed my mind that they had 'got over' their only son's death much more than I had. In a way I felt slightly offended but then wondered if they weren't doing the right thing. Getting on with their lives.

Edward's belongings were in a large cardboard box in a corner of the room.

"We'll leave you alone to sort through them," said Leonora. "Take what you like. Everything that's left will be got rid of."

"Don't you want anything?" I asked.

"We've taken everything we want," said Leonora. "Some photos of Edward as a kid, and one of both of you at that barbecue." I remembered the one—in fact I had a copy of it myself. Edward and I were standing side by side, one of his arms round my shoulder and mine round his waist. He, tall, blond and slim; me, slightly shorter and darker. We were both wreathed in smiles and looked overpoweringly happy. So happy, indeed, that I'd shut my copy up in a drawer as I couldn't bear to look at it.

They left and I started to look through the things. There were the Cocteau prints all drawn with that characteristic economy of line and, more often than not, an over large penis. I remember being slightly shocked when I'd first seen them and realized that presumably Edward's mother must also have seen them when she dusted the room or whatever she did. Edward had laughed. "Take more than that to shock Mum," he'd said.

Why he hadn't brought them with him when he'd moved into the flat we shared, I'm not sure. Perhaps it was because we had wanted to get things that we'd chosen together.

Anyway I took them out in their narrow black frames and put them on the bed. Six of them there were—a reminder of that first time we'd fucked. Actually, come to think of it, I don't think we did fuck. We'd both been a little nervous and the sex was very vanilla, a bit of sucking and finishing off, me with my prick between his legs and his in my hand. Then we'd cuddled and fallen asleep until we sort of repeated the process in the morning.

There were some clothes, obviously from his mid teens because they'd never have fitted him or me at any recent time. I'd like to have seen him as a gawky adolescent dressed in a bomber jacket and jeans. I'd have been one too and, if we'd met then, perhaps we could have had a longer time spent together. On the other hand, at that age, I was terrified that I was queer and was making every effort to pretend to be straight, boasting about the girls I'd been out with and what I'd done with them. So I'd probably have never even dared to speak to Edward if I had met him in those far-off days.

There were some books, kids stuff really, annuals. I'd never realized Edward had once been interested in football and yet there they were, the Arsenal yearbooks for 1986, 1987 and 1988. Some comics, the Beano and the Dandy, not the sort of lurid horrors you buy in today's 'comics' but innocent adventures of Dennis the Menace, Desperate Dan and Biffo the Bear. Get a good price for those now, I thought but left them.

I thought that was the lot but then noticed that there was a bit of a bump on one side of the pile of comics, hoisted them up and found a bear. Obviously it had been much loved. One of its ears was loose, a glass eye missing and the fur was rubbed almost bare on its stomach. It had a sad, hangdog appearance, as the ear drooped over and the missing eye looked as if it was winking. In my mind's eye I could see the young Edward walking around, dragging it by the loose ear but refusing to be parted from it. It smelled a little musty but not unpleasantly so and I knew that was one thing I'd certainly take.

I went downstairs with the bear and the Cocteau drawings. "The comics are probably quite valuable," I told Jack, "and I'll take these drawings just so you won't be embarrassed taking them to the Oxfam shop."

"Oh you've chosen Teddy," said Leonora. "I'm so glad. Edward did so love that bear. Once, when he thought he'd lost it, he wouldn't eat for two days. Turned up behind the radiator though we never found out how it had got there."

"Have a drink," said Jack.

"The meal's nearly ready," said Leonora.

It was a pleasant evening but when I got home again I was even more depressed. Putting up the Cocteau pictures, occupied half an hour but when I saw them lined up round the spare room which was really a euphemism for Edward's room which he never used as we both slept together in the larger of the two bedrooms, I suddenly didn't like them so I took them down and shut them up in a cupboard.

It was nearly midnight but I didn't feel tired. I sat 'Teddy' on a chair facing me across the room which sometimes was called the sitting room, or the lounge, or (geographically) the front room. "Welcome to your new home," I said and looked at the bear. 'Teddy' winked at me. Well, he was winking all the time I suppose but as I glanced at that missing eye, it seemed as if it had suddenly shut. His loose ear hung over and he looked sad—as sad and lonely as I felt.

At about two o'clock I was ready for bed and went. I pondered whether to take Teddy with me but decided against it. Edward might have slept with it but of course, he'd slept with me much more recently and taking my late lover's toy bear to cuddle with sounded too tacky for words.

I couldn't sleep and I kept thinking of that ragged toy sitting alone in the front room. Of course it had been 'alone' in the box at Leonora's and Jack's for possibly years. Eventually I went and got it (him) and

placed him on the pillow next to me. I slept like a log, better than I had
for some time.

I dreamed of Edward, not an erotic dream, but a sort of mix up of
the first time I met him.

So it seemed that the dream was set in the library where Edward
had worked and where I had taken out a gay book—*The Swimming
Pool Library* by Alan Hollinghurst, I remember he had looked at me
and smiled, that smile which, that first time and forever after always
made my heart jump and my throat catch. In my dream, though, I felt
as if I was choking. Something was blocking my nose and throat and I
struggled to wake.

And woke up to find the bear lying across my face. There was
hardly any pressure from the toy and my feelings of constriction must
purely have been psychological rather than physical. My panic died
and, as it did so, I suddenly felt amused.

"What were you trying to do?" I asked looking at the bear which I
now placed further down the bed, sitting, arms and legs stretched out,
its ear hanging loosely. It winked in the cool, dull light of dawn. The
green figures of my radio alarm clicked over. It was as good as time to
get up. As I did so, Teddy fell off the bed and I said, "Sorry" before
picking him up and felt foolish at apologizing to a stuffed bear.

In the office I sat at my desk staring at a pile of work. The telephone
rang. It was Ross, my friend whom I'd shouted at so rudely when he'd
asked me out and said that Edward would have wanted it. I
immediately felt embarrassed for, though I'd rung him back
immediately afterwards, I hadn't tried again. But he sounded as cheerful
and chatty as always. He was an incredible guy. He always knew what
was going on though where he got his information from I could never
understand. He'd have been a godsend to MI5 or any intelligence
organization. Perhaps he was. I wasn't sure exactly what he did for a
job. I knew what he did for entertainment, chasing unsuitable bits of
rough trade and very successfully apparently.

"Hear you went to see Edward's parents the other day," he said. "I
hope this means you're getting out and about again."

"How did you know?" I asked. I'd told no one and, as far as I
knew, Leonora and Jack didn't know him particularly well though they
must have met him at the funeral.

As I suspected he didn't answer but instead embarked on a long and lurid tale about some car mechanic who'd come round to attend to a defect in his car (probably self-inflicted by Ross) and had stayed for wild, raunchy sex. This had included a certain amount of S/M activity and ended with Ross being well and truly impaled on his huge (according to Ross) schlong so that he'd scarcely been able to walk for the remainder of the day.

I laughed and realized that it was the first time for a long time when I'd done so.

"Come out, Mark," said Ross. "It'll do you so much good. Somewhere quiet, a few drinks, perhaps a film."

"With you nothing's quiet. You'd probably be having it off with the projectionist and the whole film would grind to a halt.

"Projectionists aren't nearly butch enough," said Ross. "They're almost professional class. Ugh." He paused then repeated, "Do come out. Weekend."

I wasn't prepared to commit myself but I was drawn. "I'll ring you," I said.

"Any time day or night," he said. "If I'm in the middle of extreme coitus, I'll stop it for you—even make him take it out, so I can chat to you normally."

I smiled again and attacked the pile of work in front of me with something like enthusiasm. My boss nodded approvingly as he saw the pile in the out tray grow by the end of the day.

That evening though I was depressed again. I opened a bottle of wine and had a couple of glasses. Over a microwaved Tesco frozen meal—chicken pasanda with pilau rice—I stared at the bear which was sitting at the other end of the table. He stared, monocularly, back at me. For weeks past I'd been sad at living in the empty flat, now I realized that I was bored as well as sad.

"Shall I go out with Ross at the weekend?" I asked. I filled my glass again and drank it down. It was fairly foul stuff but it did its job of deadening feelings.

Teddy said nothing, though I thought his ear drooped rather more than it had before.

"I still miss Edward," I said. "It hurts like hell. In a way it would seem like betraying him to go out and try to enjoy myself."

If anything the ear drooped even more.

"What did you think of him?" I asked. "I suppose he just dragged you around by that poor old ear of yours. But you meant a lot to him." I looked at the bedraggled little monster. "And he meant so much to me."

Teddy fell over. I swear I didn't touch the table or anything. He just toppled over onto his nose and lay there, butt in the air, praying to Mecca, or perhaps to Jerusalem.

"Oh you're just pissed," I said and finished my glass. Teddy stayed where he was, well, what did I think? That he'd get up again?

"You're obviously not interested," I said, " but I'm going to phone Ross."

As it was the middle of the evening, I didn't expect Ross to be in but he was and presumably alone. At least there was no groaning and panting in the background when his clipped and effete tones announced, "Ross here at your service. How can I accommodate you?"

"Mark here," I said. "About this weekend…"

Instantly his voice changed to one of seemingly irrepressible good humor. "I'm so glad, doll," he said. "I promise you I won't do anything outrageous. In fact my sister will be here with her friend and we can send them out if you don't want company other than mine."

I hadn't been planning on extra people and I paused, glancing up across the table where Teddy was. He was sitting up watching me. I didn't remember picking him up from his prostrate position but obviously I must have done so. I was about to make excuses to Ross when the expression on the bear's face seemed to change. It must have been a trick of the light but suddenly it looked quite mean, almost savage. Of course the thing didn't have a moveable mouth but it was almost as if part of its lip lifted into a sort of snarl.

"OK," I said to Ross. "That will be fine and of course you can't send your family out. I'll look forward to coming over and meeting them."

We made arrangements as to times and rang off.

I looked at Teddy and the face was back to normal. I'd obviously been alone too much.

I left the bear down in the kitchen and had a bad night, tossing and turning, remembering how Edward and I had fitted together in that bed so that, even when we didn't have sex, we touched and held each other and the first thing I always saw of felt when waking was his warm and affectionate body, the smile on his face when he woke, that smile that ever since the first time moved me to distraction.

The following morning Teddy looked disapproving as I made coffee and burnt some toast under the grill.

"OK," I said, "I'm sorry I left you here. We can sleep together tonight." I almost blushed as I heard myself saying that. Thank goodness there was no one to overhear my foolish fancies, but, strangely enough, having made that promise, I felt better and I even took time to scramble some eggs to hide the burnt bits on the toast.

"I'll be back about six," I called back from the open door just as one of the tenants from upstairs was coming down the communal staircase. She didn't say anything but gave me a glance as if to show that she thought I'd got someone indoors. My blush must have made me look guilty and I wondered whether she was thinking, 'so soon after his friend's death and now he's got someone else.'

I pondered on that as I took the Underground to the West End where I worked. Of course there was no one in the flat, and no one likely to be, but would it have been 'soon' if I had wanted to bring someone back? It had been months since Edward had died. How long exactly? I worked it out. Seven and a half months, give or take a few days. Of course some people mourned for years. Look at Queen Victoria. Her Prince Albert died in 1861 and she never really came out of mourning until she died in 1901, that was forty years, though of course there had been the 'relationship' with John Brown, whatever that consisted of.

The train was full and I was strap-hanging surrounded by morning commuters who were forced into intimate contact. Some tried to ignore the intimacy; others perhaps enjoyed the contact. I was suddenly aware that someone standing with his back to me was pressing his backside into my groin. I tried to move away but the crush was too much. I couldn't see the guy full face but from the back and side he was young and not unattractive. It was obvious that he was pushing intentionally. Though the train moved, his body movement was much too pointed to be unintentional. I started to get an erection. It was months of course since I'd had any sexual release, or even wanted one. Now my body was reacting and the guy could obviously feel my hardness for he pushed even more and moved his buttocks against my cock. He turned his head and smiled. His hand snaked back and grasped me between my legs and I felt a sexual shock of pleasure, something which I hadn't felt for ages.

I shouldn't be doing this, I thought, Edward wouldn't like it and then I realized how stupid that was. Edward probably would have liked it. He'd have come home and told me what had happened and we'd have laughed about it together. But of course nothing was going to happen here and the train drew into Green Park station, people started to push to get out and it was my station anyway. I gave my 'friend' a smile and he patted my cock before we parted forever.

I emerged into the sunlight. On the other side of the railings the grass looked green and lush. Parks are the lungs of London and this one was at the moment anyway overcoming the petrol and diesel fumes from the street. It was almost like being in the country. Some pigeons strutted on the grass and a blackbird sang in the branches of a tree. I suddenly felt the urge to walk in but of course I didn't.

My boss said, "Glad to see you're getting on top of the work, Mark. I'm looking for someone to visit our Dover branch next month just to check on things. If you feel up to it, perhaps you'd like to go."

I made enthusiastic noises feeling that I'd been letting him down over the past months and that anyway Dover, not a very exciting town but at least by the sea, would be a change, and perhaps a welcome one. I did quite a bit of work that day.

That night true to my promise, I took Teddy to the bedroom and sat him at the foot of the bed. I'd told him about the guy on the train and also about Dover and, it seemed to me, he'd looked approving. I slept beautifully.

Saturday evening I went round to Ross's flat. His sister was an almost exact replica of him, slim with dark, short hair and deep blue eyes. Only his slightly squarer jaw line and, obviously the masculine shape of his body made the difference. "Polly and I are twins," said Ross. I hadn't known anything about Ross's family, our conversation over the years I'd known him had usually been concerned with his conquests, of which there were legion, and snippets of gossip and information, of which there were even more.

Another surprise was his sister's 'friend.' Although Ross hadn't specified the gender I'd assumed that the friend was a she. In fact it was a 'him' and the most beautiful 'him' I'd seen for many a long day. He was a slim young man with glossy black hair, the sort that looks good even when you've just got out of bed in the morning after an athletic night's uninhibited sex. Even across the room I could see that his eyes were blue-grey, those sort of very light, come-to-bed eyes which I find very attractive. And he was gay. That was made clear right from the start when Ross introduced us and he came straight across and kissed me—on the cheeks certainly but it was more than a casual continental kiss. It wasn't a come-on, just a generous greeting from one gay guy to another.

His name was Leander. And the three syllables tripped off the tongue, contrasting strangely with my monosyllabic, Mark.

After providing us with generous drinks, Ross and Polly, brother and sister, disappeared into the kitchen to prepare the food leaving Leander and me alone. It was an obvious move and I felt slightly embarrassed but he was a pleasant guy—as well as being ravishingly good looking—so that we soon found ourselves chatting companionably together as if we'd been friends for years. He told me about his job—he actually worked for the Forestry Commission and knew a fascinating amount about our native trees and the animals and plants that grew amongst them. We talked about Polly and Ross—I wondered whether looking after trees was a sufficiently 'butch' occupation for Ross to be interested in, but didn't quite dare ask that. Leander and Polly though had known each other since school days and had remained friends ever since—platonic, he mentioned casually so I didn't need to ask. The only thing we didn't mention was Edward and I suspected that Leander and Polly had been well-briefed about that by Ross before my arrival.

We talked of our interests, his were vaguely outdoor—he skied every Easter in the Austrian Tyrol, mine more bookish, books and films and we occasionally coincided when he and I both admitted to liking American musicals.

The return of Polly and Ross bearing viands and more alcoholic beverages after what seemed a very short time interrupted our conversation and I caught Ross raising Leander a quizzical eyebrow to be answered by an ambiguous smile. No doubt they'd be 'tete-a-tete'ing after I left.

But whether it was a plan to get me back into the romance arena or not, I enjoyed myself immensely. We had planned to go to a film but, by the time we'd finished the meal which took a long while because it was accompanied by the most salacious anecdotes of Ross's adventures which were if not sometimes a bit chilling—he took enormous risks—usually wildly funny, it was much too late.

"I must go home," I said when I realized it was well after midnight. "I haven't been out this late for months." It wasn't mentioned that I hadn't actually been out at all for months.

"We must do this again," said Ross.

"And next time make the film," said Polly.

"We must indeed," said Leander.

I kissed them all good-bye when the minicab arrived to take me home, this time though Leander aimed for my lips.

Half-asleep I told Teddy about the evening. It was obviously my imagination but I thought he looked disgruntled when I had come into the bedroom alone. Though I'd been sleeping well for the past nights, I woke up suddenly. My radio alarm showed it was 3:23. Sleepily I reached out to the other side of the bed feeling for a warm body. "Edward," I said but the face I conjured up wasn't blond, the hair was lustrous black and the eyes, pale blue.

I was horrified that I could have been sexually aroused by a stranger on a train, that someone I had met only the evening before could have supplanted the love of my life in my mind's eye.

Was I losing my memories of Edward? Obviously not because I could remember the things we had done together, the big things like the holiday we spent in Florence and the small things like staying in in the evening, me reading while he watched the TV.

The shape of Teddy at the bottom of the bed was silhouetted against the window lit by the street lamps from outside. "I won't see Ross again," I promised to the bear, though when I said 'Ross' I think I meant 'Leander.'

I didn't think I'd be able to sleep but almost immediately I dropped off. I dreamed of the time Edward and I had gone to Epping Forest, that patch of woodland just outside London. It had been a beautiful day. We had wandered along the paths through the trees and eventually struck off into a thicker patch. There amongst the oaks and ash and beeches, far away from everyone else, we had made love on a grassy bank sprinkled with white wood anemones. This time though something was wrong. I reached out for Edward, wanting to hold him close but he held up his hands. "No," he said. "No!"

The rejection made me feel almost sick, something rose in my throat and I was choking. I awoke threshing around. Like the previous time, Teddy was lying across my face. There was no pressure but as I pushed him away, I couldn't understand how he'd got from the bottom of the bed to the top. Perhaps I'd kicked out in my dream and moved him— but a distance of five feet? And towards me? Impossible—yet how else could it have happened?

At breakfast the following morning, Teddy looked distinctly cross. There were some 'frown' lines on his forehead that I hadn't noticed before. "What's the matter with you?" I asked but he just glowered at me, his one remaining eye looking almost balefully accusing.

"I'm going to Dover at the end of the week," I said. "If you cheer up, I'll take you with me." That didn't seem to make any difference and I left for work without saying anything else.

In the Underground I looked out for the young guy whom I had 'met' the previous week though whether it was to avoid him or to carry on from where we had left off, I didn't want to ask myself. In any event, of course, I didn't see him.

I went into conference with my boss about what I needed to do at the Dover office—basically make sure that everything was running smoothly—the annual inspection he called it. The annual 'snoop', they would probably think of it as.

"There's a guy called Jim Daniels who will look after you," said my boss. "See you're all right. Show you around, if you know what I mean."

I knew Jim Daniels from e-mails and conversations over the phone though I'd never met him. His voice sounded sibilant and I thought he was probably gay. Was everyone trying to get me into bed with someone else?

So there I was, in Dover, on the Friday evening, walking along the Marine Parade, the sea on my right, waves slowly rolling in and breaking, tall Victorian houses, mostly turned into hotels on my left, ahead the road rising to the tops of the White Cliffs and Dover Castle.

It had been a long day. Jim Daniels, his gayness confirmed though not predatory—he had a long-established live in lover to whom I had been introduced—hadn't been the slightest bit upset at my probing into what was in fact HIS part of the business. What I had seen had been perfectly kosher. He was doing a good job and my report to the boss would be, after I finished the job on Monday, very creditable. Probably result in a rise for Jim.

He'd been a good companion too, taking me to lunch—with the boyfriend—at a very good vegetarian restaurant and offering to show me around in the evening. But I thought I'd explore on my own in spite of Jim's protestations. In the end he'd agreed, given me a list of gay places obviously, with a wink, assuming that I wanted to do a bit of trawling on my own and wished me good luck.

I left Teddy in my hotel room, which was like all hotel rooms, comfortable enough but obviously a commercially decorated and furnished room with bathroom en suite. The evening was fine, the air, to my town-accustomed nostrils, fresh and ozone tinted. Ozone of course is a gas given off by an electric discharge and has nothing to do with the seaside, but the smell of the sea and probably rotting seaweed gives a deceptive imitation of the aroma. Gulls screamed and floated overhead in the air currents.

OK. I was lonely. I was away from home where I'd been for months, alone certainly but there surrounded by familiar objects so that I had been sad but not with this completely alone feeling. I wondered why I had refused Jim's offer which now seemed stupid, but the thought of gay bars or clubs, heaving with liveliness and mankind on the desperate hunt for a dream, was equally repellent.

So I wandered along the street, which was full, it being still early evening, of people on their various missions, looking for a good time, on their way to meet friends, loved ones or, perhaps equally lonely as I was.

My mobile phone rang. I had switched it on during the day in case my boss had wanted a 'private' word with me rather than using the public telephone in the office and had forgotten to switch it off. Ross's number showed on the screen. For a moment I thought of switching it off without answering but after all he was fifty miles away and I felt the need to talk to someone.

"Hi, Ross," I said, "Sorry I haven't been in touch. Been busy."

But it wasn't Ross's slightly nasal twang that answered. Instead a voice I remembered and which gave me a jolt of alarm (was it?) or pleasure. "Mark, Leander here. Thought you might like to meet up again."

Suddenly I realized that that was exactly what I would like to do, wanted to do. "I'm really sorry," I said regretfully. "I'm not in town at the moment. I'm in Dover. It's a bugger. I could do with some company." What was I saying? But I knew I was safe with all that distance between us.

And then of course I wasn't.

"Dover," he said. "But that's just down the M20. I know it quite well. I could be with you in under an hour. Where are you staying?"

I couldn't protest. Perhaps I didn't want to. "The Kensington," I said. "It's in Townwall Street."

"I know it," said Leander. "I'll meet you in the bar. Seven thirty at the latest."

And here I am. Waiting. Feeling slightly scared. I've changed into a blue shirt and tight white trousers. I know they're a bit old-fashioned but they show me off to my best advantage, I think. I'm really feeling quite nervous and shy which is idiotic. It's not as if I'm a teenager on my first date. I'm experienced, know my way around. I won't stammer and stutter when I see him, look gauche and terrified. I'll manage things with suave sophistication, look him straight in the eye.

I don't know what Leander and I will do, whether we'll go out and have a meal, or go to a club, or—possibly I'll ask him up to my room. I think that's what Edward hopes—I mean Teddy. What a stupid mistake to make.

I told Teddy about Leander coming all the way from London and the frown lines have gone. Honest. And it almost looks as if the corners of his mouth have turned up a bit. Smiling? Course not, but that's what it looks like.

Oh God. Here he is, just come in through the door. He's smiling. I think of Teddy—I mean Edward. And I smile too.

What Two Men Do In Bed

Bryn Marlow

I crawl into bed, pull the covers up over my head, scrunch my knees up to my chin, stick my arm out at an odd angle over my leg, hold up the blankets on that side. My husband Dave finishes brushing his teeth, comes into the bedroom. I lay very still, try not to breathe. His soft snicker is the reward I've been hoping for.

Dave's gentle laughter means several things: "Up to your old tricks again, hey?" and "You'd better not be waiting to reach out from under the bed and grab my ankle" and "So you're not in bed. But where exactly are you? And how long before I find out? And what is going to happen to me if I do? If I don't?"

I hold very still. Again the snicker, for me an expression of exquisite joy, of being in the moment, suspending blankets and time, waiting, watching, aware of my breath, aware of his unseen presence. Aware of the love that cords between us, a shared bond 10 years strong, seven times that in dog years, twice that again in gay male couple years.

"It'd be some sweet life," Jack tells Ennis in the movie *Brokeback Mountain*, proposing the two men make a life together. Ennis refuses point blank. "Told you, isn't going' to be that way." Jack's heart fails, hopes fall. He knows a life is built in part on choices made. "Some sweet life" has become a catch phrase betwixt Dave and me, a reminder of what we have, of the hard choices we've made to get here, the pain we've walked through, this very present blessing of our shared life.

Nights like this, when I actually am under the covers, I try to make it look as if I am not. Other nights I artfully arrange pillows and extra quilts in the shape of my recumbent frame. After 10 years, Dave's getting harder and harder to fool.

I successfully employed a new stratagem the other night. I arranged the buffalo robe under the sheets, crouched on the floor beside the bed, slipped my arm up under the bedclothes, let my hand stick out beside the pillow. When Dave turned in, turned out the bedside lamp, I withdrew my hand. He snuggled up against me only to find it wasn't me at all. He burst out laughing, as did I. After so many years together, new tricks are both hard to come by and doubly appreciated.

There are several old stand-bys. Dousing the lights before he comes in, so he has to walk through the dark to reach the bedside lamp. (Prime the imagination and those few steps can be harrowing.) Hiding in the closet, under the bed, beside it, in it or in another room altogether. Calling out to him, "I'm going to bed now. I'll be waiting for you." Even when I am. Slipping out the far side of the bed as he slips in the near side. Laying in bed—and staying there—upside down.

These antics are by now a ritual between us. A way of showing affection. Of sharing laughter. Being playful with life. Of reminding ourselves that all is not what it seems.

In coming out as gay men, whole worlds closed to us. Society's easy acceptance and approval. Relationships with spouses, children, family, friends. Our religious communities. Employers.

We chose to face our pain, feel our feelings. Discovered that deep pain hollows out a place inside that may later be filled with deep joy. Learned that what lurks in fearful darkness may after all be love. Learned not to trust the initial form of things but to ask: *Does this warm to my touch? Does it hold life for me?*

Whole worlds opened to us in our coming out as gay men. Love. Vitality. Laughter. Living in integrity, true to our deeper selves.

Tonight my breathing gives me away. Dave sees the rise and fall of the covers. I am found out. This my consolation prize: "I didn't think you were in bed," he says as we snuggle in together, share each other's warmth, our sweet life.

Great Uncle Ned

J.R.G. De Marco

He was dead, there was no doubt. He could see that from his vantage point high atop the dark armoire. Ned peered at his body thinking he looked older than his ninety-five years. Thin, white hair mussed and stringy; every wrinkle permanently carved into his face. *Should have dyed my hair,* he thought. *And had that facelift. Could've looked ten years younger.* He shook his head sadly, or what felt like his head. He wasn't sure he still had a head in his present form, whatever that was; he had yet to see this new self.

Ned was so disarmed at seeing himself dead in bed, he hadn't even considered the reason he was still on earth and not en route to some other locale. He hadn't really expected to be shipped anywhere; he'd long ago ceased believing in anything. This life beyond death was his greatest shock. But here he was and there was his body; he'd have to deal with it.

"Do I stay here? Or do I move on?" Ned asked the air, automatically looking toward the ceiling. There was no answer. "Well?" He insisted. "Isn't there anyone around to help?" No reply. Ned edged forward, still gazing at the ceiling, which was laced with cobwebs. He made a mental note to fire the cleaning ladies, then remembered he wouldn't be firing or hiring anyone anymore. "This is a fine pickle," he grumped. "I want answers!" Agitated, he slipped off the armoire. He felt himself falling and panicked; in his fright he wiggled his arms and waved his hands and found he could fly.

"Oh… I can… I've learned to fly!"

"There's more to learn, Ned." The voice came out of nowhere. Ned smashed into a wall when he heard it. "What?!"

"And you'll need an attitude adjustment before you can move on." The voice was mellow, slightly effeminate—just the type Ned hated.

Was the afterlife made up of nancy-boy angels? he wondered, then fluttered his arms.

"What did you say?" Ned was trying to avoid the walls and to pay attention at the same time.

"You heard me the first time," came the sibilant response.

"Are they all like you... uh... wherever it is you're from?" Ned frowned.

"Not that you deserve an answer. But, no. You'll learn more if you're lucky," came the disembodied reply.

"Lucky? I don't need luck. I'm dead. I've earned the right... to go... wherever it is you go... when you've gone!"

"Some of us earn it more quickly. All you've earned up till now is money. If we gave merit badges for cantankerous insensitivity, you'd get several of those. As it is you'll have to learn a few things and make some adjustments before you can move on."

"Who are you?! Who's your supervisor? Who can I talk to? I've got money, influence... Maybe there's someone who understands the power of cash."

"We don't use money and there isn't anyone else to talk to, really. They'd all say the same thing. I'll not say anything more. Calm yourself. Sooner or later you'll figure it out. Give us a ring when you do."

"How?" Ned demanded, but the room felt emptier than before. He realized he was completely alone. He knew it would be useless to argue, rant, or rave. So he settled himself in the dark-paneled reading room of his house, in his favorite red leather rocking chair, near the window. But neither the room nor the chair felt the same. He could see and hear, even smell, but none of it was the same.

He sat rocking back and forth trying to figure it all out while waiting for events to take their course: the servants would discover his body; the lawyers would be called; a funeral would be arranged. Most of all, Ned tried to understand what he needed to do to move on. It wasn't that he didn't like the house; it was large, well appointed, and comfortable. But he had to admit to a certain curiosity about a place he believed didn't exist.

In the days that followed he moved about the house watching the servants, lawyers, workmen, and delivery boys. He realized he could hear the buzz of their thoughts. Or he thought it was their thoughts. Everything was so jumbled and indistinct. Except once in a while, when there was only one person, he could discern a murmur like a radio low enough to hear but not loud enough to make out what was being said.

It was lonely. As if a scrim had been pulled between him and the world—he could see them but none of them seemed able to sense him. At least he thought so, until one deliveryman, a light-in-the-loafers kind of guy, seemed to stare in his direction when handing the maid a flower arrangement. Ned chalked it up to his loneliness getting the better of him.

Several tiresome weeks later his will was processed. While waiting, Ned had perfected the use of his new form, exactly the body he'd possessed at eighteen or twenty. Except now, no one cared because no one saw. He'd tried everything to be noticed. He went to his favorite bar, Finocchio, and stood along the wall making passes at all the guys but he might as well have been wallpaper.

He tried The Inn Downtown, his favorite restaurant, to see the waiters he had lusted after in life. Entering, he spied the back of Mario's head—the cutest waiter and Ned's favorite sat at a table taking his dinner break. Ned felt his stomach flutter remembering Mario's lopsided smile and the sexy scar above his eye. He sauntered over, if that's what you'd call it in his present form. Closer now, he saw Mario with another guy and flirting shamelessly. A surge of jealousy rattled Ned as he pushed in next to Mario and across from the newcomer, a gorgeous man, no more than twenty. He reeked of some perfume, and though he had a gym-sculpted body, he moved in graceful, precise, and too-prissy ways. *Not my kind of man,* Ned thought.

Suppressing his jealousy and summoning up all his courage, Ned turned to Mario and kissed him on his smooth, olive-toned cheek. Nothing. Though he knew no one could sense him, this stung. He felt he might as well not be there at all. As he floated up from his seat, Ned peered at Mario's new friend and was shocked to find him staring back. Ned was startled but the boy looked surprised, even frightened. Nevertheless, he continued to stare into Ned's eyes until Ned felt a tingly sensation deep in his soul, something else he had thought didn't exist. The young man's cornflower-blue eyes were sad and knowing and invaded Ned's very being.

Stop looking at me! Ned directed intense rage at the boy. The young man blinked, his eyes widened, then he looked away. *Disgusting!* Ned huffed. Just the type of man he hated. A muscle-bound, nancy-boy. *My life is—was—about men!*

With that Ned floated momentarily in mid-air, surveyed Mario and his friend, then shot off like a comet through the ceiling. Rushing through walls and buildings, trucks and cabs, zipping over clouds and under streets, he finally reached his home. Melting past the walls he curled, like a ball of mist, in his chair by the window, where he could sulk in peace. He was so put off by Mario's friend, the idea that someone had actually seen him had totally escaped him.

Some days later a calmer Ned watched his lawyers assemble his relatives around his prized walnut long-table, a gift of the government of Lithuania for services rendered. Who among his relatives could appreciate such beauty, he wondered, balancing himself on the crystal chandelier above them. Who indeed? There were six: Elma Vight, a distant cousin from Virginia whose only virtue was she'd never asked him for money. She still used too much lipstick and rouge. Sammy Scales, a not-so-distant cousin, was a lounge lizard getting too old to be anything but a ward of the state. There were three nieces, all nearing retirement, all childless; they each wore a flowered print dress making them appear no less fat but at least cheerful. The last relative was great nephew, Ben Stone, a handsome boy of thirty-one, who was as gay as a goose and for whom Ned had love-hate resentful feelings. Three servants stood a dour, silent watch and remained invisibly available.

Ned surveyed the small crowd with gleeful anticipation, knowing his will contained something that would be like a stone in their shoes. He laughed aloud (though no one could hear) when he thought of his joke—a stone in their shoes! They all despised Ben Stone because he was gay. They had probably despised Ned himself for the same reason, though none of them had known for certain because he hid it so well. Only Ben had shown him respect and, Ned suspected, that was because

Ben had correctly guessed at their connection but had always been too discreet to mention it.

Ned had decided to leave everyone something (the servants and even Mario getting more than the relatives) with the bulk of the money and the mansion going to Ben. The Stone in their shoes! He rolled off the chandelier laughing in his new silent way. Not one of the sparkling crystals even trembled as he bounced over them.

Ben, surprised to hear the stipulations of the will, began crying, which made Ned wince. Ned rejoiced at the angry, disgusted looks on the faces of the cousins and nieces.

"Gotcha!" Ned said, though no one heard.

That night, alone, lonely, and remembering the sibilant words of the angelic phantom, Ned wondered if his bequest to Ben was enough to get him past the stasis he was in. Impulsively, he flew through the ceiling, straight into the air, out into space nearly hitting the moon, but there was no nancy-boy angel to greet him. No one magically materialized to offer him a place in some better afterlife. He floated down, defeated, to his lonely warren on earth.

Moving day was exciting for Ben. Ned, better at reading thoughts, even captured some of Ben's enthusiasm. Ned's happiness was tempered by the realization that he'd have someone living under his roof who would never really know he was there. He distracted himself by ogling the hunky moving men who by Ned's accounting were all straight and oozed masculinity like sweat. Ned did an otherworldly version of a swoon when they passed close to him.

When the day was old, Ned found his nephew sitting on the yellow silk-upholstered settee in the drawing room. The servants were gone, the house was quiet. Ned gazed at his dark-haired, brown-eyed nephew and a roiling emotional wave overtook him. He resented the fact that Ben had lived a freer life than he had. Perched on the cold, marble mantelpiece, Ned honed in on Ben's internal voice, thoughts, and feelings.

Almost at once, Ned felt run through by sadness and sorrow.

"Jamie." Ben's thought wept the name. "Jamie." Ned wafted down to sit next to his nephew. Closer now, Ned found he had complete entree to Ben's mind—he could hear thoughts and see mental pictures. When Ben thought "Jamie" an image appeared: a young man with dusky blond hair, green eyes, soft lips, an angelic face. Ned felt an instant yearning for this beauty and couldn't quite distinguish if it were his own feeling or his nephew's.

Ben's gray and cloudy thoughts were slashed by the sun-like image of Jamie. Ned tried nudging his nephew's mind in other directions without success. It was always Jamie—precious and apparently lost. Ben gave no clue as to how or why Jamie was gone.

Ned tried cuddling closer to Ben, tried placing an arm around him for comfort. A look of fear transfigured Ben's face and he shivered. Ben's reaction startled Ned and he slid away to sit on the floor. There was little Ned could do except sit, watch, and listen.

Eventually, Ben took himself off to bed in a room overlooking the city. Seeing the cityscape only reminded Ned of what he had lost. Ben flopped listlessly onto the bed, Ned lay along the windowsill, hungry for company even if Ben never knew he was there. The searing loneliness made Ned feel like a shriveled walnut, bitter and unwanted. Not unlike the way he'd felt in life.

The stars pressed down through the window like a shower of tiny diamonds, rich and promising. Bored, Ned glided around the room, each time he passed close to Ben, the young man's dreams blared like a loud TV. Ned learned he could see, hear, even enter Ben's dreams. At first, Ned just watched, amazed at the weird, shimmering worlds the young man's mind constructed; but Ned was reduced to tears when Jamie appeared and replayed a scene that was obviously a nightmare for Ben. They'd had a terrible, hurtful argument and had broken up. Curious to know more, Ned entered the dream once Jamie had left.

"Who was he, Ben?"

"The love of my life. But who...?" Confusion colored the dream.

"Don't worry. I'm... a... friend," Ned was gentle, not wanting the dream to end. "How long has he been gone?"

"Weeks. I'll never see him again. I don't think I can live without him."

"Not even in this wonderful house?"

"Especially not in this house. I'll rattle around like my Uncle Ned. I'll end up lonely, unloved, and dead without anyone. Just like him."

"Was this uncle of yours unloved?"

"As far as I know."

"And, was he so awful?"

"He wasn't bad at all. Just bitter. Disappointed. I always thought he didn't like me. I can't understand why he left it all to me."

"Perhaps he was a kindred soul."

"I always suspected but he never allowed me the opportunity to ask. He had closed himself off. I'm afraid I'll shut down the same way."

"And Jamie can help?"

"Jamie is everything for me. And… I thought I was everything to him, too."

"Where is the boy?"

"I don't know." Ben gasped in his sleep. "I hope he's safe. I'm going mad trying to find him."

A sudden noise abruptly ended the dream. Ben whimpered and Ned saw a tear slide down Ben's cheek. Deeply touched and a little ashamed at intruding upon the dream, Ned flew out the window, circled the rose garden, swooped over the pond, shot into the sky, and floated down again.

Eventually Ned found himself in the cloister which he had had built to mirror part of Hadrian's palace outside Rome. It was a memorial to Rico, whom he had met, loved, and lost long ago. Remembering Rico, he thought about Jamie and what this could mean for Ben's future. Ned paced the cloister, ghostly tears tumbling over his cheeks and disappearing midway to the ground. He could feel the earth beneath his feet but saw that he left no impression in the soft soil. Staring at the undisturbed ground, Ned wept harder. He had so wanted to make an impression in life, to touch someone with his love. Now he desperately wanted one more chance. His dark thoughts were broken by Ben's wrenching sorrow, from far on the opposite side of the mansion. He didn't wonder that he could sense him from so far away, he and Ben were connected now in loss.

Ned bolted, unable to stand both his and Ben's pain, and flew to the city. The gay bars of downtown were not the same ones he remembered but they were the same nonetheless. The Trading Post, the 215, and on and on. He entered Mercutio's because of their purple neon sign. The music pounded making the darkness shiver.

The thoughts of patrons came in a cluttered jumble like TV static but he separated and filtered them and honed in on certain patrons.

He stopped next to a sweet-faced, dark-haired boy gamely trying to start a conversation with an aloof redhead. Eavesdropping, Ned heard the dark-haired boy's thoughts: *He doesn't like me. I can tell. He'll walk away. Why doesn't he like me? I'm just as good as...*

Ned saw the redhead turn away; at the same time he felt a sharp sting pass through him and knew it was the pain of rejection felt by the dark-haired boy. Ned stood by helpless, when suddenly the boy turned in his direction.

"Hi."

He sees me? Ned thought and as there was no one else around, it had to be. The boy could see him!

"H...hi," Ned stuttered shyly.

"I've never seen you here before." The young man licked his lips absently, ran a thin hand through his long hair, then flicked his head.

"Don't live... around here," Ned answered, realizing he didn't like the kid. The guy was a swish. No wonder the redhead had rejected him. *Men want real men,* he thought. "I'm looking for someone," Ned said turning away. From deep within the boy, Ned felt the same knife-like pain cut through him as he moved off. Surveying the crowd he noticed another guy who seemed to see him. The man winked and blew him a kiss making Ned shiver.

Another one. I can't get away from it, he thought, frowning. *The guys I like still can't see me.* Filled with sadness, he floated through a wall and onto the street. He circled the downtown then swept back to the mansion and the shelter of the cloister. Shuddering at the thought of the dark-haired boy, he gazed at the white marble columns and the green marble flooring and thought of Rico. *Where did you go? Why did you go? My Rico!* His tears started again as the familiar pain of rejection knifed through him.

With Rico potent in his mind, Ned streaked through the grapevine canopy and across the sky. The sun was edging up and coloring the dawn with roses, purples, and blues, but Ned hardly noticed. He concentrated on the city below and the thoughts he could pick out of the jumble: arguing and crying, moaning and sighing. He felt their passion and hatred, love and joy. It was overwhelming.

Passing over the gay neighborhood once more, he was struck with an image of Jamie in someone's thoughts. Flying closer the image became clearer and Ned saw a house, a road, and landmarks all around.

He knew where to find Jamie! Ned left the city behind and entered a region of trees and meadows. Birds flew through his insubstantial form and he cast no shadow though the sun was high and bright.

Suddenly Jamie flooded his mind as Ned swooped over a cabin in a sheltered grove. Clear, blond, and fresh. Jamie.

Hurling himself from the sky through the cabin's roof, Ned found himself in a sleek but rustic home. Light wood paneling and ochre living room furniture clashed starkly with the dark thoughts pervading the place. Ned sensed softness and sorrow there, too.

But no one was home.

Ned sat on the lumpy couch and waited. He had no doubt this was where he would unravel the puzzle. Birds twittered outside and a breeze soughed in the trees. Finally the door opened and Jamie, like a vision of light and gold, entered.

"Who are you?" Jamie seemed more surprised than fearful.

Ned was shocked speechless. Here was another guy who actually saw him. He sputtered a few times. "I'm…." About to mention Ben, he thought better of it and changed course. "I was passing through and saw your place. I need some help."

"Well, I think you'd better leave. There's nothing here for you. This place belongs to a friend. I can't…"

"Maybe you can. May we speak?"

Jamie sat in a soft chair. His movements vaguely disturbed Ned. Something about him… That was it! Jamie was just like the rest of the nancy-boys he couldn't stand. What could Ben see in him? Ned decided to leave.

"On the other hand, maybe I don't need anything here." Ned edged toward the door realizing he shouldn't let Jamie see him exit through a wall or fly through the roof.

"You've come from Ben. Right?" Jamie sat forward. He looked like an elegant golden ball of light. A prissy golden ball. It was all Ned could do to keep from showing his distaste.

"Ben?" *How could he know*? Ned thought.

"Come on, it's written all over you," Jamie's voice was sweet and full, like honey. Another quality Ned found disturbing. How could his nephew pine away over this creature?

"I've changed my mind. Maybe Ben doesn't need you as much as I thought. Now that I've seen you."

"I know what you are." Jamie smiled mysteriously. "I've seen your kind before."

"What are you talking about?"

"You're a ghost. You've got all the telltale signs. For one thing, you shimmer. For another, you looked like *you* saw a ghost when I was able to see you."

The kid was smart, effeminate but smart. Ned fumed. "So?"

"So, like, who are you? A relative of mine? Or, wait! I know, you're a relative of Ben's. A brother. Come to give me a message. Well, forget it."

Ned whisked up to the ceiling, no use disguising things now. Jamie's gaze followed his flight as though Ned were an insect buzzing around the cabin. "I certainly will forget it!"

"And if you see Ben, tell him…"

"I'll tell him to forget you. You're not worth all his crying. The sleepless nights. Those dreams… you've no idea. You can't imagine his pain. I will certainly tell him a nancy-boy like you isn't worth one of his tears. He needs a man."

"He had a man. Me."

"You're half a man. Ben deserves better." Ned spun about the cabin like a miniature whirlwind trapped indoors.

"Ben said that?" Jamie seemed defeated.

"No. He thinks he loves you!" Ned looked down at him. "The rest is my opinion. Guys today have lost the art of being men. You're all busy being in touch with your feminine side. Learn to be men. But maybe it isn't something that can be learned. Maybe you've just got to be born that way. My Rico was a man. A man any man could love."

"Ben thinks he loves me?"

"It's foolishness. I'll wise him up. He can do better."

"Who are you to say so? If Ben loves…"

"Stop right there. I said he *thinks* he loves you. I can make him think otherwise. I won't have you make him a nancy-boy, too."

"You're a strange ghost, aren't you? You're so backward." Jamie relaxed and sat back.

"Me? Backward? What are you talking about? You can't even master the art of being a man and *I'm* backward?"

"Well, I mean you obviously haven't learned very much. You new at this?"

"Well, yes, I just died maybe three months.... Why am I telling you this? It's all personal. How could you know I'm new at anything? I'm more than four times older than you and... oh what could you know about anything?"

"You must've been a really self-hating person when you were alive. You don't seem to have learned much in three months. That why you're still here? On earth, I mean?"

"That's none of your affair. Self-hating? I was a living, breathing homosexual before your parents were born. Learn things indeed."

"I didn't mean to offend you," Jamie showed not the least sign of fear. "But your views are kinda sick. Y'know? All that stuff about nancy-boys. Who thinks like that?"

"I do... did. It's perfectly normal. You guys are so into bodies and looks. But real masculinity is deep inside."

"You mean there weren't 'nancy-boys' and sissies when you were young?"

"Of course there were. Didn't like them then, still don't."

"You mentioned someone named Rico, was he a..."

"Don't even utter his name. You couldn't come close."

"What happened to him?"

"We...we...didn't..."

"Didn't what?"

"We...weren't on the same wavelength after a while."

"He wanted something you didn't?"

"He was wonderful. A real man. A *real* man. As masculine as anyone could..."

"So you keep spouting but there's something you're not saying."

"Like what?"

"Like maybe Rico wasn't as ideal a man as you wanted him to be?"

"Not true! He was a man. He just had odd ideas."

"Didn't fit with what you thought was manly?"

"I always told him, didn't I?" Ned blurted out the words.

"Told him what?"

"To walk like a man. To stop holding himself the way he did. He was so beautiful, so sweet and loving. I wanted him no matter what."

"He didn't listen?"

"No! He never listened. He loved to dance, to fuss with clothes and look pretty. It was too much. I tried to dissuade him. But...." Ned's voice trailed off.

"You left him?"

"Never! I would never have done that. I tried to change him. I wanted him to improve. He was such a manly-looking man. I just wanted him to *act* more like a man."

"And?"

"He left me! I never understood that. I wanted what was best for him. I wanted him to be what he should be. I came home one day and found his letter. It was all perfumed. I hated the smell. The letter..."

"Told you he was leaving?"

"Yes. Said he couldn't stand my attempts to change him. Said he had to leave. Even though he loved me more than anything."

"Ben wants me to change, too. Says I should be more intellectual. Says I should go back to school instead of waiting tables and trying to make it as an actor."

"Ben... well... he's got some odd ideas, too."

"What did you say?"

"Nothing wrong with working as a waiter. Some of the cutest... er... nicest people I know... um...knew... were waiters." Ned thought about Mario and sighed.

"Well, I won't do it. He has to accept me as I am or I... but I love him and this all hurts."

"Maybe Ben needs a lesson. You could call him and..."

"We've argued enough. I thought if I went away and didn't speak to him, he'd be desperate and want me back no matter what."

"Oh, he wants you back."

"On his terms."

"I wouldn't know about that. Maybe he wanted you to have a better job because he was worried about money."

"That was the excuse he used."

"He doesn't have to worry now. He can do anything he wants—including supporting you and your career."

"How?" Jamie's eyes grew glassy.

"Me! I died and left him all my money."

"You? Are you some kind of fairy godfather?"

"Sort of a fairy uncle. My name's Ned and.... Did he ever mention me?"

"Ned. Yes..." Jamie became silent.

"That bad."

"He said you were an old closet case who hated him. Said you two should have been better friends because you were both gay even though you never admitted it!"

"A little harsh but he was right."

"But you left him everything anyway?"

"Not for the right reasons. Partly because he's gay but partly because I wanted to stiff the rest of the family."

"I'm sure it doesn't matter exactly why you left it to him. The fact is you did."

"Anyway, he's got it all now. Money's no longer a problem."

"It's more than money, I think." Jamie sat down and began crying. Great heaving sobs shook his body.

There was something familiar about his crying. Ned dredged his memories. Then it hit him. Rico! The tears, the sobbing, the timbre of Jamie's voice—it was all just like Rico.

Ned, still floating near the ceiling, felt something inside him melt. It was as if there had been a blockage in his shriveled heart that just dissolved. He felt his own eyes well up. Easing himself down, he sat beside Jamie. Awkwardly he placed an arm around Jamie's shoulders. Overcome with sadness Ned held the boy tight. Jamie felt good in his arms. It reminded him of... but he couldn't bear the thought. Still, Jamie's sorrow touched Ned. He took Jamie's face in his hands and turned him so he could look at his tear-stained cheeks.

Gently Ned wiped away the tears, Jamie's skin yielding to his ghostly touch. After a while, the boy stopped crying and rested his head against Ned's chest which felt as if it were on fire with wonderful sensations Ned hadn't allowed himself to feel in years. "I still can't believe you can see me, touch me." Ned tried keeping the tears out of his voice; he felt like crying for everything he had allowed himself to miss. *It's all too late*, he thought. *All too late.*

Jamie sniffled, then lifted his head to face Ned. "I'm just one of those people, I guess. I don't know what you call them. I can see ghosts. I can talk to them. There've got to be more people like me, don't you think?"

Ned looked into Jamie's green eyes and thought of Mario's friend and the dark-haired boy and the others. "There are others. Other little sissies..." Ned cursed his sharpness. "I'm sorry. Other guys."

"I knew I couldn't be the only one."

"Well, what're we going to do about you and Ben?"

"We? I thought I wasn't good enough for him. You were going to tell him to find someone else." Jamie sniffled again and sat up.

"I was." Ned felt foolish. "I've changed my mind. And I'm going to change Ben's mind about you. If he hasn't changed it already."

"How?"

"Never mind. You've got to do something, too." Ned felt himself floating again.

"What? I'll do whatever you say."

"Don't say that, I don't know if I could control myself. Just do one thing for me—give Ben another chance. Go to him tonight."

"I don't know."

"Please." This was not an easy word for Ned.

"All right," Jamie hopped to his feet. "I'll get my things."

"Pack it all, you won't be coming back." Ned slid toward the window and halfway through he turned. "I'm going now. Will you do me one more favor?"

"Name it," Jamie stared, green eyes bright from crying.

"Think about me once in a while." Ned peered deep into Jamie's soul. "I'd like that."

"Me, the nancy-boy?" Jamie smiled broadly. "I could never forget you, Ned."

He liked the way Jamie said his name; he flew down and planted a kiss on his nose. "I know you'll be happy."

Ned flew swiftly back to the mansion. Ben, bent with sadness, sat staring out an open window in the den, letting night breezes and the hum of insects wash over him. Ned swooped in and sat on the arm of Ben's overstuffed wingback chair. Ben sat up, shuddered, and peered around at the darkened room. As Ben slumped sadly back into the chair, Ned filled his mind with images of Jamie, golden and beautiful, but equally sad. One crystal tear slid down Jamie's cheek causing Ben to wince.

Knowing he had to work quickly, Ned spied a scrapbook on his old desk. He'd never had such a memory book. There hadn't been much he'd wanted to remember of his loneliness. Silently peeking at the book's contents, Ned found a theater playbill, with Jamie's name in big red letters. And inside, there was a smiling photo of Jamie the actor.

Ned wished for a sudden gust of air and, as if on command, a forceful breeze blew through the room, riffling the pages of the scrapbook. Ben looked up, confused and fearful. The wind continued flipping the scrapbook pages wildly back and forth, until, with Ned's help, the playbill came loose and fluttered into the air. It floated gracefully, supported by Ned's careful hand, coming to rest at Ben's feet. Upon seeing Jamie's name, he began to weep. Ned quickly introduced thoughts of love. He let Ben see that Jamie needed to be himself. He instilled the idea that true happiness could be theirs, if only Ben would understand and accept.

Ned continued placing thoughts into Ben's vulnerable mind; it was all he could do and he spent himself in the effort. When he was certain Ben would truly think on those things, Ned slipped out of the room.

Later that night, Ned stood outside the mansion, Ben's mansion. Inside, Jamie and Ben clung to one another like lost puppies.

It'll work; it's got to, Ned thought. *Besides, I've planted enough thoughts and ideas in Ben's mind so he'll figure it out and make it work.*

"Nice job, Ned," said a vaguely familiar voice.

Ned whipped around. "Who's there?" Out of the shadows came a figure Ned recognized instantly. "Rico! You're alive!"

His sweet, familiar laughter filled the air. "I don't think so, Ned. Do you think I'd look this good at the age of eighty-five? No, I'm as dead as you are. But there are some advantages—we look our old selves again. And you do look good, sweetie."

"Me? Good? You're the one who looks delicious." Ned paused, composing himself. "Rico, where were you all those years? I loved you."

"As I love you. You never came for me, Ned. You never looked. I figured you decided to let me go. It hurt but I was too proud to ask you to take me back."

"You wanted to come back?"

"I would have even if you continued to try changing me."

Ned hung his head. He'd wanted to look so many times. His stubbornness and crust-bound attitudes always stood in his way.

"I was stupid, Rico. Hide-bound and ignorant. How can you even talk to me now? After all I didn't do?"

"Love doesn't die, Ned. Sometimes it isn't allowed to flourish but it never dies. Never."

"Are you saying that..."

"I love you, Ned."

Ned put out his arms wanting to embrace Rico and the whole world. "I don't deserve it."

"Well, you have a point there," Rico said without moving.

Ned froze. "This is all a joke then?"

"Do you remember that voice you heard—argued with actually—right after you died?"

"Yes?" Ned's arms slowly dropped to his sides. "What about it?"

"He said you needed an attitude adjustment and other things, right?"

"So he said," Ned snapped.

"You've made lots of progress and they're almost ready to let you in," Rico smiled one of his bright, toothy smiles.

"But?" Ned said. "There's always a 'but' isn't there? Now what? They gave me no help. No direction. I didn't know what I was doing."

"Yet you did something that showed you have a beautiful soul. You did something very unlike you and made two people happy."

"And now...?"

"Just do whatever comes naturally. They told me to tell you that."

"But no specifics, right?"

"Just one."

"What?" Ned asked.

"This time, I'll be waiting for you. When you arrive. And you will."

Beyond the Blue Bardo
Manhattan Island 1965

Sterling Houston

The Walking Blues is the mother of all
unified opposites. And our double-spirited sissy holds the key.
The slings and arrows of this outrageous fortune in men's eyes
get knotted and tossed over the shoulder like a silk Hermes scarf;
misery transformed by style. This strut of which I sing has
naught to do with fatherlessness. Though in truth, the love of a
good man is essential if a man is ever to be any good at loving.
The black sissy has earned the right to strut, no lie. I know
I did, paid for it with years of denial and shame. The head tosses
left as the knee shoots right and the buttcheek switches right
under it in perfect tempo and then reverses in a sweet rhythm
that is beyond nature. Reverses and transcends. Transcending
ridicule while reveling in foolishness, this sissy is both king and
queen, and knows her royal family by the singing of the song.
Winds of disdain whip past her ears and get incorporated into
the music, translate themselves into a sphincter thrust that has
become the envy of the civilized world.
To attain that hierarchy of black sissydom it is not required
that one develops the capacity to love being fucked, but it helps.
Nor is it necessary that one be an ardent and skillful cocksman,
but that helps too, and rightly so. When both these attributes
occur in the same fine brown frame, well Honey, the dance floor

burns down; the nightclub explodes. What has this got to do
with the worried blues you wonder? Well, everything.
You better come on in my kitchen, baby, 'cause it's going to
be raining outdoors. I sing the song of the blues. These were
lessons for the future, understood only by instinct.

One day in the kitchen of the house on Olive Street when I was eight years old, living with my aunt, a little sissy boy, way cuter than I needed to be, curly hair, long movie-star lashes and a soul that had learned through hardships death and abandonment, to look beyond the obvious—Honey, I was way too smart for my own or anybody's good—out of the blue a question took shape, and I asked: "Why do people have to die, Lollie?"

She rubbed her hands together when she spoke and the friction made a whispering like the sound of dry leaves over parchment. "The good Lord took my little baby Ray Earl, took your mommy and then made a way for you to come to me."

Seeing the look in my wide old eyes, she went on: "I don't know, sugar. They just have to. It's the Lord's way, nobody can help it."

"Why would the good Lord do a thing like that, Lollie?"

"Lord knows, sugar pie, Lord above knows." She grinned and showed three lower ivory teeth that remained in her mouth. They were enough to help her chew her meager meals.

"But I'm so glad he did, 'cause I got you out of the bad luck." An etched tracery of lines both thick and fine crisscrossed her thin face. Her ash colored hair was pulled tight and twisted into a loose bun held in place by two real tortoise shell hairpins. She bore the look of a stern grandmother though she was sweetly kind, more than a little foolish and was only forty years old.

Lollie, Miss Lu, Aunt Lula, had been the only one to take me in after my mother died. Lula the elder of two sisters, had had the horrible privilege of seeing her sister (who was my grandmother) and her niece (my mother, of whom I remember almost nothing), hauled off by the TB wagon, all in the same sad year.

"Hauled off by the TB wagon never again to return," she would tell anyone, savoring the drama.

Yes, baby, I do get my drama queen genes from Miss Lula. She had to take me, aged seven; there was no one else. These tragic events ironically resulted in the end of a long period of mourning for Aunt Lula; mourning for her own dear dead young baby Ray Earl, taken in 1918 by diphtheria.

In the torturous mountains of Tibet, the holy men have evolved a practice of fanatical detachment. The joys and sorrows that worry us to death down here only blow past the tall tops of their yellow caps like the razor-sharp killing zephyrs that whip those Himalayan summits.

This is the ultimate going beyond the going beyondness into a zone of utter arctic indifference. It became my quest to be like those monks.

To keep exclusive council with the unspoken.

Calvin was fine as wine. We met at The Old Reliable, a neighborhood bar on East Third between Avenue A and Avenue B. It was the night of the day he got out of Rikers Island. Something about some forged checks, never was quite clear what. Who remembers anyway? A young project-living black man, then as now, was likely to get the maximum for whatever and Calvin had got six months, for some petty nonsense.

The Old Reliable had been a working man's neighborhood bar on the Lower East Side since the Depression. It was now run by a middle aged Ukrainian couple, Speedy and Margie, and their dog, Cornflakes. Speedy tended the bar. Margie kept all in order, busing tables, wiping up spills. Cornflakes, a brown and white shaggy mutt, worked as the bouncer. He was a good one, too. That dog was a fine judge of character. If voices were raised in anger, or somebody didn't look quite right, Cornflakes would bark at them and they would be asked to leave in no uncertain terms by Margie who, at nearly five feet tall with a head of hennaed Brillo hair, resembled an aging Orphan Annie.

The O.R. was the place, you understand, that only-in-New-York place that captured the decisive moment, that defined the magical time we were all lucky enough to be a part of.

The truly hip New York scene had migrated completely by the winter of 1965 to the Lower East Side from the fabled Greenwich Village haunts of earlier decades. As the neighborhood had changed, and young musicians, artists and models, cultural adventurers moved in, Speedy and Margie, although they were neither artists nor could they be in any way defined as hip, made all welcome. They were content to see the place full night after night from happy hour till 4 a.m.

For "who was who" in those days, this was the place, I'm here to tell you. A warm and welcoming mishmash of art stars and fans of art filled the narrow barroom. Pagans, mad queens, lost poets, pansexual players, revolutionaries, characters once found only in the West Village at the Riviera or the Café Figaro or the White Horse had now taken the place over. The Old Reliable, often referred to as the "O.R.," the "Old Horrible" or the "Un Reliable," by wags of the day, was no less a hub of intellectual and flirty intercourse than Café Flore had been in early 20th Century Paris.

My first impression of Calvin was not good. He sat across from me in one of the bar's small wooden booths, frowning with his cheek resting on his open hand.

"You talk just like one of them white boys," he said to me. "Where you 'spose to be from? Harvard? Trying to sound all grand and shit."

Right, Calvin. Under-educated me, who'd barely finished my Texas high school, only to flunk out of Community College. Lollie had always taught me to "talk proper," it just stuck, I guess. Also, with an actors' ear, I'd sponged up the accents of most of my artsy boho acquaintances. I guess, to his pretty black man Brooklyn Bed-Sty ears, I no doubt, sounded like what he identified as "white."

There was deep new snow on the ground that night, and the square-paned grid front windows of the Old Reliable had little white wedges piled in their corners like a Christmas card. The juke box was pumping hard. "Sugar pie honey bunch," Levi Stubbs and the other three Tops chirped over the relentless beat, "Don't you know I love you."

The place was jumping with the reliable old cast of pre-superstars, jazz musicians, painters, poets, paupers, and queens, typical 1965 Saturday night, smoking, drinking, laughing, cruising, but most of all living the life we had all once only dreamed of. New York City, baby! I had been told it was cold and rude, but in truth, it was very easy to meet people. Sometimes, too easy.

"Harvard?" I said cleverly, hitting hard on the first syllable, trying to sound all haughty and street. I wanted to give the impression that I was insulted, but Calvin was just too cute for words.

"You must be from the country, or something."

"I been in jail, like it's anybody's business," he said, rolling his big eyes away from me.

"Now I'm really scared." I said, and sipped from a thirty-five cent mug of Rheingold draft. Calvin's skin was like a smooth bittersweet chocolate bar. He had a perfect round head, round as a little pumpkin, and a bright white smile graced by a chipped front tooth that he tried to hide with a curving finger when he laughed. Eyes the color of black coffee flashed intelligence and mischief.

"Can't help myself," Levi pleaded on the box, and he was so right. "I love you and nobody else!" Like me and thousands of others, Calvin had come to the city to do his "thing," to get high, get laid and become legendary by whatever means necessary. Being from the Borough of Brooklyn, he had not so far to travel as I did, to reach this Mecca for wonder-children. But the East Village was as far removed from the realities of Brooklyn as it was from San Antonio.

Under the narrow table, I felt his knee rub against the inside of my thigh, lightly. So very lightly.

I had fled San Antonio as soon as I could. Took the Greyhound and never looked back, at least not for a long time.

"Hey! Want to go to a party?" Calvin said.

There were always parties after the bars closed at 4 a.m. Usually in somebody's basement crib or walk-up tenement three room flat. Jug wine in paper cups, good smoke and music and a couple of more hours to do some serious socializing.

"Maybe. Yeah. Where's it at?"

"Over on Eleventh and C."

"Come on, then. Let's get out of here before last call."

We walked out into the frosty crazy New York night. Lonnie Redmond who lived in a one-room studio in Harlem was house-sitting a flat in Manhattan while the flat's owner, the mysterious piano genius Cecil Taylor, was touring Europe after the release of his Blue Note LP. We headed to Lonnie's.

I recognized many of the people in the room there from the O.R., the Annex and other haunts. Madeline Moore caught my eye and moved toward me. She was the designer for the underground movie "Flaming Creatures" who had got me a part in the play "The Life of Juanita Castro" when one of the actors got busted.

"Let's get wicked," she purred as she pulled a torpedo shaped wheat straw joint from her powdered cleavage. "Come, young Calvin. Let's smoke this good boo, darling."

She beckoned us from the clump of party talkers and dancers in the tub-in-kitchen living room and led us toward the piano wedged into the street-front bay windows.

I had seen photographs of flats like this in old LIFE magazines. They sprang up like mushrooms after the first wave of immigrants streamed into the city from Russia, Poland, Italy. These downtown neighborhood tenements had been built for them in the rat-infested flatlands between two polluted rivers, to keep them—the rodents and the immigrants—from spreading into more desirable environs.

A few years before we had met, Madeline had been a very successful Ford model. She still sported a trademark thick bush of Halloween orange hair that surrounded her dead white face and dramatically penciled eyes and lips. Penelope Tree stole that look from her. Miss Jean Shrimpton copied Penelope and got it on the cover of Vogue. So much for originality.

"Right here?" Me and Madeline ducked underneath Cecil Taylor's battered baby grand, then Calvin bent down. "Hey make room for me? Y'all trying to bogart, or something?" Madeline took an extra sharp toke and held her breath as she handed the yellow wheat straw joint to Calvin. The nearness of him was making me warm to hot.

We were surrounded by a forest of legs and feet, booted girls and men in bellbottoms covering all but the tips of their toes.

"Darlings, do be discreet. Not that I really give a shit…"

It was the sonorous voice of the poet Jackson Williams, Jacki to his numerous acolytes and devotees. Along with a handful of other bright young black things, Jacki had started Penumbra Press, a loose collective of poets and writers whose inspiration had been Claude McKay, Bruce Nugent, Wallace Thurman and the Fire poets of Harlem in the Twenties.

"...but what are you sissies doing under Cecil's piano smoking reefer? You ought to at least have the courtesy to go out on the fire escape with that mess."

"Jacki, hush up and get your black butt down here." It was Calvin.

"And watch who you be callin' 'sissy,' punk."

Jackie dipped low with a one note laugh, pushing back the wide brim of his pale green Borsillano to better check us out. "Is it you, young Calvin? Darling, when did you escape from the Bastille?"

"Good behavior," mumbled Calvin, as he playfully pulled Jacki by his ebony hand crowded with silver and turquoise rings.

Jacki squatted down and sat with us, Indian style. "My, my. Isn't this a cozy little playhouse, like elves sheltered under a mushroom cap."

"Did you miss me, while I was on vacation?" Calvin asked with a fake pout.

Ignoring his question, Jacki inhaled and spoke through a held-in toke. "Who's your new beau?" he said tilting an arched eyebrow toward me.

Jacki and I had seen each other before at the bars. And I'd gone to one of his poetry readings at Judson Church, but we had never spoken until this. We hadn't been introduced, you see. Old school queens.

"This is Simon. He's not my 'beau,' whatever that is. 'Least not yet." He put a hand on my shoulder. "He's from Texas, so better be careful. The all carry weapons down there."

"Yes, I'm sure he's packing quite an arsenal. Ha! Simon, my dear..." He whined, looking me over. "Come by and see me sometime, everybody does, you know." He knowingly aped prime time Mae West.

It was true. Besides being the editor of Penumbra, Jacki was a formidable poet and essayist, who had attracted the attention of no less than James Baldwin. He was the possessor of a nearly lethal quantity of charisma, and most fatefully for me, he was an accomplished and practicing Yoruba priest.

"Simon is an actor, Jacki dear," Madeline said. "He replaced Noel as Juanita Castro in Ronnie's play. I discovered him."

People were always discovering people in those days.

"Indeed. Do come have lunch with me, little Simon. And do me a favor, my dear. Please stop pursing your lips as though you just sucked an under-ripe persimmon. You needn't pout so. What have you to be pouty about?"

I felt myself flush, even though I managed to smile.

"I don't know you very well, my dear, but you are clearly a star. So relax. A star has but one real responsibility, and that is to shine. Relax into it." This was sage advice, and I never forgot it.

"How old are you?" He asked as if it had just occurred to him that I was a mere baby.

"I'll be twenty in a month."

"Just nineteen! We'll have a party for you on your birthday. It'll be fabulous! I'll make collard greens and buttermilk biscuits. Southern boys like collard greens, don't they, Calvin?"

This request had the weight of a command, and in truth, I was quite curious. I would later learn that though he was from the West Side of Chicago, Jacki was well versed in soul cooking. And in those days a good home cooked southern meal was rarely available.

"I'd be very much obliged," I replied, mock-batting my eyelashes at him.

Little did I know that this formidable character would become my mentor and my nemesis over the next year. A charter member of the coterie of Negro intellectuals that held forth authoritatively on all matters Afro, Jacki was a rebel even among those rebels. His eloquence—and some would say arrogance—on such volatile issues as religion, sex and race matters was good for pumping up the volume at even the loudest party.

"Please!" Jacki changed his tone with me, and started in on one of those eloquent lectures. "You know, black folks have always had a love/hate relationship with the reality of an enslaved past."

"Love?" Madeline objected. "That's a strong word to use about four hundred years of…"

Jacki clarified: "No, not that we loved being kidnapped and enslaved in any way, shape or form, having our humanity raped and trashed with such cruel abandon for all those nasty centuries. But we do love—you hear me? *love*—that we survived it so triumphantly.

"Not only were we not destroyed. We kept the drums, and remembered how to use them and move with them, and came to dominate all music in the western world!"

Madeline responded like a Baptist choir. "You have a point there, baby, although a bitter one."

Jacki went on: "And the astonishing restraint displayed when full knowledge dawned of the deliberate and continuing atrocities committed against us in body, mind and spirit, the restraint that every black person shows on a daily basis by managing to resist the temptation to strangle on sight each and every white person he encounters! We should all get the Nobel Peace Prize."

"Hell, I'd settle for my forty acres and my mule!" Madeline drawled on, playing with Jacki's head.

"And me? I's just pleased as punch to be livin' in New York City mah-self," I spoke up through the cloud of reefer smoke induced enlightenment. "This present generation is sho' better off here than back in Africa."

Jacki showed his perfect teeth framed by plum-colored bow-shaped lips and gave me a wink like a flash of lightning.

From their icy high mountain fastnesses the Tibetans could see far and deep. They think they can see from one lifetime to another.

The Tibetan Buddhist sages say when you die you start a journey from one life to another. The space between lifetimes they call the bardo. They say you have a choice — or the misfortune of having to choose — which kind of incarnation you'll have next by the path you take through the bardo.

When the lama reads the Book of The Dead to you — while you're lying there all dead with your soul slippin' out of the body, all confused 'cause this ain't never happened to you before, 'least not in this ego's memory — he'll tell you to go for the clear light. That way Buddha takes you in his arms and you're in that golden nirvana forever. But if you miss that — and everybody does, honey — then go for the blue light, 'cause that path'll bring you back human and you get to play the whole thing over again. Maybe you get the gold next time.

If you take other paths, with other colored lights, you're liable to end up sufferin' in one of the Buddhist hells or huntin' hopelessly for some kinda happiness as a hungry ghost or even wind up a storm god blowing for endless eons down some steep Himalayan valley.

In their aeries at the top of Himalayas, those Tibetans sure saw a lot of blue sky. You can see why they'd thought the blue tunnel was the one leadin' back here to life as a human bein'.

So go for the blue light. Come back to the flesh.

Yeah, just as I was sayin' you gotta walk the blues 'fore you can see Buddha—or feel yourself loved and cuddled by the man you love.

Calvin and I spent more and more time together. We were natural born lovers. That's it, nobody planned it. We fit like, well, find your own metaphor, sweetheart. We indiscreetly found beds and floors, not always able to wait for comfort. He showed me his secret hiding places in Central Park; the old livery stables was a favorite, we could smell the pale perfumes of long gone horses. In Central Park, a place so erotic that brushing against a tree trunk, a leafy branch touching the skin, could cause a rock hard that had to be dealt with.

I even met his mother in Bed-Sty. She was sweet, very skinny and exhausted at thirty-eight. We made heat and sweat in the back bedroom of a ground floor apartment of a project high-rise, to the music of a crying child, a barking dog, the Puerto Rican radio, a siren crying in the afternoon sun.

Little did I understand it then, but fucking is always a political act. One either has sex in a way that reinforces the status quo, or threatens it. The lovemaking between two black men, free men freighted with ugly histories of forced entry absent of desire—this loving possesses a tenderness like none other.

Conquest and surrender without battle, without prisoners. Questions of power, based on received white skin sexual privilege become moot between those equally despised, equally feared and loathed, and coveted. Brown on brown love allows a concentration on the celestial nature of coupling that many take for granted. Nothing to be proved, see.

Nothing to be gained but ecstasy itself. Flesh and firm luxuriant spirit twists and twines and tumbles and rolls.

"Wait, Calvin, I don't think I can do that. I really want to but..." I held the solid arc of him between my thighs to delay entry. It curved up gently like the prow of a mighty and determined ship.

"Just wait. I'll be slow, so sweet, here... let me."

We kissed, sucking spit and tongues. Calvin put two fingers into my mouth swishing them like candy. He took the sweet fingers and, kissing me deeply again, slipped them slowly into my now opening pucker. "Yeah, that's it baby, just relax, relax, like that see. Ain't that good? Yes, that's hot. Ahh..." In one motion, he removed his fingers and guided in the first few inches of his proud pretty penis.

It hurt, but just a little, and I knew that soon it wouldn't hurt at all.

"There I go there I go there I go. Pretty baby, you are the soul that snapped my control..." King Pleasure's voice crooned over the late night jazz show. "Wrapped up in your magic... don't have no fear, oh..." he went on gliding, singing merrily over James Moody and strings.

Calvin, his skin shining like raw black silk and smelling of hot apricots, arched forward and curled around in a position that let his lips caress my cock, lick and caress and kiss, and rock in rhythm, rock me all night long.

We burst together in an unsolicited yelp, shuddered and shook a moment, then laughed out loud.

This was the first time in my life that I felt sex lived up to its billing. Now I understood why everyone made such a big fuss about it, what all the songs really meant; what mourning, rage and sorrow were produced by the loss of it. I would never be the same.

Was it love? I can't say. Who is really wise enough to know such things? Not me, honey. I was practicing the walkin' blues.

But what I know is that I was learnin' to love myself. And beyond pain and fear, there was surely joy. I felt it inside me.

Like Calvin.

It became clearer and clearer with each passing eon of sweeping winter into frigid spring, from millennia of births and lives to stony death and back again—that there must be something more (or less?) to this celestial arrangement of molecules and nothingness.

Better to recognize this photoplay for what it is: false and unreal—a projection on the screen of the senses. A projection which has no more relationship to the true nature of reality than do shadow puppets that love and fight and die by the flicker of oil lanterns. No more real than the projection of movies on the screen of old theaters. The real, the actual musicalcomedydrama is invisible and inaccessible to all but the most subtle of mind.

Sad to say, the way that can be followed is not the way to it.

Those Tibetan Buddhists did not think they were in Shangri-La, darlin'. No indeed. The jagged spiked mountains there made them think, not of heaven, but of the hell of the Evil Genius. They were hung up on transformation, you hear.

The lean bitter ecology of their glacial existence inspired no fantasies of wondrous bountiful harvests. No milk and honey, no grapes and grains piled as high as the pyramids. Instead those girls worked another alchemy. Taking the wind and the snow with the lamb and the yak, they made straw into delicious spiritual gold.

          The Walking Blues, I say, is a way to keep the real blues at bay. Rather than say "Good morning, heartache, sit down," say, "This black sissy has earned the right to strut."

Is the Walking Blues preventative medicine?

Yes, of course it is.

The Verse

Jay Michaelson

> *"And with a man you shall not lie as with a woman;*
> *it is an abomination."*
> —Leviticus 18:22

On the day the verse was erased, I was asleep, nursing a Friday-morning hangover. It was my sister who told me the news, waking me from my sleep with a telephone call.

"Did you hear what happened?"

"What," I muttered.

"Turn on the TV. Something strange has happened to the Torah."

I imagined, in my groggy and half-awake mind, a particular Torah: the one in the ark of the synagogue where I was Bar Mitzvahed. That Torah was *the* Torah, I assumed, sitting under fluorescent light in a small ark set into a blank, beige-painted wall.

"I don't get it," I said.

"There's—it's hard to explain. I just wanted to make sure you're okay. You should really turn on the news." I had been caught, asleep after eleven on a weekday. I felt guilty. I made my way over to the television set, still half in a dream.

"Scholars across the globe are dumbfounded at what can only be described as a miraculous event," said the inflected voice of the local anchorwoman.

I changed the channel.

"It occurred shortly before the onset of the Jewish sabbath in Jerusalem—"

"Impossible to say—"

"It was, ironically, on this sabbath that the portion containing the verse was to have been—"

"We turn now to Rabbi Yossi Baruch, author of the book *Sacred Lust: Sexuality in the Jewish Tradition*. Rabbi Baruch"—she pronounced it *Baroosh*—"explain to us what this verse is, and what has happened."

"Well, Sandy, as you know, and, we don't have all the information yet, but Leviticus 18:22 inexplicably—some would say miraculously—has disappeared from every extant Torah scroll on the planet. Not every text of the Torah, mind you—only the scrolls. The verse that has disappeared is—or perhaps I should say *was*—generally understood as the Biblical injunction against homosexuality."

"Now, Rabbi *Baroosh*, it's been a long time since Sunday School—can you explain for our viewers what the verse actually says."

"Well, Sandy, the King James Version says: *Thou shalt not lie with another man as thou liest with a woman; it is an abomination*. Now, Sandy, that the verse in Leviticus is rather narrow, prohibiting, on the surface, only one sexual act. But what you must understand is that every letter, every stroke of every letter in the Torah, is extremely important. Every word contains a wealth of hidden meanings, legal implications, even mystical significance. So, this verse was understood to mean much more than simply the, uh, act of intercourse between two men, and was expanded over the centuries to cover the entire range of homosexual activities—between men or women."

"So what does it mean that, now, somehow, the verse has effectively—disappeared?"

The rabbi had made a career of explaining Jewish law as it pertained to sexuality. He had grown popular, and not unwealthy. But how to answer this question? The legal issues were simple: the verse was unambiguous, and clear, and no matter how much the activists had excoriated him on the talk shows, no matter their arguments about biology or genetics or morality or so-called human rights, there was no getting around it. He had stood firm. He had remained steadfast despite those gossips who whispered about him when they saw him in shul, tittering like embarrassed schoolchildren in their first sex-ed class. But this was something new. A verse—removed from the Torah?

This was a miracle, not a legal argument. What the verse said is secondary—couldn't they see that?

I looked away from the television and out my window. A large cloud was passing over. Twenty blocks south of me, Rabbi Berel Weintraub perceived it to be an evil omen.

That cloud, he thought, is too low. It is a sign of judgment. The messianic days. Everything must be interpreted.

Berel stroked his white beard, and allowed himself to fall back into his desk chair, which rolled to the wall. He had been on the phone continuously since 10:15, when the news broke and the phones began to ring. Now it was almost noon, and still the phones rang. His wife Chava was his only source of strength, Chava who now parried on the telephone with rabbis and community leaders from across the country, all demanding an answer from the esteemed *posek* and scholar—an answer that Rav Weintraub knew he could not give.

Rav Weintraub's first thought had been: For this? Two thousand years of waiting, and God gives us a sign *for them*?

Because he knew it was a sign, and that it was from God. The backlash that had already begun to be articulated in some quarters—allegations of a massive plot by the homosexuals around the world—was an absurd denial of the obvious. This was an act of the supernatural, just as we had been waiting for, but not in the form we expected. The contortions of the supposed plot were impossible to entertain. How could the homosexuals—even if there were some secret cabal among them all—have snuck into the museums, the genizahs, the locked *aronei kodesh* in a thousand shuls across the world? And even had they gained access to every Torah in the world (an absurdity!) how could they have perfectly erased, without a single trace, and without even a gap, a verse written in permanent ink on parchment? The verse didn't just disappear, leaving a blank space—*it seemed to have never existed at all*. Berel had seen it with his own eyes, as soon as the first story broke, now almost two hours ago. Where the words *v'et zachar lo tishkav mishkevei isha, toevah hi*☐used to be, now there was nothing. The Torah went straight from *ani adonai* in verse 21 to *uv'chol behema* in verse 23. The section break a few lines down was almost imperceptibly larger than it had been, but that was all. No, this was not a conspiracy.

Rav Weintraub thought: when a man of faith is presented with overwhelming evidence that contradicts his faith, he nonetheless chooses belief. This is the meaning of faith; that it is the ground of reality that stays true despite that which shifts. The man of faith may cease to explain, because explanation may fail; even expression may fail. He may even outwardly deny the impossible proposition, that God cares, that God exists, that God acts in history with love. He may even *inwardly* deny it. But ultimately he knows in his deepest heart that he believes. And there is love there, and peace.

Yet when a man of faith is presented with overwhelming evidence that *affirms* his faith—what then? Of what value is a man's faith when it is faith in the obvious?

At least, Rav Weintraub thought, allowing a smile to creep up the corners of his mouth, this showed the feminists.

"What do you mean?" Gloria asked when Naomi made the same remark, twenty miles away, in Queens.

"I mean that for generations we've been fighting this battle, and yet it's *them* that God chooses to endorse with an inexplicable sign. It's an outrage."

"You're being ridiculous," Gloria said to her lover. "Look what God has given us! And besides, this is our battle too, remember?" she added tenderly.

"I know. I know it is. I know it is, Gloria. But—"

"It's the same battle, it's the same fight, with the same enemies who now have nothing to say to us. God has spoken out against them… God has spoken! And on our side! This has changed our lives!"

Naomi said nothing. Maybe, Gloria thought, Naomi had never wanted God to approve of their living together, because God's approval would mean one less reason to leave.

"God spoke about us," she said. "God spoke about *humanity*, Naomi, what we've been saying all along, that the Torah *must* change, *has to* change. Usually not this way. But this is only the beginning! If God has taken out this verse, then what are we to do with the sexist verses, the ethnocentric verses, the cruel verses about slavery and injustice—well, obviously, we have to imitate God! It doesn't matter whether it's one group or another, it doesn't even matter—what matters is God spoke on *our side*. Somewhere there's a man, right now, someone

who used to believe that we were all *nuts*, that we were just *heretics*—
and he's in *doubt*, Naomi! Do you see the irony? He's in *doubt*□because
God has spoken. For us the conflict is natural. But what that must feel
like to a traditional Jew…"

Shaya Porush was one such Jew. Throughout shabbos services at
his shul in Jerusalem, there had been a hush over the *kehilla*. No one
dared venture a theory. The Torah had been unwrapped—the Rebbe
himself had authorized it—and, sure enough, the verse was gone. Like
it never existed! If this was an act of human beings, it was the greatest
blasphemy ever to be perpetrated. The death penalty would not be
enough. And to make such a disgusting point, such a vile point!
Everyone had his suspicions about who in their community might
indulge in such… abominations. And if they were responsible…

But, like Berel, Shaya had to admit that this could be no act of mere
human beings. For him, it had not been difficult to accept the notion of
Divine intervention: Shaya believed—no, he knew, because he had
read—that God intervened in human affairs all the time. He steered
the bullets in the Yom Kippur War, guided the SCUDs in the first Gulf
War. If Jews suffered, it was because God willed it, and because through
their sins the Jews themselves had earned it. And when they were
protected, clear and convincing evidence could be marshaled for the
direct intervention of God, if only one was patient enough and careful
enough to look.

But that God has done such a thing *with this verse*! The Rambam
had taught that in the time of the Messiah, some *mitzvos* would endure
and others would be set aside. But was this really one of the *mitzvos*
that was so important to merit Divine intervention? And what of the
hundreds—no, thousands—of years of tradition? There is no distinction
between the chain of tradition and God. It was God who wrote the
Torah, God who taught the interpretations of the Torah. So what now?

Shaya looked around his apartment. The candles had been lit for
shabbos, and his wife had prepared the table as she did every week. But
the *davening* at shul had been perfunctory, almost silent, and even now,
when the Karliners' kids should be screaming on the other side of the
paper-thin wall, everything was quiet. It was as if everyone in Jerusalem
had been stunned.

Of course, none of them knew any homosexuals. There were misfits
in the community, like Mendel, who never married, and who lived

with his parents until they died. People spoke about him. But that was all *loshon hara*; no one had any proof. And Shaya was the first to reprove the gossips when they spread their filth. But what was next, Shaya wondered as he looked at his oldest boy reading quietly on the couch. He wanted somehow to protect him. Shaya opened the bottle of kiddush wine and called out to his wife and children.

At the same moment, across town, Oren Shalev opened a bottle of champagne and called out to his husband Shamir.

"What are you doing?" Shamir asked in Hebrew, entering the room when he heard the pop of the cork.

"I'm celebrating. Kiss me." And they kissed.

"I'm not so sure it is something to celebrate."

"Shamir, this is what we have wished for all our lives."

"Maybe you wished, with your love of the old superstitions," Shamir said, breaking the embrace. "But I have no use for their Torah, their verse, or their God. And now, uninvited, he has broken into my house and insisted that I recognize him."

"Shamir, it doesn't matter whether we believe or not. What matters is that, for the people that do, what this must mean for them. What they must now recognize, about us, about the times we are living in."

"I don't want it to mean *anything* for them! I want them to leave me alone! I don't need their god's approval. And now, now we will hear about nothing except the miracle! The miracle this, the miracle that! The messiah is coming! This is a huge step backward, Oren. What now, so every other verse in the Torah is now true because this one was proven false? It has to be! Otherwise God would have deleted them as well! So the world was created in six days? So God slew the firstborn of Egypt? Chose Israel to be His nation of priests? Now all of that is true? Do you see what a catastrophe this is? Only because we are selfish do we think this is a good development. Oy, *baruch hashem*," Shamir said in the accent of the religious, "now being a faggot is okay. *Baruch hashem*, as if I needed their approval. Needed their *hechsher* to tell me that your dick is kosher, Oren. I didn't need it. I didn't *want* it. And what about the other three thousand verses of their ridiculous and tribal Torah?"

That was the question Professor Michael Wigand was asking in the *beit midrash* of the Jewish Theological Seminary in New York. The scrolls were out, and being closely inspected by Professor Wigand's rabbinical students. "Every letter of every verse," he instructed them again. "I want you to check it against the chumashim, against the Septuagint, everything. Don't trust yourself that you know every letter."

How can I be of use? Wigand thought, as his students pored over the scrolls. Leave the speculation to the speculators. Plenty of them. My job, what I can do, is make sure we've got the story right. Those popularizers, rushing onto the talk shows. What if there's more missing that we don't know about? It could be more subtle—a letter here or there, or a word. No one seemed to be checking. My job is to check. Let the others guess as to what it means. I can tell you what it says.

Rachel looked around at the students in the *beit midrash,* who all seemed to be in shock. And she knew why: they had spent most of their young careers in dialogue with sacred text, and navigating the tension—a dynamic, vital one, Rachel thought—between the constant words on the page and our changing conceptions of what it meant to be human. But they were used to having an opponent who played by the rules. And those rules were that while the words are on the page, it's up to us to make the Torah a living document. *Lo bashamayim hi,* Rachel had been taught—the Torah isn't in heaven, and we don't listen to voices; we listen to reason and to conscience. Now the rules were suddenly thrown out the window, and the game seemed to be over. She looked around, at these earnest young scholars, cross-checking every line of the Torah, and thought: they can't handle it.

And Rachel knew, despite his certainty, that Wigand couldn't either. He wasn't a spiritual man; he was a scholar, a rationalist. Who knew what he even *believed?* Textual evidence, linguistic analysis—the Bible could have been the Code of Hammurabi for all that Professor Wigand talked about God. Privately Rachel suspected he was an atheist. A professor of Bible instead of a rabbi. And yet—not a professor at a university, but here, at a seminary, so that Wigand could surround himself with believers but never admit to being one himself. Maybe that was it. And now, his feverish accounting allowed him to maintain, in the face of it all, that what was important was not God but exegesis and hermeneutics. Maybe, come to think of it, he was gay too.

Rachel's thoughts were interrupted by the sound of someone shouting. "Is this the God in which we believe?" Rabbi Doctor Millman asked no one in particular as he strode into the *beit midrash.* "To change our interpretation of this law—fine! I published an article suggesting just that. But to accept that God has acted—and that God has chosen to act only in the Scripture of the Jews—this I cannot accept! That after Auschwitz and Stalin, that after Hiroshima and the Middle Passage, that this is when God has chosen to act! Chosen to speak to us, like we are madmen in the street who hear voices! The God in which I believe resides in the human heart, from whence we hear the voice of conscience. That is the voice which tells me to revise the law with compassion. But this? This lowers us all. It dehumanizes us, reduces us to children who have no choice—*no choice*—but to obey the father's will.

"And why only the Torah? Why not the Koran? Why not the New Testament? Are we to recover our ethnocentric notions of chosenness now, at precisely this moment of revelation? Is this what the Israelites felt when, encamped under Sinai, it seemed that God was speaking directly and only to them? Are we infants now, as then?"

Reverend Patrick Doyle was making the same point, looking out over Boston Harbor, by now exhausted with the debate and regretting that he had missed lunch. "God has always chosen the Jews to be the bearers of his message. What is significant is that the Jews have chosen not to listen."

"Nonetheless, Reverend," said his junior colleague, "is it not odd for God to choose the Jews—again?"

"Perhaps, but perhaps not. We have always taught that the Jews would have a role to play in the end times," Reverend Doyle replied, looking out at the harbor. "Perhaps they are nearer than we think."

But Reverend Doyle's mind was not on the Jews, or on the apocalypse. Rather, Reverend Doyle, himself a man who had mastered his homosexual inclinations for over forty years, who had only recently dismissed two gay priests in the wake of the sex scandals engulfing America's churches, thought of his deeds. It was true that the sins of the priests were not homosexuality, but abuse and pedophilia. But he had treated them as violations of Leviticus, he realized in his own prayer, because he had thought he understood. These were not small children that the two priests had allegedly molested; they were young adults. Vulnerable teenagers, yes, but not children. Reverend Doyle knew the desire that he punished. And he also knew that if he could master it, which he had, faithfully, without even a single lapse, for decades, he knew, even if he could not say, that the gays and lesbians were wrong. Sexuality may not be a matter of choice, but sexual behavior is. The will is stronger than the body's inclinations.

So Reverend Doyle chose his next words carefully. "What I cannot fathom is why this particular verse was singled out. We will have to reflect on it, over time. It may be, as I suspect, that the teachings of the Church on this subject are built upon sound doctrine, regardless of the verse in Leviticus. Or it may be that their teachings are rooted only in the Scripture that has now, it seems, been deleted, in an act of grace which we cannot understand."

The Reverend thought back to when he was an altar boy himself, in a time when the sexual behavior of priests (or anyone else, for that matter) was not a matter of open conversation. He had thought that Father Monahan embraced him with more than fatherly affection, noticed how he looked at him at points in the service. But he loved Father Monahan, and would have given his body over to him had he asked. And yet, because Father Monahan didn't ask, his love was all the more holy. To master one's urges, and to yoke them to a holy cause, was the greatest service. To take away this unique mission—to love only God, because all other love was forbidden—would be a great loss.

Reverend Doyle looked at his colleague, and out at the harbor again, where Arthur White was working one of the last independent fishing boats in Boston harbor. He'd heard about the news but didn't care. There were no fish, that was a bigger problem. The pollution, that was the shame of it, that was the cause. And now Arthur, Jr., wasn't going into the business, and who could blame him? The boy would have more of a future going to college, learning a profession. The news of the verse didn't affect him in the least, Arthur Sr. was sure. Let God help with what matters.

And there were farmers in rural China, there were guerilla fighters in central Africa, there were entire nations for whom the news meant very little. Some thought it was a fake—a ploy of the Jews. Some thought it was superstition.

Marshall "Mack" Henry absolutely would not hear of it discussed, no matter if his wife brought it up, or the men on the rig. The thought of two men together absolutely stirred his stomach.

The news shocked twenty-six-year-old Sholom Berger, who had willed it to happen, unknowingly, with a pure, selfless love that cut through complications, pleading for a miracle at the propitious time, at the dawn *hashkama minyan*—silently, so that no one else would hear. "Please, God, make the verse disappear. Just make it gone. I wish it would disappear. I wish it never existed. I wish I could be what you want me to be, but I can't. I wish I could be normal, could be straight, but you won't let me be. You won't let me, as much as I have tried. You have created me as you have. So you force me to disobey you. You make me, you push me away. Why? And I don't want to try to change myself anymore, God, to fight your will, to fight myself. You have made me this way, and that was your will, and I don't want to deny You or how you made me. This is your doing, and I won't reject it any more, God. I'll tell my mother, I'll tell everyone. I'll come clean. But I don't want to rebel. I don't want to hurt you. I don't want to leave you. I want to love you. You give me no choice but to disobey you. Why? It can't go on. God, just make the verse—one verse; one line; eight words; twenty eight letters, and it would all be as it should. Twenty eight letters! Make them disappear, God, unwrite the verse. Say you didn't mean it. It was an aberration. A misunderstanding. It was nothing, really—the scribes got it wrong, they didn't hear clearly. It happens. God, please make it disappear, allow me to love you as you have commanded me— with all of my self and my strength, all of it, my eyes and ears and my cock, too, yes God, even that, even my sex, my whole body—let me love you with all of myself, as I want to do, as you commanded me to do: *b'chol levavcha, u'v'chol nafshesha, u'vchol me'odecha*, God, with all my heart, with all my soul, with all my might. If you won't change me, change the verse. If it just, if only the verse just... didn't exist!"

No one at the shul could hear Sholom's prayer. It is told that in such cases the gates of heaven open, Sholom had learned as a boy, as they did to the cries of Ishmael. But he would not hear the news for hours, and so he wiped away his tears, and continued with the *amidah*. Unbeknownst to him, David Weiss was praying just as fervently, on the other side of the synagogue, for the will to somehow find the strength to be able, again, night after night, to face his wife, wanting to confide in her and yet unable to do so. The accomplishment of the physical act was no longer such a challenge; he had mastered the art of fantasy, and with only a few well-worn images, or even phrases, could bring himself to completion. But the desire he felt now was not sexual. It was for something everyone should be entitled to, he thought: he wanted to share everything with his wife, in order to love her fully. And that meant expressing that he could not love her fully. But it seemed impossible. Cruel, even—cruel to the very human being he wanted to love most gently. And so David prayed to be able, somehow, to continue, and maybe someday find an answer.

David's wife knew. Of course she knew. Even David thought she knew, but wouldn't say. They had been married three years. David had tried. He had tried because it was commanded, and tried because he wanted it to be true—wanted to believe that if he pleased her, if he had sex with her, that it would turn into love, and that the images in his head that he used when he was with his wife would disappear. They would become irrelevant, because he would come to love her. And even if he didn't—so what if he didn't. So what. The inside matters less than the outside, David believed, and he would be kind, and caring, and compassionate. He loved Aliza. She was beautiful—but objectively, like a painting or a sunset.

Aliza knew, but had not decided whether to do anything about it. She respected David's decision to marry, to live a *halachic* life, and could not pretend that she hadn't suspected the truth before they were married. Aliza was older than David—thirty-four now, thirty-one when they wed. Old, by Orthodox standards, even in their modern community. She was lucky to be married at all, and to an intelligent, sweet man. Ten years she had waited for a man who would love her completely and whom she could love in return. Ten years, and stupid men, fat men, pushy men, sexist men, men who didn't seem to shower in the morning. Was a gay man such a bad deal after all? She had watched her friends marry increasingly defective husbands. This one never looked you in the eye, that one had greasy hair, that one was, well, when someone reaches a certain level, it becomes impolite to call them "stupid." You begin to search for euphemisms.

At the weddings of good, smart girls, all with careers, all with stable personalities and decent souls, it seemed the grooms got lousier and lousier. Misfits. Nebbishes. Clods. At first it was kind of a joke, but it had long since ceased to be amusing. Would she have to choose, herself, between settling and living alone?

So when David came along—she asked him out—she wondered why someone so eligible was still... eligible. It occurred to her immediately that he might be gay—again, first as a joke, then less so. They were not *shomer negiah*; they kissed on the second date, and did more on the third. David was tentative, but passionate nonetheless. Sometimes he seemed to try too hard; Aliza remembered on that third date wondering if he was "compensating." But she couldn't be sure, and, frankly, she didn't want to be. Here was a man who could hold an intelligent conversation, who had a great job and a great sense of humor, and who was good looking besides. Everyone has an inner demon they wrestle with; it is what makes religion. So maybe this was David's.

She had only known for sure in the last year. Yocheved had been born a few months already, and yet, David still seemed uninterested in sex. It almost seemed as if he were enjoying a sort of reprieve. This is normal, Aliza had read, for all couples to go through such a period. But then, one Sunday, David was relaxing and watching a football game on TV. Maybe it was the way he was sitting, with one leg crossed over the other, or the way he was holding his glass of soda—or maybe it was how he seemed to look at the men on the screen almost with a look of longing. But in that moment, Aliza knew.

And when she heard the news—her mother had called her in a sort of apocalyptic panic—she instantly thought of her husband, and cried. Whether the tears were for his liberation, or hers, or for the inevitable dissolution of their jointly-held dreams, Aliza could not be sure.

"*Lo bashamayim hi!*" roared Eliezer in the rabbis' private *beit midrash*. "It is not for God to change the halacha!" There were only twelve men there, but he spoke as if to a congregation. "Even when the *bat kol* from God shouted in agreement with Rabbi Yehuda, nevertheless the Rabbis ruled according to halacha, *as they understood it*. We do not throw out two thousand years of halacha because God suddenly changed his mind."

"Don't be a fool!" answered Moshe. "You know as well as I that this is precisely what the *maskilim* use to justify every innovation away from Torah that they desire. Every bone in my body detests the homosexuals and what they do. But I am not so closed a man as not to see! This is more than what Daniel received, more than Yirmiyahu

himself merited in the valley of the bones. If you would have told me
that there is an argument why a man with a man should not be a *toeva*,
I would have said you are crazy. No, worse than crazy—*rasha*. So this
is what it takes. This is what it takes."

"First of all—" Eliezer began.

"First of all, we should do nothing," interrupted Pinchas, who had
been listening to both sides. "It's shabbos. Let's have shabbos."

"But it's shabbos *Achrei Mos!*" Moshe responded. "What should
we *lain* tomorrow? Should the verse be included or not?"

"Since very kosher Torah in the world has the verse missing, the
verse is missing," Leib Wolf said. Rabbi Leib Wolf was eighty-three
years old, a survivor of the camps, and a respected authority throughout
the community for over forty years. The room fell silent. "The halucha
we can discuss next week. Who knows but that this may be the
birthpangs of the Messiah? Maybe a decision will not be necessary."

"Rav Wolf," began Reb Moshe. "Should we say nothing?"

"Saying there is nothing to say is not the same as saying nothing. *A
wise man keeps his counsel, but a fool—*"

"But, Rav Wolf, the *feigelehs*?!" Eliezer dared to interrupt. The other
rabbis glared at him in shock.

"Reb Eliezer," said Rav Wolf patiently, "we should always
remember to hate the sin and not the sinner. If there is no sin, there is
nothing to hate. But this is for later. In the meantime, we read the Torah
that God has given us, and tell people to wait. As of now, everything
that was *ussur* is still *ussur*, because no rabbinic authority has said
otherwise." Eliezer smiled. "But," Rav Wolf added, "it is only an evil
man who denies what is obvious."

"So now it's a double mitzva," Gary said to Jonah, smiling, as he
watched the sun set through the apartment window.

"It's shabbat already?" They had been in bed for hours, since all
the shops were closed and since they had nowhere else they wanted to
be. "Wow."

"I love you."

"I love you," Jonah answered.

God, otherwise, was silent.

My Last Visits With Harry

Bill Blackburn

I first met Harry Hay in 1985 when he was seventy-four years old, nearly twice my age. From that time, his friendship and mentoring have been a blessing–a charm–in my life, even after his passing.

Harry was an originator of the Mattachine Society, the first substantial national homosexual rights organization that grew out of his progressive, idealistic politicking at the end of the 1940s. He is honored by many as the "Father of Gay Liberation." In 1979, he and several colleagues called a gathering of similarly idealistic gay men to meet in the Arizona desert to explore gay consciousness and vision. From that gathering and fairy cirlces around the country arose the Radical Faerie Movement.

Harry has long had a message for gay men, and the message he brought constantly evolved. He was not simply an historic icon; he was a living visionary and a reformer. But beyond each of those merits, Harry was also very much a human being and that is another aspect of him that I hope to present here.

I had the great gift of visiting the ninety-year old Harry many times in the last months of his life, 2001 to 2002. We visited as longtime friends and as collaborators in building community. But there was a special quality to our last visits after his diagnosis of metastasized cancer as we knew that Harry was in the last days of his life. He had a message to deliver and I was one of the conduits that he was going to pour it through.

I visited Harry in his home in the Castro district of San Francisco on October 1, 2002. Harry's purpose, he believed in his last years, was to reach gay men with one message, a new way to move toward achieving our acceptance as vital members of our culture. And to be clear, he was not going against his long-held opposition to the assimilationist position that we are the same as heterosexuals except for what we do in bed. Harry believed that we are unique people with unique qualities and gifts. This integration was to be as homophiles—a term Harry often used to indicate "a lover of" or "having an affinity for" (*philia*) the same (*homo*) to differentiate from the only-sexual focus of homosexual—remaining the singular beings he conceived of us being. And therein lay his final message for gay men.

"No group in American history has gained widespread acceptance without showing that they brought a gift for society with them," Harry asserted. "All the successive waves of immigrants did this, whether they built the railroads and highways or provided whatever labor was needed. We know that there are many gifts we bring, but they are not well articulated for the general public. So we must tell them and in order to do so, we must first figure out what they are.

"Bring gay men together in Circle to discover the specific gifts that we bring, things that the larger culture needs. And once you have a consensus as to what those gifts are, begin letting the culture know exactly what it is that they are getting from us. It is in this way that we will be given respect and acceptance, not by simply demanding 'rights' nor asserting that we deserve them."

Harry preferred that these Circles draw up the list but when I pressed him, he stated his opinion that one of these gifts is the ways we have found, beyond the standard male models, for men to love and be tender with one another.

Harry repeatedly stated that delivering the vision of this Circle was his final mission and that he had dedicated his remaining time to this effort. He was also clear as to how we must create this Circle.

"Remember that one has to give oneself permission to enter the Circle, to live in one's Heart. [Harry wrote and even thought in capital letters and so I assert their accuracy here.] The Heart is the fourth dimension and there isn't an easy way to get there. One has to work to do so. One has to really want to—need to—get there. And one person can't do the work for someone else, or give another an easy hand up."

"In Circle process, you have to watch the energy very closely. Sometimes you may think you have a Circle but what you really have is a square. If someone becomes dominating, if two or more have become contentious, if the level of participation has become too intellectualized and not from the Heart, and so on, you no longer have a Circle. If the Circle has become squared, call a break: everyone take a walk, climb a mountain, have a meal together, whatever it takes to re-enter as co-equal members of the Circle."

Harry talked about what had first moved him to action around calling together the Mattachine Society. He said that two events had awakened him. One was biologist Thomas Huxley making the statement that "No negative trait [i.e. one that does not have an obvious benefit such as reproduction or food gathering] ever continues to appear in a given species millennia after millennia after millennia unless it in some way serves the survival of that species." That, Harry said, indicated to him that homosexuality must have a positive societal effect.

The other awakening event was his encounter with Kinsey's statistics regarding men who have sex with men. Harry said: "You must understand that in that era, those of us so inclined never imagined that there could be more than a few hundred of us anywhere on the planet. But Kinsey's statistics alerted me to the fact that there were millions of us in the U.S. alone! I immediately realized that there was a tremendous injustice in the repression and harassment of so many people."

Harry was tiring from our visit and I saw it was time to take my leave. I said: "Harry, it's been a privilege to know you." Harry looked quickly, startlingly, up into my eyes. "I mean, it has been pleasing to know you."

"Yes!" said Harry with a grin. "You see, the term privilege would imply a subject-object relationship. To be pleased to know me implies a Subject-Subject relationship, a mutual pleasure." Subject-Subject consciousness, a concept Harry developed, maintains that gay men (he would actually prefer the term faerie men, differentiating from unawakened gay men) have a special quality of relating to one another as extensions of oneself, as subjects rather than objects.

"Bill," he said as I walked to the door, "light as many candles in your work as you can reach, and even those candles that appear beyond reach."

He wasn't talking paraffin.

I next visited ten days later. Friends warned me to expect a change: hospice had been brought in and Harry truly was in his last days. They had begun a small dose of morphine sublingually to control the pain and he was sometimes sleepy and foggy, though sometimes as clearheaded as ever. I didn't know what to expect as I approached his room. He lay there looking in my direction but I had no way of knowing if he recognized me or could even see me. I stood quietly at the doorway collecting my emotions before approaching his bedside. I leaned over and said softly, hopefully: "Harry, it's me, Bill Blackburn."

"Yes, I know," he said. "I'm glad you're here." And not skipping a beat: "Now, Euclid of Alexandria, the great mathematician, is said to have told Ptolemy the First: 'There is no royal road to geometry.' You know what that means?"

I didn't know what anything meant at that point but that I was here. I was trying to settle my emotions, to really be present with my dear and dying friend, to be able to even talk, and now I was being confronted by Euclid and this other antiquarian guy? I was not ready but Harry, heedless, plunged on.

"You see, Ptolemy was the ruler of Egypt. He felt that the privilege of his status would entitle him to knowing mathematics automatically. That Euclid should give it to him outright, that he shouldn't have to do the work of learning it. That he was privileged to know Euclid's art."

I responded with something profound like: "Uhhh, okay…"

He went on: "Euclid said: 'There is no royal road to mathematics.' That is, you can't simply be given it. You have to do the hard work of learning it. You have to study it, and that takes time and effort. There is no shortcut."

Now something was starting to sink in. I was waking to what he was trying to tell me.

"You see, some people want to lead others, or push them, or even worse, intellectualize them into their Hearts. But that will never work!

There is no royal road to mathematics and there is no royal road to the Heart. You can't even teach others the steps. It takes hard work to get to the Heart, and each person has to do the work himself. And the last part of getting there takes a leap—a leap in the dark."

"It takes a leap to get to Subject-Subject consciousness. There is no knowing the way, no intellectualizing your way there and no intellectualizing others there either. Once there, you can sometimes see the steps that it took to get there, but they're not the steps anybody else can take or duplicate."

Harry then said: "You know, some people tell me that I can relax and let go, that my work will go on without me." Harry knew damn well that I was one of those who had been telling him that. He didn't forget a thing.

"You know, that isn't what is worrying me, whether my work will go on. What is worrying me right now is that I've made mistakes. I've made too many mistakes. I find myself laying here in my bed counting them."

My heart sank. Here was this icon of gay liberation, this man who had done so much for the liberation of gay people and for Native Americans, and for so many other social justice issues, who had the gratitude and admiration of many, many thousands of people, and he was caught up in his mistakes. Something was very wrong here.

"Harry," I said, "you know, you're very close to that place where you get to be perfect. On the other side, you get to be 'God.' But here, you get to make mistakes just like the rest of us. Your feet are in the dirt, just like the rest of us. You walk, you stumble and learn, you pick yourself up and go on. We need you to be human, Harry, or we couldn't approach you. You couldn't be a model for us if you were perfect. You would intimidate and overwhelm us."

Harry quickly changed the subject, going on to talk about—what else?—the latest genetic research. He said: "A finding such as the fact that the hypothalamus of gay men is found to be smaller than in other men, as it is small in women, is misleading. An isolated fact such as this can be over-interpreted. DNA research shows us that there are hundreds of gauges or causes of behavior, and each one carries more information than we can know. Any single, isolated factor therefore becomes meaningless."

We went on to other topics. As I was sensing his growing exhaustion, I said: "Harry, I want to go back to something we talked about earlier. Honey, you have got to forgive yourself." Then I caught myself. "I'm sorry, that's not what I want to say. You don't *have to* forgive yourself. I would *like* you to forgive yourself. It would please me if you would." And he looked up at me like a school kid with a great big grin—or was that a school teacher?—I assume because I had caught myself using a term inappropriate for Subject-Subject relationship.

"Oh, I heard you already," Harry said. "I'm laying here thinking about it." And I'm sure he was. We said our farewells, telling each that we loved the other. "Come back soon," he said. "If I'm still here, I'd love to talk more with you."

I walked into the front room and spoke with John Burnside, Harry's partner since 1963, before I left. John asked me about the course I was about to fly to Boulder to take. It was a course in "Spiral Dynamics integral," a model of the evolution of culture and consciousness developed by Clare Graves and Don Beck. I gave John a quick overview of its stages of development that transcend and yet include the stages before.

"Oh," said John, "have you read Emerson's essay, 'Circles'?" He went on to tell me, "Emerson uses an image of a tower with a winding staircase. We are the tower. And at the bottom of the stairs, we can see things in great detail, all the phenomena of the world. Yet as we ascend the staircase, we gain broader views." It was a perfect analogy to the Spiral Dynamics model. It was also a metaphor for the years these venerable men had lived.

John also spoke of categories, that Emerson said that categories are useful only in commerce and war. He said that this merges beautifully with Harry's teaching that we are all unique, that no category can define us. We are each our own individual. And this excursion through John and Ralph Waldo brought me back full circle to my conversation with Harry on hypothalamus research and DNA.

I went to my car and, finally free from intellectual challenge, I again found my emotions. When I had cleared my tears, I sat for twenty minutes taking notes and marveling at these two amazing, gentle, brilliant, vibrantly alive and fragile men.

My last visit with Harry was 4 days later, October 16. He was indeed in his last days and having a hard time of it physically. I mostly worked with his caregiver, John Campbell, to keep Harry clean and warm. But before I left we had a chance for a bit of dialogue.

Harry said: "Goodbye, Bill. It has been very good to know you. I'm pleased to know that you will be carrying on the work. Now you know what to do. Get Circles together of gay men and have them discuss what gifts we bring, what we contribute to society. We have to be clear, ourselves, about what we bring. Then we need to tell the world that we are here to offer those gifts. That is the way in which our place in society will be assured."

I left the physical presence of this great man, my Elder Brother Harry Hay, for the last time, unable to distinguish between my tears of sadness and my tears of joy and gratitude.

And so, in the Radical Faerie tradition of Calling, I call these Circles into Being and call upon others to call forth these Circles:

Let us join together to look deeply together and bring our Gifts as Gay and Faerie Brothers into the Light. Indeed, I Call on all of us, Lesbian, Gay, Bisexual, Transgender, Straight, of every Race and every other Dimension of Diversity!

Spend time searching in your Hearts and in the Circles of your Communities, discovering and developing the best Healing Gifts that you bring, and Offer them out to this Beautiful World that needs us so desperately.

The Earth needs us, all Life needs us, and Harry urges us on. Let us rise to our Highest Consciousness, to Vision and Work Together to create a new culture of Inclusion, Justice, Prosperity, Peace and Liberation.

Another World is Possible!

Reversing Vandalism: How the San Francisco Public Library Turned a Hate Crime into Art

Jim Van Buskirk

I am a lifelong lover of books, a voracious reader, a gay man, writer, and librarian at the San Francisco Public Library. Over three years ago, SFPL staff members began finding books hidden under shelving units throughout the Main Library. The books had been carved with a sharp instrument: covers and inner pages were slashed and odd almond-shaped pieces were cut out, and then stuck into other books. Offending words and/or images of eyes, mouths, and other body parts were carved away.

Staff members united to stop the culprit by watching the bookshelves. One afternoon, a librarian on her day off saw someone shove damaged books under a shelf. The vandal was caught and arrested. Ultimately, more than 600 volumes were desecrated. Because most of them related to gay, lesbian, bisexual, or transgendered themes, or HIV/AIDS, or women's health issues, the perpetrator was charged with, and found guilty of, a hate crime.

When the crime was reported, an outpouring of support came from sympathizers across the country, including offers to help replace the vandalized volumes. After the trial, the books were returned to the library. Most of them were determined to be beyond repair and had been withdrawn from the collection. Before the books were actually discarded, we began taking digital photographs to document the destruction. The more I handled the volumes, the more I realized that throwing them away would only complete the vandal's crime.

During conversations with artist friends, the idea emerged that these ruined volumes might serve as raw material for artistic responses. Discussions with library staff led to the Reversing Vandalism project. Initially I imagined that some librarians might want this embarrassing situation swept under the rug, so I was very proud when the entire library ultimately committed so many resources to ensure the project's success.

We circulated a public call for participation in the project. The response was immediate and intense. Some who answered were members of the Gay, Lesbian, Bisexual and Transgender (GLBT) communities; some were visual artists, and many were people who fell into neither camp. People quickly understood that this vandalism was not a local issue, or solely about gay and lesbian concerns, or even about books—it was an opportunity to address a social climate increasingly filled with fear and hate. Artist Mary Bennett coordinated the participation of the Center for Contemporary Arts in Santa Fe where 44 of the vandalized books were offered to local artists for an exhibit set to open that summer.

Artists have always used art in response to tragedy or hate, knowing intuitively that creating a visual image through any medium can produce physical and emotional benefits for both the creator, and for those who view it. Many artists created something beautiful from the shreds of a ruined book. Some of the responses are whimsical, sad, angry, or political. Others added humor to the situation. Most impressive was the wide variety of responses. Using the same raw materials, artists contributed an unexpectedly diverse range of expression as they participated in proselytizing the importance of reversing vandalism. Some people got stuck along the way. One woman told me that working with the book brought up too many emotions; they overwhelmed her, rendering her unable to finish her artwork. I imagine that her story is not unique.

This wanton act sought to deprive others of much-needed information. My own response to the tragedy, like that of many of the visual artists, was initially one of fear, outrage, frustration, and sadness. This was quickly coupled with confirmation that queers continue to be grossly misunderstood by people in our midst.

In 1996, with Susan Stryker, I co-authored a book called *Gay By The Bay: A History of Queer Culture in the San Francisco Bay Area*. Seeing a stack of several copies of my own book defaced, I thought about a perpetrator threatened by ideas, and how he might feel about the people who embody those ideas. What, I wondered, is the leap from carving up books to carving up people? The murders of Matthew Shepard and Gwen Araujo sprang to mind, symbolizing the verbal, physical, and psychic abuse that queers frequently endure.

People ask me about the perpetrator and seem frustrated when I respond that I am less interested in theorizing about what makes him tick than viewing his actions as symptomatic of an underlying erosion of respect for others' differences in contemporary society. This energy explodes unexpectedly, like a volcanic fissure, releasing hot hatred that is deemed an anomaly. It is not. Since the new Main Library opened in April 1996, we have found the words "Kill Fagots" carved into the top of a customized wooden table in the library's James C. Hormel Gay and Lesbian Center. We have also seen the initials "HIV" carved into the mirrored surface of three of the library's four public elevator cabins as well as into tables, and the bar-code labels sliced out of dozens of books on GLBT issues.

Rather than immediately repairing the destruction, hoping it would go away and pretending it would never happen again, I want to acknowledge it, try to understand the fear and ignorance that ignites hatred. I recognized it as an unfortunate fact, a function of the strides in the struggle for the civil rights of all minorities and marginalized people, sexual or otherwise. Rather than bury it, I want to bring it into the light, to demonstrate how we all share this experience and can learn from it.

The Reversing Vandalism project was envisioned as activism—an attempt to move from being victims of an assault to empowered creators. It is appropriate that not all the artists involved identify as queer, because this was not just a crime against some of us but also a crime against us all.

Seeing the colorful cover of my book appear in several of the artistic responses to this horrendous crime illustrates the resilience of the human spirit in the face of adversity, and in the ability of art to point the way from hate toward healing.

Grandfather's Photograph

Neil Ellis Orts

I have an old photograph on my wall. This is its story as best as I can reconstruct it. I have so few facts to go on.

My mother was an only child, raised in a single-parent household before there was such a term. Her father died very young, under circumstances that she never understood. My mother was two at the time and didn't have any memories of the man herself. Grandmother didn't talk about him. Grandmother never talked about the past. "That's over," she'd say and stomp away.

When my mother was thirteen, a man, a little older than what her father would have been, appeared at their house one August day. Grandmother was cold to the visitor and hushed, sharp words were exchanged. All my mother got from the conversation was that the man was asking for a photo of her father.

After he left, empty-handed and angry, Grandmother went into one of her rages. She began digging through a closet until she pulled out a small box. She was a mutterer, a trait that I had assumed she developed in her old age, when I knew her, but apparently manifested much earlier. As Mother watched and listened from a doorway, she realized the box held photographs of her father, photos she never knew existed. When my mother told this story to me, I could hear the hope and excitement in her voice as she discovered that there existed some tangible evidence, finally, of her own father. I also heard the heartache as she told of watching Grandmother take the box to the wood-burning heater. One by one, Grandmother lit each photo and watched it burn.

Mother fought her fear of Grandmother and tiptoed to the box while Grandmother's back was to her. She reached into the box, intending to grab a handful, but Grandmother turned just in time to see Mother's reach. Mother's hand retracted with only one photo, which she managed to conceal from Grandmother. "Get out of here and mind your own business," Grandmother told Mother, as if the photos had nothing to do with her. Mother ran from the house, into the backyard, behind the woodshed, and looked at the pilfered photo.

Her whole body collapsed. In the photograph was not one man, but five. Her father's face was revealed and yet remained a mystery. Grandmother had cast a spell of secrecy and silence and it was so strong that Mother never told Grandmother that she had saved this one photo.

The silence was broken a few months after Grandmother died and still I could feel Mother's fear as she revealed her secret treasure.

Now Mother is gone and I have inherited the photograph, but I do not keep it hidden away. It is framed and on display. After all these years, it feels useless to search out Grandfather's family. Even if I found them, it seems unlikely that anyone is still alive to identify him or any of the men in the picture. I am almost glad.

Of the five men in the photograph, two are seated very close to each other, slightly leaning into each other's shoulder. Their hands are properly in their own laps, but their arms overlap. I try to convince myself the one on the left looks a little like me, if only because I think he is the most handsome. I also pretend the man on the right is the August visitor who started an August fire, all by asking for a photograph. Perhaps, I imagine, this very photograph.

I spend much time before the photograph, almost like a holy icon. No revelation comes to me through this window to heaven, however, so I use it to create myths to explain my family.

This is the story of how Grand-mother's heart was broken and why she cast the bitter spell.

This is the story of how Mother became a fatherless child and came to keep secrets and fear questions.

This is the story of how I break Grandmother's spell and why I keep this photograph in the open.

I don't care if the stories are factual because, in the end, they are true.

Gay Spirituality?

Will Gray

At a gathering to celebrate the New Year with a group of gay men there was a discussion about the place of spirituality in our lives. One man asked: "But what do you mean by spirituality? Because, if it's a belief in god, I see nothing to make me believe in his existence." His voice was clear, but there was a tone to it that made me think he was hoping that, someday, someone could refute his argument, like someone who once believed quite strongly and felt a strong desire to believe again.

I think he raised an important question. As a non-practicing atheist (how do you practice unbelief?) I regularly wonder why I feel so welcome among men who describe and sometimes define themselves as spiritual. I've even wondered about the level of rejection I would face if I were to come out about my non-belief in a group of the self-identified spiritual. But I conclude that they would continue to welcome me and, in fact, that they would contend that I was quite spiritual.

What leads me to think that? Because of what I know about the human capacity for awe. Some examples from my life:

1

On the last morning of a one-week Outward Bound canoe trip I woke at 4:30, lit the stove and brewed a pot of coffee for the other people in my patrol, whom I had come to care for over the days of the course. They rose and accepted mugs of hot brew without words, but smiles of thanks, because we had agreed to a silent start for this last morning.

We quickly broke down camp, loaded our canoes and paddled out from the mouth of the river on whose banks we had camped into a large lake flecked with wisps of fog. Out on the water we brought our canoes together in a ring and waited until the rising sun filtered through the mist. The only sounds were those of the woods and the water. At sunrise our instructors read a poem to us and, free to talk, we remained silent for a long moment, savoring our experience, our companions, and the beauty around us that we often fail to notice. For me it was a moment of awe, for others it was spiritual. What the difference is between the two I can't say.

2

When I was thirty-one I registered with an adoption agency and within a year I met the boy who became my son. Over the course of a summer we visited for progressively longer periods, moving from a half-hour initial introduction through lunch at McDonalds, half-day visits to my neighborhood, overnight stays and then weekends, finally reaching the day he arrived to live permanently. That night, after the long ritual of getting him settled into bed, I sat out on my porch and my emotions danced into accepting that this new life was a reality. On my way to bed later I peeked in on the six-year old boy asleep in the room next to mine. In sleep his face was relaxed and his skin seemed to capture the glow of the night light. I had never understood it when people talked about being willing to give their lives for someone before. Now it seemed both natural and surprising. The power of my emotions filled me with awe. How that differs from a spiritual experience I have no idea.

3

I'm not sure about love at first sight, but I can attest to the power of lust at first sight. At the end of August many years ago I spent a weekday at the beach by myself, mulling over problems and feeling alone. As I was heading towards the bus that was the first leg of my trip home, a handsome man passed me and flashed a glowing smile that I couldn't help return. I continued on reluctantly, transferred to the train and found a seat. I put my bag down, sat, looked right and saw the same man across the aisle from me. Soon we had made a date to get together that night. We recently celebrated our 21st anniversary. But that first night, before any thought of love had entered my mind, still stands out. Long, tender, playful, hot; it was revelatory. For the longest time after our first orgasm I was unable to speak. Not because I was so tired but because for that brief interval I just forgot how. I don't imagine there is any difference between that kind of ecstasy and the rapture of a spiritual moment.

So, I accept these moments of awe, reverence, ecstasy—whatever label we choose to apply, and view them as experiences I share with others that might be called spiritual. Like the man asking the question at the New Year's retreat, I see no existence of a god, but that doesn't prevent me from sharing moments of transcendence and gratitude. Maybe that's all that is needed to be considered spiritual, or to seem so to others.

"Charmed, I'm Sure"

Mark Thompson and Malcolm Boyd

It is a cliché right off the top of Snoopy's doghouse, but I get to say it here: It was a dark and stormy night.

I had arrived in Los Angeles the day we met on an assignment for *The Advocate*, the national gay newsmagazine. I had begun my professional career at the publication in 1975, drafted out of the journalism department at San Francisco University the week I graduated. Now, I was Cultural Affairs Editor. After years of dutifully reporting on just about every story imaginable—from gay revolt in Spain to gay plumbers coming out (believe it or not, that was a big story in 1977)—I was finally able to choose my own subjects. And there were no two people I wanted to talk with more than Christopher Isherwood and Don Bachardy.

The legendary couple had long been a pillar of Southern California's sprawling gay community, exemplary role models open and accessible back in a time when the closet door shuttered the lives of most. By 1984, the year of my visit, they had been together 31 years. Christopher, of course, was the author of many books, plays, and memoirs, including the work that would later be immortalized as the film *Cabaret*. Don, his junior partner by three decades, was an equally talented portrait artist with a new exhibition opening soon.

The stated purpose for our visit was to publicize the show. But the real reason was a rare opportunity to ask them about their faith, the Hindu philosophy of Vedantism, and one of its leading practitioners, their longtime friend and spiritual guide Gerald Heard.

I had anxiously anticipated our meeting for months, even though I knew there was another, less savory aspect of my trip from San Francisco to Los Angeles. *The Advocate*'s wealthy owner wanted to move the magazine lock, stock and barrel to the Southland where he figured it would have a better time prospering. The last nine years had been mutually beneficial for us both. And so, in the manner of some noirish movie, the publisher made me an offer "I could not refuse."

As a proud third-generation Northern Californian, the idea of moving south was about as appealing as an amputation. I loved living in San Francisco, not just for its thriving gay life, but for its opera and theater, its sensuous beauty and grand sense of place. The running joke up north about Los Angeles was that it held less culture than a Petri dish.

In time, I would happily find that not to be true. But on the chilly February day of my visit—a trial run deciding my future—I could not have been more miserable in my unshakable low regard for my future home. This story is about how one other man made a difference, and in no more than a few hours time. Funny how fate swings on the most fragile of hinges.

⁓⁙⁾

When I met Mark I had no idea we would end up as a gay couple together for more than twenty years.

Ours was a casual coming together. A mutual friend set it up. Mark and I had certain things in common (we're both writers) but I realized immediately how different we are in many other ways. For one thing, there is a thirty years age difference between us—I being the older. Mark was a Boy Scout as a kid on the Monterey Peninsula in Central California and had a stable early childhood. Also he grew up with siblings. I was a Manhattanite kid, an only child, and experienced a difficult upbringing because my father was an alcoholic and my parents divorced when I was ten.

I think Mark and I would never have met if our friend hadn't arranged it. We moved in such different circles.

⁓⁙⁾

Different circles, to say the least. Actually I had "met" Malcolm once before—through a television screen while watching "The David

Frost Show" one afternoon in 1968. I was a high school sophomore, already an editor of the campus paper and an avid fan of Frost. As righteous a reporter there ever was, no one slung a meaner clipboard than he did.

I had rushed home from school to see his featured guest, the great Indian musician Ravi Shankar, whose music I adored, only to see him bumped by this best-selling author and noted civil rights activist in a clerical collar. It was Malcolm, of course, and I had never heard of him before. Was I ever peeved to see my satir-playing guru pushed aside by some overly earnest priest. East could not possibly meet West. Not that day!

So, here I am 16 years later, fishing through vague recollections while talking to the man himself. I had just returned from a glorious afternoon conversing with Christopher and Don in their lovely ocean-side home. The glow of the occasion was considerably dimmed by the rush-hour drive across town to my temporary quarters—a shabby gay motel on the city's eastside that exchanged rooms for ads in the magazine.

Thank God, I told myself, it was for one night only, and then I would be home.

Apart from my interviewees, no one knew I was I town except for one other friend, a much respected community leader. So respected, in fact, that I had no choice but to comply with his message left waiting for me at the motel: Malcolm Boyd was staying at the same establishment and wouldn't it be nice if I popped by and said hello?

Once a Scout, always a Scout. Tired, grumpy, and already homesick, I picked up the phone and did as I was asked. It startled me when a voice came immediately on the line and said, yes, a short visit would in fact be welcomed. He was here on an emergency time-out from a dysfunctional boyfriend. Much to my surprise, my courtesy call lasted three hours. We talked about everything under the moon that night. As I left, the thought that I would never again see this fascinating, talented, complex, and very charming man crossed my mind. What could I have been thinking?

⌒∴⌒

It turned out that Mark made the move south after all, and we embarked happily on a two-year courtship that didn't involve living with one another. Our weekends were shared and we traveled a lot of places together—from Hawaii to New York, Vancouver to Cancun. Slowly we grew together. Mark (very correctly, I think) felt we shouldn't establish a permanent relationship until—or unless—we were ready for the long haul.

~~~·⁓

Long haul? Hell, what was I doing with a famous Episcopal priest thirty years my senior? Age difference aside, there was the religion factor to consider as well. I still remember the first time I was invited to the church where he worked. Someone thrust a communion wafer into my hands and I thought, *Now what am I supposed to do with this? Put a dab of cheese on it?* Asking a confirmed Zen Buddhist to partake in the "body and blood of Christ" can be a very daunting thing. *But at least the songs are okay*, I recall thinking.

~~~·⁓

Finally, one night in an elegant restaurant, I got up and knelt by Mark's chair and offered him a ring I had purchased. He accepted my proposal. Then we went house hunting, found a place that has been perfect for us over two decades, and—voilà—became a gay couple, and, indeed, a gay extended family.

It's been a great experience. In May 2004 our relationship was blessed by Episcopal Bishop J. Jon Bruno in a ceremony at Los Angeles' Cathedral Center of St. Paul with five other bishops present in a wonderful crowd of friends. We had embarked on yet another phase of our life together.

~~~·⁓

Six bishops! That's a lot of purple shirts. It was the first time in the history of the United States that a reigning bishop had blessed a gay couple in his cathedral. It was the most beautiful day of my life and everyone else was deeply moved by the simple elegance of the occasion. Instead of exchanging rings, we decided to have our hands bound together by a lustrous silk scarf that Malcolm's mother, Beatrice, had painted with a family of white cranes around the time he was born. The birds symbolize long-life and happiness. My younger brother, John, presented the scarf at the altar in a richly carved wooden box. More than a marriage, we saw our union as the uniting of two families. And now, as Malcolm says, we are an extended gay family encompassing a multitude of friends, family, and even former lovers. We are very proud of this.

⸺⁚⤸

What's it been like? I can only say INCREDIBLE... WONDERFUL... LIFE SUSTAINING. Anyhow, it's far beyond words and I am immensely grateful for it. We share a deep love. At the same time, we're not two peas in a pod or carbon copies of one another. A hard but important lesson, I've learned, is to give up control (never easy) and be flexible and open to life and willing to change and also embark on new adventures.

Mark's later childhood had witnessed family disintegration and domestic chaos (as mine had). So we'd both suffered through a lot of pain and argument and loud disagreement. This background came to the fore when, beginning our life together, we once got into an ugly kind of fight. But then we looked at one another, paused, stopped, and admitted we wanted nothing more like this in either of our lives. Since then we have never "let the sun go down on our wrath." We've always embraced and let an argument or misunderstanding die with a dying day. The next morning we never look back. We accept the freshness of a new day.

⸺⁚⤸

My favorite silver screen icon of all time is Bette Davis, and over the years I've learned to channel her nervous fury pretty well. Of all her immortal lines, I especially like the one from *Cabin in the Cotton* (it was her favorite too): "I'd love to kiss yah, but I just washed mah hair." It's utterly hilarious to me, but not to Malcolm I discovered one evening early on. I was trying to end that famous fight of ours with a touch of absurd humor, but then found out—much to my dismay—that my witty, adorable gay lover had no sense of camp. What, a card-carrying homosexual of a certain generation not knowing what camp humor is? Well, you can just imagine how quickly I got to work fixing that. It's still a foreign tongue for Malcolm, but I do give him an "A" for effort. A little camp (not too much) can be just the right spice for making the bitter parts of life go down easier.

Humor plays a huge role in our life together. Both of us understand the absurdity and irony of many aspects of life. We like humor and practice it. We also like a genuine structure in life, tenderness, being part of a community, starting new projects that keep life interesting and a strong appreciation of beauty as much as possible in everyday living. We work hard and play happily. We share a strong sense of supporting civil rights and justice and involvement in a number of related issues.

Life *is* serious, but it should never be too much so. One simply must stop and smell the roses. And we literally do. We have family memberships in every Southern California public garden of note. That and going to the many excellent art museums in our region provides our major source of entertainment and sustenance to the soul. Being makers of beauty while also inhabiting a world of beauty wherever it can be found is essential—even serious—business for us. We could not live otherwise. Where else is the charm of life better discovered than in nature, or in the depths of a great painting? We refresh our senses so we can continue to spiritually nourish one another.

A major focus of my life is supporting Mark in whatever his new endeavor is. He returns the favor. Mark is one of the best human beings I've ever met and he has raised friendship to the level of an art. I don't simply love Mark; I also like him. He is the best gardener. He is the best cook. He is the best writer. He is the best therapist. (You can see that I have a strong opinion on this.)

In my view, he is the best boy friend/lover/partner/mate. "What a difference a day makes" runs a popular song. I'm genuinely happy Mark and I met on a particular day. (What if we hadn't?) I realize all this stuff is clearly in the hands of the gods. What fools we mortals be. Yet I think it helps when we hold positive attitudes about love and relationship, are willing to work at it, maintain laughter, keep growing instead of prematurely checking out, and offer real thanks for real blessings.

I agree that keeping it real is what it's all about (old movie lines notwithstanding). Not everything about our relationship has been perfect. (Ouch! You mean roses have thorns?)

But getting stuck, even bleeding a bit now and then, is part of the divine process of getting older and wiser—hopefully together. Those thirty years that once seemed like such a big divide, is now but a heartbeat away. I look at Malcolm's face and I do not see the lines of age, but the stellar beauty of a tremendous soul. Every time I look even further into his eyes my heart breaks wide open yet again. How deep is the sea? the philosopher asks. As far as you want to go.

So, we're charmed, I'm sure. My journey to visit Christopher and Don was not only a portal into what can truly and honestly happen between two men in love, but a fated foretelling of those possibilities in my own life. How completely magical and perfect it all has been.

Among other things, we are blessed with the friendships of many "fellow travelers," those who walk down the same paths of creativity and peaceful self-expression we tread. A favorite neighbor and friend is the Los Angeles poet and teacher Terry Wolverton. Recently she sent us an excerpt from a new work-in-progress, titled A History of Love. She talks about the changes that happen midway in a life. I like her writing so much, I want to share a few lines from it here.

"Something shifts—a definition or need," she notes. "Hunger fades to ash or the memory of ash. Heat of your blood cools. Upper regions of your spinal column awaken. All the old stories, somehow no longer useful, you release to wind. Renounce suffering. Love no longer something to crave but to give. A boundless fountain of cool water from which anyone might drink. Live now to be that source."

We so admire those words, know their worth and meaning in our own lives. A fated meeting can be charming, indeed. But to keep the charm intact one must hold and expand upon the belief that at its root lives unconditional love. And it is to the playing out of its endless motifs and potentials that we have surrendered our lives. At once an act of faith and utter devotion, there really is no other better reason for living.

Viewing the Statue of David

Jim Toevs

In the Galleria dell' Accademia, Florence, Italy.

I step into the room, David, and there you are, icon of men who've loved men, icon of manly beauty, standing in your famous pose, so full of life, as you have always been.

Encased for eons in a vault of stone until Michelangelo found you there, discarded and overlooked by so many, but recognized by the Master. For as he said, "All I did was chip away what wasn't David."

You are my mirror; for I too am engaged in the process of chipping away that which is not truly me.

At times, I experience moments of dancing playfully through life, knowing all there is to life is love.

You remind me that you slew your Goliath with a single stone. Yet, too often, I forget, and I go seeking my Goliaths; engaging them in battles which I can never win.

Too often, I concentrate on the refuse of who I never was. Those chips of stone, signifying nothing.

But when I look into your eyes, I remember: "I am the light of the world." "I am the creation and the reflection of the One."

And when I remember, I am free! Free to be in the NOW! The present moment, which is the only time I have.

All of my anger is about the past, and all of my fear is about the future, but in the NOW, this moment, I can accept everything in my life as being exactly the way it is supposed to be.

Thank you, David, for being my mirror. I am David. David is me. We are One.

The True and Unknown Story of Albert Gale, told by Himself

Andrew Ramer

"Say, you related to *Dorothy* Gale, the one who went off to that Oz place?" people ask when they hear my last name, which I try not to say too much.

"Distant relation," I always tell, which ain't exactly a lie.

"Gosh she was brave, wasn't she? And had all those amazing adventures." They always know a few I haven't heard about. "And her Auntie Em and Uncle Henry. What a rough life they all had. But they were mighty good to her, weren't they?"

"Sure were good to *her*," I always say, thinking back on how it was. When Pa died not six months after Ma, Fred Hammersmith, the county sheriff, wrote to Aunt Em and Uncle Henry telling them. Well, Em and Henry wrote back real fast, "We want the little girl, but not the boy. Boys like him are nothing but trouble." That's how I ended up in the orphanage in Abilene. Fred took me there himself, real sorry to do it. Said he'd keep me if he could. Asked his wife. But they had four boys and three girls already. Had me for dinner once a month on Sunday. Not like being back at home, but nice. Around the corner from it, so I'd always walk the other way. Too sad to see the porch and the windows and that new family, and all the happy places I once knew plain vanished into air when Ma and Pa died. Money from selling the house went to Em and Henry. They built a new barn with it. Not that it did them much good.

"And Dorothy was so pretty, too," people say, recalling pictures of her they've seen in books. We always called her Dot, but no one wants to hear that. And even years later, on one of my bad days, hung over and with a black eye, I was a hell of a lot prettier than she was. Which's what got me into trouble at the orphanage. By day the older boys would push me around. Tell me, "You're sweet as a girl," and call me Alberta. By night in the spring house those same boys would be shoving their woodies down my guzzler or corn-holing me, me not able to even shoot yet when they started. Lucky for me I grew up real tall the second year I was there. After that when one of them boys came after me I would say, "You want it, you pay for it." Most did.

Would have made a hell of lot of money in that place, but I had to light out of there real fast one night after the preacher lay hand on my right posterior and I swung around and knocked him out. But every Christmas I was there I'd send a fancy card to Dot, along with a gift of some kind, a doll or a game or a pretty bonnet. But not once ever did I hear back from her, even before she went off on her wanderings which you've heard so much about.

So I hitched a ride east from Abilene and then north by stage, heading up to Lincoln in Nebraska. The coach was full so I hopped up next to the driver, lanky man in his thirties with sad dark eyes and a big droopy mustache. Sidled right up to him as the sun set, rubbing my thigh on his thigh, then sliding my hand up between his legs. By nightfall he was sharing his bed with me. Fed me all the way to Lincoln, took real good care of me, just as long as I took care of him each night.

I stayed in Lincoln. Shavetailed, inexperienced, I got a few jobs doing this and that, but found out there was better money for a pretty boy being kept. Lincoln's a good town. People there all mind-your-own-business, till I moved up from a bank clerk to the head of the grade school, Mister Ryland Walker. Figured it would be a good way to finally learn myself a thing or two, but mostly in the end it was him that did the learning. Virgin till we met, with lots of years of hungering to make up for. Could have been nice. House full of books and fancy Greek statues. Me helping out at school. Was always good with numbers. But one of the teachers in the school was a curly wolf and got jealous, so they ran me out of town.

How I got myself to the Dakotas and then out to Montana, now that's a long story. Took up with a fancy man from Back East by the name of Jim Hodges. That was in Sioux City, where I landed after Lincoln. Jim ran a rooming house with his sister Evvie. I liked that, having had a sister once myself. Well, one night the two of us were doing our usual in bed when the marshal and his men broke down the door. Landed us both in jail, me and him. That's how I found out he was a bunko artist, wanted in Boston for embezzlement at some kind of insuring place. Well, they chained him up and sent him back to Massachusetts. Me they would have kept there, what I did being such a big crime against moralizing. But then the head guard started visiting me, and he kind of forgot to lock my cell one night. Hope he didn't get in a too big a fix. Him the one told me that Evvie could deal with her own flesh and blood being a thief but not a fornicator with young men— so she turned him in for the reward money. Made me sad. Would have stayed with Jim for a long time, just the way we were, starting to feel almost like a family, something I thought I'd lost forever.

Took me a year or two to get to Butte, and a couple of hundred men. I was good at what I did, and I knew it. Pretty don't last long, so you have to be good, and I was good, front and back, top and bottom. Had something of a reputation in that town. Got me a nice room, upstairs in a saloon run by Joe Wheelwright, one-time runaway slave, and his partner, one-eyed Izzy Goodman. The two of them watched out for me, fed me. Theirs the first place that was truly home to me since my own family. Butte was a small town back then, but people came through, prospectors, claim strikers, folks heading West. Men when they came into money would find me for a night or two at Joe and Izzy's before they turned around and went back out again. Drank too much sometimes, got myself roughed up a bit. Black eyes, like I told you before, and a few broken ribs. But mostly they were good years, drinking and sexing and playing too much cards. Nothing like my sister's adventures. Just the kind of ordinary things no one writes books about. Stories that get buried with you when you die. Where sunrise is the most magic thing you know, sunset, a good mate and a pot of stew slow cooking over a fire.

Anyhow, one night I was down at the bar between customers when a man walked in. Tall and fine as cream gravy. A half-breed with coppery skin and the brightest blue eyes I'd ever seen, like sky on a perfect day. Took one look at him and something melted inside me. Never happened before. He looked me back real good and motioned with his head out the side door. He went first and I followed, a minute later. It was dark and I didn't see him, till he took me in his arms, pulled me to his chest and kissed me, long and slow, like no man ever kissed me before, not even Jim. And the doors to my heart swung open faster than a bank vault being robbed. Figured that he being older, things would be like they always were. He'd be wanting to pull my britches down, turn me round, press my face into the wall, and push in.

Inside the saloon, Joe was behind the bar and old one-eyed Izzy was doing what he did each night. Picked up his fiddle and played one of those tunes he brought all the way from Europe, one of those sad-sweet Hebrew tunes I never heard nothing like before, till I got to Butte. And then that half-breed did the damndest thing. He took me in his arms and spun me around that alley like it was a dance floor, cheek pressed to my cheek, stubble rubbing stubble. Now I'd learned all kinds of things since I'd left Abilene, but dancing weren't one of them. And I guess he knew that, but each time I stumbled or tripped on his feet, he just twirled me again, boots shuffling on the dirt, me caught in his arms, my arms wrapped tight around him.

After six or eight songs, old Izzy stopped fiddling and the two of us pulled apart. I asked the stranger if he wanted to come up with me, but he said no. Had some other things to attend to. I felt like I would crack inside. Didn't want to show him. Started to turn to go, when he reached out a hand, put it on my shoulder, pulled me back to him, leaned close and kissed me again. Funny, after all the men and boys I'd been with, but it was out there in that dark alley, for the first time in all my twenty-six years, that I knew what love is. And I liked it. Turned away two customers back inside. Joe, from his perch behind the bar, gave me a curious look when he saw. Went up to my room and thought about that feller. Hoping he'd come back, which he did the next night, night after that, and the next one. To dance me and court me for a full long week, come with flowers and candy from the General Store, shiny buttons one night, a pocket watch, a flask, a chess game. Till I was yearning in a whole new way, till he knew that we were ready.

His name was Sock. I learned that on the second night. Half Chickasaw, quarter Swede, quarter English. Real name Ben Townsend but everyone called him Sock for the dark red birthmark on his right cheek. From far away it just looked like an L, but up close you could see the heel and the toe and everything. Top of that sock right under his pretty right eye. I could look at that man all day. Did, those first few weeks when he was courting me. He'd been out to sea. Ranched and farmed. Lived a time in New York City, working for a newspaper, laying type. Been married and widowed and spun with other men. But Sock was the husband type. Knew about my business and didn't want to share me, not that I ever wanted anyone else after I'd been with him. So I paid off Joe and Izzy, and said my good-byes. Danced one last fiddle dance with Sock in the saloon, everyone clapping for us till we all were crying. A wedding dance, Izzy called it. Him and Joe sent us off with a set of sheets Joe embroidered himself, a shaving mirror with a pearly edge to it, and planting seeds to last us years. So we took out from Butte, did some prospecting up in the mountains, and made enough from silver to buy us a nice piece of land and a few more horses.

Sock knew the land better than any man I've ever met. Times I'd swear he wasn't part Indian, but part fox, part eagle, or part deer. He could walk through brush without making a sound, and smell hunting a mile away. Said he learned it from his mama, out on the prairie. That man could find water with a stick, and coax plants from a rock if he wanted to. He knew some other ways too, ways of courting that I never heard tell of before, which won my heart from the beginning, and then the rest of me. Courting ways he said the Indians knew, ways of men being with men that make most White people afraid. That opened me up like a sunflower, turned toward the light. Like a good story, bending toward a campfire.

You'd think, after all those town years and all of those men, that I'd be lonely for bars and streets and stores and people. Truth is, after all of that sexing and drinking and traveling, it was good to be alone with Sock, alone on our own piece of land. Every season or so we'd go down to sell our findings, buy what supplies we couldn't make ourselves. But our life was good. Hard but good. And we lived together close to thirty years. Worked. Laughed. Screwed each other loco. And lay out under the stars and talked till we were drunk on words, till our stories were woven together like ivy and the tree it climbed. Till you couldn't tell where one of us started and the other one stopped.

My Sock was a good man. Real good man. Took a fever, just as the summer was heading south, just about a year ago. Nearly seventy years old. Not as strong as he once was. Fever went into his bones, and he couldn't shake it. So I nursed him, fed him, cleaned him, holding his hand and stroking the cheek that named him, dancing him into the big jump the way he danced me into love. Till the squeeze in his hand let go, till the seeing in his eyes dropped down and away. Then I washed him one last time, his midwife into dying, wrapped him up in an Indian blanket his grandma made, all black and red, and buried him up on the ridge, just as the leaves were turning. "My favorite spot in the world," he always said, ridge, valley, trees, snake of river in the distance.

Well, up till now, with you reading this, Sock was the only one knew the whole truth about my life and Dot and where we came from. One night, just before he took ill, we were sitting side by side on the hearthstones, staring into the fire as it was crumbling to embers. Suddenly a burst of emerald flame shot up from a last bit of log. "Looks like what we've heard about Oz," I said, laughing. Puzzled by my amusement, Sock took my slim hand in his burly one and asked me, "Albert Evans Gale, that big sister of yours is famous all over the world for her grand adventures. Don't you ever wish that you could be in her shoes?"

"Hell no," I said, looking deep into those sky blue eyes of his. "I lost a lot more than my sister when Ma and Pa died. But truth be told, Sock, looking back on everything—I'd rather be here with you, any day, in this two room shack of logs we built ourselves, than living out there in some fancy green glass castle, with wizards, and witches, and a crazy bunch of flying monkeys."

Tom
or An Improbable Tail

Ruth Sims

This is the tale of the naked god / boy / man William found in his apartment. When he told it to me he swore on his mother's grave that every word was true. The oath didn't mean much, though, as I knew his mother was alive and well and playing the slots in Vegas. There are a few things you need to know about William before you read his story.

One: He hated making decisions. If his mother would come every morning and lay out his suit and tie and socks for him it would make him happy, as long as she didn't stay long enough to nag him.

Two: Well, actually, it's part of No. One. He's a lawyer because his father wanted him to be a lawyer and he didn't want to bother making a decision about what he wanted to be when he grew up if he ever did. Lawyering was okay. It paid damn well, and there was a certain snob appeal to being with Rutledge, Rutledge, Kirkwood, Jones, and Connaughton. He didn't yearn to be a white Johnny Cochran or a reincarnation of Clarence Darrow. Which was good, because he did corporation work. Mergers, contracts, corporation minutes of meetings that never take place, that kind of thing.

"As the corporation goes so goes America," Rutledge Senior was fond of saying in stentorian tones. That gives you some idea of RRKJC. William often said he was the only one in the office who didn't starch his underwear.

Besides being indecisive and not very ambitious, he was cursed with being 'cute.' He hated cute. If he thought shaving his head and wearing a nose ring would help, he'd have done it. But RRKJC did not allow lawyers with pierced noses and he did have bills to pay. RRKJC was so conservative they made the millennium Republicans look like "bleeding-heart flaming liberal pinko card-carrying members of NAMBLA" as Connaughton put it.

William wondered what they'd do if they knew that he was gay? He knew what they'd do. They'd soil their $900 suits, that's what they'd do and then they'd can him.

Now that the background is out of the way, on to the good stuff which will involve the beautiful naked god/boy/man and… well… Maybe you need a little more background first. Be patient.

Nobbyville, Illinois, Pop. 60,000, had always been William's home. Women's liberation and gay liberation didn't even stop there for a potty break until the mid-1980's. There were only about a hundred Black families and fewer Hispanics, so race relations weren't much in the news either. But it was his hometown, warts and all, and he could never decide where to go if he left.

I know, you're salivating and want to cut to the chase and the naked god/boy/man. Hold your horses. Or anything else that needs holding. This can't be hurried.

By a lot of peoples' standards, William didn't have much of a social life. He rented videos and DVDs frequently, went to church when he felt like it, which wasn't often, visited his mom and his sister, indulged his Inner Thespian by appearing in local amateur theatrical presentations. He also spent a lot of time with Mary Palm and her four sisters, and sometimes wondered why it wasn't called Myron Palm and his four brothers. No, not what anyone would call a very exciting life.

Now, you may get the impression that Knobbyville was a kind of large Hooterville or Mayberry. In a way it was. It was a bedroom suburb of the university town a half hour away. The streets were clean. It was mostly crime free, and the Neighborhood Watch signs were for show. The police force was small and snappily dressed. The three fire stations had brand-new buildings and trucks. Garbage was picked up twice a week. Rent was high. There were waiting lists of nervous city dwellers wanting quiet places to live. William's apartment was in the most expensive complex in the city. Within its wrought iron perimeter were two swimming pools, a sauna, a tennis court, and a resident chiropractor.

William had been on the waiting list nearly a year before he lucked out and somebody died. He was willing to sell his grandmother to get in. Only a cemetery could have been quieter and more serene. There were strict Tenant Rules in his complex. No loud music. No children. No pets other than very small birds. No Persons of Opposite Sex Sharing Living Quarters, as the Census Bureau put it. And *certainly* no Same-Sex Live-In Roommates! In all likelihood God would have rained down brimstone if that had been allowed. Helen Blathersage was manager of Shadyland Estates. The renters referred to her simply as Helen Hellhound, when she wasn't listening.

William didn't mind the restrictions. He liked classical music. He had no pets and no plans to get any. He wasn't likely to have children. He had only one real friend, Dudley Osmyn, who was the prototypical science nerd, a six-foot-three Woody Allen only not quite as virile.

In fact, Dudley was more than a science nerd. He was an actual, "It lives, Igor!" bona fide mad scientist. At least William thought so. In the fifteen years since they'd left high school, Dudley hadn't changed at all. In high school he had been tall, thin, and weird. At thirty-three he was just taller, thinner, and weirder.

Nobody in high school ever thought William was gay. Why would they? He played football. Everybody thought Dudley was gay but since they were afraid he'd blow them up they left him alone. William didn't know if Dudley was gay or not, but he thought Dr. Dudley Osmyn, with a whole alphabet of degrees after his name and award certificates on the wall, probably had less sex than he did and he didn't even want to imagine with what.

They didn't hang out a lot, but every once in a while William would pick Dudley up in his BMW and they'd tool to the next town, where Dudley would get drunk and listen to William massacre "Impossible Dream" at a karaoke bar called Casablanca.

One night, as Dudley opened the door to get out of William's car, a cat dashed from a nearby driveway and sailed in, immediately flattening itself to hide under the seat.

William groaned and cursed and fished under the seat. He could see the cat's face, its eyes topaz and enormous. He pleaded with the creature. It grinned at him. At last he grabbed it and dragged it out by the scruff of its neck. It dangled limply from his hand. It was a beautiful animal with long, tawny hair. And it hadn't even scratched or bit him. And instead of squirming and fighting for its freedom, it looked mournfully at him. He wondered why.

Gently he put it on the pavement. In one seamless motion it leapt back into the car and flowed under the front seat again, where it made itself as small as possible with no visible handholds to grab. Sighing, William decided to go on home and coax it out there. Then he could fling it over the fence and it could go pester someone else.

As he drove, the cat came out from under the seat and snuggled up next to him. It rubbed against him and shoved its head at him until he scratched its ears just before he pulled into the parking lot.

"All right, all right," he said. The cat purred until William thought his eardrums would burst. "I won't toss you back on the streets tonight. I'll just sneak you in for the night. But come daylight you're on your own."

Of course, like all cats, that one knew a sucker when it saw one. And it settled in for the duration.

The cat and William seemed to be made for each other. William explained to it—him—the need for silence and he never made a sound. His manners in the litter box were impeccable. He draped himself on William's knees by the hour, purring and kneading his legs with his paws. After the first night the cat slept curled up against William's belly as he lay sleeping on his side.

So then William had two big secrets from the firm: his gayness and his little friend with the furry balls. He also kept him a secret from his mom and sister, because they were real blabbermouths. And of course he was a secret from Helen Hellhound and the other tenants. That meant smuggling in cat food and smuggling out lumped litter.

The day the cat followed him home was May 1.

⌒⁚⊃

On June 22 William came home to find the naked boy in his apartment, calmly sitting on the sofa. *Boy?* He was a god. He was every calendar boy who ever lived. He was Apollo and Ganymede come to life. He was perhaps twenty or so and

William wasn't but who cared. The boy / god / man was lithe rather than bulging with muscles. Every inch of him was beautiful.

William's reaction could've been used for a tomato stake.

"Oh," he gasped. "Who—who—"

"Did you sit on a fence post all night?" the boy asked, grinning. And yes ohgod his teeth were made of pearl and he had a deep, deep dimple in his cheek.

"Who are you? How did you get in here?"

"You left me in when you went away this morning," the boy said, looking puzzled.

"I did no such thing! I've never seen you before."

The boy looked hurt. "Of course you did. I was asleep in your bed this morning."

"Hush!" William hushed him. "This is the day Helen Hellhound makes her rounds. Places this great are impossible to get into. You've got to get out of here!"

William's mouth said the words, but his heart wasn't in them. The boy was so incredibly gorgeous. His ripe mouth trembled just slightly. He stood up. "I don't know why you don't love me anymore," he said sadly, and reached for the doorknob.

"Wait!" William screamed. "You can't go out of here like that! Where are your clothes?"

"Well… I don't have any. Why would I?" His eyes were elongated, with an almost Asian slant to them, and they were an odd topaz color, sexy—and—and—feline.

William clutched the door. What he was thinking was preposterous, mad, impossible. He gulped and asked the boy his name, hoping, praying, he would say Reginald or Ronald or Lester… anything but what he said.

"Tom," the boy said with a slight smile.

"Stay there," William ordered. "Don't move anything." He frantically searched the apartment, desperately calling, "Kitty, kitty, kitty. Where are you, you goddam cat?"

Finally he went on wobbly legs back into the living room. *I am a mature man*, he said to himself. *I can handle the explanation, whatever it is.* He gulped, staring at Tom. Then he dashed to the bedroom and grabbed a bathrobe. "Put this on," he ordered. "You're making me crazy. I'm only human."

"I wish I could say the same," Tom said with a sigh. He took the robe but did not put it on. Then he sat on the sofa, his arms wrapped around his drawn-up knees, which did nothing for William's composure.

"I am hallucinating," William announced. "I don't know why, but I am. I think my beer was drugged last night. LSD. That's it." He glared at Tom. "You're a figment of my drugged imagination."

Tom studied him, unblinking. "No, I'm not. You're not hallucinating. You're not dreaming. I'm here. I'm were. Get used to it."

"Were…? As in werewolf?" Then William saw the joke and started to laugh. "Oh, for—! Of course! It's a joke. Dudley sent you over here for my birthday, didn't he. That sonofabitch. Oh, this is a good one! I never thought he even had a sense of humor. Ha-ha! I don't know how he snuck you in here without a key, but he is a genius, after all." William knew he was babbling. "How could he think I'd believe this shit for a minute? OK, Tom, you little ol' 'wereperson' you, let's go to bed, celebrate my birthday, then you can clear the hell out and go tell old Dudley it worked."

Tom's wide-eyed unblinking stare was nerve-wracking. "Dudley who?"

"Oh, right. Like you don't know. What did he do? Order you from U Meet Bods of Gods?"

Only Dudley, William's oldest and dearest friend, knew that William's favorite website was umeetbodsofgods.com, which featured prurient pictures of boys-to-go, with whom one could "get acquainted," if one had the money. William had never inquired as to the price, but he was sure it was plenty.

"Admit it!" he ordered. "You're an online hustler!"

"I told you," Tom said, plainly bewildered, "I don't know who Dudley is and I'm not a hustler, whatever that is. I told you the truth. And I don't know what 'online' is, though I've been on lots of fences. Twice a year, at the solstice, this happens. I don't understand it. It hurts and it's scary. I go to sleep a cat and then the pain comes and everything goes black. When it's done, I am a human being. And then when the next solstice comes I have to go through it in reverse and become a cat again. It's only happened two other times, and I don't know if I want to live if this is what it means!" He started to cry, silently, with big tears filling his beautiful eyes and spilling over. "I don't know what I should be or what I want to be. I just wish I could stay the same, one way or the other, forever."

"There are no such things as werewolves or were-whatevers," William said coldly.

"You're wrong," Tom said in a low voice. Looking defeated, Tom lowered his feet to the floor and started toward the door.

"No!" William said sharply. "Get your clothes on."

"I told you, I don't have any."

William stared at him. It was true he didn't see another man's clothes stashed anywhere during his frantic search of the place. And yet... He sighed. OK, this was a dream, maybe, though he didn't remember going to bed. Well, the only thing one could do was play along with a dream until it changed or you woke up.

"Fine," he said, spreading his hands in a gesture of resignation. "Fine. You take it easy and I'll go pick you up some clothes, okay? Meanwhile, you just make sure Helen Hellhound doesn't see you or hear you."

Tom nodded and sighed. "I'm tired. I'm going to take a nap." He stretched out on the sofa, on his back, right arm and hand relaxed at his side, the fingers of his left hand tented upon his sternum, one knee bent, eyes closed, the long silken lashes making a fan upon his healthy pink cheeks, his coral lips moist and inviting and his relaxed morsel of manhood lolling sweetly to one side, so lovely, so tempting—

Sweat popped out on William's forehead. *Anytime now,* he said silently to the Dream Machine. *You can change the DVD any time now. Come on... Not going to do it, huh? Well, then I'll just wake myself up. Take that!* He doubled up his fist and whacked himself on the nose.

"Oh, shit! That hurt! Ow—ow—!" He dashed to the kitchen for ice cubes, tripped over his own feet and fell on his face. Groaning, he got to his feet. As he put a Baggie filled with crushed ice upon his sore nose he had to face the truth. He knew in his heart that Dudley was too cheap to hire an expensive hustler, and in dreams nothing hurt the way his nose did. The only other explanation was that this whole thing was real.

He wished he had time to sit and think long and hard about the situation, but he had a dinner meeting with Connaughton in a couple of hours. He showered and put on his best up-and-coming-young-lawyer suit and tie and raced out with one final, longing backward glance.

The meeting was a disaster. He couldn't keep his mind on Commonwealth Plastics vs. Gilgood Condominiums. He kept seeing the—cat?—asleep on the couch. The third time William said "Condoms" instead of Condominiums, Connaughton's jowls quivered with suspicion.

"You know," he intoned, "at Rutledge, Rutledge, Kirkwood, Jones, and Connaughton one's personal life is not allowed to intrude into one's professional life. We prefer you to have no personal life at all."

"Yes, sir. I agree, sir. And I'll get right on the Com-Plas v. Gilgood Condom—mmm—iniums right away, sir. I'll work on it at home, sir."

"See that you do. You know, there might just be a junior partnership in it for you."

"Yes, sir!"

Connaughton blabbed on for a while longer. Finally William was able to escape.

He made a mad dash to the Mall, to a young man's clothing store. There, he was in a quandary as to sizes until he saw a sweet-faced lad who appeared to be about Tom's size. The clerk helped him pick out everything from socks to shirt and shoes, and when he reached for a package of tightie-whities, the kid smiled, shook his head, and handed him a very small shimmering lavender garment consisting of a couple of strings and a pouch.

William's jaw dropped at the price for such a flimsy piece of goods. "Kind of expensive, isn't it?" he asked.

The clerk rolled his eyes. "What price Heaven?" he asked.

William paid, thanking God for the guy who invented credit cards, and left the Mall. Just to be on the safe side, just in case this was all real, just in case he got lucky, he stopped at a drugstore for condominiums. He screeched into his parking place, ran into the building and bumped smack into a bulky, solid object. His plastic bags of goodies went flying.

"Do you have a woman in your apartment?" asked Helen Hellhound, blasting him with her fetid breath.

"Uh... no." William was frantically picking up his parcels.

"I thought I heard someone moving around in there," she said.

"No. I swear to you on my mother's grave, Mrs. Hel—Blathersage, that I do not have a woman in there."

"A likely story. I'm watching you. Don't forget I've got a waiting list. Your lease is about up and if I see a woman coming out of there…"

"My mother's grave, Mrs. Blathersage. My mother's grave."

Clearly she didn't believe him, but she lumbered on her way with a snort of disbelief. William burst into his apartment.

"Tom!" he cried. "Tom?"

He was nowhere in sight. Oh, dear God. He'd left. He was wandering the streets of Nobbyville naked as September Morn, with all his tawny-haired, graceful beauty exposed for all the world and the police to see… "Oh, Tom…"

"Here I am," said a voice behind him. He turned to see Tom emerging, yawning, from the closet. He was… coming out of… the closet. William wondered if he dared hope it was significant.

He dumped the clothes from the bags onto the bed and urged him to try them on. Watching Tom stretch and bend and preen was… was… The cute kid in the store had the right word for it: Heaven.

When he finished, Tom was Michelangelo's David in tight stone-washed jeans and a soft blue shirt with an open collar, and loafers, and under it nothing but that stunning little bit of underwear.

There has to be some way, William thought, *to keep him like this.* Without realizing it, he had come to believe every word Tom said.

As the days passed, having Tom there created some peculiar difficulties.

He was curious about everything. He often forgot he was one-hundred-thirty-five pounds heavier than he had been and not nearly as footsure. One night he jumped up on the television set, flapped his arms to regain his balance, teetered, and fell off right on his splendid tush. Another time he caught himself in mid-spring as he planned to leap to the windowsill.

His eating habits took some getting used to. He preferred Kitty Nibbles and a saucer of milk to anything else, the exception being tuna fish of any variety.

William tried to be as accommodating as he could, though he drew the line at Tom's version of bath time and shoved him into the shower.

All that while, as the first week and then the second and third passed, they co-habited chastely. William's hints that the co-habitation become a little more unchaste met Tom's unblinking puzzled stare.

Time, William thought. *If I just had the time I know I could convince him.* But time was what he didn't have. All too soon Tom would change again, if the whole thing were true.

In desperation William made an appointment with Dudley, and took Tom to see his old friend.

Dudley listened, pondered, uh-hummmed a few times, and then took Tom into a room alone. At one point William heard someone screech as if in sudden pain and several minutes later they emerged. Tom had a peculiar expression of well-being; Dudley had an awkward gait and a scratch on his cheek.

"Are you sure you want to keep him like this?" Dud asked, dabbing at the scratch.

"Damn right."

Dud asked Tom to wait outside. "Look, you're my oldest friend," he said, putting his hand on William's shoulder. "I have to ask. Have you had… um… sex with this… uh… person… yet?"

"No. He won't even consider it. I'm not sure he knows what it is."

"Will, you're aware that cats, even the little kitty in your Aunt Nellie's kitchen, are at heart savage, untamed creatures, aren't you?"

"Dud, forget the cat stuff. He's a man. A beautiful man and I love him. I just want to keep him that way. What I want to know from you is—A—is he crazy? And—B—if he isn't crazy, is there anything I can do about it?"

"No, he's not crazy. Definitely not crazy. He's a wereperson, all right." From the bottom of a credenza, Dudley hauled out a thick manuscript. "Were-phenomena have always fascinated me. In my spare time I've been investigating it since high school." He laid the manuscript on the desk and opened it. "I wrote this seven years ago. It represents my life's work. But not a publisher or scientific journal will touch it." He flipped pages, showed photos. William gasped at some of the familiar faces he saw.

"That's Senator—"

"Yes. He was a hyena. And this actress was a greyhound bitch. And this one—"

"Oh, yeah. Him. The televangelist with the shit-eating grin. I always figured the grin stayed in the air after he was gone."

"Well, he was a jackal. I sure wish I could have done something about that nasal twang of his, but that's not my field."

"But—how did they find you?"

"There are always underground rumors if a person wants something bad enough. They all came to me because they'd heard rumors of my research."

William stared fixedly at another picture. "My God. That's the manager of my complex!"

"Oh, yes. Hmmm. That was my first attempt. I didn't do it perfectly. I wish I could have left her out of the book, but, well, one must include one's less-than-perfect results or it's meaningless."

"Assuming I believe this, which I don't, what was she?"

"A pit bull."

Then, William believed. "So she really is a hound from hell."

"Most assuredly. With a nose to match."

Almost as an afterthought William caught the most important part of what Dudley had said. "What did you mean—your first attempt? At what?"

"At un-wereing."

"Come again? You mean it's a psychological thing? You hypnotized them or something?"

"Do I look like a shrink?" Dud turned more pages in the manuscript and explained.

"It's strictly a surgical answer. Nothing voodoo about it. See here?" He pointed at a detailed computer-generated image of the base of the human brain. "This is the pituitary body, right here. Irregular development or disease can cause such things as dwarfism and gigantism and problems with the sex organs. There's tentative evidence it may even have something to do with homosexuality."

"So? Everybody knows that."

Dudley turned to another image accompanied by several photographs. "Those were normal brains, normal pituitaries. Now this, my friend, is the answer to your problem."

The brain in the pictures seemed to have some kind of corkscrew arrangement running down the middle, like a crooked zipper, and it ended at the base of the brain in a flat thing like a tiny beaver's tail.

"A brain with a zipper?"

"That's not a zipper, you moron. That's a Galdogenes gland, named for the first-described were-person, 'way back in the time of Hippocrates. It was actually discovered in 1632, but the Church suppressed the knowledge and it was lost. I rediscovered it. But I never dreamed there were so many—"

"Dudley, you're giving me a headache. So it's got a name. Now what?"

"We take it out. If we schedule the surgery immediately, Tom will remain the lovely boy he is now, albeit eventually subject to sags and wrinkles like the rest of us. For a long time he will probably be naive and—ah—more or less innocent."

"And gay?" I said hopefully.

His eyes got a faraway look, like that of someone wistfully revisiting a very recent memory. "Well… there's a distinct possibility." He frowned slightly. "Back to Galdogenes. If, on the other hand, you delay the surgery until the next metamorphosis, then you will have a handsome tom cat who will be your companion, one who will love you and trust you without reservation, and he'll never question your whereabouts."

"Like I ever had any whereabouts to question! I didn't know you liked cats, Dud."

"I hate the little buggers. But people tell me they're everything nice."

"I'll have to talk it over with Tom. I can't make that kind of decision for him."

William peeked out into the adjoining room where Tom was scrunched into an impossible-looking position on one of the chairs, sound asleep. He did sleep a lot. But even taking into consideration the awkwardness of his pose, he was so beautiful William couldn't bear the thought of losing him. Not even if it meant giving up an apartment for which he'd sell both his grandparents and throw his mother into the bargain for good measure.

"I'll let you know," he told Dudley. He took Tom home, stopping at The Colonel's on the way for a pint of chicken livers. He was a little annoyed that he didn't get even one of his favorite snack. By the time they got home, Tom had eaten them all.

"More?" Tom asked plaintively, his eyes shining as he licked his lips.

Those lips! William had never been much for poetry, but at that moment he could have echoed Oscar Wilde and said, "Those red rose-leaf lips of yours were made no less for the joy of kissing than for nibbling chicken livers."

That night William sat Tom down and talked to him. He told him he loved him and was willing to even give up his apartment for him. He explained about the Galdogenes gland and the surgery, pledged his eternal love and pleaded with Tom to have the operation. Tom didn't say anything for a long time after William was finished.

"Well?" William prompted.

"I don't know what I want," Tom said slowly. "I like being here with you. I think I might even like doing the beast with two backs with you. But I don't know if I want to give up being a cat. You can't imagine... the freedom... the careless life... the swaggering... Oh, the *swaggering!* Humans don't have the slightest inkling how to swagger." He sighed. "I'll leave it up to you. I love you too. You took me in, gave me a home, bought me tuna and chicken livers. For that I would die."

William was elated. "No. No, not die. Live. First thing tomorrow I'll make arrangements for the surgery. Oh, Tom, just think—you'll be a man, a real man, for the rest of your life!"

Later that night he felt something was wrong. He got out of bed and found Tom sitting naked beside the open window. His posture was tense, as if all his senses were alert, and he was growling softly deep in his throat, a sound very much like a hiss. Below, a scruffy tomcat with a missing ear was yowling at something unseen.

"It's just a cat, Tom," William whispered, kissing his ear. "This is your chance to find out once and for all what you want. Try being completely human while you can. You might like it."

Tom looked at him, startled, the pupils of his eyes dilated. They went into the bedroom.

It took William a week to get over the experience, not to mention that the scratches and bite marks on the back of his neck were hard to explain to the doctor at the walk-in clinic.

Tom had seemed to enjoy the experience and yet... William often noticed a wistful expression on the beautiful face, sometimes accompanied by a mournful sigh.

Six months after he first set eyes on the stray cat, William made the first major decision of his life. It was the hardest thing he ever did. In that short time he had fallen head over heels in love with Tom, but he had to let him be what he had to be. It was a simple matter of patience. And it was torture. On December 21st William held Tom's hand through the night, soothing him as his form slowly, painfully, became smaller, softer, furrier. When, in the morning, Tom climbed to his shoulder and purred in his ear William reached for the telephone and called Dudley.

"Dud," he said, "it's time for the surgery."

William's new apartment doesn't have the amenities of a swimming pool, sauna, or tennis court. What it does have is a cute guy named Larry across the hall. He's friendly. He's funny. He's smart. He's as crazy about William as William is about him. He even has a rainbow flag on his bedroom wall. And he never comes over to visit without bringing chicken liver for Tom.

It's a good life. William no longer regrets his decision. And he's sure Tom doesn't either. With his head high and his tail perpendicular, Tom's strut is struttier and his swagger is swaggerier than ever. He sits on the television set, peers down from the tallest bookcase, and at least once a day gallops madly through the apartment as though possessed. If he takes the notion, he vanishes. And sometimes, as if in remembrance of things past, Tom looks up at William and gives him a smug cat-smile. Then in one graceful leap he reaches William's lap, stretches out, purrs happily, and goes to sleep.

free Speech

Martin K. Smith

At East 8th, Chuck saw some cops arresting a street person on the opposite curb. The man writhed in their grip and cried out, wild-eyed. Chuck stayed where he was, looking at other things, until the man had been taken away. Chuck feared and avoided homeless people, though he'd never say so straight out.

One of the man's plastic bags had split open in the struggle and been overlooked by the cops. Among the crumpled newspapers and foul old clothes lay a picture: a wedding photo, bride and groom with bad Seventies hair, the glass clean and the metal frame polished. Chuck knew it wouldn't last long if left on the street; it would soon be smashed or stolen. He took the picture home for safekeeping.

"He'll be back out in a couple days," Chuck told his boyfriend. "They always are. I know the guy: he's usually in Tompkins Square selling weird homemade incense, or trying to sell it; and if you can't get away he tells you these long stories of how he's been to Goa or Nepal or Tibet. Though I bet the furthest east he's ever gotten is Rikers Island."

"Still, it's really nice of you," Jeff said. He gave Chuck's shoulders a rub and his head a nuzzle. They'd been dating for two years, sharing the apartment four months.

"But he'll probably think I'm his best buddy, and be all over me every time he sees me."

A week later, the incense-man had returned. Chuck brought him the photo. "You dropped this last week when the cops got you. It looked important."

The man snatched the picture and clutched it to his breast like a teddy bear. Chuck turned to go, but the man grabbed him and thrust a paper bag into his hand. It contained a clutch of what looked like homemade tea bags. "I want you to have these. You did me a good turn so I want you to have these. Karma, you know. Know what it is? Kalpataru tea. Really rare, really really rare. It'll—"

A beat cop appeared at the walk's far end. The incense-man scuttled into the bushes and vanished.

∴⁓

Chuck would say that while he didn't exactly dislike his parents, they had the unique parental talent for grating on his nerves, so the less time he spent with them the less stressed he was. They came to the city several times that month, because Mr. McDonough was participating in a study at Columbia, something to do with nicotine's effect on intelligence. Chuck could have made some pointed remarks on that subject, but restrained himself.

"You oughta get yourself a car," Mr. McDonough said to Chuck, lighting up and puffing like a chimney. He was looking over his shoulder, one hand on the seat, other on the wheel, trying to back the Chevy into a tight space. He still wore his fading blond hair in a Fifties pompadour.

"Ty, they don't like you to smoke until you get to the clinic," his wife meekly reminded, but he ignored her.

"What is it with you not wanting a car? Means you gotta ride the goddamn subway all the time, with all the freaks and crackheads." A horn blew behind them. "Out your ass, buddy!" he yelled out the window. "Doll, get out and tell me how much space I got."

Mrs. McDonough scrambled out and peered along the street. "Ty, look, there's a space, closer to the clinic! See, they're just pulling out."

"This one's still got time on the meter! Dammit, how much space've I got?… Screw this damn study anyway,' Mr. McDonough said under his breath. "If she wasn't on my ass about it, I'd cut out and go find a titty bar."

(If she wasn't on your ass.) Chuck thought, *(and if they didn't pay you a hundred bucks a pop. And with luck you'd get your fat ashtray-reeking ass mugged. That'd be payback. And maybe you'd come back and find your car stripped to the rims.)*

"I don't have to parallel-park the subway," Chuck allowed himself to say.

Once Mr. McDonough was checked in, Chuck returned to work, while his mother went for an afternoon's shopping. She was at the apartment when he got home. She'd found the kalpataru tea and made a pot. *(I wish she wouldn't go rummaging in our cabinets as if the kitchen were her own.)* She asked in her timid way if he'd tried any, and when he said no, offered a mug. It tasted like regular tea but with a slight herbal edge, a faint astringent, sinus-clearing aftertaste.

His mother looked around. "This is so much nicer than your old place. It was so dingy, it about broke my heart to see you there. Here you've got a nice clean kitchen, and even two bedrooms. And since you both sleep together in the one, you could use the other for a den… or an office."

Chuck nearly dropped his mug. His mother was from the sort of Southern family where blood was thicker than water, but denial was thicker even than blood.

She looked hurt. "I wish you wouldn't glare at me like that, it frightens me so."

"It freaks me out that for once you admit something that's been staring you in the face for years."

Usually when his mother found she'd blundered into a topic like this she'd back right out again, changing the subject as quickly as possible. This time she didn't. "I'm always afraid to talk to you about things like… like you and your boyfriends. You get so *angry*. You glare at me and look like you're going to explode!"

"It's because I don't *want* you asking me about it. It's none of your business anymore, for one thing. And another—" Chuck couldn't stop himself. "I know I can't trust you with it. Since I was five I've known. Because you kept saying you 'loved me' and 'wanted me to be happy,' but you'd tell Dad everything and then stand by and let him bully and humiliate me and treat me like shit, nonstop for twenty years, and never once even *tried* to make him stop. That's how I know."

"That's hateful, and it's not true. I *do* care. You never heard all the nights I argued with him, begged him not to be so mean to you."

"No, I didn't, and they didn't do a damn bit of good."

"He's a hard man—"

"He's an asshole. He's unhappy all the time, and takes it out on everybody else. He smokes too much. He's probably cheated on you."

"I don't know and I don't want to know."

They were spared further pain by the street door buzzer, announcing Mr. McDonough's return from the clinic. "I'll see you out," Chuck said. Neither of them dared speak another word.

~⁚⁾

Jeff laughed in amazement. "She actually *said* that? We sleep together? Oh my god. What did you say?"

"Nothing. I was too stunned."

"What was she drinking—anything?"

"Just that tea the guy gave me."

"Well, there must've been something in it. What is kalpataru, anyway? Is it a place, like Kathmandu?... That is just so funny. After two years she finally gets it, and then just totally blurts it out. And it's not like you haven't been telling them. You *have* been telling them?" he grinned.

"I've mentioned us."

He had made passing remarks, carefully casual, about "this friend of mine," then "my friend Jeff," then "Jeff and I." His mother, father and conservative older sister never replied, though their respective faces proclaimed worry, contempt and disapproval. His younger sister, always a loyal ally, was delighted, but didn't press for details until later, when they were alone.

"You *better* have told them," Jeff was saying.

Later Chuck came into the bedroom and found Jeff already asleep. He was sprawled across the bed naked, face down, arms out; a picture of content. Chuck was drawn to the bedside, to sit beside him. The golden hair and profile against the pillow. Smooth curve of arm into shoulder; muscles, powerful and lithe. The miracle of his very existence, his presence, of two years—two whole years—with him. Chuck's hand went out, caressing the broad back. Jeff very slightly opened one eye. "What?"

"Nothing."

The next morning Jeff found they were out of coffee. Chuck liked to take a thermos-full to work, so Jeff brewed some of the tea instead. It wasn't caffeine, but it was hot, and the February temperatures were nasty.

At Holland Printing Chuck had his hands full: one of the older presses broke down in the middle of an important job. When Mr. Ventana, the manager, came in at his usual late hour of ten, Chuck had the machine dismantled on the shop floor. Ventana fancied himself a hardass; he liked not spending money, and not having people disagree with him. He demanded an explanation.

(The thing's broken, stupid. It's dead.)

"The problem," said Chuck, taking a last swig of tea, "is that this thing's deceased. It's shuffled off its mortal coil and gone to join the choir invisible. This is an ex-printer." He listed all the parts that were stripped, frayed, worn, eroded or corroded. "It leaks more ink than it prints with, and every 20 pages or so we have to realign it by hand. I babied it as long as I could, but you're gonna have to bite the bullet and get a new one."

"So when the clients come asking for their job what am I supposed to tell them?"

"Ashanti Press is doing the job for us. Tommy took the masters over an hour ago. Rhonda's paying us back the favor they owe." (*Rhonda, who you've had a hard-on for for three years.*) "I know you wanted her to pay you back personally, but tough." (*Besides, you're married to Mr. Holland's daughter, so you have to keep it in your pants.*) "You married Mr. Holland's daughter anyway, so chill. Now, here's specs on new presses. Most of these, the dealers can have here, up and running, by this afternoon." (*Holy shit, I'm gonna get myself fired.*)

Ventana scowled and looked through the faxes. "All of a sudden you think you're General goddamned MacArthur."

"I'm assistant manager—you promoted me yourself. So I'm assistant managing."

⌒⋮⊃

"Then what happened?" Jeff asked eagerly.

"Nothing. I avoided him the rest of the day. He called the dealers, then he called Mr. Holland, then he ordered a new press. And he didn't fire me… yet. And Mr. Holland did say I'd picked the right model, the one he would've chosen."

They were in bed that night. Jeff was house masseur at a gym, which sometimes scheduled late clients for him, and hadn't gotten home until 10.

"At lunch I searched 'kalpataru,'" Chuck went on. "I didn't find much. It's some kind of mythical sacred tree that grows in the garden of an Indian head-god. India Indian. It grants wishes—prosperity, happiness, boy children, the usual stuff."

"So what were you wishing for when you told Ventana off?" Jeff smiled.

"Nothing. Except that he'd buy a new printer."

He did not tell how after work he'd gone to a Village bar, one of his old haunts. There he fell into conversation with a guy named Clyde. Clyde wore a Civil War soldier's cap. He had dark blond hair and a dark blond beard and a dirty happy grin, particularly when he eyed Chuck up and down. He had a lean little body in a tight white T-shirt and jeans. He was from North Carolina, and Chuck had gone to grad school in Chapel Hill, so they traded stories about clubs there. Then Clyde grinned his dirty happy grin, and asked Chuck did he have any plans for the night? Chuck felt a hard-on rising.

He thought a long moment before he spoke. "I'm going home to wait for my boyfriend, who's working late. I'm sorry, I should've told you sooner that I'm taken."

"That's cool. How long y'all been together?"

"Two years, and counting."

"Two years, that's damn near old-married. But he still lets you out to play once in a while."

"I let myself out." Chuck reached for his coat. Clyde extended a hand. "Alright then. Been nice talkin' with you."

"Likewise. It's been nice cruising you."

"You were cruisin' me, eh."

"I was, and enjoying it way more than an old-married should. So I'm leaving, before I say dangerous things."

"Like what?" Clyde smiled. A little of his tongue showed.

(*Like, are you blond down there too?*)

"There's a pickup line I always wanted to try: is your other hair the same color as your beard?"

His hard-on stayed hard all the way back home. In the bedroom he jacked off, quick and intense.

Now, lying on his back, he let his hand glide gently down the length of Jeff's chest, into the curve of Jeff's stomach. (*I shouldn't have beat off. I should've waited; should've saved it for you.*)

Jeff's hand covered his own. "I'm really tired," Jeff said. "The last client they gave me was this enormous fat guy, it was like kneading dough trying to find his muscles, I was *exhausted*. I'll feel better in the morning, I promise." He rolled over and lay his head on Chuck's chest. "I wonder what your mom was wishing when she talked about us."

Chuck looked at the ceiling. "Probably the usual—that I'll meet a Nice Girl and Get Married."

"Maybe she'll settle for a Nice Guy instead."

(*I'm an asshole. I almost cheated on you. "I don't know and I don't want to know."*)

⌣⋰⌒

When Chuck came home from work a few days later he found his mother in the apartment with Jeff. She appeared to have been crying. A pot of the tea sat on the table, with two mugs. Chuck pulled up a chair and, with some dread, awaited an explanation. All she said, though, was that she'd had to return something at Gimbel's, they'd given her the wrong size; then she'd called a friend and they'd done a matinee at one of the revival houses. They'd wanted to walk in Central Park but it was just too cold out. And, she added, could Chuck come home this Sunday, for dinner? (Chuck's parents ran a motel, the "Star of the Sea," in Point Pleasant on the north Jersey coast, living in rooms behind the office.)

"Can you do that?" Chuck asked Jeff.

"Sure," Jeff agreed. He'd never been to Chuck's family's home. The invitation itself was a surprise.

Chuck walked his mother to the subway, and hurried back. "Well, what did you talk about?"

Jeff blinked. "Us? Oh, family stuff, family trees and ancestors and stuff. How far back my family can trace…"

"Did you both drink the tea?"

"Yeah, but I don't feel any different. I didn't go around blurting stuff out. Like… oh, like how sexy you are in the mornings with your boner sticking out." He grinned at the memory. "But, she didn't ask. So you *do* think there's something in the tea."

"I don't know—"

"But you think there might be."

"She looked like she'd been crying about something. That worried me. It's always a bad storm warning. Big-ugly-family-argument kind of storms, I mean."

"Well, we were talking about you—"

"Oh Lord."

"—and she said how something you said last week was true, and how she wished she'd done more to help you."

"What did I say?"

"It was, um—Oh, I was talking about arguing with my dad. Like when my older brothers'd trick me into doing something they weren't supposed to, and then let me take the blame when the thing broke or whatever. I'd get *furious*. But Dad was always pretty smart about guessing whose fault it was. Then she got upset and said how she hated it so when you and your dad fought, and how much it hurt her."

"Hurt *her*, huh." Chuck picked up an empty mug and looked into it. "That's like crying crocodile tears over fucking Hiroshima." He looked into the teapot. "Truth serum," he muttered, wishing he'd never found the incense-man's picture.

"Don't worry, we didn't say anything bad about you." Jeff had risen to stand behind Chuck and massage his shoulders. "She asked me if we think about getting married. I told her I didn't know, how hard it is sometimes for me to tell what you're feeling." Chuck leaned back sharply to look up at his lover's face. "I can tell when you're happy usually," Jeff went on, "and I *always* can tell when you're horny. And I told her I can tell when you're mad, 'cause even though you don't say anything you get this kind of death-ray look in your eyes. She smiled at that."

"And what am I feeling now?" Chuck inquired.

"Tired from work... and... No, you tell me." Chuck didn't answer. Jeff bent down and kissed him. "I love you, you know that."

Chuck gave him a skeptical look. "Death ray and all?"

"Death ray and all."

Chuck's family always drank iced tea at dinner. Mrs. McDonough would set a large glassful at each place before calling the others in. At the center of the table, besides ketchup and mustard, there'd be a pitcher of tea, a bowl of sugar cubes, another of Sweet-n-Low, and a bright yellow plastic lemon full of lemon juice.

Mr. McDonough was watching football in the living room, so Chuck and Audrey, his younger sister, sat in the lobby. Jeff had gone to Mrs. McDonough in the kitchen and offered to be helpful. Chuck could hear them talking and laughing. (*What are they doing back there?*) When they came in to sit, Jeff was just setting the tea pitcher down.

Mrs. McDonough said grace, and began serving the roast chicken. They ate in silence the first five minutes or so, as usual, everybody concentrating on their food. Then Mrs. McDonough spoke up, in her timid, artificially "social" voice that always got on Chuck's nerves. "Do you ever cook Charlie dinner?" she asked Jeff.

Jeff looked puzzled for a moment. "Oh, you mean *Chuck*—I never hear anybody call him Charlie. I do sometimes. I can grill a steak, or make hamburgers, and, like, basic sandwiches and stuff. And I can put things in the microwave."

"He was a tough kid to feed," Chuck's father said. "Every time we fixed something he didn't like, he'd throw a tantrum and say we were trying to starve him."

"Our older sister force-fed him mud pies when he was little," Audrey said, "maybe that had something to do with it."

"And if it wasn't about food, it was about chores or about school. Always something, for eighteen years until he went to college."

"I learned it all from you," Chuck said back, and instantly hated himself for the slip. He never let them see they'd gotten to him; he'd vowed they never would. His hand was on the glass of tea—and a sudden suspicion came to him. Chuck looked at his lover and thought, *I am going to fucking kill you when we get home.* Then he thought: *In for a penny, in for a pound.* He took a long drink.

"Like hell," his father was saying. "I bust my ass keeping this place going so you'll have something to eat, but every time I asked you to do something, even just change the vacancy sign, you gave me this whole song and dance, on and on—"

So Chuck opened up and said the first thing that came to mind. "Cork it, ashtray-breath." Then he returned to his food.

His father did a double-take. "Excuse me??"

"You heard me."

"Uh-uh. What the hell do you—"

"I don't live here any more, so I don't have to listen to you complaining. Especially not when I'm eating. It's ancient history."

His father gaped. "Don't talk to me like that—"

"I call 'em as I see 'em. Learned that from you too."

"Ty, stop!" Mrs. McDonough pleaded with her husband.

"Twenty years I bust my ass so this ungrateful little shit can give me grief and whining and bullshit, telling me I'm a lousy, worthless…"

"Tyrone Edward, I said *stop it!* That's *enough!*" Chuck's mother jumped up, snatched away her husband's dinner, and dumped it in the garbage, plate and all. She stalked away down the hall. The master bedroom door slammed shut.

"Jesus Mary and Joseph—" Chuck's father said, in helpless bewilderment.

"Looks like you'll have to eat takeout," Audrey cracked.

Then Mrs. McDonough reappeared. Without a word or a look at anyone she picked up her own plate… and a fork from the silverware drawer. Then back down the hall. The bedroom door shut again.

Chuck laughed, probably to keep from crying. "She never misses a meal. There could be a nuclear war, and she'd still insist on having dinner." He made scraping motions with his knife, as if over burnt toast. " 'It's just a little fallout. You can't really taste it…' "

Mr. McDonough, with useless gestures, wandered towards the bedroom muttering. "Jesus…"

Audrey said, "Let's go somewhere and have a drink."

Chuck and Jeff walked towards the back parking lot. Audrey had gone ahead to her car, which in cold weather was reluctant to start. They heard the frustrating *ur, urr, urrr* of an engine not catching.

"You want truth, I'll tell you truth," Chuck said. "Last week when you had that late client, I went to a bar. I met a guy named Clyde, from North Carolina. We cruised each other—seriously. I came that close to tricking with him." Chuck's voice broke, and he shuddered, and squeezed his eyes and hands tight shut. "What the hell did you think you were doing??" he cried.

Jeff seized his arm. "I didn't do anything. What'd I do?"

"The tea," Chuck said in a tiny voice. "You put that tea in there…"

Jeff was mortified. "No I didn't. I wouldn't. I saw you looking at me and thought 'Oh my God, he thinks I've dosed him with that tea!' But I'd never—Chuck, look at me—I'd never, ever, *ever* do that to you. Never, ever."

There was a creaking sound. The jalousie window of the master bath was slowly cranking open. Chuck's mother stood there, veiled and indistinct behind the screen. She motioned them over. "I threw out the tea Jeff made," she whispered. "I was afraid it was that special tea, that makes us say all those hateful things. So when you went to the bathroom I threw it out, and made some regular."

"That's just what I was telling him! It was regular tea," Jeff exclaimed.

"God," Chuck said. "This is like bad Agatha Christie—'Who Poisoned the Cocoa?'"

They could hear Mr. McDonough knocking at the bathroom door, his voice plaintive. "Margaret? Come on out, okay? Look, dammit, I'm sorry…"

Audrey's car started up. Audrey gave a feral cry of triumph.

The three of them went to a bar near the train station. They took a booth at the back. Audrey tried to lighten the mood. "So when're you two gonna get married? I want to help plan the wedding. I want it to be a cookout. With hot dogs. And balloons."

"Tell me about this Clyde guy," Jeff said.

Chuck was looking at the room: shabby, long and narrow, with a few patrons huddled at the bar beneath a flickering TV. A blue curtain filled the front window, dimming the lights of passing cars. It looked like the sort of place where affairs might suddenly end. He had a feeling he might be about to find out. *In for a penny...*

So he told about Clyde—the dark blond hair and dirty happy grin, the lean little body, the eyeing each other with frank enjoyment. "He said, 'Does your husband let you out to play sometimes?' and I said 'I let myself out.' And there's this pickup line I always wanted to use. I asked him 'Is your other hair the same color?'" Audrey gave a shout of laughter, then covered her mouth.

A huge smile spread across Jeff's face. "Oh my god—what did he say?" he asked. "Did he show you??"

Chuck stared.

Jeff exclaimed, "Listen—didn't I ever tell you what happened at Shaun's last party? Kevin propositioned me! These friends of ours," he explained to Audrey, "Keith's this little Chelsea boy, but Kevin, he teaches at NYU, and he has that whole professor thing going on, you know: he's quiet, smart, he tells these really dry jokes out of, like, Jane Austen. And Keith's the wild one, I always thought. But at the party, *Kevin* sees me in the hall and says—he was drinking martinis but you couldn't tell he was drunk unless you really knew him—he said: 'If you're ever interested, Keith and I could do a threesome with you.' "

"Coming from Kevin, that is a surprise," said Chuck.

"And honestly, Kevin's hot. They're both fun and Keith's cute— we dated for a month once. But Kevin—it's something about that quietness, the whole professor look..."

"Tweed jackets with leather elbow patches? Bushy eyebrows? I'll be damned," said Chuck.

"I've never seen a tweed jacket with bushy eyebrows," Audrey remarked.

"They're all the rage," Chuck replied. He could not help but contemplate the idea of Jeff in a three-way with Keith and Kevin. Or perhaps even a four-way, with himself included. The logistical questions—who would do what and to whom, and how—fascinated and aroused him. And somehow the emotional complications didn't feel like they'd be all that complicated. (*Well, if we are going to break up, at least it won't be in this dump.*)

When they reached home Chuck went to the kitchen for hot chocolate. He opened the cabinet door, and said "Goddammit!" A mouse had gotten in and shredded open the kalpataru teabags all over the shelf along with a garnish of mouse droppings. "So now there's a really truthful mouse running around somewhere," Chuck said as he cleaned up. And later as they lay in bed he remarked, "Now we'll never know if it really was a truth drug. Unless I see that guy again and get some more."

"I don't really care, you know? You didn't need it. You totally blew your dad off without it."

Chuck shuddered. "God. I'll be getting fallout from that for years."

"But you've been wanting to do that for years. For as long as I've known you. And you did. Didn't the Indian myths say kalpataru grants wishes? Maybe it wasn't a truth drug."

"Well, I told some truth anyway."

"You kicked ass." Jeff nuzzled him. "I bet he'll respect you more now anyway." But Chuck sat up in bed. "What?" Jeff asked.

Chuck took a deep breath. "It's something… that I wish I knew what the truth was. About getting married. What with my mother asking… and Audrey asking… I want to marry you. Very much. But I'm scared to, because of things like Clyde. I was that close to betraying you. If I'd had a few more beers… I was walking right on the very edge of the cliff. I *wanted* to hook up with him. I was even thinking logistics: if he's staying nearby, we could have a whole hour to play, and I could still get home before you. While another part of me was saying, screaming, 'You disgusting betraying piece of shit horndog, how can you even be thinking this??!' And afterwards I came home and jacked off, fantasizing about him."

"That's why I told you about—"

"Because I figure I can propose all I want to, but I can't expect you to give me an answer until I can give you an honest yes or no as to whether I can handle it."

Jeff took him by the shoulders. "Listen," he said. "Listen. That's why I told you about Kevin coming on to me. I've got fantasies about him just like you do about Claude—"

"Clyde."

"And I don't know either if I can handle it. I mean, like, if somebody I've always wanted for years came along, like Dan Haggerty—"

"Dan Haggerty??" Chuck laughed in spite of himself.

"Shut up, I'm serious. Grizzly Adams?? Didn't you think he was hot? If he came up to me and said 'Let's go!' what would I do?"

Chuck thought. "What *I* would do if that happened… I'd tell you 'Go for it, have fun.' Just come home to me afterward. With pictures we can sell to the National Enquirer."

Jeff slapped him, gently. "You sleaze. Making money off my all-time fantasy. But listen, if you meet him again—Claude, Clyde—do bring him home, 'cause I want to see what he looks like. If you think he's hot, he probably is."

They lay quiet a while, holding one another. "Okay then," Chuck said, "some night we'll have Kevin and Keith over, and Clau—I mean, Clyde; and Dan Haggerty if we can get him. And we'll play naked Twister. And we'll have hot dogs and balloons."

"No, save those for the wedding. Martinis. They're what made Kevin ask me," Jeff said.

" OK. Hot dogs at the wedding it is." said Chuck.

All the same, Chuck searched for the incense-man during the next few weeks, but never found him. One day he spoke to a local activist who knew the Tompkins Square denizens well. She too had noted the incense-man's absence, and had inquired among his fellow transients. They told her vague rumors that he'd gone to Kathmandu.

This I Know
Roads to Heaven: Reflections on Redemption

Dan Stone

"Jesus loves me/this I know/for the Bible tells me so…"

That verse was as familiar to me when I was a kid as "Mary had a little lamb." What's more, being the good fundamentalist Christian preacher's kid that I was, I believed it. Jesus loved me because the Bible said so. Those twin messages—one about love, one about the law—seemed inseparable. As I grew older the balance between the two seemed to shift. That sweetly ringing bell about unconditional love grew dimmer and dimmer compared to the increasing clamor of biblical rules and regulations.

The first time I had sex with a boy, when I was 17, felt as natural as waking up with an erection and as electrifying as any thunderbolt from heaven. Teenaged clumsiness aside, it surpassed everything I'd feared or fantasized about what could happen between two bodies colliding and converging in the gasping darkness. Then, as quickly as my blood had boiled, it froze, passion crashing like a renegade wave against the punishing rocks of a young and unyielding faith.

I saw a lake of fire light up in my mind's eye as surely as if God Himself had doused me in kerosene and struck a match. Fearing for my eternal soul, I begged the Lord—and my bewildered playmate—

for forgiveness. I shoved all my "unnatural" affections back into the closet for another decade and nailed the door shut. The nails on that closet door held securely all the way through the first five or six years of a seven-year marriage that would end in ruins.

"Didn't you know you were gay?" Too many have asked. The best answer to date remains that it was a moot point. At the time, in my biblically bound little world where homosexuality was a fast train to hell, being gay meant that I was, literally, doomed.

Many of us—maybe most of us—have had to find our way downstream to a place where the waters of tolerance and self-acceptance can begin to dissolve those unforgiving barriers often erected by the faith of our fathers (and mothers). In the process, many of us also discover that there are multiple roads to heaven. Some of us choose the most familiar route we can find, seeking out a community of believers whose faith feels just enough like home. Others choose a journey that takes them through the wilds of completely unfamiliar landscapes and unfamiliar terrain, embracing spiritual practices and traditions that bear no resemblance to their past and that offer no reminders of their pain.

Others make less formed choices, opting instead for an unstructured faith, a lingering distrust of any institutionalized belief, any organized spirituality. Some choose to focus more on the questions rather than rigorously pursuing the answers, to accept and celebrate the mysteries of soul and spirit rather than seeking to solve them. Part of the paradoxical beauty of believing is that you can't really be sure. Whichever road we choose out of despair and into the loving self-affirmation that is ours to claim, it is a choice worth celebrating.

Sometimes these days when I meditate, when I allow myself to relax into the inner knowing that is one of the real gifts of any faith and allow the lovely, loving voice and images that inhabit my true self to appear in my mind's eye, I see Christ—or someone Christ-like... walking with me on a secluded beach. In my meditation this Christ looks more like a Greek warrior than a martyred Jew... He's beautiful, virile, shirtless with long hair flowing down a sinewy back. He is a calm, detached presence, and I don't know if he's a figment of my imagination or an inner guide or some remnant of my former faith that I'll eventually outgrow—or if it even matters. What does matter is that he listens, and that he has a loving way of answering questions with questions, of pointing me in the direction of my own truth, or at least, the quest for it.

"Worship at your boyfriend's feet if you want, not mine," he has said.

I've taken his advice as much as possible. I've held the feet of a lover in my lap or in my hands and, all fetishes aside, felt the simultaneously humbling and exalting attraction to and reverence for another man. It always leaves me feeling chosen in some way, called to experience a life truly charmed by such a profoundly felt love and desire. In those moments while I am holding another man close to me or being held by him—or sometimes merely having a handsome stranger catch my eye on a beach—I remember the little boy I was before I knew that anyone could ever find fault in me. I also remember the man I've become who knows that the love he feels is perfect, and that the man who feels it has no need for redemption. In those moments, the bad movie that is all that's left of the Hell I used to fear is forgotten.

Sometimes the Christ I see in my meditation says nothing at all. He just sits beside me on a quiet, private shore. He offers no sermons, no admonitions, no beatitudes or parables, no mention of sin or of salvation. Whoever he is—this Christ in me or in my lover or in the sexy stranger on the beach—he is the one who teaches me about heaven. He loves me, this I know—and not because the Bible tells me so.

Musuko Dojoji

Mark Horn

I fell in love the week I arrived in Japan. I was already enamored with the country—I had felt drawn there from the time I first discovered Japanese cinema in college—everything from Kurosawa's samurai slash-ups to Ozu's claustrophobic family dramas. Tokyo felt more like home than the Brooklyn I'd known all my life. I knew I had to go.

My new apartment came with the cushy ex-pat job I'd taken with an ad agency. From the terrace I could see Mt. Fuji when the air was clear of smog. Just outside my building there was a local ancestral Shinto shrine to the trickster-fox god, Inari. Just beside the shrine's stone statue of the fox stood a small army of life-sized plastic statues of Colonel Sanders, waiting in a warehouse parking lot. I wondered if Inari would lead these hollow men in white suits in a Pied Piper dance to Mt. Fuji, and free Tokyo of American fast food. No such luck. The tradition of my Jewish ancestors taught me that stone gods don't move. But that didn't stop me from finding my own trickster god to follow. His name was the equivalent of John Smith for the Japanese, since there was no name more common in the country than Hiroshi Aoki. It was the only common thing about him.

He wasn't anything like anyone I'd ever been attracted to before. He was a little shorter than the average Japanese man, and when he walked, he had a strange kind of hop that had him lurching in unexpected directions every few steps. His small body somehow managed to hold up a large head with eyes that burned with a fierce intelligence. Framing those eyes was a mane of wild, thick black hair that was often askew and sometimes hid the occasional acupuncture needle he'd forgotten to remove after his classes in Oriental Medicine. And that was one of the things that hooked me—he shared my interest in the culture that most of modern Japan seemed to have jettisoned: kabuki plays and acupuncture, Buddhist myth and Shinto folk tales. So it didn't seem so strange that he reminded me of nothing more than a *kappa*—a mythological Japanese creature that seemed part child, part monkey, part frog and all mischief.

He had taught himself English by reading Shakespeare and personal ads in the back of gay magazines. In this way he'd made English a language all his own, combining words I'd never heard used together before, like the seductive incantations of some ancient priest of love. And before I knew it, or could explain it, I was under the spell of this Japanese frog prince. He would come on Friday nights dressed in full formal kimono to give me the pleasure of slowly unwrapping the layers, always leaving a surprise for the last—would he be wearing a traditional loincloth or skimpy French mesh briefs? In this Japanese version of the dance of the seven veils, there was no resisting this Salome.

It became part of our routine every Saturday morning to go off in search of history down the street and around the city. We'd find a historically significant site, and he'd tell me the legends associated with it—he seemed to know them all.

One morning, he took me on a walk past Tokyo Tower, that imitation Tour Eiffel that the Japanese will proudly tell you stands 40 feet higher than the original in Paris. And unlike its Parisian progenitor, Tokyo Tower offers the cultural advantages of a bowling alley in the building at its base. I'd only seen the tower in black-and-white monster movies, so the reality of it in hideous industrial orange paint made it thoroughly understandable why Godzilla destroyed it every time he returned to town.

Just as we passed the crest of the Tower's hill Hiroshi stopped and fixed his gaze on the goal of our outing, further down the slope yet still under the tower's looming shadow: Dojoji Temple. From this vantage point we could see the whole of the huge walled compound—from the main temple hall with its pagoda-style sloping roofs to the labyrinthine monastery complex twisting around a courtyard with a copper bell tarnished green and as big as a Toyota pickup. We walked through the fortified gate without a word or story from Hiroshi. We passed the crypt of the Tokugawa shoguns—Dojoji was the family temple, and most of them were buried there. But Hiroshi walked past that as well without stopping to mention anything of interest. Finally we came to a bench next to a large cedar tree in the courtyard by the monastery quarters. A plaque in front of the tree said that President Grant had planted it on the first trip to Tokyo by a U.S. President, in 1879. This wasn't the kind of story Hiroshi was usually interested in sharing. Then I noticed that on the flagstones in the courtyard before us there was something odd: a circle about fifteen feet in diameter appeared to have been burned deep into the paving stones. People who were walking straight across the plaza would avoid stepping into it, walking around to give it a wide berth.

When Hiroshi saw that I had noticed this he said, "You know, there's a story told about that circle…" and this is the story he told me:

About four hundred years ago, when the Dojoji temple monastery was a great center of learning, two monks who studied here went on a short pilgrimage to visit the statue of the great Buddha in Kamakura. The elder of the two was a saintly man, and the younger, Anchin, was his disciple.

As was customary, the monks only ate what they received from people they met on their way. And they slept under the stars unless some villager offered them shelter. One day they found themselves outside a small hut on the edge of a village just as the sun was setting.

A woman opened the door of the hut—she was a young widow who lived alone. When she saw the young monk Anchin, her heart ached with loneliness. And her body stirred with desire. She invited them in to spend the night.

She served them a humble dinner, not simply because they were monks, but because, as a widow, her means were not great. The elder monk offered her the Buddha's blessing because he understood her generosity. And then the monks retired for the night, bedding down separately in the small entrance room of the hut.

After midnight, the woman snuck into the bed of the younger monk, and he woke up with a start. She ran her hand across his chest to calm him down—but never having known the touch of a woman, this disturbed him even more

*and she could feel his heart beating hard, whether in terror or desire she did
not know, though she hoped it was desire.*

*"Please," she said. "Do not send me away. I am so lonely. My husband
died so young and it has been a long time since I have felt the touch of a man's
hand."*

*She wound her leg around his and then, taking his hand, she put it be-
tween her breasts. He pulled back and hissed his protest quietly, trying not to
wake his master.*

*"Stop, please. I have taken a vow of chastity. Please do not cause me to
break that vow — there are hell realms that we would both be condemned to for
lifetimes." And he tried his best to meditate on these Buddhist hells as she
continued to wrap her body around him, writhing in her own desire as she
sought to arouse him.*

*Just before dawn, as Anchin thought he might give in and break his vow,
he pleaded with her once again, and made her a promise: "Please, at least let
me complete my pilgrimage. I cannot bow down before the great Buddha of
Kamakura having broken my vow. Let me at least do that, and on my return,
I will stop here and satisfy your desires."*

*With this promise made, she slipped from his bed just before the sun —
and the old monk — rose.*

*Anchin mentioned nothing of what happened to his mentor, and they
continued on their way south to complete their pilgrimage. Once they had
fulfilled their vow, they started the return journey. But Anchin, who was
terrified of seeing the young widow again, suggested to the elder monk that
they take another way back to Dojoji, stopping to visit the shrines of the seven
gods of good luck along the way. The other monk agreed, unaware of the promise Anchin had made to the widow.*

*The young woman counted the days it would take for the monks to arrive
at their destination, and to return her way. As the time for their return grew
closer, she prepared to give herself to the young monk. She imagined his strong
hands taking her, his firm flesh pressing her against the futon. As each day
passed she grew more fevered in her desire.*

*When it was past the time she calculated for his return, she went out into
the road, and stood searching the horizon for him, until after a few days, she
began to ask passing travelers whether they had seen the two monks on their
journey. Oh yes, she was told, they had been headed this way, but had taken a
turn to stop at another shrine along the way.*

*She knew then she had been deceived. Filled with the mad rage that only
one whose lust has been thwarted can know, she shut herself within her small*

thatched hut. No one saw her for three days. Then, from inside the hut the villagers heard a deep hissing that was accompanied by an unhealthy smell, as though the earth below the hut had cracked open, unleashing a sulfurous cloud of steam.

They gathered outside, but were afraid to approach the door. A good thing too, since while they stood there, reciting prayers of protection from the Heart Sutra, the wooden door of the hut cracked open, and out slithered an enormous serpent. The villagers fell back in amazement, and the beast, more than thirty feet long, shot off down the road in the direction of Dojoji temple.

Word spread even faster than the serpent could travel, and soon the two monks heard of the great beast that seemed to be headed in the same direction they were. Anchin realized that the serpent had to be the avenging spirit of the young widow, and he confessed the whole story to the elder monk.

When the elder monk understood the situation, he hurried Anchin as fast as they could travel back to Dojoji, arriving at the temple just as the serpent could be seen on the horizon at the top of Nogizaka hill. The abbot of the temple had ten monks bar the great gate of the temple compound, and directed ten other monks to lower the copper bell over Anchin in protection. Then they waited.

It didn't take long for the snake to reach the gate. And the walls of the compound, as tall as they were, were no match for the serpent as it slipped up, over, and then down the other side.

Slowly it made its way around the temple compound, its tongue flicking in and out to catch Anchin's scent. It slid through the monastery quarters, and into the temple itself, darting this way and that, in its frantic search for the young monk. Then it raised its head and turned with a wild focus towards the copper bell, sitting on the flagstones in the center of the courtyard.

The serpent was on the bell in a shot, coiling its body around it, squeezing the thick metal with all its might, trying to crack the bell open like a great green egg.

When this proved fruitless, the serpent began to beat its head against the bell for hours, until tears of blood ran from its eyes. Finally, after one last heave, the snake fell dead, a foul stench rising from its steaming body.

The terrified monks slowly came out from their hiding places and tried to pull the body of the snake from the bell, but it was too hot to touch. So they formed a chain, like a fire brigade, and splashed the body of the demon and the metal of the bell itself with water that evaporated into steam until it was cool enough for them to be able to pull the body away and lift the bell.

There was nothing left of Anchin except for a few bone fragments and a small pile of ashes.

The abbot had the body of the serpent burned, and then the ashes of the young monk and the serpent were mixed together with ink that was used to write a copy of the Lotus Sutra. Once this was done, the abbot had a dream in which Anchin and the young widow appeared before him, thanking him for bringing them together in this way. They told him that they had courted each other in the past, throughout many lifetimes in the divine play of searching for one another as they sought enlightenment. He was told that because he had joined their ashes in the writing of the sutra, that after a period of a few hundred years of separation in different Buddhist heavens they would be re-born and meet again, finally able to consummate their love together on this earthly plane.

Hiroshi paused in his telling to turn and look at me. Then he looked out again across the courtyard at the circle burned into the flagstones. The story was over. Or so I thought. Because then he took my hand, threading his fingers tightly through mine and twining his arm around mine. Then he said quietly, "So four hundred years later they were reborn, and this time, I got the man I wanted."

For just a moment, I was afraid. And then I looked at him and smiled at the way he'd artfully sewn together this legend and our romance. I wriggled out of his arms, jumped up and ran across the plaza.

"Don't be so sure," I shouted with a laugh, trying to convince myself that this was just a tale, struggling to quiet the insistent pounding of my heart. He didn't give chase, but simply narrowed his eyes and tightened his mouth in a smile that was both sexy and scary at the same time.

That night, in bed, it felt to me as though Hiroshi was everywhere at once, the sheets knotting up as he twisted and turned all around me, with a ferocious hunger that I'd never seen before. As we made love he arched his back, his eyes rolling up in his head, taking him somewhere I couldn't follow. Or was too afraid to go.

He must have sensed this, because in a moment he came back— looking straight at and through me with a strange and tender fire burning in his eyes as he asked, "After all this time, why do you still hold back when heaven awaits us both?"

The metal bands of fear that bound my heart melted in that moment, and together we transformed the wild fire of lust into the pure light of nirvana.

Epilogue

The story is based on one of Japan's oldest folk tales, first recorded in the 8th century C.E. The location was a famous temple known as Dojoji in Wakayama prefecture, not Tokyo. I have moved the location of the temple and its tale to Tokyo's Zojoji Temple, which was within walking distance of my apartment and where we often went on New Year's Eve to hear the tolling of the great copper bell 108 times at midnight.

The folk tale is well known in Japan, and is the basis for a kabuki play called *Musume Dojoji*, or Daughter of Dojo Temple. For that reason, I've titled this story *Musuko Dojoji*, or Son of Dojo Temple.

I wrote this story to honor the memory of Hiroshi Aoki, who once told me that the real reason I went to Japan was to meet him. I know in my heart this is true. We were together for ten years. The magic, mystery and love he brought into my life lives on even though Hiroshi died unexpectedly in his sleep in 1997.

People often ask when I tell this story in performance what really happened. The facts? I did live in an apartment with a view of Mt. Fuji that overlooked both an Inari shrine and a KFC warehouse where statues of Colonel Sanders were stored. Hiroshi did teach himself English by reading Shakespeare and Advocate personal ads. He and I often went in search of hidden history and folklore all across Japan. Tokyo's Zojoji temple, in the shadow of Tokyo Tower, is the site of a tree planted there by President Grant. As for the rest? Well, as I like to tell my students in the class I teach on folk tales and mythology, just because it didn't happen, doesn't mean it isn't true.

A Path of Mirrors

Don Clark

It could be that our *spirit guides* are not hidden from normal sight or cloaked in great mystery. It just may be that they are unrecognized at first sight, only to be revered in hindsight, standing in plain sight always, figuratively acting as sign posts pointing the way along the path best taken if you are to have your own unique, rich and full life.

Now, three quarters of a century along my life's path, I look back and see them clearly. There are many of them, some gay, some not—none more beautiful or unusual than the first I encountered. Like him, they stand smiling, eyes locked on ours, saying "This way, not that way. *This* is your path, right this way."

My life continues to seem to me far better than ever I could have imagined it to be at any earlier moment along the way and I certainly owe most of that to them. My appreciation of their gifts makes me more watchful now, hopeful and ready to recognize the next guide. As always, he or she will be someone who sees something in me that I do not yet see in myself. I know that I shall learn first to trust this person, then to sense the love between us and, consequently, to see the next steps along my path as I peer into trusted eyes as one might look into a mirror, able finally to see what this guide sees in me.

My eighth grade teacher was not the first guide to appear but the first whose guidance was clear to me. I was the tall, stooped, skinny kid with glasses and bad teeth, the last of five to pass through the school from a family on the wrong side of the tracks—the sickly boy skilled at hiding from the notice of teachers and school yard bullies.

At the end of the first week she moved me to the front desk in the row farthest from the windows, no more hiding or daydreaming my escape into the sky and treetops outside. She was going to teach us correct English grammar she told us. Her eyes were on mine often as she opened the world of nouns, verbs, adjectives, adverbs, tenses and dependent clauses. My terrible spelling seemed to trouble her little and she was delighted by my quick mastering of the game of diagramming sentences.

She appointed me chairman of a committee to create a yearbook for our graduating class. I rewarded her with an anecdotal history of the class in one long rhyming poem. The final day of school she wrote her "best wishes and good luck" in each student's autograph book. Her neat handwriting covered the entire page in mine:

> *Dare to do right,*
> *Dare to be true,*
> *You have a job*
> *No other can do.*
> *Do it so nobly,*
> *So full and so well,*
> *Angels will hasten*
> *Your story to tell.*

I had been someone special to her—someone *different*. Maybe what charms a life is exactly *that*—being seen as different. People are wearied easily by sameness. For better or worse, someone who seems different catches interest.

A year earlier it had been my oldest sister who appeared as an unrecognized guide. She had gone to Washington, D. C. in the summer of 1942 to answer the war effort call for government office workers. A month later I started seventh grade and three weeks later developed a ruptured appendix that was followed by pneumonia.

There was a long recovery at home after leaving the hospital. As a get-well gift and to help fill the empty time, my sister enrolled me in the Junior Literary Guild. The first book was a biography of young Abe Lincoln. I liked it a lot and read it twice.

By Christmas I had recovered but then developed sick headaches that kept me out of school. My sister was lonely in Washington and suggested that I come back with her for a month to keep her company and to give me a change of scene.

We shared her rented room and ate our meals in the Government Workers' Cafeteria. She bought me a public transportation pass and, though only twelve years old, I was free to wander wartime Washington, finding my way to the Smithsonian, National Archives, and Lincoln Memorial—even into the Supreme Court. Some days I just rode streetcars, looked at buildings, wandered into stores and watched people. At the end of each day I told her what I had seen. I was learning to be a storyteller.

In high school my first year English teacher was fresh out of teachers' training. She asked each of us to try writing a poem. I brought her a long story poem about an old, unwanted hobo. When she returned it with spelling errors corrected, she quietly asked if I would give her permission to show it to some other teachers. No teacher had asked my permission for anything, ever.

In my junior year another unlikely guide appeared. Alan, seated next to me in Spanish class was overweight and suffered with acne. He wore glasses and had braces on his teeth. "Which colleges are you applying to?" It was asked casually, in a tone he might have used to ask me if I had done the homework assignment. "It's tough getting in anywhere with all of the returning veterans on the G. I. Bill." It was as if he was speaking a native language that was foreign. I did not know anyone except teachers who had ever been to college.

The school guidance counselor thought it was a bad idea. "You should be thinking about trade school, if anything," she said after quickly looking me over.

But Alan persevered. "You have to go. First get your grades up, get on the Honor Roll and join some school clubs. You can write away and get your own college catalogs. My father says he'd be willing to give you a reference. He's a dentist."

Antioch College in Yellow Springs, Ohio was the college I chose. It was a school with a work/study program, an honor system that worked, community government, a dedication to social justice in the world, students who could have gone to any college and a monument to its founder, Horace Mann. His words, inscribed beneath his likeness were taken seriously. "Be ashamed to die until you have won some victory for humanity."

Wayne, my next guide, was one of the returning vets. He became my closest friend. Some people thought we were lovers but we were not. I was hiding my attraction to other males, or believed I was. Homosexuality was thought to be a mental illness or, at the very least, symptomatic of inferiority, an arrested stage of development. I wanted to become a writer or a psychologist if possible. The latter would be out of the question if I could not conquer or at least hide my affliction. I needed to put those feeling out of my mind.

Several years older, Wayne had seen a larger world and seemed to know something about everything. He was attracted to all that was unusual, had a knack for meeting important people and had a definite talent for interior design. We were roommates often, on campus and off. He could transform the ugliest rented room in the dingiest part of a city with paint, crates and a few scraps of fabric. He could also ask endless provocative, argumentative questions that required a fund of information I did not have and gave me headaches as he expanded my intellectual horizons.

He also introduced me to Grace, a powerful guide to point my way with the acceptance and wisdom of a Buddha. She was the director of a prestigious private progressive elementary school where Wayne had worked and I was to have a work/study year. When we met I saw a woman with short-cropped white hair wearing jeans and carrying a pail of garbage, amused by the shock she read on my face. "Well, someone always has to take out the garbage," she said with a laugh. "I'm no different from anyone else."

During the years that I knew her she demonstrated, without fail, an ability to be concerned about my troubles with sufficient intensity that I was forced to find my own next step out of the trouble. Her empathy and compassion were natural, part of a deep reservoir formed by her life experiences. She seemed to think I could handle just about anything.

Turning to her just before entering the army as a draftee during the Korean war, she listened. At our parting, she kissed me, took my hand and said, "You know, they can't take away who you are no matter what they do." Without knowing it, that had been my worry. I feared that I might lose the person I had become during my college years and be sent back to the bottom rungs of the ladder.

Her faith pointing the way, I read nineteenth century literature during my two years in the army, declared open argumentative opposition to the destructive foolishness of Senator Joseph McCarthy and his witch hunting, and spoke out in army forums against the insanity of war, especially the mere consideration of such weapons as atomic and hydrogen bombs. Armed with the prospect of a subsequent security net in the form of a slimmed down G. I. Bill for educational benefits, I dared to apply to several doctoral programs in psychology.

Jack appeared in my first year of graduate study. This guide was a dapper young bachelor professor who lived in a penthouse on the fashionable East Side of Manhattan. He took an interest in me and invited me to his cocktail parties with socially prominent people.

It was a big jump for a kid from the wrong side of the tracks. "People naturally like you," he said. "You're interested in people and treat them with respect. That makes you interesting to them. Go ahead and ask them questions. Let them see that you're interested in who they are." He was right. If I let them see my interest, they responded by letting me know some of their innermost thoughts and feelings.

He seemed surprised when I married a young woman who had been my friend since our freshman year together at Antioch. We had grown to love one another. She assumed that I would be a good husband and father. I could see that belief in her. She too was right, I was. She had pointed the way. She had seen qualities in me that I found in myself by looking into her.

My mentor in graduate school, Gerry, was another guide to whom I remain indebted. He seemed to believe that I could be a competent psychologist and even offer something unique to the field. It was he who pointed to a path in the academic world, ten years on the faculty of Hunter College and Lehman College of the City University of New York

My guide, Asya, who was a clinic consultant at Hunter, appeared in my first week there. She was a colorful, astute Russian émigré—an unorthodox psychoanalyst. I had become better able to recognize my guides by then. "You are at your beginnings, my darling," she said in her unique accent during our first consultation. "Where you will go we are going to see but you are going somewhere."

She was delighted with the births of our two children, acting as a self-appointed grandmother to them. I agreed when she said, "You are seeing real miracles as these babies are coming into this world."

The children too were guides. They showed me absolute trust and truth free of guile. I saw it in them and they saw it in me. Looking deeply into them, again I saw what was being seen in me. I owed it to them and to myself to be whole in truth, to achieve integrity by freeing myself of all deception.

It was the 1960s and the human potential movement was underway. I plunged into it without hesitation, flying off to the Esalen Institute when I could and accepting an offer from the Carnegie Corporation of New York to investigate the promising ideas this new movement might hold for education and psychotherapy. The basic idea inherent in the human potential movement was that each of us should become more true to ourselves and become all that we could be as individuals using untapped hidden reservoirs.

Taking that premise to heart along with the faith in me shown by my guides and loved ones, I accepted and began to embrace my long suppressed homosexual desires and nature. I reviewed the supposed psychological research on the pathology of homosexuality and found it to be a house of cards, illusory opinions as misleading as the emperor's new clothes. The *experts,* professionals presumed to be healers, had been harming us and making a handsome living while doing it.

I began to come out. Gay students appeared and made administration officials at the college uncomfortable. I had rank and tenure and they could do nothing. But my train had left the station. I was inhaling and exhaling truth. It was addictive. It was a short journey from there to leaving the university and starting a private practice aimed especially at helping gay men and lesbians as well as their families and friends, first in New York, then back in San Francisco where I had done my internship.

I was fully out of the closet personally and professionally in January of 1971 when we moved back to San Francisco. I was made uneasy by reminders that I could lose my psychology license both in New York and California because of my admission since I was guilty of *moral turpitude* as defined by the laws at that time. I had a wife and two children to support. But I was pulled forward by my lust for truth. I was made uneasy also by the responsibility when told that I was the first licensed mental health professional in the United States, perhaps in the world, to be public about my gay identity.

But I had learned by then that the best defense is a good offense. Reserved by nature, I had to force myself to take every opportunity to be the expert and lecture others on truthful, respectful, professional care for gay men and lesbians. By four years later, in 1975, I had learned enough that I needed to share it. I wrote *Loving Someone Gay*. It was difficult to find a publisher willing to touch it but the first copies appeared in December of 1976 and sold out immediately. Early in 1977 it collided with Anita Bryant and her *Save the Children Crusade* as well as with the legislative *Initiative* witch-hunt proposed by John Briggs aimed at finding and firing all gay teachers and their supporters in the public schools of California. Reserved me was in demand for television, radio and newspaper interviews. I had to do it. The National Gay Task Force could not have dreamed of paying for all of the airtime and print space suddenly made available to me.

There were frightening threats in response to public appearance sometimes but more guides appeared, pointing the direction for next steps. Friends, lovers and well-wishers filled my world. Change was everywhere.

The inevitable divorce was civilized but painful for us. Writing my memoirs during the past two years I have been able to revisit those years, see their value in lighting my path and be glad that they are behind me now.

After that frantic period came the best and worst years for our gay communities as the AIDS epidemic caused an unbelievable number of friends and loved ones to fall into sickness and die. It tested all of us. We rushed toward one another with compassion while our governments and others rushed away from us in fear.

The entire landscape of my world changed again. Like many of my peers I felt depleted. Guides disappeared and I was left to guard the guidance they had given to me and others.

I have wondered how my life might have been had I failed to notice and heed the directions of my spirit guides. What if I had failed to look deeply into them as into the mirrors they were and failed to find myself? It is a dark prospect that I am unable to summon the courage to imagine. But, fortunately, I had no choice. It all began in such an unlikely and impressive way when my quite beautiful first spirit guide appeared.

I was only four years old. The family had driven from New Jersey to Miami Beach in an old Buick, looking for work during the Depression. We lived in a shack but that did not matter to me. The warm air and sunshine felt good. Food grew on trees.

One wonderful, bright afternoon he appeared. He was a young man probably in his early twenties, tanned and fit, cheerful, smiling and laughing. We were at a public beach. He stepped into a shower stall that had louvered wooden doors designed to hide that which bathing suits otherwise covered.

I was drawn to him as if to a magnet, yet I knew I must not go into the shower to touch him though I had a strong urge to do so. I wanted to be close to him. I watched his swimsuit drop to the wet wooden slats of the floor, watched as he soaped his hair and watched as suds cascaded over strong shoulders and arms, then on down tanned legs to his feet. He opened his eyes and saw me looking at him, probably seeing my desire. He gave me a dazzling wide smile and winked at me.

It was strange. I felt connected to him—as if I knew him. It was a sudden bond, stronger than I felt with anyone in my family. I looked into his eyes. He seemed to understand what was happening though I did not.

But our time was not ripe. I was too young. There was nothing either of us could do about it. He could and did welcome me to my tribe with that wink and smile. He could show himself as love, my first beautiful spirit guide pointing a direction, pointing to a future as if able to see that I would find my way and that there would be help.

Forty-one years after that fateful day in Miami Beach I met a young man in San Francisco who seemed eerily familiar. Ten years passed before we were to meet again—once again drawn to one though not yet remembering our earlier meeting.

There was a very strong feeling of familiarity that second time we met—as if he was someone already known to me, as if we had been intimate long ago. It was a puzzle. Later, I told myself that the feeling must have been due simply to our having met ten years before.

More than half a century had passed since meeting my first spirit guide in Miami Beach but now I realize *that* was the feeling. That young man in the shower had been much older than I then and younger than this man to whom I was so drawn at our two meetings, who in turn, was younger than I. A distracting confusion of ages obscured a truth that was the key to the puzzle. The feeling I had experienced those many years earlier was the same—a knowing, a familiarity.

The essence of that first spirit guide had reappeared and I had sensed it. Full circle, the time was ripe. Life had prepared us. We were free at last to join together—ready to be guide to one another. We had stories to tell, tales from lives lived apart and a life yet to be lived together.

Lines

John McFarland

I was at the post office late in the afternoon on December 31. I was in a long line waiting to buy stamps. When I finally stepped up to the counter the clerk tried to foist unsold Christmas inventory off on me. I wasn't having any of that tired old story. I wanted the ones with a flag, fluttering. I got those and was off to hook up with my honey Lenny.

I must have been radiating good cheer at a really irritating level as I exited the post office, though. The first person coming down the street screamed at me, "You're nothing special."

I could have shot back, "If that smart remark was supposed to ruin my day, hon, you'll have to get to me much earlier because I am under heavy fire from professional assholes from the minute the sun comes up." Instead, I laughed. I didn't care what the man thought, and frankly, he was wrong.

At the crowded lounge where I met Lenny, we ordered drinks with flames and discussed how we'd spend the evening. New Year's Eves, we spit on them! We hate them! We decided that we'd cook dinner, open some very cheap wine and watch a video, something effervescent, something sure-fire for the end of the year. I suggested the one with Dennis Quaid as Jerry Lee Lewis, the one that everybody panned even though it is only fabulous. Lenny didn't have anything better in mind so we marched out to get it. At the video store hordes of people were badgering the help for recommendations and decisions. I started searching the shelves for the movie on my own. I looked under Rock 'n Roll. I looked under Musicals. I looked under Dennis Quaid. I looked everywhere. I couldn't find it.

I took my place at the end of the very long line to wait my turn for help. When I finally made it up front to the counter I was face to face with this very cute guy I'd never seen before. Lenny was sort of standing beside me. The line behind us was huge.

I asked the guy, "Do you have *Great Balls of Fire*?"

Lenny leaned against me and whispered in my ear, "I can't believe you said that to him."

The guy didn't blink and said, "It's in Actresses, Felons, under Winona." He motioned us to follow as he charged toward the shelves.

Lenny said, "If I had known you were going to make a public spectacle..."

I said, "He didn't think I was asking about his balls. He knew I was talking about the movie. The title, you know?"

"Nobody else here thinks that, Joel. Everybody else thinks you are such a big slut you couldn't stop yourself from putting the moves on some poor kid who has to show up for work on New Year's Eve and put up with cheesy come-ons from the likes of you."

"Hey!"

"On New Year's Eve! In a crowd! Fuck!"

"Look, he's taking us straight to the video. He didn't think I was talking about that. And I wasn't. He and I are the only two people in this store with our minds on the business of renting a video while the rest of you gutterbunnies are somewhere else," I said.

So, we got over that and we went home. We had a terrific dinner. The wine wasn't bad either. The video *was* fabulous. Don't believe what anybody else tells you. Plus, now we understood, really understood, that it was only right to file the movie under Winona. As Myra, Jerry's child-bride third-cousin, she stole the show out from under the noses of all the rest of them.

As midnight neared, we were ready to turn in. We went to the window to close up and pull the blinds. The air was crisp. The stars were out. A full moon hung over us.

"What doesn't look better by moonlight?" Lenny asked as he wrapped his arms around me from behind.

I was about to say, "Nothing," but my eye was caught by movement in a window on the first floor of the apartment building across the street. I pointed my finger for Lenny to check it out too. Our sightlines gave us a clear shot of what wasn't visible from the street. Two guys were sprawled on a couch. They were as close to each other as they could get without merging. One had a remote on his crotch. They were laughing and pushing against each other.

"They're watching a movie just like we were," Lenny said. "Maybe it's another one from Winona's long line of star turns."

"That would make them almost our twins," I joked as the one with the remote hit a button on it and tossed it aside. He rolled over on the other guy and laid a serious lip-lock on him. His hands were moving so fast that clothes that had been on bodies seconds before were suddenly on the floor.

Lenny tightened his grip around my chest. "Those jeans came off so fast," he said, "they must have been watching *Edward Scissorhands*, and Mr. Remote picked up more than a few pointers."

I turned around and held Lenny as tightly as he was holding me. "A good movie, moonlight and someone as close as your own skin," I said and nuzzled Lenny's neck. "Will our neighbors' very fine example be wasted on us?"

One thing led to another, and we ended up having an exceptionally good New Year's Eve, even though your average man coming down the street might say it was nothing special.

Two days into the new year as I was vacuuming the carpet in the bedroom, I decided to just go for it and wash the windows too. I went to town on the panes with Windex and paper towels. When I was wrapping up the job and checking for streaks, I noticed some movement on the couch in that famous window on the first floor across the street. Two feet were propped up on the coffee table. White athletic socks. Bare legs. Mr. Remote was wearing boxers. He was reading a book and laughing so hard that his whole body was in convulsions. I kept buffing away and watching the scene. Without warning, Mr. Remote glanced up and our eyes met. He stopped laughing and held his place in the book with his finger. He didn't glance away. Breaking eye contact was not his style, but raising his free hand and waving was.

I waved back with my cleaning hand. The funky paper towels flopped around like old socks. This sent Mr. Remote into gales of laughter and what looked like a serious coughing fit. He stood up and got himself under control. Then he walked right up to the window and blew me a kiss. What choice did I have? I blew one to him too. The windows had never looked this good before.

I had cleaned up enough for one day and decided to go to the local bookstore for a restorative browse. Maybe I'd even run across something that would send me into gales of laughter. The place was mobbed, and the line that started at the cash register snaked around the store. As I leafed through photography books, I heard a woman who'd made her way to the counter ask a clerk, "Do you have *Celebrate Yourself?*"

I looked over to see this sweet, sort of wounded-looking woman. I imagined all the devastating things somebody nasty could throw back at her. I wanted to cover my eyes and run from the store to avoid seeing one more ugly thing happen to a person that vulnerable. But I should really have more faith in the brotherhood. The clerk simply smiled and came around the counter to help her. "I love that book," he said. "I can't tell you how many times I flip to a random page in it and I am restored."

"Oh, really?" the woman asked, almost breathless with anticipation. "Then I'm on the right track?"

"With me, you are," the clerk said and laughed. "I'm certified."

The next person in line yelled at the departing clerk, "Hey! Do I have to just hang out here while you go off to *flirt* with her?"

The clerk touched the woman's arm to have her wait a moment. He turned back toward the counter. "Sir," he said cheerfully, "someone will be available to flirt with you very soon. If you could please be patient…"

The man sputtered a little, but the woman directly behind him said, "I can flirt in an emergency. I'm certified, too. Is this an emergency?" He had no alternative but to laugh.

With that crisis apparently taking care of itself, the clerk then led the woman to the self-help shelf. Of course, I followed them like a dog, but at a discreet distance. The clerk handed the woman a copy of the book and smiled. "May it bring as much joy to you as it has brought to me," he said. He wasn't kidding her, and she knew it. If moonlight had all of a sudden appeared in the store, she could not have looked any better. She beamed at her new book as if it were her first-born.

I bought a book too, not that I needed another one. No, it wasn't *Celebrate Yourself*. And no, I didn't ask the clerk who had turned a run-of-a-mill mob scene into a party if he happened to have great balls of fire. I already knew that he had a great heart, which is even better. He also had these amazing big gray eyes. When he handed me the book I bought and my change, he said, "Hasn't today been beautiful?"

Left with Love

Lewis DeSimone

I used to run the weekly bingo game at an AIDS hospice. At the time I didn't find any irony in that—a game of chance where, with one spin of the wheel, your number is proverbially "up." If anything, I was uncomfortable only with the competitiveness, the way the game—for a few players, at least—seemed to center on the jackpot, a paltry sum of cash raised from staff and guest donations. Terry, for one, a middle-aged woman who was legally blind, came alive during those games—anxiously prodding her volunteer companion to scan her cards to let her know how close she was to winning, goading me to spin the wheel faster, call out the numbers faster, bring her closer to her winnings.

Maybe Terry was charmed. Maybe her enthusiasm encouraged Fate to pull for her. Or maybe the other players were just too sick and tired to attend carefully to the game. Whatever the reason, Terry won three out of four games each week, stacking her winnings—wrinkled dollar bills, tight rolls of quarters and dimes—on her side of the table. We all knew that she would spend the money on cigarettes from the store around the corner. In a hospice you don't bother warning people about the dangers of smoking.

Only a few of the residents consistently showed up for the game. Most simply retired to their rooms after dinner, having had enough of other people during the day—staff, visitors, and an endless stream of volunteers all looking for some way to be of use. By the time I arrived, they were ready to call it a day.

Wayne never joined us for bingo. I couldn't imagine him sitting there with the others, eyes fixated on arbitrary numbers. Somehow I knew that Wayne had no interest in games.

I wish I could tell you the details of Wayne Porter's life, but I don't really know them. I know that he was born and raised on the East Coast (New Jersey springs to mind, but he never discussed it much), that he lived off a trust fund most of his life and never held what the rest of us would call a normal job, that he was a consummate gardener, that he worked for a time as a sexual surrogate in San Francisco's permissive heyday; and I know that on a beautiful Easter Sunday not long ago, he died in a sunlit room on Maitri's north side, just minutes after I had kissed him goodbye.

I don't know the details of Wayne's life. Wayne taught me that details merely get in the way.

Finding Maitri was almost accidental. I had lived in San Francisco for four years and still didn't feel quite at home. The going joke is that you become a native after five years—rather like earning back your virginity after a long bout of celibacy (and only marginally more credible). An East Coaster at heart, I still found California—despite its charms, despite the fairy-tale livability of San Francisco, in particular—wanting somehow. As beautiful as the place was, as comfortable as my life was, all the good seemed to hover on the surface of things. Something was missing—something at the core of me and my relationships. I needed to make contact with people on that deeper level. Volunteering had worked years ago, in Boston; I had met most of my friends through my work with an AIDS organization there. Surely, I thought, the same strategy would work here.

So I visited the San Francisco Volunteer Center, to see what options existed. One of the first listings I found was for Maitri AIDS Hospice, a facility that had recently expanded from a small house in the Castro, the home of a Buddhist monk who had one day brought a dying person inside out of simple kindness, to a state-of-the-art facility on the outskirts of the neighborhood. *Maitri*, the flyer said, was Sanskrit for "compassionate friendship." I wrote down the information, but knew I would never call. The idea of working so closely with the dying intimidated me. If they had wanted clerical help, someone to write their newsletter, I would have called the next day. But sitting at someone's bedside, looking at lesions and emaciated flesh, changing the diapers of the bedridden—no, I couldn't do that.

And besides, it was Christmastime. I was too busy to start any volunteering just yet. First I had to get my holiday cards mailed. I called a new friend, Joe, to get his address. I caught him just coming in the door; he had been to a board meeting for a nonprofit he had recently agreed to help. Which one? I asked. "Maitri," he said.

That was the first sign. And wisely, I listened. I was just beginning to listen.

There are fifteen beds at Maitri, intended not just for the dying but for those fortunate enough to be recovering their strength, now that protease inhibitors and other drugs have given a whole new meaning to the word *cocktail*. The initial hope was that 40% of the rooms would be occupied by people who had been ill but were preparing to return to full functioning. But in the entire time I worked at Maitri, only one resident left to pursue an independent life. Others left for different reasons—an unwillingness to abide by the house rules; a visit to the hospital that unexpectedly became permanent—but the majority of rooms had become revolving doors for the dying.

In the beginning, I spent most of my time with Harold. Everyone's favorite, Harold was lively, musical, funny, and quite demented (I mean that clinically—hospice humor). He was restricted to a wheelchair, and his arms were unreliable. Most Thursday evenings, my job would be to feed him dinner. He loved everything—and everyone. I have never known anyone to say "I love you" more often and less discriminately than Harold. And he was never more grateful than when someone said it back. It made his day, brought out the most beautiful, toothless grin I'd ever seen.

Having Harold to visit at dinner gave me some structure in those first few weeks at Maitri. I didn't have to wonder what I would do each Thursday evening, didn't have to take the initiative to knock on someone's door or strike up a conversation with a stranger. At the training, an experienced volunteer had told the intimidating story of his own naïve first days on the job—asking one resident, a rather formidable drag queen, how she was feeling. "I'm dying of AIDS, asshole," she snapped, "how do you *think* I feel?"

I never had an experience like that at Maitri, but I knew that it could happen any time, from any quarter. Even Harold was known to say nasty things from time to time. My greatest fear was appearing intrusive—toting a patronizing smile to someone whose problems were beyond the scope of my comprehension. I girded my loins, reminding myself that my hurt feelings were nothing compared to what was going on around me: emotions heal, and at the end of my shift, I would go home on steady legs, look in the mirror and see healthy pink cheeks. In the morning, I would go back to work, among the living, and my greatest frustration would be finding a seat on the subway.

I had been at Maitri for a few weeks before I got up the nerve to knock on a single closed door. Wayne was new; he had moved in just a couple of days ago, and I was assured he was eminently friendly and eager to get to know anyone who expressed an interest. So, after feeding Harold and finishing up the bingo game, I tapped tentatively on Wayne's door.

A lanky man in his early forties—only a few years older than me— he was lying atop his bed in the corner of the room, watching television. Short-cropped hair highlighting a round, open face, he greeted me warmly and invited me to stay and watch with him. His favorite movie—*Gone with the Wind*—was about to come on. I hadn't seen it in years, so I eagerly sat in the armchair to join in for an hour or so. The dresser stood between us, so for the most part we watched in silence. During the commercials, we chatted, on subjects as varied as the antebellum economy and Vivien Leigh's love life. It was a pleasant, casual evening, but somehow I still felt I was intruding. How would I feel if a virtual stranger came into my room and plopped himself down in front of the TV?

An hour or so into the film, just after Scarlett had become a widow for the first time, I got up to leave. Spontaneously, Wayne rose from the bed and offered me a hug. The gesture startled me, and I suddenly had the urge to change my mind, tell him I could stay a little longer. But I couldn't allow him to think I was pitying him; that would be more of an insult than leaving. I had to be nonchalant about it—for his sake.

Outside, walking toward the trolley stop on Church Street, I began to cry. Wayne was upstairs, alone with Scarlett and Rhett and Aunt Pittypat, and I could have kept him company, for at least a while longer. Something had entered the room just before I left, and only now, on the street, did I feel its presence. In standing up for that embrace, Wayne had offered me love, and I had walked away.

2

After that first night, I spoke with Wayne briefly from time to time, but we didn't have much chance to talk at length. Harold always needed to be fed; there was a bingo game to run. But one Thursday evening, I arrived to find a small crowd, staff and volunteers, in Wayne's room. He had developed a fever and wasn't feeling hungry. When the others left, I sat with him throughout the evening—most of the time cross-legged at the foot of his bed, listening to the story of his life.

I don't remember it all now. The story itself wasn't the point; it was the telling that mattered. There was an openness in his manner as he related scattered anecdotes from his life, a casual demeanor that assumed I would understand, assumed we were equals despite our very different backgrounds. And charm. Wayne was nothing if not charming.

Every now and then a note of regret would creep into his voice. He'd never gone to college, and he wondered how different his life would be if he had. He seemed to think he hadn't been productive enough, hadn't settled long enough on any one thing to see it bear fruit. But those were just momentary lapses; for the most part, Wayne seemed to be at peace with his life—and more important, with his death, though that subject never came up.

I didn't say much, only venturing an occasional invitation to elaborate on something he'd mentioned—his mixed feelings about the rural northern California town he'd lived in, his obvious fondness for gardening. He wasn't just rattling on, though; clearly it pleased him to have someone to talk to, an ear to absorb what he was saying, to validate those pieces of his life that he dared to share.

Listening, I found myself falling under a spell of sorts. It was more in the way he spoke than in what he said—the quiet, calm voice, a monotone of unwavering gentility. The fever increased the effect, slowing him down, settling him. He looked at me so earnestly as he spoke, it was hard not to feel intimately connected. Even now, it's embarrassing to admit that I grew somewhat aroused, drawn to him in a familiar way, as if this weren't a hospital bed but a candlelit table in a romantic restaurant, the evening only a beginning, full of possibility. His tone was unintentionally—naturally—seductive. And I believed, for a moment, that I was falling in love. I wondered what that would be like—to fall in love with a man on borrowed time. He talked about fetching his car, which he had left upstate, and taking a weekend drive into the country with friends, and I pictured us together in the car, as on a date. I imagined being his lover, whatever that would mean at this point in his life; I imagined being his widow.

I'd been in love before, my heart opened by passion, slammed shut by pain. I'd felt this inexplicable sense of intimacy before, this disbelief in the separateness of souls. I had jumped at the chance more than once—entangling myself in the complexity of another human being, ignoring the warning signs. It was hard to read the signs after a while, each situation rich in its own palette of fantasy colors, its own denial of the rational world. Passion, I'd learned, thrived on denial, insisted on impracticality. And yet, looking back on this night with Wayne a few days later, I realized that the love I felt for him was much larger than the sexual and romantic passions of the past. It was, instead, a generic love—an all-encompassing feeling that pulled both the platonic and the sexual in its orbit. I *was* falling in love—but with something much larger and more significant than any one man.

Wayne had a prescription for marijuana—thanks to California's new and precarious law allowing the drug for medicinal use. I joined him in the courtyard of the building so that he could have a relaxing smoke. He offered me a hit, but I declined; in my position, it seemed unethical to get stoned with a resident. So we continued our conversation—in the darkness, in the chilly San Francisco spring breeze. Wrapped in a fluffy robe, he toked on his pipe in the corner while I, clutching my jacket around me, watched and listened.

Wayne had redesigned the courtyard—repotting the plants, rearranging the greenery boxes. As we sat, he pointed out his handiwork, noting that certain plants did well together, others strangled their neighbors' roots. In the corner, bookended by the greenery he had nurtured, he seemed completely at home. But through the darkness and the gentle curls of smoke, his tired voice revealed his growing weakness; the fever was taking its toll.

After a while, I walked him back inside, his hand in the crook of my elbow. We parted just outside the living room, beside the Buddhist altar where votive candles were lit in memory of lost residents. We embraced then, for a good long time—not the abrupt hug of that first night, but something deeper, more substantial. Smiling, he told me what a nice guy I was. And coming from him, with nothing to gain, I believed it. Shuffling in his worn slippers, Wayne returned to his room while I raced downstairs to catch my train and, as if it were now part of a ritual, sob my way home.

I received a call on Saturday morning from Grace, Maitri's volunteer coordinator. Wayne's fever hadn't abated. He had, in fact, refused medication for it, and now he was moving in and out of consciousness, struggling for breath. I put off going in, not sure what to expect, not sure of my ability to handle whatever it was I would have to face. I had never witnessed death before, only its sterile, funeral-director aftermath. The truth, I feared, was radically different. In the raw, I imagined, death was ugly, horrifying, and I feared looking into its eyes.

In the end, I didn't really have to force myself to go. I simply made the decision that visiting Wayne would be a part of my day—one more item on the to-do list. It was that matter-of-factness that made it possible for me to climb the stairs at Maitri in the middle of the afternoon. I thought of the yoga class I had taken a couple of years before. When introducing a new pose, no matter how difficult it was, no matter how stiff her students might be, the instructor always said soothingly, "Don't *try* to do it. Just *do* it." To "try" was to admit the possibility of failure—as if only one right way existed, as if the physical positioning of one's toes or back or arms alone determined the success of the pose, as if the pose were merely a function of the body, of time and space. And so, I didn't *try* to put on a courageous face, I didn't *try* to survive the moment. I just did.

Though his eyes were wide open, Wayne seemed unconscious— not looking at anything, not listening to anyone's words. All his effort seemed focused on breathing—another lesson from yoga, I thought, a skill I'd never mastered.

We were alone most of the afternoon. He lay on his back, angled toward the window, toward me on my chair beside the bed. I gently held his hand and strove for the same degree of presence he now exhibited—not doing, not becoming, simply being. I closed my eyes and, guided by his loud, hoarse breathing, I focused my energy on the contact between our palms, his rougher, sweatier, and so warm. I held his hand and prayed, meditated at his bedside. I prayed for the power to pass love, joy, and peace through my body and into his. I thought of beautiful things. I thought of love. I prayed, a prayer of thanksgiving— thanking God for the people in my life and the gifts I had received: my parents, who had given me life and, more or less, unconditional love; previous lovers, who had awakened feelings in me or had given me the pain I needed to grow; my toddler nephew, who had taught me the purity and simplicity of love. I thanked God for all of them, and many others. And I thanked Him for Wayne, the occasion of my prayer, my reflection. And for the first time—despite the months of yoga and my other, more private attempts—I actually lost myself in meditation, a kind of trance that I came out of minutes later in complete shock, surprised that I had been able to let go for even that long.

I gave up trying to speak to Wayne. The silence seemed so much more eloquent than my feeble attempts at conversation.

I sat with him for a few hours, his heavy, broken breath the only sound in the room besides my own occasional shifting in the chair. Finally, his eyes grew a bit more aware and he stirred slightly. "There you are!" he said quietly, nonchalantly—as if he'd never considered my being anywhere else. Or perhaps, I thought, he thinks I'm someone else, someone he needs to see. And almost instantly, he fell back into that unresponsive state, deep inside his own world. I took his words as evidence that the fever was breaking, that this particular crisis was over. I was late for a dinner date, and so, assured that he was sleeping safely, I left for the night.

That dinner was like crossing into another world, whose language I had somehow forgotten—the casual cocktail chatter of a second date (first, if you don't count a beer between strangers at a bar who an hour later tumbled into a silent bed). That first evening had been about sex, the topics of conversation no more challenging than physical compliments and sexual preferences. Tonight, Kevin was telling me about work, his family—doing his best, playing by the slow rules of comfortable courtship. I couldn't help thinking how ironic it all seemed: we hadn't thought twice about physical intimacy—but here, with a table and dinner plates between us, we fumbled for connection, as if we had never met. The words came haltingly on my side of the table, stumbling over fresh memories that left everything else in dull shadow.

Thankfully, dinner ended, and we continued the evening without speech—in the subtler, more comfortable language of nakedness and simple, primal urges. I couldn't be alone that night. Only the hard reality of Kevin's body—this insistent evidence of life—could provide the slightest consolation. I accepted it gratefully. I held my eyes and ears open, glided my fingers across every muscle, burrowed my nose into every sweaty crevice, licked the salt from his skin—to open all the avenues of sensation, every stimulus my body could contain, to focus every nerve on this single moment.

I got home the next morning to find another message from Grace. Wayne had gotten worse, she said; the nurse expected him to die that afternoon.

I made breakfast, read the paper, called my parents—all Sunday morning rituals, though they now served the added purpose of procrastination—and got to the hospice at around 1:00. Wayne was completely nonresponsive now, breathing with the harsh, stentorian rumble of machinery—not the softness of the gentle man I had come to know. The sheet pulled down to expose his bare, feverish chest, he lay completely still except for a disturbing flutter just under his sternum—as if an inch-long caterpillar were scuttling back and forth just beneath his skin. The people seated at either side of the bed introduced themselves as a cousin, Joel, and an old friend, Della—a vibrant fiftyish woman with too-red hair, lots of jewelry, and an incongruously serene expression. I sat with them for a while. For some reason, my fear of intrusiveness was gone—I had learned to be invisible in the room. And I had to be there, I couldn't leave.

Joel and Della, I learned, had been there for much of the morning; they soon left, expecting to be called if there were any changes. Their places were soon taken by Alan, a veteran volunteer I had met at my training a few months earlier. We sat on opposite sides of the bed, Alan staring into Wayne's eyes. He asked me for a swab on the nightstand at my side. He passed the pink sponge along Wayne's gums and lips to moisten them, and something in the gesture struck me to the heart— the gentleness, perhaps, the matter-of-factness, the sheer kindness it displayed. I left the room hurriedly and made my way toward the courtyard.

"Hey!" a loud voice called as I raced down the hall. It was Harold, alone in an alcove by the nurse's desk. The nurse's aides often wheeled him out here and sat with him. Harold was entertaining, and so they freely honored his craving for attention. I often had to stifle an impulse to read this as somehow exploitative, since Harold seldom found himself as amusing as they did.

I stopped, gulped down a sob, and went over to him.

"You got a cigarette?" he asked.

"No, Harold," I said. "I don't smoke."

And so the routine began—a dialogue that replayed itself each week.

"Why?"

"Because it's not good for you."

"Did you ever smoke?"

"No."

He threw me a flabbergasted look—utter disbelief. "Never?!"

"No, Harold."

Harold had a habit of digging into people's pockets—perhaps in search of cigarettes, perhaps out of idle curiosity. Ordinarily, I had the presence of mind to stand back far enough, to keep myself out of reach of his fluttering hands. But I had no presence of mind today, and already Harold was going for my pants.

"Show me your wallet," he demanded.

In the beginning, afraid to refuse him anything, I had offered Harold my wallet, watched him methodically pull out each credit card, my driver's license, a photograph of my two-year-old nephew. He had looked at each item with the fascination of a toddler and, I thought, the poignant nostalgia of someone who had once defined himself by those very objects, someone who had once carried his own identity in his pocket.

But today, I pulled back. "No, Harold," I said, drawing his hand away as gently as I could. "Maybe later, okay? I have to go do something now. But I'll be right back, and then I'll let you see it."

He looked up, cocking his head to one side, dull hair sloping over his brow. "Really?" he said. "You'll be right back?"

"Yes. I promise." And, disentangling myself at last—frankly astonished at how easily Harold accepted the lie—I rushed around the corner, toward the quiet safety of the courtyard. But now, added to the burden of what was happening in that room down the hall, was a fresh guilt. I had lied to Harold—a sweet, helpless, dying man who looked to me for support, for reassurance. Of course, he would instantly forget my promise. There were no real repercussions to reneging. But that wasn't the point somehow.

I pushed open the glass door to the courtyard—the garden that Wayne had landscaped, the spot where we had sat just three nights ago, sweet smoke rising around his head in the cool night air. I sat in a rocking chair, facing the corner where he had sat that night, and I wept. My back to the glass, so no one could see, I sobbed. I felt my heart shatter and the tears of love spill around me.

Recovered after a few minutes, I took the long way around, to avoid Harold, and returned to Wayne's room. I've lost track of most of that afternoon, and am left with the general impression of a steady stream of people moving in and out—mostly staff and other volunteers who sat for a few minutes, or stood by the bed, smiling at Wayne, stroking his hair, smoothing their hands over his pale chest. At one point, a volunteer named Karen sat across from me, each of us gazing down at Wayne. I suppose I'd grown used to his heavy breathing by then, for the memory of that moment is nearly silent until, in her sweetly modulated voice, Karen pointed out that Wayne looked amazingly beautiful. "Maybe it's just that it's Easter," she said, "but he looks like Jesus."

And I saw it. It *was* Easter Sunday, and the cover of *Parade* magazine (which I'd read on the bus coming here) had been a detail of Leonardo's *Last Supper*—a close-up of Jesus' face, which had finally been clearly revealed during the painting's long restoration. Karen was right. In the nose, the downward tilt of the head—which, in the painting, prefigures the posture of the crucifixion to come—I was looking at the face of Jesus. And the eyes—so blue, so achingly azure blue at the center of bloodshot orbs. Wayne's eyes, open the whole time, were bright, alive, despite the slow fading of the body beneath them. And I knew— I *knew*, I did not imagine, I still *know*—it was Jesus' eyes I was seeing. Jesus was speaking to me through Wayne's eyes.

I wanted to tell him it was okay to let go. But that seemed presumptuous. It wasn't my place to tell him any such thing. He would let go when the time was right. And for now, all I could do was hold on.

The room got crowded later. Alan and I were by the window, Karen beside the bed when Leslie, whose brother Greg was dying across the hall—*O holy day*—came in to visit, to escape from her own private grief. She bent over the bed and murmured, "Oh, Wayne," idly caressing his bare chest. "Oh, Wayne." I didn't hear everything else she said, but one, final line made its way clearly across the room: "Say hi to Greg for me."

Karen went round to the other side of the bed and held her. I turned away, toward the window. When I turned around again, tears begging to fall, Alan—a perfect stranger—pulled me into his arms. I held him close, pressing myself against him, and sobbed into his shoulder. I think we both were crying—or all four of us—two pairs of embracing strangers, sharing love and death.

The others left, and for a long while Alan and I sat on either side of the bed, holding Wayne in silence, or sharing our thoughts about any number of subjects, profound and mundane. It felt strange to discuss movies, books, work—the ordinary details that make up a life—while Wayne lay beneath us, between worlds. I tried to get distracted by the conversation, but it was as if there were subtitles beneath every line— *Wayne is dying. Hold fast. Wayne is dying.*

Eventually, Alan, too, had to leave. A new volunteer replaced him at the bedside, someone I'd never met before, someone who had never met Wayne. The nurse had just suggested that he come in, to sit.

The nurse had told us what to look for as a sign. Wayne's breathing would slow down, she said—more space between inhalations, a shallower sound. But still his breath came hard, labored—as if he weren't quite ready. It had been a long day, I told myself. They would call when he got worse (no longer did I allow the word *if*), when the time drew near.

And so, a few minutes later, I left Wayne in the care of the new volunteer, whose name I no longer recall. Leaning over the bed, I kissed Wayne goodbye and whispered, "I love you" in his ear. I had never told him before.

I was making dinner when the phone rang. I was terrified—as scared as I'd been with Wayne, when each pause in his breathing stopped my heart. I answered in a subdued voice, and was relieved to hear my sister-in-law on the other end of the line. We talked about Easter, my parents, my nephew. She passed the phone to my brother, and we chatted for a while longer before Mary Kate got back on the line and said, "I have to tell you the good news, because Doug apparently can't." She was pregnant again, the baby due in October.

Instantly, a tear rode down my cheek. Somewhere along the way, I had forgotten that Easter was a day for new beginnings.

Clicking off the phone to call my parents and discuss the baby with them, I heard the telltale tone that signaled a message on my voicemail. I put off checking it; I needed to be somewhat upbeat when I spoke to my parents. When we were done, when the joy was sufficiently spread, I braced myself and called for messages.

The call had arrived at 6:01—perhaps, I thought, the very moment when Mary Kate had been giving me the good news. Just twenty minutes or so after I left his side, Wayne gave one final shudder and was gone.

Wayne. My favorite. The one who taught me that the walls of bullshit we put up between each other are unnecessary. The one who taught me that intimacy is simple, that it can happen in an instant.

He went so quickly, whereas the others, who seemed so much sicker—Tom with his incontinence, Harold in his raving dementia—still lingered. Wayne, the healthy one—the one who, one evening in the dining room, had asked Tom if he needed help eating; the one who had fixed up the garden for everyone to enjoy. He had just been waiting, I suddenly realized—waiting for us all to leave, the people he loved. He died with a stranger at his side, so there would be no tears.

3

No, I didn't really know Wayne Porter. Not as he would be described in a biographical dictionary or an obituary—age, occupation, how many survivors he left behind. When obituaries list the survivors, they count only relatives and spouses. The truth is that Wayne Porter left behind 5 billion survivors—a whole planet full of people who were still breathing when he left us.

Like all Maitri's residents, Wayne had had ample time to prepare for his death. He had had years of the ticking clock—as we all do, really, if we would only tune our ears to listen. Through him, I came to see death less as a sudden rupture than a natural process, a gradual stripping away of things. To make way for death, he had let go, one by one, of the accoutrements of life. He relinquished, first, that sense of himself as immortal. Possessions went next: to come to Maitri, he had had to give up his home, his car, everything that couldn't fit in a 10 x 12 room. And in those final days, he gave up the rest—first and foremost, the pain of desire. When he drifted into that coma-like state, unable to respond to a look or the touch of a hand, he essentially was giving up on human contact—narrowing his scope, focusing down to the core of himself. But before the final surrender of breath, he reached that core, and when I looked into his eyes—Jesus' eyes—I saw it. When you strip away all the layers that life on this earth imposes, you are left with the essential thing, the thing that is the foundation for it all. You are left with love.

At Wayne's memorial service a couple of weeks later, several small glass bottles full of ashes—little parcels of Wayne—lined a table, next to photos from various chapters of his life. His cousin wanted to share Wayne with all of us, anyone who had been touched by him, however briefly. I hesitated, but finally took a bottle from the table and held it tightly, greedily, in my hand.

I had always been a city boy, never one to venture outside without an explicit invitation and much prodding. But not long after taking possession of that talismanic bottle, I crossed the bridge to Marin, to a beach on the far side of the Headlands, where the Pacific crashes loudly to shore. And there, in a tiny cove surrounded by boulders and glittering, pebble-strewn sand, I scattered the bottle's contents—a surprising mixture of gray-brown ash and bleached-white bone—into the sea. I didn't know if Wayne had ever visited this beach. I didn't know if he had even liked the water. But it didn't matter. His soul now belonged to the world, to the sea and the rocks and the sky. It was all his domain.

I lifted my hand and watched the ashes spill, floating gently on the breeze for a moment before being absorbed by the retreating tide. And beside me, against the boulders lining the shore, I saw a white flash— a ghostly figure running, dancing on the waves.

Before that Easter Sunday, I hadn't believed in much of anything. But now, after so many signs had made themselves known—after so much love—I had no trouble seeing that flash of light as Wayne's very spirit, dancing, inviting me to dance, inviting me to believe in something—to believe in myself and my capacity to love and to be loved—at last.

To this day, that image still flickers occasionally just at the edge of my peripheral vision, usually when I most need reassurance, most need to know that I am not alone, that whatever I'm going through at the moment will surely pass.

After a few waves of my arm, the bottle was empty. I refilled it with multicolored pebbles from the sand at my feet—a memento of the scene, as the ashes themselves had been a memento of Wayne.

I cradled the bottle all the way home. And back in my apartment, as I searched for the perfect spot—calm, unobtrusive—I somehow let it slip between my fingers.

The bottle crashed to the floor, glass broken into large jagged pieces, pebbles strewn in all directions—a three-dimensional Rorschach blot I didn't need to analyze. It was Wayne again, this time telling *me* to let go.

Get Thee Behind Me

Christos Tsirbas

The Devil rises out of Lake Ontario and, like the Nazarene, walks over the waves toward me. The water churns beneath him and steam billows in his wake. I am sitting on a bench watching him. Bathed in moonlight, he is regal, his every step forward measured, his posture perfect.

I am starting to sober up after spending the night drinking at one of Toronto's more fashionable bars on Queen Street West then taking the streetcar to the edge of the lake.

I'd left just before closing, after sitting at a corner table, swilling pitcher after pitcher of a potent micro-brew from Montreal. I was drinking to get depressed; it's a habit. I don't feel right without the occasional descent into despair. It's like a reset switch, an escape from my life. Most people take vacations. I get drunk and depressed, sometimes for days or weeks on end.

And being depressed makes me happy. It's a paradox that I don't question, just as I don't question the sight of the Devil before me. I've taken enough drugs to know I'm not hallucinating. That's why I'm calm and seated as the Devil alights on the quay and makes his way toward me. I'll take his reality over chemically altered perceptions any day. After all, it's easy to walk away from reality but I can't walk away from my own fevered brain.

I listen to the clipped sound of his cloven feet against the concrete walkway and admire his clothes. He is wearing a suit of fine leather that drapes his body like silk, veiling and accentuating its contours at once. I shiver delightfully at the sudden thought that the suit is made of human skin. I find the idea transgressive and yet appropriate. After all, humans are animals so why not make clothes out of our skin too?

He stops before me and looks down. He's seven feet tall, with a lean, sculpted face of bright crimson. His cheeks are hollowed, and a triangular patch of beard under thin lips punctuates his sharp chin.

The air temperature before me rises. His body blocks the cool breeze that blows in from the lake, dissipating it and replacing it with the scented warmth that rises from his skin. It is a carnal, spiced smell that lingers before me like the odor of an exotic meal or a sexual conquest lying sated by my side. But it is also the discomfiting stench of carrion and rotting plants; of forests razed to the ground. It is a whiff of the end of the world.

The Devil's eyes are obsidian, dark and luminous at once. His breath is visible: wisps of steam curl from his lips and nostrils. The air around him shimmers with his body heat. He smiles and his teeth are perfectly white, sharp.

I taste his breath in the air. It is dream and nightmare combined, a distillate of everything I've ever drunk, smoked, snorted, popped or injected into myself. Is his kiss the ultimate drug? Are his lips the key to that elusive junction of joy and sorrow that I've sought by plunging myself into depression time and again?

His mouth opens and the Devil speaks with a resonant voice that seems to emanate from the depths of the Earth. It cradles me, wraps me up in sonorous phonemes as if it were more than mere vibrations in the air.

"Show me something that matters," he says.

The tone is imperative but without urgency. It is a command spoken in the regal tone of one who expects rather than demands obeisance. I should be scared, I tell myself, but I'm too wrapped up in self-pity to feel fear.

I shift in my seat and pull the wallet from my back pocket. I hold it up to him like a schoolboy holds up his homework for inspection. "This is what matters," I say, rifling through the bills it contains. "This is all that matters."

I know that my answer is a cliché but how dare he, or anybody else, disturb my misery with a silly question?

The Devil grumbles. His eyes grow wider and he leans down toward me. A wave of sulfurous air overcomes me and I gag. "Show me something that matters," he repeats. His voice is forceful. It pulses against my skin, causing the hairs on my arms to stand. It resonates in my bones and I am made aware of the hollows in which my marrow forms.

His voice cuts through my alcoholic stupor. I know what he wants: something to take from me.

In my self-loathing, I want to give it to him. I want to lose everything and fulfill the dire imaginings that drive me to spend nights drinking.

"Follow me," I say as I start to rise.

The Devil smiles and wraps his meaty fingers around my wrist, speeding me to my feet with his searing grip and leaving my arm throbbing after he releases it. I start toward the wide concrete avenue and streetcar tracks of Queen's Quay. I hear his hooves behind me, then beside me. I glace over and above my shoulder at his massive horns, then down to his tiny cloven feet. The Devil matches my pace, though his single stride is nearly twice mine.

I strive for words but find none. Questions come to me, but I choose not to voice them. Perhaps the alcohol prevents me. Maybe I fear the answers that he'll provide. Or could it be I don't care? The being that walks next to me is proof of something; confirmation that reality is more than I've chosen to accept.

I've no wish to expand my reality.

The Devil walks by my side without speaking. His rasping breath, his clipped gait and his gunpowder scent signify his presence. His arm brushes mine and I feel as if I've been branded, as if a mark of possession has been burnt into my shoulder. I imagine myself a low-rent hustler who's been lured into the passenger side of a Mercedes. The thought excites me. The humiliation of the sex trade plays well with my lack of self-worth.

We reach the intersection. Stoplights hang above us. At our feet is a lattice of streetcar tracks. The moonlight loses itself in the orange glow of streetlamps and the harsh fluorescent illumination of office buildings. The lights of the passing cars speckle the street. It's late and there are few of them on the road. I hail the solitary cab that advances from the east. The driver speeds past us and loops around, bringing the car to a halt before us. I open the door for the Devil, who stoops, squeezes into the back and closes the door behind him. I step to the front of the cab and sit next to the driver. He'd rather I sit in the back but I ask him to consider my companion. "He's far too big to share the back with," I say and tell him our destination in midtown.

He punches the meter, heads east and takes us under the Gardiner Expressway onto Yonge Street. The temperature in the vehicle rises as we proceed. Steam starts to form on the windows. The cabbie leans into the console, switches on the defoggers and air conditioner. He watches the Devil through the rear view mirror. He can't see past the demon's bulk to the cars behind him. He casts accusing glances my way and crosses himself at stoplights. He does so discreetly, bringing his hand up to his nose and making the sign of the cross with tiny strokes, as if he were scratching an itch. He doesn't want me to see his fear.

Sweat drips down the driver's face. The fetid scent of his sweat and the tobacco on his breath commingle with the Devil's burnt meatiness. I am gagging, close to throwing up, and I don't know if it's from the stench in the car or from the excitement of riding with the Devil.

It's not that I'm scared of the Devil. He's proven himself to be real, and reality doesn't scare me. It's possibility that terrifies me. And his sudden realness makes so many other things possible.

The ride up Yonge Street seems like forever. I think of damnation: his never-ending stench would be a never-ending torment. I imagine the absence of all the fragrances that populate my life, all the delicious aromas that cohabit my every waking moment and inform my being– I think of them gone, forever replaced by a suffocating odor like the one that permeates the walls of this cab.

The Devil taps my shoulder. I feel a short, sharp stab of heat at the pinprick of his fingernail. I turn around to see that he is grinning. I've seen that self-satisfied knowing grin on countless faces in my lifetime, but on the Devil's face it is terrifying. I wonder if he can read my mind and sense what I'm thinking or where we're going. His grin widens as I mouth the word, "Why?" He leans back and closes his eyes in response.

I turn and look out the windshield again. As I do, the driver fixes me in his gaze for an instant. His deep brown eyes are moist with fear. His skin glistens with sweat. He shakes his head sadly, and without words damns me. I've seen that look before too, on other nights such as this, when I've been too smashed to leave a bar or just sober enough to make a scene.

Is that why the Devil is here? Because I am thus damned? Has he come to collect me and escort me to Hell? Am I so far gone as to merit his especial escort? Is this my last night on Earth?

"No." It is a simple answer to my unasked question. I hear the Devil in my head and my numbness turns to a dread that cuts much deeper than fear.

I feel like someone has slit my stomach and shoved the cavity full of coal. Bile and acid rise in my throat. In the reflux, I taste the bitter alcoholic tang of the night's beer. I squeeze my eyes shut and clench my teeth. I lower my head and clutch my stomach. "Hurry up," I whisper to the driver. "I don't feel so good."

The driver accelerates. There's little traffic to slow him down and the city files past us, obscured by steam. I see Yonge Street deconstructed, reduced to color, light and intimations of mass. It unfurls like an out-of-focus movie or series of impressionistic paintings. For a moment, in its lack of form, it feels more real than I and my companions in the car.

And then I see my reflection in the windshield and the reality of my situation confronts me: I want to stop the car, to run out screaming into the street and forget the entire night, starting with the second that I left my apartment, intent on nullifying myself in drink, and obliterating my ego in thoughts of self-pity. I want to forget all the assumed slights, oversights, and attacks that brought on this latest bout of anger and self-hatred. I want to pull off my skin, rip out my veins, and leach the vitriol from my bones. I welcome death if it means oblivion, but the possibility of joyless eternity spent contemplating the transgressions of my all-too-brief earthly sojourn fills me with dread.

The thought is made even bleaker as we pass Mount Pleasant Cemetery.

We are almost home. I live in a high-rise that overlooks the graveyard. On any other night, I'd think the fact funny, but on this night, nothing seems funny: The very idea of humor seems cruel.

We turn on Davisville. The driver slows to a crawl before alabaster high rises. "Right here," I say and he stops in front of my apartment building. I hand him a couple of twenties, almost triple the fare, and tell him to keep the change. The generous tip fails to elicit a smile or any words of acknowledgement. The Devil squeezes out of the back and as soon as he shuts the door, the vehicle speeds away. I imagine the cabbie crossing himself as he accelerates.

Riding the elevator up, I see myself and the Devil reflected in the mirrored walls: Infinite recursion. Eternal repetition. The same thing over and over again. This is hell in a nutshell, encapsulated in chrome and glass.

We come to a halt on the tenth floor and I lead him down a carpeted hallway that stinks of industrial strength detergent, the type that smells faintly of lavender. With leaden hands and swollen fingers, I unlock the door to my apartment. My head feels like it's floating, physically disconnected from the rest of my body.

The Devil ducks and enters my apartment. I hear the cat hiss and scurry down the hall. Before me, out of windows that rise to the ceiling, I see the lights of downtown Toronto, a jigsaw construction of orange, yellow and white, rising into the blue-black sky. Tiny red lights on rooftop antennae warn off low-flying aircraft. Curly dark masses between buildings signify trees, the green underpinnings of the city, sprouting haphazardly where concrete has yet to take root.

The apartment is softly illuminated by the city and the living room is a play of grey shadows and pearly patches of ambient light. Its familiar shapes—rectangles and ovals, the sofa and bookshelves, the tables and lamps, the paintings on every wall—are an intricate chiaroscuro construction. It seems alien to me, foreign and distant, a far-away place that I'm seeing for the first time. I've lived here ten years and have never considered it home. I've never wanted to name it thus, because that would render it far too real and things that are real are far too easy to lose. I am terrified of loss: scared that I'll be abandoned and that everything that I hold dear will vanish into the ether, forever lost.

The scent of the evening meal—a pot roast—still lingers in the apartment. It blends with the Devil's spicy bodily aroma and the mixture makes sense, as if he belongs here, a full-time inhabitant of the apartment.

I lead him down the corridor to the bedroom. The door is half-open. The cat is tensed at the foot of the bed. Her eyes fall on the Devil and widen; she whimpers, scurries under the footboard and crawls under the bed.

The Devil opens the door all the way and ducks into the room. I follow and together we both look down at the queen-size bed.

"This is something that matters," I say pointing to my partner, who is naked and sleeping on his side, with his back turned to us. The curtains are drawn apart and the windows are open. A fan circulates the summer air.

In the moonlight, he seems like a sleeping statue. The room is a study in charcoal, as if he'd stood outside his body and sketched his own portrait. His skin is pale: creamy, and smooth. He's kicked off the top sheet. It lies bunched and furled around his ankles.

I admire his strong shoulders. My eyes linger on that sweet spot at the nape of his neck and then follow the trace of his spine to his buttocks and legs. I watch him breathing, his forearm, folded over his abdomen, rising and falling. I can smell him. His scent is not lost in the Devil's aroma. It is a familiar and comforting perfume that hangs in the air before me, rising above and beyond the dour odor of damnation.

A smile forms. The thought of his arms around me floods me with feelings of safety and happiness, pushing aside my revulsion and fear, casting out the hurt that I've allowed to wash over me all night, dissipating the sense of self-pity that had caused my outburst and driven me out of the apartment, not caring a whit for his feelings.

I feel the beginnings of an erection.

How long did he sit in the living room, wondering about the root of my latest display? How long did he wait for me before going to bed? How often had I done this and hurt him? And why does he stay, excusing my behavior?

Is he desperate?

"No," whispers the Devil. "He loves you but you're still not convinced."

I turn and look up at him. The Devil smiles. He bares his sharp fangs and bores his eyes into mine. "But I don't think it's love you want." He whispers seductively and I am ensorcelled by his lascivious tone.

Curling his finger around my collar, the Devil pulls me toward him. He sucks the breath out of my body and scorches my lungs. I sweat and gasp for breath and follow as the Devil backs out of the room, leading me forward. My stomach muscles spasm and my legs quiver. My hips buckle, my buttocks clench as we move in a *pas de deux*, my steps forward echoing his steps back.

He draws me onto the balcony and stands with his back pressing the railing. We are millimeters apart, and I feel him against my skin. I am on the verge of climax. I want to let go, and in that momentary explosion, forsake my lover and forfeit my life.

This is what I've been courting.

The Devil tenses, expectant. His breath burns against my shoulder. His odor swaddles me and feeds my hunger. His muscular bulk draws me.

I almost whisper, "Take me." Instead, I squeeze my eyes shut and clench my teeth. I ball my hands into fists, tighten my scrotum and tense my entire body. I stand motionless, firm and let the excitement wash from me.

When I open my eyes, I fix my gaze on the Devil and smile. "He loves me," I say.

The Devil smiles back as I push him off the balcony.

As he falls backward to the ground, he blows me a kiss that sears my cheek and then he's gone.

I reach up and probe the burnt skin with my fingertips. I know the scar will be permanent.

Behind me, I hear the curious mewling of the cat. I turn and step back into the apartment. She rubs against my legs and scurries ahead of me to the bedroom. She jumps onto the bed and I crawl in after her, my clothes and shoes still on. I wrap my arms around my partner. His skin feels soft and cool against me. He registers my presence with a muffled moan, but doesn't wake. He presses back against me and I pull him closer, spooning.

I've spent far too much time pondering Heaven and Hell, life, the future, eternity. I've wasted years, plumbing the depths of despair, finding reasons to feel sorry for myself; discovering an endless succession of ways to sabotage my efforts and derail my life. I've contemplated the meaning of things to the point of inaction, crippling myself through self-examination.

It's time I stopped. No more of these excursions into despair. It's time I grow up and let myself be happy.

I lose myself in the warmth of my lover and his familiar scent. The odor of sulfur lingers in the air and on my clothes, a reminder of how far off-course I'd gone. My lover turns to me, half-awake with partially open eyes. He slides a hand under my shirt, the other one under my belt.

"You smell good," he says.

I smile and kiss him.

His Paper Doll

Steve Berman

"**R**ichie, what are you doing?" Han flopped down on the bed next to me. I nearly ruined the delicate cutting job I was intent on.

"Making voodoo dolls." I hadn't turned around when he'd come into my room.

"Yeah, right." I should have expected the blasé reaction. He picked up the magazine I had been using as source material. "This the latest *XY*?"

I nodded while trying to trim with scissors around the curve of a forearm I liked. It had a neat tribal tattoo around the bicep. The boy it had once belonged to looked up from the page and seemed blissfully unaware of what I had done to him.

"You're trashing it!" Han held up one glossy page I had already performed surgery on. He peered at me through the cut-out.

"Han..." His full name is Han-Kyoung. His father's American and his mother's from Korea. That makes him a gorgeous mutt. I'm taller than he is, but he has all this spiky cool hair, so I guess that makes us even.

He turned a few pages, coming to another photo spread of gorgeous guys being playful on the beach, laughing and grinning on the sand while they practically groped each other. I hadn't cut that one yet. "I want to look like those boys."

"You already do." He truly did. He was a boi with an i that stood for "i can't believe he's so yummy." 'Cept that he was my best friend so he was only sorta yummy. More like small-print yummy.

Me, well, I'd probably never be pictured in any mag. I'm the sort that you focus on a feature. Nice green eyes. Good smile. Never the total package. Han's a total package.

"Yeah, but they all have their arms around other beautiful boys. I have no one."

Inwardly, I groaned. This again. What had it been, three weeks since he hooked up? "So make a doll with me."

He rolled over on his back. "Nah. You're so weird." He began paging through the magazine.

I'm constantly being asked about Han and me. People don't ever get that we're just friends. The closest we've ever come to doing anything was hanging all over each other, sweaty and rolling in a pile, at this one rave.

They don't see that Han needs someone who won't screw him over, who will be true if that word even means anything anymore. He needs a friend, one who won't care if he does something stupid or wrong.

I tore off a strip of clear tape and added the arm to the pretty little Frankenstein in my hands. I needed Han as a guide through queer teen life, as someone who I could share all my thoughts and feelings with.

"So why the doll?"

"I told you, it's a voodoo doll. I read this book on them. Sympathetic magic, they call it."

I looked up to see him giving me that sad smile.

My creation had the face of a blond angel perched on the torso of a tasty bare-chested jock. I sighed. "Does he look like a personal portable wishing well?"

"That's going to get you a boyfriend?" His eyes squinted a moment at the doll, then shook his head. "We def need to get out."

"It's Tuesday. There's nothing to do."

"Let's go somewhere." He leaned over and made a playful grab at the doll. "You could bring your date along."

"Be serious." Now that I had finished, I felt sorta silly holding it.

"How about getting tattoos?" He lifted up his T-shirt a little to expose his flat stomach. "I could get some black flames around here." His finger circled his belly button.

"I've got no scoots. I bet your wallet is nearly empty too."

"So piercings are out, then."

I gathered up all the excess pieces that had fallen on the floor into a small neat pile. It looked like the scrapped photos from some weird manikin shop. "My mom won't let me pierce anything but my ear."

"Maybe you need to get something pierced that she won't see." He smirked.

"Gack. Think not."

Han pulled my pillow under his head. "I know what. Let's check out the Copy Center."

I rolled my eyes. "You mean check out that guy working there."

He smiled, not the least bit ashamed that I had known what he was really after. "Dana told me he's still there."

With Han there's always another "that guy." This one was an ultra-cute boi working the counter. Our little fag-hag friend Dana swore up and down that the guy was gay. Of course, she liked to think that any thin little boy who uses a lot of gel in his hair and has more than one piercing in each ear was queer. Her track record was pretty damn good though; she figured both of us out.

"C'mon, c'mon, let's go. Just come out there with me." His voice neared a whine, the last thing I wanted to hear on a dull night.

But I never could say no to him, which was probably another reason he liked to hang with me. "All right."

"You're not bringing that along?"

Actually, I hadn't been thinking of bringing the paper doll. But I still held in forgotten in my hand as I reached for my fleece vest on the chair. But the tone of his voice, so queenly sarcastic, just made me want to be contrary. "Yeah, that way when you start flirting with that boy, I won't be lonely."

"So weird." He dashed for the bathroom and spent fifteen minutes making sure his hair and face were perfect. When he came out, he looked the same.

Han wasn't due to get his permit for another six months, so we had to walk or bike everywhere when we couldn't get a ride. Thankfully, my house is not that far from the strip mall where the Copy Center was. Seems like no suburban house in Jersey is ever far from a mall.

The boy at the counter was nice. No doubt. With that certain tint of bleached blond hair all the boys in the city had—the dye box must be labled Queer #5—swept up over his forehead. He wore a necklace of thick silvery links that drooped down on the t-shirt he wore underneath his unbuttoned work shirt. His cheap shiny name badge read Bailey. I turned my head to laugh a little; with that name he never had a chance of being straight.

Han went into action, starting with a grin when they made eye contact. I decided to amuse myself by making some copies of the voodoo doll and went over to the boxy machines by the wall.

I glanced up to see how things were progressing. Han and the counter boy were leaning over the counter and chatting. Han tapped the boy's name tag playfully. It never took him long to hook up.

I made faded versions of my voodoo doll, moving the switch to Utter Light, and a Goth edition with everything pitch-black by reversing. I wasted another fifty cents on expanding the cute parts. Everything went into the recycle bin.

Boredom quickly set in.

Han came over just before I succumbed to the temptation to discover what "optional automatic duplexing" would do.

"So?"

He held up a bright yellow Post-It note with a welcome seven digits alongside an email address. Han wore the smug smile of success. "I think I know what my Friday night will be like."

I tried to look like I could care less, even though I was envious about how easy he made being gay seem.

"C'mon, let's go," I muttered, and started to trudge out of the shop. I heard him follow behind me.

Then came the jingle-jangle of the bells at the front door. I stopped in my tracks. Han bumped into me. He started to complain but then went quiet. Blame the guy who'd just walked into the Copy Center. Too much, just too much.

I fought to keep from staring at him, deciding to turn around and drag Han out with me. And maybe take a peek back at him just before the door.

Han, though, I saw, was already following the guy's every move with his eyes as he walked by. My friend almost smacked his lips in hunger. "Look at that," he whispered to me. "Bet his screen name doesn't have 'boy' in it."

I nodded, lost in admiring thought. The guy couldn't have been much older than us, but def he was no teen.

Han started towards him, but I reached out and grabbed his arm. "What are you doing?" I hissed.

He looked at me and smiled, trying to seem helpless. The same look he gave whenever he ditched me to talk with some new boy. "But he's so damn hot," he whined in my ear.

"But you just got Counter Boy's number," I said with a tip of my head towards Bailey.

Then he said it. In a voice that seemed almost innocent in its eager-puppy happiness. "There's always one more."

Both Bailey and I watched Han walk over to where the guy stood at the copy machines. I wish I hadn't seen Counter Boy's reaction. It made my stomach, maybe even my heart, sink when he went all pale and then tore up a little piece of paper in his hands.

Then I watched the guy lift up the lid to the copier... and find my doll. I had forgotten all about the thing. How stupid! I wanted the floor to rip open and swallow me up. No such luck. I blushed and looked away and quickly found that worse and had to look back.

He was showing the paper doll to Han, who smirked and pointed over at me. Again I had to blush and turn away, feeling more embarassed than humanly possible. I didn't dare look back. Bad enough Han had landing another. This guy knew me for the silly kid I really was.

"Excuse me" came over my shoulder.

He was there, standing next to me, holding out my voodoo doll. "I think you left this in the machine." He smiled, not the sort of grin you give some dumb kid to share in the awkwardness of the moment, but the sort where you truly are smiling at him—at me, I mean. I felt suddenly warm and, yeah, tingly all over.

"Thanks" was all I could manage to say. As I took the flimsy thing from him, I couldn't help but notice some weird connection... idea... I'm not sure. It's just that I was so aware how my doll had blond hair and blue eyes and so did he. Not the store-bought kind, but the real deal. So what, though, right? I mean, millions of others do too. But he also had the same trim, hottie build, and his sand-washed blue jeans were close to the same color as the turquoise of the doll's swim trunks.

"He's cute."

That startled me—I had been staring at the guy's dimples—and for a moment I had the awful sinking feeling that he was talking about Han. But his eyes never left me. The doll again.

"Thanks." I wanted to groan at my dead vocab.

I risked a glance over the guy's shoulder and saw that a dejected Han had made his way back to the counter but Bailey ignored him.

"This is going to sound weird, but just a few blocks from here there's this awesome coffee house and... well, do you like coffee?"

I didn't know what to say—I wasn't even sure right then whether I did like coffee, but the last thing I wanted was to hesitate, so I nodded and stammered out a "Yeah, sure." When was the last time I'd had a cup of coffee?

"Great." He smiled again and everything inside me went warm. I almost giggled.

He opened the door for me and I barely remembered to wave a "see ya" to Han, who stood there with his mouth both open and pouting. I had never seen him wear such an expression before.

That made me chuckle. The guy told me his name was Cameron, which is a sexy not silly gay name. He led me through the parking lot to his Jeep. A Jeep. To my mind, that meant he was fun—at least, that's how I always pictured boys that drove them. Especially when they had the top down in autumn.

The wind was strong. He pulled out fast and showy, driving wild, and I laughed at the speed. The doll flew out of my hands. I honestly didn't care.

Desiring St. Sebastian

Donald L. Boisvert

For Catholic gay men of my generation, growing up in the middle years of the 20th century—before Stonewall and the public affirmation of gay identity—devotion to male saints often provided an ideal and acceptable venue for learning about homoerotic desire, particularly since we did not really have any other culturally-validated icons of positive male submission. All the heroes of the heterosexual world-at-large were big, brawny, aggressive top males: Superman and Batman, GI Joe and the Marines, Joe McCarthy fighting off the effeminate Communists. Saints were the ideal anti-heroes for us sissy boys. Under the guise of Catholic devotion, we could indulge our most secret same-sex fantasies, fixated on glorified saintly bodies.

It was precisely their difference that was the source of their heroism. These saints had achieved their greatness by doing things that very few manly men would choose to do, largely because religion was understood as the tepid domain of women and effete males. Significantly, of course, they had attained their saintly glory by giving themselves over totally to another male, Jesus, who himself had submitted to the wishes of the most powerful of all males, God. These saints had been men in love with men: speaking, writing, declaring, and acting out their love in ways that were highly eccentric, if not at times downright suspicious. How could I not in turn love them and be attracted by them? How could I not want to be like them?

My world has always been populated with saints. When I was younger, I would play with my collection of saints' statues as one might with dolls. I loved to touch and fondle them, care for them, brighten them up for their namesake's feast day, bow to them in reverence. To this day, I still collect all sorts of statues of saints. Though I do it now for apparently more serious "scholarly" reasons, I suspect that something of my earlier playful mood persists. The Catholic Church proposed masculine saintly models to me as exemplary of how I should live. I filled in their foggy and other-worldly traits with my own emerging need for intimate male companionship. I projected myself onto them, and found myself surprisingly and pleasantly turned on by them. What more could a pious queer boy ask for? Or desire, for that matter?

Even today, though I teach and write about religion more often than I practice it, my imagination remains inhabited, if not haunted, by the richness and attractiveness of saints' lives. They still turn me on, though now the romance is colored in distinctly academic tones. I have learned to live with my hagiographic obsessions; they have sustained me. In a wonderfully perverse sort of way, much like a pornographer's luscious secrets, saints have become my private delight. But there are saints, and then there are saints.

Like so many gay men throughout the ages, I especially responded to the iconic image of St. Sebastian. Tied to a tree, semi-naked and pierced by suggestive phallic arrows, this warrior saint is the classic homoerotic symbol—not simply because he has been painted so much in Western art, most often by homosexual artists, but primarily for the desires that his imagery embodies: desires bordering on pain and ecstasy, but also on the savage and transformative allure of masculine beauty. The traditional iconography of St. Sebastian also overflows with powerful touches of deep artistic longing for youthful male beauty. The saint is always depicted in a provocative pose, flirtatious and inviting in his vulnerability. He appears to flex his torso suggestively, inviting us, as it were, to touch his alluringly saintly military flesh. This potent conflation of homoerotic beauty and holiness is what makes St. Sebastian so unique amongst saints, and it is precisely this that has transformed him into such a perennial gay symbol. He holds out the promise not only of enticing beauty, but more daringly of his body, and our devotion to it, as the locus of redemption.

St. Sebastian was above all a military saint, a member of the Roman emperor's personal bodyguard. Part of the legend that grew up around him hinted at his having been a sexual favorite of the emperor. In the countless images of the saint, this subtext is clearly evident in the manner in which his beauty is transformed blissfully through the symbolism of the phallic arrows. Here stands a saint penetrated violently, and ecstatic because of it. Equally powerful in its appeal is the suggestion that the pain "on display" was the result of a spurned lover's sexual hunger. The love of men for other men can sometimes be a dark and dangerous affair. When I gaze at a picture of Sebastian— and he is almost always drawn or painted with an attractive, muscular body—I respond to a very pressing hunger. I too want to violate such exceptional beauty, and claim it as my own. Knowing that this is the sacred body of a saint only makes my desires that much more gratifyingly perverse.

Sebastian was an elite soldier, and therefore a dominant male. Almost certainly, he would have claimed the cultural privileges accorded him because of his high standing, particularly in patriarchal Roman society. Yet the Sebastian of Christian iconography is anything but a dominant male. He is the vulnerable victim. Precisely in this passivity is found his strength, and also his attractiveness in the eyes of so many gay men. His death, so heavily charged with erotic overtones, resonates with our own sexual experience. We subject ourselves to the longings and hunger of other men, and in this submission is often found our own completion. I learned desire from this saint because he taught me to yield. He taught me that passion is above all a matter of letting go—slowly and deliberately.

In our individual and collective gay imaginations, the most enticing aspect of Sebastian's iconography is without doubt his well-proportioned muscular body. This handsome masculine beauty touches us deeply—engaging us not only aesthetically, but also at the far more visceral level of our deepest erotic fantasies: those of possession and submission. As experience has so often taught us, these are flip sides of the same coin. In submitting, we possess; in possessing, we submit. The special grace of gay life is often found in a fine and delicate mixture of the two. Sebastian issues a challenge to conventional forms of heterosexual masculinity, as do, in many significant ways, all gay men. The image of the pierced saint is unequivocal. His power emanates from his weakness. Yet what an exceptionally beautiful, affirming, and liberating weakness this is! What saintly grace!

I did not come to an appreciation of St. Sebastian until considerably later in life, once I had come out. Part of this no doubt had to do with assimilating the canons of a certain normalized homoerotic culture. By claiming our sexual preference, we learn to see and read certain commonly-accepted imagery, symbols, and clues differently. We "translate" the figure of the pierced saint into the gay icon, and we come to understand him as somehow reflective of our own identity and values. This experience, in my case, was both a Catholic and a gay one: Catholic by virtue of its focus on a traditional saintly figure, yet gay because of what the saint embodied.

At the heart of such an experience lies a paradox. On the one hand, the Roman Catholic Church continues to denounce and reject homosexuality in increasingly strident tones; on the other, its clerical culture and ritual life remain defiantly homoerotic in the extreme. In reality, this may not be a contradiction. In order for the Church to persist in its male-centered ways, it must, in the same breath, strongly condemn any suggestion or possibility of some element of homoerotic attraction within its ranks, the better to deflect unneeded attention. But such homoeroticism does not ever go away quietly; it becomes transformed into something else: hidden perhaps, but still very much there. It should therefore come as no surprise that devotion to saints—a central motif of traditional Catholic culture—should become a conduit, an alternative venue, for same-sex longing and attraction. What I was doing in seeing these male saints as vehicles for my desires was simply tapping into something already there, something powerful and lasting that the Church itself had enabled and encouraged, and for which I was and am more than a little thankful. Re-imagining male sanctity as same-sex longing is essentially subversive work.

Something deep and permanent continues to draw me to the saints. In my youth, I wanted to be one, like many Catholics of my era. We were expected to try to become so; the call to sanctity was universal. In my innocent adolescent quest for holiness, I was only responding to what Catholicism expected of all it adherents. But a nagging question remained: how could I possibly ever reconcile my attraction to other boys with some broader life purpose? How could I like men and somehow be spiritual at the same time? This question, I believe, lies at the very heart of the gay presence in the world, and of gay spirituality and sanctity more specifically. It summons us to consider why we are as we are, and why we do what we do. Why are we so concerned with beauty in the world?

It is possible that any number of male saints may have been homosexual, though this can really never be fully proven in any traditional way. Perhaps the question needs to be considered differently. Why would it not be possible to imagine that many of these saints struggled valiantly and heroically with their same-sex desires, and that their truly exemplary lives and grand works of Christian virtue and charity may have been, in fact, the means for them to channel their homoerotic hunger? This does not negate or deny genuine sanctity; it simply gives it more depth. And why can gay men not partake of this sanctity through their own inspired quests for order, creativity, and service in this world?

The great discovery—the resolution of the paradox—is that it is precisely by being true to my homosexuality with its longings for beauty, harmony, and intimacy with equals, that I may indeed have achieved a kind of saintliness. This isn't what the Church thought it was teaching, but this is the ultimate truth: being a good gay man could be one way of becoming a saint.

Avalokiteshvara at the 21st Street Baths

Toby Johnson

One night in the late 1970s, I checked into the 21st Street Baths a few blocks from my San Francisco Noe Valley apartment. Within five minutes I felt I'd made a mistake. There were very few people in the place. None of them looked attractive to me and nobody seemed to find me attractive.

There was only one guy I was even vaguely interested in. He was boyish-looking, with short-cropped, dusty blond hair, a round face, not really pretty but appealing in a wholesome way; he was thin, but with solid shoulders and a tight abdomen. He wasn't exactly my type, but cute. I passed him coming out of the locker room area, then saw him again walking the long hall of mostly empty cubicles. He didn't seem to even acknowledge I was there. That's the way the baths are, I told myself.

I watched TV awhile, delaying departure in case somebody else showed up. In night-life time, the evening was just starting. I wondered why I'd come. Earlier I'd been feeling lonely. I really need to be touched, I told myself as I'd headed out down the backstairs and into the dark night when everybody in the building should be asleep. I could still feel that neediness all through my chest; my heart still burned with longing. It had led me here. I wasn't ready to go back home yet.

I wandered around the place, checking out the wet area, then the hall of cubicles again and back through the TV room. Interesting, the different smells. I wasn't sure I liked them all. I went upstairs and into one of the common rooms. A red spotlight illuminated the entrance, but otherwise the large space with cushioned platforms around the walls was pitch dark. It was impossible to tell just how big—or how small—the room really was. Of if there was anybody in there. As I made my way into the darkness, a hand reached out and touched me on the thigh. I looked, but could not see who was there. I automatically resisted. What if I were being groped by somebody unattractive?

Well, no wonder you're lonely, I said to myself. If anybody chooses you, you assume you wouldn't want them. You're caught in the webs of karma: getting rejected because you reject others.

As my eyes adjusted, I saw it was the guy I'd noticed earlier. I moved closer. We started in on the kind of impersonal play that goes on in the orgy room at a bathhouse, but then soon changed tempo. We lay down on the platform, side by side, facing each other, holding one another tenderly. Violating the stolid silence, the young man introduced himself to me as Jim. "You seem sad," he said.

Realizing the opportunity for communication, sensing the openness on Jim's part, and wanting more from this meeting than just sex, I told him about my earlier loneliness, my longing for love and my disappointment with the baths as any sort of remedy. Jim listened carefully. Occasionally he murmured or squeezed me to let me know he was paying attention.

I surprised myself talking out loud in such a place. There wasn't anyone else in the room, so we weren't disturbing anybody, but still... Wasn't this a breach of bathhouse etiquette? Though wasn't it wonderful? And I surprised myself with the depth of honesty I displayed. I started talking about my interior life. I recounted several major spiritual experiences in my life, acknowledging that I found the clash between my spirituality and my liberated gay sexuality confusing.

We lay together in an embrace that was not entirely sexual, but was not unsexual either. His body felt so good in my arms. His skin was soft and smelled slightly sweet. His chest felt supple and warm as we pressed together. We shifted in one another's arms sliding slowly against each other, gently belly-frotting to keep renewing our arousal. I was vividly aware of his flesh, slightly electric, against my chest and of our cocks lying full but not quite hard between us.

He said he was a switchboard operator at Langley Porter, the psych hospital at U.C. San Francisco. But otherwise didn't say much about himself—other than that he too struggled with joining his spirituality and his sexuality. He commended me on being spiritually inclined and coaxed me to talk some more.

I told him about my past as a Catholic seminarian and my conversion, by way of Carl Jung and Joseph Campbell, to a kind of New Age Buddhism. I told him of my effort to live a good life, to be compassionate and sensitive to other people, to participate in my culture and in my society, to pursue a right livelihood as a gay counselor, to be politically and ecologically aware, to live responsibly, and not to cause harm or pain—to discover how to be a saint as a modern gay man. I told him about the sorrow that seemed to come to me, in spite of my good efforts, instead of joy.

Almost lecturing him, assuming he wouldn't know about such things, I explained how Buddhism teaches that all existence is sorrowful. I lamented the pang of sorrow I found in being gay—not from guilt or negativity, but from the frustration of seeing such sexual beauty all around me and feeling—on the ego level—inadequate to participate, but beyond that—on some metaphysical level—simply unable to possess it all.

"So many men, so little time," he joked with one of the war cries of the Sexual Revolution.

"But on a much deeper level," I replied. "It's like I want to be everybody and know their lives from inside and feel their flesh as my own."

I told Jim about my fascination with a particular Mahayana Buddhist myth. "The Bodhisattva Avalokiteshvara was this enlightened being who chose to renounce nirvana and remain within the cycles of reincarnation. Out of generosity, he vowed to take upon himself the suffering of the world in order to bring all beings to nirvana with him. He's a world savior—a little like Jesus.

"When I first came across this myth, maybe without realizing what I was doing," I said, "in a burst of fervor I committed myself to this story. I made the bodhisattva's vow. Does that mean I'm doomed to suffer? And is the suffering a gay man gets these days the loneliness and isolation that comes with living in a sexually active environment, maybe getting sex but never quite finding the love, just the frustration and disappointment?"

This was in the 1970s, before AIDS. The metaphysical suffering of the gay community had not yet become physically manifest in sorrowful deaths all around us, as it would in a few years. I was later going to see just how appropriate the bodhisattva's willingness to take on suffering would prove. If Buddhist monks down through time had emulated this story by making the bodhisattva vow, a lot of them were certainly likely to get reincarnated in the nuclear age and as homosexuals in the days of AIDS.

"Is this a holy way to live?" I asked.

A long silence ensued. We slid against each other and roused the pleasure in our bodies again.

"That's a pretty dismal interpretation of the story," Jim answered finally. "Isn't a better interpretation that since the bodhisattva took on everyone's incarnation, he is the One Being that is reincarnating? You can rejoice that he accepted your karma. You are him. You are everybody. The Being in you is the Being in everybody else. Embracing the suffering of the world doesn't mean being unhappy. It means deciding that everything is great just the way it is, that life is worth choosing—in spite of sorrow. That'll actually bring happiness.

"The Bodhisattva took on the suffering of the world in order to transform it and save sentient beings from suffering, not to glorify suffering or get people to feel guilty about being happy and punish themselves. That sounds more like a Christian misinterpretation of the story than the bodhisattva wisdom."

I was surprised by his answer. "You know about the bodhisattva?" I asked.

"Yes, I know," Jim said and smiled enigmatically in the faint red light of the orgy room.

"You mean you know about Buddhism?"

"I mean, I know about accepting everyone's incarnations."

"You know about Avalokiteshvara?"

Jim looked into my eyes with a profound gaze. "I know I am Avalokiteshvara," he said.

"You mean like we all are?"

"Like I am."

All of a sudden, to my dismay, I understood this man to be saying not simply that, like all beings, he was a manifestation of the Central Self that in Mahayana Buddhism is mythologized in the story of the

Bodhisattva Avalokiteshvara, but that he was, in a unique way, a specific incarnation of that divine being.

I felt my world whirling out of control. I was in the presence of one of my most beloved of gods—right there in the flesh: Avalokiteshvara holding me close, in the orgy room at the 21ˢᵗ Street Baths. A thrill of excitement, mystical wonder, bewilderment, and consolation coursed through me.

I experienced linking my soul with that of this other man, chakra by chakra. In my mind I could perceive a red-orange light surging back and forth between us, connecting us at each of the energy centers, brightest and hottest at the level of our hearts. I felt an enormous rush pouring through me—body and soul. In a certain way you could say I was falling in love and feeling love's joy. I could feel that flame burning in my heart, but now not as longing but as bliss.

My head spun. I seemed to have entered into some truly "underworld" state in which the gods took on real flesh. I wondered if I'd gotten delusional. I wondered if we were both just playing a game with one another, spinning out the implications of a mythology we both happened to know about. Maybe he was just another stoned hippie like me carrying on with all this new age stuff.

What did it matter? Whatever was happening, it was marvelous. Far more than just having found somebody to have sex with. This wasn't even exactly "sex," but it was fully satisfying of the loneliness I'd felt earlier. Whoever he was, he was manifesting the bodhisattva truth. What did it matter?

As if addressing my bewilderment, Jim said, "Have faith."

"What do you mean?"

"Faith that things are never totally true or totally false, faith that life won't destroy us, that nothing really matters because it's all okay." He laughed. "Live in the present. Don't try to possess the world, have faith in the world.

"You said you made the bodhisattva's vow in a burst of religious fervor. I think that was transcendental memory. In your soul—in who you really are—you remembered making that vow as Avalokiteshvara. That's how you came to be incarnated in this particular life."

"Wow."

We both breathed deep and rolled over so he was on top. Squirming together, we rekindled our arousal. It was very loving. Very affectionate—maybe he kissed me on the neck. And very intense. Then we both relaxed, pulled apart and looked into each other's eyes. He smiled. "Time for me to go."

"Can I see you again?" I asked, already feeling bereft.

With a tone of gentleness in his voice, "Don't cling," he replied. It sounded more like wisdom teaching than rejection.

A pang of loss struck me, but I understood the spiritual lesson to live in the present and not to be attached, to enjoy the joy I was feeling without trying to possess and hold onto it.

The story of Avalokiteshvara is a charming savior myth for gay people. Maybe better than the story of Jesus. The problem with the latter story is that Jesus's saving act was being sacrificed to an angry God in atonement for sin. And in traditional Christian belief, sexuality, the thing that defines our gay lives, is manifestation of that sin. Besides, for that story to make sense you have to believe in a God who can be angry about human behavior, who makes rules and who demands suffering as atonement. The bodhisattva's saving act was being sensitive, feeling compassion. In this story, suffering is just part of life, not a punishment for anything. And his saving act wasn't about who God was, but about who *we* are.

On the mystical level, though, the stories of these two "world saviors" are not opposed to each other, indeed, they're complementary. Christians are supposed to see Christ in every person they meet, Buddhists to realize Avalokiteshvara is the one soul incarnated in everybody. The reincarnation mythology does explain the mechanics of how Avalokiteshvara could become everybody. The mechanics of Jesus's presence, through grace, isn't as obvious, though is clear in his teaching: "Whatsoever you do to the least of these, that you do unto Me." This was Jesus's own realization: that he was one with the Central Self. And this is a recurring motif in Christian mysticism. In fact, the experience of meeting a sex partner in an unlikely place and discovering him to be an incarnation of one's savior—as I just described—is the only slightly veiled story of the most famous mystical poem in Christian history, "On a Dark Night" by St. John of the Cross.

The Bodhisattva Avalokiteshvara is described as lovable, attractive and appealing. He is often shown as a young man sitting bare-chested in a casual meditation pose, one leg curled up under him in a half lotus, the other hanging relaxed over a wall. He's sweet, sensitive, gentle, kind, handsome. He's loved by everyone who knows him. He delightfully blends masculinity and femininity, demonstrating the best of both.

He sounds like an archetypal ideal gay man, doesn't he?

The story tells that just as he is about to enter nirvana, he hears a groan go up all around him. He comes out of his trance to ask, "What's this groan? I was about to achieve my goal of lifetimes of meditation." And all nature answers in a single voice, "O Avalokiteshavara, we are happy for you that you are about to achieve your goal of lifetimes, but we are also sorry. Life is hard. Your presence among us has been such solace. We all love you. We're going to miss you. And we are sorry to see you go. It is for ourselves that we groan."

So Avalokiteshvara vows to remain behind to let all the others enter nirvana before him: "Better for one to suffer than for all." That's how he becomes all beings: out of compassion, out of sensitivity to the pain of others, out of generosity, and out of human kindness.

The basis for ethical behavior is to realize that the self in each of us is the same self, the Self of Avalokiteshvara. That's why we ought to treat one another well, because it is ourselves we are treating. Therefore the reason for being good isn't because we *ought* to, but because, seeing who we really are, we *want* to.

There are four virtues associated with the Bodhisattva. These describe how we'd naturally live when we realize who we really are: compassion, loving kindness, joy in the joy of others, and equanimity. Isn't "joy in the joy of others" the basis of the Sexual Revolution?

Offering a lovely image and myth for meditation, this story is rich in meaning for gay people. There are said to be "Three Wonders of the Bodhisattva." Joseph Campbell—the great light and "wise old man" of my own spiritual journey—wrote glowingly about this myth, calling it The Way of Joyful Participation in the Sorrows of the World.

The first wonder of the Bodhisattva is the androgynous character. Avalokiteshvara pleasingly blends masculinity and femininity, transcending gender distinctions.

The second wonder is the annihilation of the distinction between life [*samsara*] and release-from-life [*nirvana*] symbolized by the Bodhisattva's renunciation of nirvana and willingness to remain in the rounds of incarnation for the joy of seeing all others saved.

The third wonder of the Bodhisattva myth is that the first wonder (namely, the bisexual form) is symbolical of the second (the identity of eternity and time).

So the first wonder is that there is no difference between masculine and feminine. The second wonder is that there is no difference between earth and heaven. And the third wonder is that the first two wonders are the same.

Overcoming the distinction between male and the female is a clue to overcoming the distinction between time and eternity. To be free of gender roles and obsession with duality is a step in seeing that life in the flesh is the experience of being in heaven now. The religious quest isn't about escape from reality into an otherworldly paradise or judgment against other people's sin, but the "joyful participation in the sorrows of the world" right now.

We've got it backwards: we tend to think the world is outside us and that we're inside. In fact, "we" are the phenomena that are happening in our experience. We—our egos—are made up of all these events going on around us. And it's all really going on inside our heads along the surface of our brains as we perceive and cognize the phenomena that is generated by interacting with other beings and that is then projected as outside. *We* are what's outside.

What is inside, the Being having the experience, is God. God is the witness of the universe, perceiving from every possible perspective. Each perspective is the lifetime of a particular incarnated sentient being. And Avalokiteshvara has taken on the incarnations of all beings.

His multi-syllabic mouthful of a name, parsed one way in Sanskrit, means "The Lord Who Looks Down in Pity"; parsed another way, it means "The Lord Who Is Seen Within."

So who is really down inside each of us, having our experience— sensing our bodies with their organs of taste, smell, hearing, sight, and touch that respectively generate the world of 5-dimensional spacetime, feeling our feelings, thinking our thoughts, perceiving our conscious- ness—is this cute, sweet, sensitive, kind, generous, sexy, sensual, lovable young gay man who blends masculinity and femininity so attractively that he comprises all possible human incarnations.

At the heart of the cosmos is Avalokiteshvara. And we gay people are like him and radiate his good traits when we honor our homosexuality as our experience of oneness with God.

Maybe what we human beings, incarnated in these physical bodies, experience as pleasure in the flesh is our souls' recognition in each other of our common identity as the bodhisattva choosing to reincarnate in all flesh. Maybe pleasure is Avalokiteshvara's recognition of himself in his other incarnations.

After Jim disappeared into the dark of the bathhouse, I lay there on the platform with my heart beating like crazy. "Avalokiteshvara's real," I kept saying to myself. The longing and neediness in my chest was gone. The fire that burned was happiness. What a wonderful night!

How odd that a bathhouse would be the locale for such a deep spiritual experience. But maybe that was just perfect. What an important insight: sexuality and spirituality are really just different faces of the same affirmation of life-force, *élan vital*. In heterosexual contexts, this life-force reveals and manifests—and creates—the duality in nature and thereby procreates new life. In homosexual, it reveals and manifests—and creates—the unity of cosmic consciousness and empowers us to love the world and each other, and strive to make it a better place for all our other incarnations. For all it can be a source of love, joy and affirmation. We just need to see things differently. There is no difference between time and eternity. This *is* heaven here and now. That's the secret.

That incident at the 21ˢᵗ Street Baths changed me. Here I am, thirty years later, still telling the story. It affirmed my belief in a healthy spiritual life lived in the styles of modern gay culture. It caused me afterwards in gay settings to bless the other men and women there, seeing their beauty—like Jesus's lilies of the field, wishing them grace, perceiving them all also as manifestations of the One Being, intending for them that they also discover their god manifesting to them in the form of another gay person to show them love and bring them joy.

Manifest Love

David Nimmons

Manifest Love was born on a Fire Island dance floor in July, 1999. The day before, I had received word that my father had died suddenly. After a day of solitary grieving, the next evening I went out dancing with my lover and friends. I went among men as my rite to bid goodbye to the first man in my life. Over the evening, friends came by, offering a hug or smile. Feeling the support of my tribe, buoyed by the radiant joy of the room, looking out over the throng of sweaty, shirtless men, I began to really see how sacred is the experiment we were involved in. In that room were many of those I held most dear; men who had cared for each other and for countless ones we had lost. I felt myself in community bonded heart, soul, and body in an intricate dance with our forms of love. As I danced, I communed with my father, friends and feelings. As the night rolled into dawn, I silently asked that his spirit transition in peace, sure in the knowledge that his youngest son was in such good hands. Then, as a parting benediction, I opened up and asked: "Dad, do you have any last message for me?"

As clearly if they had been spoken in my ear, in that way we have of knowing fully without hearing, two words echoed: manifest love. It felt electric. The words seemed to carry both a description of the scene before me—an example of what love, manifest, looked like—as well as a commandment, a consecration to action. That night began a process of first seeing, then naming, then embodying, what it is that makes this tribe of men so special. It opened a window on the soul beneath our collective skin, and began a quest to help us enlarge the truths that we—and the larger culture—know about what it means to be gay. From that moment grew the project, Manifest Love, which has now come to include several thousand men here and abroad.

For forty years, gay men have conceived and defined our primary cultural work to cleave out social space for our sex lives and create institutions and venues for supporting sexual experience and adventure. What has developed is nothing short of amazing. Yet the possibility that such innovations may hold anything important, humane, or liberating goes largely unaddressed in majority culture and media. At best, our practices are viewed with studied silence; at worst, with wide-eyed alarm and ferocious distrust. Our culture is everywhere misrepresented, even to ourselves, always presented in the dimmest light. In the cliché, the glass is always shown as less than half empty when it is really more than three quarters full.

Consider: the sensationalized statistics that a third of gay men fail to practice safer sex equally means that two thirds of gay men in those studies do consistently practice safer sex. When you look at the motives for such behavior, you discover it is often based in altruism, compassion and concern for other gay men as brothers, not out of fear or avoidance of sex and intimacy. Perhaps we're not those promiscuous, uncaring sluts recklessly endangering our own and others' lives, but caring and compassionate comrades seeking bravely to reach out to one another with a new vision of sexual connection.

Consider: the early headlines about HIV being spread by gay men who donate blood or about homosexuals who want to be Scout Masters, soldiers, teachers, or priests actually show that gay men have notable tendencies to volunteer, to be caretakers, social servants, indeed, saints and prophets. Yet when do we hear about gay men's uncontrollable urges to volunteer or help the needy?

The scary headlines that domestic violence is a scourge in gay communities mask the reality that, in every other situation, we demonstrate a remarkable absence of public violence. To be sure, any domestic violence is too much, and for those involved, the human cost is as real and hard as a clenched fist. Yet two facts ring with absolute clarity. First, that it is hard to make the case that gay men's domestic violence levels are any higher, and they may in fact be lower, than in the dominant society. But second, and far more important, is that when one widens the analytic lens to include the full range of violent assault behaviors—not just domestic violence but public violence, bar brawling, street violence, mass gatherings, and bias violence—one conclusion emerges clearly: we have created one of the most peaceable populations of males on the planet.

Gay worlds are a complex patchwork, shaded with different colors and hues, intersecting stripes, as interwoven as they are distinct. It is not, as the media—mainstream and our own—present, all white, all pumped, all employed, and all in the same Castro zip code. As you gaze deeper into this rich male mandala, read the studies, sift the weight of factual evidence accumulating in sociology, criminology, anthropology, public health and epidemiology, hear men's stories and dreams, hang out in gay environments, you cannot help but be struck by the variety of innovations in the lives of these men.

If gay men were simply finding new ways to be with each *other*, it would hold some descriptive sociological interest, like a treatise on Mennonite or Hopi Indian customs. But upon examination it becomes clear that the breadth and scope of gay male social innovations have no clear parallel in contemporary culture. Most males just do not relate to other males in the ways we do. Yet the virtues and strengths of our connections with one another are often dismissed as marginal and insignificant.

Imagine that another group of men, say a previously little-known order of devout monks, has been discovered living scattered among the populace in our major cities and countryside. Social scientists document that these brothers are characterized by a virtual absence of public violence, high levels of service and volunteerism, and novel forms of caretaking with strangers and each other. Researchers further note that they manifest an uncommon amity across gender lines, enjoy distinctive rituals of bliss, worship, spectacle, and public play. Their patterns of friendships are deep and powerful, with wide-ranging networks of intimate and intertwined social relations, whose members often live in closely woven networks of intentional communities.

Were such a hypothetical band indeed found, the discovery would arouse keen excitement. The brotherhood and its members would be lauded, lionized, hailed as role models, if not canonized. The President might cite them in his State of the Union address; the Pope would praise them as moral exemplars. Before you know it, Time Magazine would put them on its cover and they would be trooping onto Oprah for their fifteen minutes of media spotlight.

Yet although every one of those attributes has been well documented in the cultures created among gay men, the wider culture seems to have missed the story that these homosocial laboratories are brewing a set of values experiments without modern precedent. We've gotten no calls from *Time* magazine, no invites to the White House, not a peep from the Vatican. Not even a message from our pal Oprah.

Objectively, we are innovating in areas of male care and nurture, altruism and service, brotherhood and peacefulness. We are crafting powerful changes around bliss and ecstasy; gender roles and sexuality; intimacy, friendship, and communalism. Yet because it is homosexuals who are both the innovators and subjects in these experiments, their dimensions have gone largely unremarked, their meaning virtually unseen.

The metaphor of the monks is closer to truth than it might first appear, for one would have to examine highly determined male cultures—religious orders, intentional spiritual brotherhoods, fraternal organizations, places where rules and codes are formalized and enforced—in order to observe such similar male patterns. These habits, customs, and practices in our communities, this gay culture of male care, pacifism, intimacy, and service, recall a range of spiritual teachings. Yet in gay neighborhoods from San Diego to San Antonio to Seattle, one sees these habits arising natively, as everyday social practice, as indigenous manifestations of chosen social norms.

It would be easy, and wrong, to read these observations as a smug brief for gay men's superiority. Instead, we can put forth a more nuanced set of claims. First, that the lives that many gay men have been building do indeed hold demonstrable, culture-changing implications both for ourselves and for the larger society. Second, that we have long overlooked them in part because the accustomed stories offered to, told among, and accepted by gay men dangerously obscure central truths about the values evolution we are engaged in. Third, that viewed together, these queer cultural experiments can best be understood as a new, evolving public ethic. They are complex and contested, they do not happen everywhere nor uniformly, and not all of us are included in them. But throughout, they have a rich ethical basis in thought and theory, in action and relation. They represent the birth of a new set of male possibilities, outlined in lavender.

The fourth implication may be, to some, the most provocative of all. Far from describing some latter-day Sodom, a society of sluts and sybarites, many of the customs of gay enclave cultures echo traditions of Judeo-Christian brotherhoods and intentional communities. Stroll down Eighth Avenue, La Cienega Boulevard, or Halstead Street, and you can just hear echoes of utopian philosophic traditions of caritas and beloved community. You may well feel you've stumbled into a postmodern rendering of Whitman's "dear love of comrades." You might almost imagine we are a society of friends, if only we knew it.

Queer-inspired practices, from Radical Faerie gatherings to AIDS volunteer buddy teams, shimmer with notions of communal caretaking and altruism. At their best, they recall nothing so much as New Testament teachings of *agape* and *caritas*, male embodiments of service and nurture, nonviolence and gender peace, brotherhood and friendship, all spiced with equal dollops of sexuality and spectacle. Only in this case, the apostles are wearing Calvins or Abercrombie and Fitch... and sometimes not even that. Yet look at the soul beneath the skin, and you see we are rewriting the defaults of what a culture of men can be with and for each other.

Obviously, the conventional wisdom that gay men are narcissistic sex addicts and sinners living in a marginalized demi-monde of drugs and disease, creating nothing but problems for police and public health authorities (a set of opinions diametrically opposed to the facts) makes sense only if one believes that our larger culture gained nothing of value whatever from explorations of sex and gender in the 1960s. Or that, even if it did back then, that America has nothing further to learn about sexuality. But if either of those isn't true—if we're not in sexual Jerusalem yet—then small wonder gay men's sexuality frightens the culture's horses in such a big way. For we embody a far more subtle and unsettling truth.

Perhaps sexual explorations bring not just costs, but unsuspected collective and individual benefits. At this historical moment, gay men are so troubling precisely as living, breathing proof that a subculture can play by different rules. We bring erotic tidings that many would prefer stay unheard: that humans are blessed with open hearts and willing bodies, the better to enjoy a robust erotic communion with each other. In a larger society that has resolutely held its erotic fantasies and desires at bay, we are a reminder that one could instead invite them in to sup—and have them stay the night. Even more disquieting, that maybe, just maybe, we could all awake in the morning to find our humanity not only intact, but vastly enriched. What then?

Our queer sex narrative is less a mere morality play of wanton hedonism than a stunning cultural accomplishment. It presents a systematic cultural elevation and recognition of the power of the erotic, a celebration of collective carnality. At its best, it is bounded by ethics and informed by care, and nurturing of relationships. It can open doors, personal, dyadic, and collective—although we have work to do to fully realize those promises.

Millions of gay men have built the planet's most unabashedly sex-affirming culture. We have done it in a few short years, in a nation moving away from erotic pleasure, conflicted about sex, ashamed of bodies, and increasingly vocal about our suppression. Yay for our side. But what if it turns out that sex is just a proxy? We built such unparalleled sexual cultures when we imagined that sex was what made us unique. Our sex and bodies were how the larger society saw to name us as different, and for years, they were how we ourselves grasped our prime difference. So we manifested that into being, big time. But our sex may be just the most visible marker of our cultural invention. The sex is the part the world has most easily seen: the iceberg above the water line. But what if it blinded us to something else all these years?

What if all that sex—that lovely, magnificent, sticky, daring, tender, piggy, bold, sweaty sex—is but our opening act, a way to learn what we can do together, a dry run for the glorious transformation we can make when we put our will to it? Given our unnamed habits of nonviolence, service, caretaking, altruism, intimacy—the hundred ways that we rewrite the rules of men—our deepest cultural innovations may be less about male bodies than about male hearts.

It's time to ponder the F-word at the center of gay lives. No, not that one. I'm talking about friendship, silly. But you went there, didn't you? Of course you did. Our sexual exploits often steal the headlines, yet when you cast an eye beyond the bedrooms, backrooms, and baths, a far more profound set of gay affectional innovations comes into view. For we are rewriting the rules and habits of intimacy. The very practice of friendship is being reinvented in gay worlds.

In a remarkable essay, "Friendship as a Way of Life," French philosopher Michel Foucault defined friendship as the core philosophical issue of queer men's lives: "Affection, tenderness, friendship, fidelity, camaraderie, and companionship. Things which our rather sanitized society can't allow a place for... That's what makes homosexuality so 'disturbing': The homosexual mode of life much more than the sexual act itself. To imagine a sexual act... is not what disturbs people. But that individuals are beginning to love one another—there's the problem."

Foucault argued that openly gay worlds offered "unique historic opportunities for an elaboration of personal and ethical creativity analogous to that practiced by certain moral athletes in classical antiquity. Only now such creativity need not be restricted to a social elite or a single, privileged gender, but could become the common property of an entire subculture."

Understanding how we do that, to more fully recognize the values we demonstrate in our actions, is now the goal of our collective effort. The first step is to name those special parts of being gay that we don't usually talk about. This does not imply an uncritical or simplistic queer rah-rah boosterism. Nothing in this discussion is intended to "build esteem" or "create" pride or "show our best face to the world." The goal is simply to tell the whole truth we know in our lives, and what we may feel in our gut. That is, to widen the analytic lens to view more of ourselves and our practices. We need to recount our wisdoms as well as we do our warts, lest we be telling only half a truth. Yet all that truth-telling is just preparation for work in the real world. Because it turns out that if we seek to feel love manifest with those in your life, we need to manifest love.

This is the work that—since that moment in 1999—I have devoted my efforts to and for which I and my friends have organized the national project Manifest Love. The goal: to help gay men find new ways to be with and for each other. We do practices, rituals and actions we call "Loving Disturbances." They are just that: innovations and experiments in applied affection, concrete real-world experiments devised to nudge the patterns and practices of gay lives in more affirming and humane directions. They are social actions that bring values into being, the action core of Manifest Love's local work. They may happen at a bar, on the street, in a sex club, online, or in a meeting, between friends or tricks or neighbors. They may happen alone or with others. The point is to broaden the habitual patterns of queer men's cultures to help us meet and interact in new ways, and have fun doing it. A Loving Disturbance aims to leave a corner of the queer world just a little better off—a tad more affectionate or less defended, slightly more in line with the values discussed here, a moment aglow with an aura of promise fulfilled. (If you want specific examples, take a look at our webpage: www.manifestlove.org or the book, *The Soul Beneath The Skin :The Hidden Hearts and Habits of Gay Men*)

I hope you will hear the invitation in my analysis of our collective culture, and join me. Together—as friends—we can live up to the promise that brought us together in the first place: a community of men who manifest love.

Neighborhood Walk

Steven A. Hoffman

My husband, Brady, looked up at me with bloodhound eyes. The over-turned feeling that had developed in my stomach knotted itself a little bit tighter. I hoped that one day it would right itself. Brady spoke so quietly that I could barely hear him under the glowing din of the local news. "Gary, let's take a walk," he said.

I looked at his gentle, yet worn face and nodded. Out in the open was the best place for us to be.

Without another word, we left our house. On the porch, Brady plucked some of the expired blooms from their stems in one of his many arrangements of perennials. He looked at the windsock hanging from the gutter above the porch. With so many houses in the neighborhood decorated with colorful banners and flags, either nobody realized or didn't care about the significance of the rainbow colors in front of our house. He gave the still windsock a gentle spin and we headed up the street.

Ed Wiley, our next-door neighbor, was raking rust-colored leaves into small piles. Watching him organize his debris-filled yard with only one arm amazed me. Ever since we moved into the neighborhood, Ed and his wife Sherry had always been friendly and willing to help us with all of the surprises and joys of first-time home ownership. Even before his crash, Ed would fix leaks, suggest the best gardening supplies and lend us his monster ladder so we could clean the gutters. He lent his knowledge and muscle on all the things my dad would do if he lived nearby.

Four months after the accident, I didn't know how Ed could think about chores let alone face the neighbors. Brady and I felt awful that he had caused so much pain to another family. While we did not pity Ed his misfortune, we always tried to show our support for neighbors who have unconditionally accepted our non-traditional relationship. The loss of his arm was reminder enough of his adversity and Brady and I did not want to add more pain to his suffering.

Ed persevered despite the tragic accident. He, Sherry, and the family who had lost their 17 year-old son had reconciled and started to attend therapy together. While Ed had been just under the level of legal intoxication, the high school senior had been quite drunk. Tragic news in small town life always fascinated Brady. He would constantly comment on the media's dramatic portrayal of a situation and then the rehashing of it even if there was no new news to report. Brady wouldn't stop bringing up this accident when it hit the newspaper and TV. He would read each article out loud and call me into the room whenever a story adding nothing to the situation would appear on television. Not just because Ed was our next-door neighbor but because it was high drama for a small town like ours.

Just last week, Brady read from the newspaper and announced that the police were still unable to determine fault. A mid-night, mid-road collision that left one driver without an arm and the other without a life.

Ed cradled the rake in the crook of his left shoulder and waved at us. We had never seen Ed wear a prosthetic arm and figured it was his daily reminder and self-punishment.

While we would usually stop and visit, Ed must have sensed that our evening walk was more serious than social and he did not greet us further.

Brady and I have always been very comfortable in our silence. Our walks would sometimes be filled with anecdotes about the day's activities or what one of us had heard about one of the neighbors, or who we saw doing what in their yard on our return drive from work, but other times were spent with only a word or two spoken. Our quiet walks were a down time when our souls held hands and no words were necessary.

As we approached the Lynch house, a few past the Wileys', our first words of the walk were spoken. Brady kept his gaze forward and started as if he had practiced his speech in front of the bathroom mirror. "I've been avoiding saying something to you. And I know that you know that something's been bothering me."

He was right.

Across the street, Mrs. Kohler peeked through her living room window curtain and the distraction suspended our conversation. Caught in her ritual role of self-appointed neighborhood surveillance chief, she let the lace drape return to its limp position. Brady and I looked away from her house so as not to further embarrass her poor espionage methods. Looking at the sidewalk ahead of us, we grinned and our shoulders touched. After ten years together, accidental brushes of physical contact still raced charges of energy through my body.

The Kohler house had always been the one the neighborhood kids would quickly ride their bikes past. For years, the rumor had been that if kids got caught peeking into the Kohlers' property they would be chased with a swinging shovel followed by a personal visit to each of their houses with reports to their parents of voyeurism, intent to steal property and/or spitting on the Kohlers' plants.

Mrs. Kohler's husband slipped on their icy driveway two winters ago and died. We learned from the Wileys that Mr. Kohler had twisted his ankle and, when he fell, hit his head on the frozen pavement. He died a couple of minutes later. But among the neighborhood kids, the rumor was that he had slipped while swinging a shovel wildly at a boy who had fallen into one of their bushes. Brady was popular with the neighborhood children and was always invited to join them in street football and hockey. With that playful connection he was also a joker and he innocently started the rumor about the swinging shovel with the kids across the street, knowing that it would reach all of the others as quickly as flu spreads in a second grade classroom. He had hoped that it would also protect Mrs. Kohler's privacy while she mourned.

Since her husband's death, Mrs. Kohler had not felt direct rays of the sun or moon, or rain or snow. The closest that she had stepped outside her home was when she ventured into her three-season room that overlooked her backyard garden. Layers of thick chicken-wire screen replaced glass in the windows and protected her from the elements and possible intruders.

Brady had approached Mrs. Kohler's door shortly after the winter thaw to offer his green thumb. He went to her house when he recognized a familiar car in the driveway to ensure someone else's presence and support. It was Mrs. Kohler's daughter who lived near downtown who opened the door. She told Brady that his offer was very generous, but said she and her family planned to come by and tend to the yard work and matters concerning her mother. When Brady returned home, he looked frantic and told me that Mrs. Kohler had chased him off her property trying to hit him with a swinging shovel. For a single instant I believed him.

"I know something's been up with you," I said. "But I knew you would eventually tell me what's going on." I wanted to look at him, to hold his hand, to put my arm around him, but public affection always made him tense.

We were again interrupted by screams coming from the Van Winkle house across the street: another one of Jim and Nancy's contests to see who could shout the most obscene and graphic words. No one ever won that contest. It amazed me that they never even cared to close their windows when they fought. As I strained my eyes towards their house without my head moving in that direction, I could see Brianna, their nine year old girl, on their front stoop. With her arms embracing her knees, she stared at her bare feet or maybe the neglected weeds coming up in the cement cracks of the walkway toward the house. Her older brother, Simon, who had sat on that same stoop and smoked dope, had been declared impossible to manage and become a ward of the State last year.

Brianna looked over at us with discomfort and helplessness. She used to step off the school bus beaming and tell us how well she was doing in school or her about part in the school play. We gave encouraging words of support and cheered her on.

After Simon was no longer in their house, Brianna had come by while we shoveled snow from the driveway and the sidewalk. She had been asked to read a report in front of the entire class. The excitement in her face could have melted all the snow on the block. Brady congratulated Brianna and commented that it was too bad we couldn't attend the program and hear her read her paper. The radiance dimmed as she thought for a second. She told us her parents were invited and that she was going to also get an award from the principal, but her parents didn't want to take time off work to go. I suggested she come back over and read the report to us sometime soon.

A couple of hours later that cold evening, our doorbell rang and Jim Van Winkle informed us that he no longer wanted us to talk to his daughter. We were a bad influence on her and we should mind our own business. I looked over toward their house and saw Nancy Van Winkle standing at the front door threshold. Through the thin winter air I was surprised how clearly I could hear her yelling at Brianna that if she wanted to tell people what horrible parents she had she could go live with her brother.

Now I smiled and waved to Brianna across the street. She grinned. Brady hesitated in his step. In that same instant the yelling from within the Van Winkle house ceased. Their screen door opened, Brianna was pulled inside, the door was slammed shut, and the screaming resumed.

Unsure what to do, Brady and I looked around to the neighboring houses and then at each other. Brady appeared anxious.

Making a turn around the block and slowly walking past a few more houses in silence, my lover, partner, and best friend stopped. I looked at him; his head drooped so low on his chest that his neck looked broken. When I saw a tear swell between his beautiful thick eyelashes and fall to the cement, I grabbed his hand. His deep pain so apparent, I wondered if my unconditional love for him was enough. I wasn't sure I was ready for whatever he had to say.

He didn't let go of my hand. Brady tightened his grip. His words were static, distant and lost. "I'm a fraud—a failure."

I sent positive energy from my hand to his—a heartbeat squeeze, a pulse of reassurance.

He released my hand and started forward on our walk again. When I caught up to his lead, his composed words continued. "I've lost the ability to make decisions at work, but that doesn't matter since my co-workers have just started to work around me and resolve things without my help. Someone must have said something to management, because they are going through the formal steps of performance counseling with me. Fred likes me and knows that I can be a great team player. I've always been a great employee—I've never had any problems." The three or four following seconds of pause were uncomfortably long. "In so many words he told me that he is sympathetic to my problems, but I need to turn things around—now. He gave me written notice that if I don't get my shit together, he'll have no choice…"

In that clear moment of silence I wanted to grab him and pull him to me—hold him in my arms like my mom would do when she knew I needed to be supported—and tell him everything would be alright. I looked at him and made a wispy throat-clearing sound to acknowledge that I understood what he was saying and he should go on if ready.

"I don't know what's the matter with me. I've never been like this. You know that. It's not me. I don't screw things up—I set benchmarks. I don't get called into an office and chewed out for being a fuck-up.

"Four weeks ago I was given a month to get it together. And, as you know, last month wasn't very productive for me at home, either. Instead of working late at night on the computer doing office stuff, like I was supposed to be doing, I would end up surfing the web every night and just chatting with people online or watching music videos on TV. I'm sure you know what time I get to bed each night. It's early in the morning. And now I don't seem to even need or want to sleep. In fact…" He paused and heavily inhaled a few consecutive breaths.

"It's ok," I told him, trying to be calm and reassuring. I wasn't really sure if it was alright though, and I also wasn't sure I wanted to hear more—at least right now as we moved past the people whose house was behind ours. We didn't even know their names, except for their dog Bailey, who yapped non-stop and would stick its nose through the common backyard fence at us when we were outside. These neighbors did not care for us, and had never returned a wave in the four years since we moved into our home. At that moment of our passing their driveway, they were at the sidewalk a few feet ahead putting leaves into a large brown paper recycling bag. As we approached, they headed for their garage, backs always to us. I was relieved that at least this was not going to be the time they finally chose to make introductions.

"It's not really ok," he continued. "I'm not there for you, Gary. I'm not here for you. I'm not here for anyone. Not even myself. I feel like I'm always about to hyperventilate and most of the time I wish I would... I... I think I've given up hope. I meet with Fred tomorrow and I don't think it's going to be a good meeting. I wanted to tell you sooner. I really did, but I didn't want to get you upset."

We rounded the final corner back to our street. "Don't you think," I said, "that I've noticed that something's wrong? That I already am upset? Not mad-upset, but concerned-upset. I have no idea what's going on in your head. I haven't been sure if it's me that is causing you stress or if it's your work. Or something else. Or many things. I've wondered for the last week if you are sick, if you're having an affair, if you're not in love with me anymore, or something worse—what that is I'm not sure. But, I don't know how to help you or us other than to be patient and know that things will work out like they always have. I've tried to let you know, with my little hints, that I love you and that I stand by your side."

He froze mid-step for a second—unsure whether or not he was going to stop or continue walking. I followed as he proceeded forward toward our driveway. He once again spun the rainbow colored windsock and sat down on our front stoop. I joined him. "It's not you at all. You're awesome. I hate that I am hurting you. I know you've been trying to help and that you think I'm ignoring you. If you weren't around and didn't love me I probably would have done it already. I feel like I'm a ghost—I could scream and scream and scream, and no one—not even you—would hear me."

For the first time in about thirty minutes I looked deep into his honest brown eyes. "Done it already? Done what? What are you talking about?" My voice trembled as much as my hands.

A souped-up Honda Civic drove by; a kid yelled something un-neighborly out its window at us. Just one more "thing" to add to our list of burdens. I hoped Brady would ignore the slur and answer me. We looked in separate directions and he started to rub his hands together. "I went to the sporting goods store after work today and was looking at guns. I picked up a handgun. It scared me how good it felt to hold, to grip. I looked around and thought that everyone in the store knew that I wanted to become a ghost and disappear. The salesperson was good at his job. He was really encouraging me to buy it and was even trying to give me a deal."

Brady reached behind him and dug his hand underneath the back of his shirt and into the waist of his pants. He pulled out a matte black revolver and, holding it like he had always had one, started to examine it—looking at it from one side, then the other. Frozen, I was speechless. I looked around to make sure none of our neighbors were watching us. I had never seen a real handgun before other than those under glass cases or attached to a police officer's hip. I had certainly never held one before.

"Hon," I said. Not sure where I found the ability, I spoke with a firm and caring voice: "Brady, you're the love of my life. Whatever bothers you bothers me. Whatever is wrong we can work out—together."

He set the gun down on the porch, out of my reach. His knee nudged mine and he took a deep breath and held it. I, too, held my breath. "Even when I bought the gun I knew I couldn't use it. It's not that I don't want to, but if I did, what would happen to you?" Brady sighed. "It's one thing to be selfish with my problems. But the thought of destroying your life—it would kill me." We both eased up a bit with a chuckle at his pun.

I put my arm around my husband's shoulder and drew him close to me. With my free hand I picked up his right hand and gently twisted his wedding ring around his finger. "We're together—forever. We made that commitment and I certainly intend to keep it—and I expect you to keep it as well. Let's find out what's happening with you right now and go from there. I'm here for you and we'll get through it no matter what."

I pulled him even closer and kissed his ear. At that moment, I knew that there are many ways people become ghosts. That we not only live in part as ghosts every day, but that we are surrounded by them. Everyone has something they want to hide or become invisible from—a walk around the block could illustrate that. Sometimes it can be controlled while other times the ghost is driven externally. In that respect, life is as much for ghosts as death. But for the moment, my husband and I would focus on life.

"I hate the rut I'm in at work," Brady admitted. "It's not what I've ever aspired to doing as a career; it's so non-descript and whenever I try to explain what I do to someone I see their eyes either glaze over or roll up into the back of their head. I turn forty next month and life is all over the place with me. The only good part of me is you."

I pushed my shoulder against his to give him a love bump and made him lose his balance on the stoop. He extended his arm to catch himself from completely falling over. "You *are* an old man," I said smiling. He was seven years older than me, yet we both joked about how I acted older. "I'm set up enough in my job that you can certainly work on a career change if you wanted. I'm here for you, Brady."

"I know you are. And I love you. I'm sorry I'm such a dork. And I'm sorry for bringing in this thing." Brady stood up and grabbed the gun. "And I didn't even have the guts to buy any bullets for it—it's empty." He held it with less confidence than before. "The guy at the shop said that I could return it for a full refund. Maybe we do that tomorrow." He opened the screen door and entered our home.

I quietly yelled through the screen, "We can do it tonight, even!" Hopefully Brady would hear the urgency in my voice—how much I hated guns—especially to have one in as personal a setting as where we live. I went into the house, and finally felt a little hungry. "After we go to the gun shop, *tonight*, how about we treat ourselves to sushi for dinner?"

While we were upstairs changing clothes to go to Sushi Masa, the best sushi place in town, the front doorbell chimed. Brady was in his boxer briefs; he held up his shirt pantomiming that he needed to finish getting dressed. I was without socks and shoes, but was more presentable, so I went down to answer the door.

Jim Van Winkle stood on our porch. His neck and face were red with anger and his fists were clenched. Not saying a word I looked at him through the screen. Our windsock was lying on the ground. He surveyed the street behind him and the houses to his side; seeing no one he tugged on the screen door and let himself into our house forcing me to take a step backward.

"I told you to leave my daughter alone and mind your own fucking business. We don't like your type in our neighborhood and 'specially don't like you talking with Bri." While he wasn't particularly tall or muscular, he showed permanent trophy scars from past fights. He also smelled of rum or whiskey or some other hard alcohol.

I was furious with his intrusion. I was also very scared and intimidated. This isn't how rational adults behaved. I started to speak with louder volume so that Brady would hear and hopefully call the police. "I hardly think that waving at your daughter is reason enough for you to enter my house uninvited and disrespect me."

Brady must have already heard Jim and came downstairs.

"Well, if it isn't the other half." Jim stumbled towards Brady on the bottom step. "You and your little girlfriend here need to learn not to think of this neighborhood and everyone livin' here as welcoming you. If I had my way you'da been out of here a long time ago. The good people 'round here are chicken-shits and don't want to get involved. So I guess I've gotta fix things myself."

Brady moved forward towards Jim. They were about the same size and Jim cocked his head down, like a bull, so that he was looking through the tops of his eyes. He pushed Brady down onto the stairs. "Maybe now you'll realize you're NOT welcome here. Maybe now you'll learn not to pry into my family's business."

Jim turned his back to Brady and faced me. He put his fists in a boxer's stance. "Maybe this'll learn ya," he said as he took a step toward me.

As Jim wound up his arm in preparation to "learn me," I saw Brady stand up behind him. Brady yelled in a tone I had never heard before. "Fuck you, Van Winkle. You need to get the fuck out of here."

As Jim Van Winkle turned around in disbelief, I finally got a full view of Brady. He held his new handgun with extended arms and both hands around the handle. I couldn't believe that this was happening to us—and in our own home. I stepped another foot away from Jim, but he grabbed my wrist and pulled me toward him. He swung his arm around my neck and put me in a neck hold. "Now what—you got enough balls to shoot me with your honey here as my shield?"

Brady looked over at me and I could feel my head becoming light from the hold. He flicked the gun tip from Jim towards the screen door and back a couple of times. "Just get the fuck out of here Van Winkle."

Jim grabbed one of my wrists and twisted my arm, forcing me to release an uncontrolled yelp. He took no steps toward the door and I couldn't hear any change in his voice, let alone one of fear. I think he rather enjoyed the game, like a dog chasing a biker. "Dude," he said. "You need to give me the gun or use it quickly or your girlfriend is going to be in even more serious trouble. You don't want that—believe me."

Brady's eyes jumped from me to him and back to me. I could see his mind trying to figure out what to do to get us out of the situation. Jim eased up on my neck but increased the pressure on my arm. I started to see stars but I worried that trying to fight him would end with either my arm or my neck breaking. Laughing, Jim said, "Don't fuck with me—just give me the gun. Kick it to me."

As Brady started to put the gun down to the ground, Jim let up on his grip. A new strength consumed me and I let all the weight in my body drop to the floor like a sack. Confused, Jim let go of my neck but still had my arm. Brady reached back for his gun as I hit the ground— I could hear a crack and felt unbearable pain from my shoulder down to my fingers. I could faintly hear two voices as I began to pass out. As I lost consciousness, I looked up and saw Brady and Jim both with their hands up in the air, Brady still holding his gun. Through our screen door I saw two policemen with their guns drawn.

Brady was kneeling beside me when I came to. Jim had already been handcuffed, and was being led from our house to the police car in front of the Wileys' house. Brady stroked my hair and spoke softly. "I am so glad you are alright. That was so scary. The paramedics are on their way to treat your arm." The pain had subsided a little.

"Nice neighbors we have here," I mumbled to my husband.

He responded, excited, "You'll never guess how the police got here so quick."

I watched as Jim Van Winkle was driven away past our front door in a police car. "Didn't you call them before you came downstairs?" I asked.

"No, I hadn't called them. And it was just luck that I had brought the gun downstairs. But you may want to take a look outside."

Brady helped me up. I cradled my arm to minimize the pain and we went out onto the front porch. Another police vehicle was parked in front of the Van Winkles' house and Nancy was being handcuffed. As was typical, she was yelling, but the police officer didn't seem to be paying too much attention. Ed Wiley approached our porch. "It appears that the Van Winkles are in trouble with the law beyond just being loud pricks. After the yard work I had gone inside, but when I heard shouting from your house I came out prepared to help."

A fourth policeman was walking towards the Kohler house and it was then that I saw Mrs. Kohler standing outside her home, Brianna in her arms.

"How is Mrs. Kohler connected in all of this?" I asked. "And, since when does she leave her house and venture outside?"

Brady waved to Mrs. Kohler, who immediately returned the wave. A moment later, Brianna looked over and gave a sad but thankful wave. Brady replied, "It turns out that Mrs. Kohler's self-appointed neighborhood surveillance position finally paid off."

Ed finished the story. "She saw Jim approach your house and then yank your rainbow windsock down. She realized that something bad was going to happen, so she called the police. Mrs. Kohler also heard Nancy Van Winkle yelling at Brianna about you and your bad influences and how Jim was at your place straightening you two out.

"After the police came, I went over to Mrs. Kohler, who was on her stoop. She's a really nice lady—just a bit nervous about being alone. She likes you guys a lot, though. Sherry and I have been friends with them for years and she always tells us how much she admires the two of you and your perennials garden." Ed bent down and picked up the windsock. "She also thinks this is a charming touch to your home."

Brady confidently put his arm around me, forgetting that we had company—and that I just had my arm almost ripped from my body. I reacted by pushing away from him, but didn't want to spoil one of his first public displays of affection, so I leaned back into him. When a ghost reveals himself to you, you don't want to reward it by retreating. Feeling like the walk helped Brady and me after all, I grimaced through my pain. "Good thing Mrs. Kohler didn't have her shovel!"

My Pride and Joy

Tyler Tone

Snippets of bare skin. Breasts exposed to the hot August rays. Naked shoulders kissed by the sun. Tattooed backs, arms, calves. Shaved chests, furry pecs, pierced nipples, others just little nubbins of flesh.

Flashes of color and texture. An orange feather, a pink tutu, white tassels hanging from nipple rings, a very skimpy red Speedo with a large white cross center front, a sequin bustier, a straw hat, peacock feathers moving in the intermittent breeze. All this stimulus and the Vancouver annual Gay Pride parade of the summer of 2005 had not even begun.

My day began, with foreign sensations on my body while I sat at my dining room table, with a half eaten zucchini walnut muffin discarded amongst the make-up strewn about the table top. My friend, a professional make-up artist, had made her way to my home very early to help with my transformation, my maiden voyage as a parade participant. A soft sponge massaged my face as my friend applied clown white foundation. She filled in my lips with a fine tipped paintbrush and then glued paper flower petals one by one to create a halo around my right eye. Paint blackened that eyelid which then was sparkled with silver. Hairpins dug into my scalp to secure an adornment: a large white Marie Antoinette-style headdress. The sage green dress, that I had spent the winter constructing, bound my torso. Once cinched into place, it reshaped my body just as the make-up had transformed the surface of my face. With some well placed sparkly jewels and comfortable yet coordinating footwear, the transformation from man to Vancouver Parade Beauty was completed.

As the parade advanced down Denman street toward our beach side destination, I was filled with prideful joy at the multitude of reactions to my costume creation. The eleven feet of light weight fabric that made up the skirt of my dress brushed the pavement as the lenses of hundreds of cameras pointed at me, state of the art, fresh from the manufacturer, the latest digital gadgets for that summer. Other gleeful faces aimed their point and shoot disposables. All these people wanted to photograph my pride.

Yet, I wore only part of my pride that day. The greatest manifestation was not on my body, but walking alongside of me, at times holding my hand, at times running ahead with a water pistol to spray admiring parade watchers.

My son, a union of complete desire. The deepest desire of a gay man and a lesbian woman to be parents. He was created out of an act of need, not an act of sex. The mystery behind his conception piques the attention of many people I come into contact with during my day to day living. Eyes widen and mouths gape ever so slightly as I launch into the well rehearsed story of his magical conception. I have used my hands to create many wonderful garments and costumes, but my son is my greatest creation.

Back at the make-up strewn table, as my new face had been applied, I could see my son struggle that morning. I wasn't entirely clear about what was going on for him and even more frustrating, how to alleviate it for him. He seemed excited and proud of the dress that I had carefully constructed for him out of men's neckties. He wore the multi-patterned garment all morning, as soon as he woke up. Yet as he stood in the living room I saw him struggling with identity, with societal norms, with his love for me: a man wearing a wig. I saw him wanting to do the right thing. I saw him perplexed and unsure. I tried to encourage him to talk to me about what was going on. He just told me to be quiet. And I have learned that this is his way of working things through. After the make-up artist's departure, I was able to focus my attention away from my new-found radiant beauty to his inner turmoil. He told me that he was uncomfortable wearing the tie dress that I so lovingly made for me. He said he couldn't wear the dress... unless... he had a wig on as well.

So I maneuvered myself around my apartment in the over-sized dress, with the two-foot high extension on my head to search out a wig for my nine-year-old son. I found a long bright butterscotch-colored wig that had been discarded in a box from a long forgotten Halloween costume. Together we combed the tangles out of it and set it with two colorful barrettes.

As my son and I made our way out the door to join the throng of parade revelers, we paused at a mirror to take in our feminine transformations. My son laughed at the fact that my chest hair was exposed above the deep neckline of the dress. He said that I didn't really look like a woman and wondered at my decision for designing the dress that way. I told him that I didn't really want to look like a woman; I just wanted to dress up like one. He cocked his head to the side to take in his reflection in the mirror, smiled, and agreed that girls have more fun clothes to wear.

I gave his hand a gentle squeeze as we marched out of the building to become a part of the color and texture of the parade crowd, confident that I'm allowing my son the ability to express himself in any form he desires. And on this day, it just happened to be our initiations as Pride Parade beauty queens.

The Bell of St. Michael's

Gary Craig

Yea, thou I walk through the valley of the shadow of death, I will fear no evil, for thou art with me....

The monks of St. Michael's in their choir stalls chanted on, but among the sparse crowd of visitors in the pews of the monastery chapel, Ramón Santiago only shook his head. Had He been with Anthony when the boy passed into the shadow?

Anthony was not his lover, only his most recent client at the AIDS project—but over the months the boy had shared his fears with Ramón, cried with Ramón, and finally died in Ramón's arms. Two weeks ago, Ramón had stood in another chapel among family who hadn't been there for Anthony and didn't want to be there then.

Though Ramón had prayed earnestly, God had not been in that chapel. Ramón had finally retreated from the city to this monastery on the bluffs overlooking a tiny coastal village and the sea. God did not seem to be here either.

The lector came forward to read the Gospel now. Ramón stood with the others and tried to focus on the words. But the lector's blond good looks brought back Anthony's face, haggard with the ravages of disease, but still with glimpses of beauty. The lector's eyes were blue, while Anthony's had been brown in spite of his pale blond hair.

When the dozen or so white-robed monks finally filed out, the visitors dispersed to their various retreat groups. But Ramón had come alone. Feeling dissatisfied and obscurely guilty, he knelt in the empty chapel and tried to pray. To him, his silent words sounded like mere complaints, and he felt no answer.

When he got to his feet, feeling older than thirty-three, he found a monk waiting patiently a little way off—the lector, still in his white cowled robe. *"Hermano mío, quieres hablar sobre lo que ha pasado?* —do you want to talk about it?"

Ramón's first impulse was to decline, but the other's shy smile turned away that response. Instead he said, "Uh... *sí, si no tienes tareas mas importantes ahorita* —if you don't have anything more important right now. And I do speak English."

The lector laughed. "Oh, I know. But I don't have too many skills to show off, so I try whenever I can. Let me get this robe off, and we'll go outside in the garden."

He hung the robe on a wooden peg in a line of others just outside the chapel, and led the way outside. The light morning breeze was cool under the oaks, but the morning sun warmed Ramón's shoulders as he followed through the courtyard and into a grove of towering eucalyptus trees perched on the bluff itself. Uncomfortable, Ramón stared out over the little harbor below and the heaving sea beyond it, trying to decide what he could say. "I don't want to take you away from your duties."

The young monk smiled. "I am helping with one of the retreat groups, but there's an hour before I'm needed again."

Ramón cleared his throat a couple of times. At last he asked, "Is it wrong to be angry with God?"

The lector raised an eyebrow and considered for a moment. "No. I hope not, anyway—I've certainly been angry with God." He frowned a little. "I got over it, at least mostly. I mean, the reasons I was angry didn't go away, but I guess I finally just understood that God is bigger than me, and knows more, and maybe there're reasons I can't understand why things have to be that way." Then he looked up, meeting Ramón's gaze. "So why are you angry at God?"

Ramón looked away, trying to pick his words. "A young guy I... cared about, was dying. And he desperately wanted some sort of sign from God—you know, if not for healing, some way to know that God at least... cared."

"Was he your lover?"

"No, just a client with the AIDS project—but he was a sweet guy, and he deserved... oh, I don't know, something. I mean, I wish I could have been his lover—I *am* gay—I hope that doesn't offend you."

"What? Oh, no, of course not." The lector waved it aside. "But, there wasn't anyone else for him?"

"Well, other people at the Project helped some. But his lover had left a long time ago, and his family barely even showed up for the funeral."

"And you—you don't have a lover either?"

"Not for a long time. I mean, a date occasionally, but then I get assigned to one of these cases, and it's like there's not time for anything else. I mean, that's my choice, I guess. But Anthony, poor little guy, he didn't have any choices at all. And God didn't seem to be anywhere around."

The young monk shook his head. "*Hermano mío*, did you never consider, you *were* God's answer to Anthony? God was with him all the time, loving him and holding him—in *you*." His eyes glistened and he blinked as he gripped Ramón's shoulders. "Did you never know that, *hermano mío*?"

Ramón shook his head. "No. No, I didn't." He swallowed, fighting off tears, and after an indecisive moment the young monk pulled him close.

Startled at first, Ramón slowly relaxed. With a deep sigh he let his head rest on the other's shoulder. The other's warmth seeped into his tensed muscles, and he started to become aware of the firm body beneath his hands.

Finally, almost regretfully, the monk stepped back. Ramón shook his head again. "No... no, I really never did think of that."

"Then think of it! You were there to be the presence of God that the boy needed—the angel, warm and strong, kneeling by his bed, enfolding him.... But now, I think it's *me* that's a little bit angry with God, for not letting you feel His presence more clearly."

Ramón smiled. "Probably He tried. I can be awfully hard-headed. So..." He looked up. "'Thou art God.'"

"And thou art God," the other agreed, picking up the quote from Robert Heinlein's *Stranger in a Strange Land*. The book had been fad reading when Ramón was younger, and he still remembered its fantasy spirituality—it felt good that the young monk knew it.

"So you grok that, too?"

"I am only an egg, so how could I grok in fullness?" That was from the book too, and they grinned at each other. "But yes, I think I do," he went on. "I mean, that's not the whole truth, as Valentine Michael Smith would have had it—that would be close to heresy. But yes, we can aspire to God's perfection even if we don't have it, and we can reveal God's perfect caring to each other, too."

Ramón met the other's gaze. "So—thou art God."

The monk looked down. "Maybe. A little bit. But all too human, too." Somewhere a bell clanged once. "I do have to get back. Come, walk with me."

As they ambled out of the grove toward the low, rambling buildings of the monastery, a breeze ruffled the monk's fine, blond hair into his eyes and he pushed it back. "Look, you don't have to worry about talking to any of the brothers here about being gay or anything. Many of us are gay too—I mean, don't get me wrong, we take our vows seriously, all of them—but we've, well, been there and done that."

Ramón grinned. "Vows, huh? I remember when I first walked up the hill from the bus station in town and saw this gorgeous place, I said 'Yeah, if this is Poverty, I want to see Chastity!'"

The other laughed aloud. "I guess we don't suffer in our surroundings—but it's true we don't own much of anything for ourselves, or... or anything."

They were approaching one of the rustic, heavy wooden doors that led to the library and meeting rooms. Ramón stopped. "Look, I'm sorry, I don't even know your name. Mine's Ramón. Ramón Santiago."

"Mark Christensen." He stuck out his hand, and Ramón gripped it. "Look, I'd really like to talk to you again."

Mark looked uncertain. "Well, uh... I'm scheduled for the rest of the day, but... well, yes, we could meet after Compline. The Rule of Silence isn't that strict, as long as no one else is disturbed. Meet me at the grove."

Ramón nodded. "Great! After Compline—I'll be there. Thanks."

Mark squeezed his hand once with a little smile and was gone.

Ramón wandered into the main building. The lounge outside the refectory was empty, but he remembered that the little gift shop by the front door was open two hours each day before lunch. Wanting to get something for his co-worker Lorraine, who had helped him with Anthony, he went inside.

A couple of visitors were looking through the small selection of books in one corner, and the plump, ruddy-faced monk called Brother Thomas seemed to be doing something to an account book on the counter, the sleeves of his robe pushed up to keep them out of the way. He looked up and nodded with a bright smile, but then went back to his work.

Ramón looked over various small craft items displayed for sale, and finally picked an owl hand-carved in wood—Lorraine had a fetish for owls. Then his attention was caught by a few paintings displayed on the wall. The first two were outdoor scenes which seemed to record parts of the monastery itself, but the one nearest the door was the most striking—it showed a white-robed monk, cowl thrown back to reveal a shock of wind-ruffled blond hair, standing in an arcade outside a row of monks' cells. You could see a part of a white-washed plaster arch behind him. He was looking down affectionately at a baby in his arms, and the baby's face was radiant in a stray beam of sunlight filtered through unseen trees.

Ramón stared at the painting. The resemblance to Mark was uncanny. Finally he turned to Brother Thomas. "Excuse me, but does one of the brothers paint these?"

"No, the artist's name is Gerhard Brandt. He does live here, but he's not a brother—he's the caretaker. Strange story—he turned up several years ago, made himself quietly useful, and eventually the abbot gave him the old caretaker's cottage, which he's made into kind of a studio. I'm sure, with that talent, he could do better for himself down in the city, but he seems to like it here. Kind of keeps to himself, but he really does help out in lots of ways. And he gives us these paintings to sell, as part of his contribution to the Order."

"So that really is Brother Mark there with the baby?"

"Oh, yes, we love that one. I remember when it was painted, or at least sketched… one of the visitors had a baby with her, and Gerry Brandt just sort of borrowed the baby for a while." Brother Thomas giggled. "The baby wasn't nearly as placid as Gerry painted him, but Mark jollied him into a smile eventually. Gerry has some more paintings in a little gallery down in the town, where the tourists stop, if you want to see them."

"Maybe I will—I was thinking I'd walk down to the harbor after lunch anyway and borrow one of your boats."

"Oh, yes, it'll be a nice day, though it usually gets pretty breezy in the afternoon. You'll enjoy that. And you'll probably meet Gerry himself—he's the one who takes care of the boats."

"Thanks, I will."

Ramón remembered to pay him for the carved owl, and took it along the arcade to his little room. He stashed it in his bag at the foot of the narrow bed and looked up for a moment at the simple cross which was the only adornment on bare, white-washed walls. Then he sat down at the little table and tried to work for a while on the training course he would have to give at the hospital the next week. He did make some progress, but thoughts of Anthony and, he had to admit to himself, sometimes of Brother Mark, kept intruding into his concentration. Finally he tossed the papers aside and changed into jeans and sneakers for the afternoon's sail before heading to the refectory.

At lunch, Ramón managed to catch Mark's eye for a moment and got a luminous smile in return, but there was no chance to even speak. He was disappointed—but at least there would be tonight after Compline. He stacked his tray with the others and headed down the twisting road toward the village.

Ramón walked out on the rough planks of the pier and found the floating dock which belonged to St. Michael's without any trouble. Three small centerboard sloops lay in cradles on the dock beside a hoist. The door to a sail locker was standing open, and a man was kneeling beside one of the boats patching the hull. He had a narrow, fine-featured face, deeply tanned, and dark curly hair sprinkled with gray. When he got to his feet at Ramón's approach, he was about Ramón's own height, maybe ten years older, lighter, but seeming lean and competent. He gave a brief nod of recognition.

"Santiago." It was a statement. "I'm Gerhard Brandt. Brother Thomas said you might be wanting a boat. Ever sail one of these single-handed before?"

Ramón looked over the boats' rigging. "Not precisely these, but close enough. Is it okay to take it outside the harbor?"

"It's going to be a bit of a challenge out there today."

"I feel like a challenge," Ramón shot back.

The other chuckled with a trace of a smile. "Tell you what—let me watch you handle it here in the harbor first, and then if it seems okay, you can take it on out."

"Fair enough." Ramón nodded. "Any rocks or reefs I should know about? And how's the bottom near shore?"

"There's one rock outcrop..." He squinted at the level of the water lapping the heavy pilings of the pier. "With this tide you should clear it, but anyway there's a buoy—just stay away from that. And the bottom's fairly steep—you can come in pretty close to the beach without ever grounding. But if you want to ride waves, go over by the point there. It's a longer run, with the wind on your quarter, and you end up in deep water again. That's my favorite spot, anyway."

He shackled the hoist to one of the boats, and Ramón helped him swing it out and lower it into the water. Ramón stepped down into the boat and shipped the rudder and centerboard while Brandt brought him a set of sails from the locker. Brandt appeared to busy himself with other things while Ramón was rigging the sails. Still, Ramón knew he was being watched unobtrusively. But Brandt seemed to find no complaint. He only came over when Ramón was ready to cast off and said, "If you do go outside, just stay in sight—if anything happens, I can always come after you in the motor skiff."

Ramón waved assent, and Brandt cast off the mooring line and pushed the bow out away from the dock. The boat drifted, sails banging, as Ramón hauled in on the sheets until both sails filled with a sharp crack. The boat yawed sideways for a moment, and then gathered way forward. Ramón was busy handling both sheets and the tiller while maneuvering in the confined space, but he had done this before. He took a turn around the small harbor, admiring expensive yachts tied up in their private slips or anchored bow and stern in the mooring area. There was a small fleet of commercial fishing boats as well. Then he tacked back toward St. Michael's dock, and Brandt waved his okay to go on out.

Ramón came about quickly, ducking across the cockpit as the boom swung over his head. On the starboard tack, he could just clear the end of the breakwater, but he had to lean far out as the boat heeled to the stronger wind. He passed close to the massive rocks of the jetty, their lower parts covered with seaweed and barnacles, and the bow rose to the first long swell of the open sea.

He let the bow fall off a point or so and eased the sheets just a bit. The boat leaped forward, scudding along the swells as if there was nothing it loved more. Ramón's eyes narrowed as he watched the leading edges of the sails. He leaned well back, controlling the boat with his body, exhilarated by the rush of wind and spray. He didn't feel cold at all. In the momentary lee of a trough between the swells he managed to pull his shirt off and fling it into the bow. Then, as the boat rose and heeled over more strongly, he leaned out again, feeling the sun on his shoulders and his smooth, broad chest.

When he could spare an instant to look, he could see a few tourists on the beach watching him. But he passed the beach area and headed for the point. Sure enough, the long swells felt the bottom there and piled up, sometimes even breaking a little before they swept around into the cove. Perfect, perfect. He sailed out to meet them.

Then, judging his moment, he snapped the boat around to the other tack and let it gather way forward as the oncoming wave lifted the stern. For what seemed like hundreds of yards, the boat flew along the face of the wave, before the swell subsided in the deeper waters inside the cove. Grinning fiercely, Ramón turned back to try it again.

He was by himself, just him and his boat and the sea. Not even any surfers had donned wet suits to brave the cold of the water today. For some time he thought about nothing at all beyond the next wave and the sensitive responses of his boat. As he was heading out to sea one more time to challenge another wave, a freak swell bigger than the rest rounded the point and raced toward him, rearing up to break. There was no time to turn and run before it, and he didn't dare lose way lest it roll him completely. Grimly he held his course, slanting toward the wall of water towering up before him. At the last possible second he slammed the rudder down, heading straight into the oncoming wave. The bow reared up and up, and Ramón almost lost his grip as solid green water poured into the cockpit on both sides. For an instant of panic, he was sure they were going under—but the hull popped out of the curling crest of the wave, seeming almost vertical, and fell with a bone-jarring crash onto the wave's back slope.

Ramón took a deep breath and shook the salt water out of his eyes. "Shit!" he said aloud. "That was something else!"

The boat answered the helm sluggishly because of all the water rolling around in the cockpit, but he was able to get stabilized on a long reach back toward the beach. The bailing bucket had been tied to the centerboard trunk, so he hadn't lost it, and by cleating the jib sheet he was able to free one hand to bail out some of the water. But his shirt was a sodden mess, and he had to put up with a now chilly wind on his naked torso.

By the time he had managed to get most of the water out of the boat, he was nearly back to the harbor, and decided to call it a day. As the boat ran easily downwind past the entrance buoys and the sun dried most of the water off his upper body, his pride revived, and he maneuvered up the channel toward St. Michael's dock and managed an almost perfect landing. Brandt caught the bow line and made it fast to a cleat.

"Not too bad," he admitted. "When I saw that monster wave come at you, I was already half way into the skiff—but you beat the bastard!"

"Well, not quite," said Ramón with a wry smile. "I'm afraid we've still got a fair amount of water to get out of this boat."

"Not a problem—just take an extra turn on the bow harness when we hook up the slings, and pull the drain plugs in the transom—it'll pour right out when we lift her up. But let's bring up the sails first."

Working together, they stripped off the sails, sprayed them off with fresh water, and hung them over the racks to dry. Then they lifted the boat and, as Brandt had promised, the remaining water poured from the drain cocks. They swung the boat into its cradle and checked the stays and hull, but found no damage.

By this time Ramón had started to shiver again. Brandt looked at him critically. "Got any dry clothes?"

"Y-yes. Where's that duffel bag I left?"

"I put it in the sail locker—you can change in there, too."

Ramón stripped off his jeans, cold and stiff with seawater, and his sodden sneakers. He toweled himself as best he could in the cramped space, but the salt water left sticky residues on his skin. He pulled on dry pants, a sweatshirt, and his spare shoes. Stepping out, he found Brandt mending a torn batten pocket in one of the sails.

"Well, thanks for everything."

The other looked up for a moment and nodded, but didn't stop what he was doing.

"Uh... I was looking at some of your paintings in the gift shop today. I mean, I'm not a critic or anything, but I think they're really good. Especially the one of Brother Mark with the baby."

Brandt's expression softened a little. "Yeah, I was pretty happy with that one myself."

"It sort of reminded me of St. Anthony and the Christ child, too—is that part of what you had in mind?"

"Maybe." Brandt bit off the coarse thread and knotted it. "Maybe so."

"Well... Brother Thomas said you had some more in a gallery down here. Do you suppose I could go see them?"

Brandt's expression remained noncommittal, but still he seemed pleased that Ramón had asked. "Gallery's on the main street, about half way back to the road up to St. Michael's, on the left. It's called Greg's Art Space—owner's name is Greg Knowles."

"Okay, I'll look for it. Thanks again."

He slung the duffel bag with his wet clothes over his shoulder and walked up the inclined ramp to the pier. Back on the street, he managed to find the gallery, tucked in among some other small shops next to a little coffee house. When Ramón let himself in, a voice called from the back, "Be with you in a little while."

But in fact Ramón needed no help in picking out Brandt's work among the other artists displayed. The subjects were more varied—there was one of the inner courtyard of St. Michael's, with the oak trees and the arcade running along the row of monastic cells, but there was also a pair of semi-abstracts suggesting boats sailing before a fierce breeze. And there were Biblical subjects, too. Ramón was especially drawn to one of the youthful disciple John leaning his head on Jesus's breast at the Last Supper. He wondered why Brandt had chosen that particular theme. He rather thought Mark might have been the model for the young disciple, but he wasn't certain.

The owner emerged from the back carrying a newly framed oil, not one of Brandt's. He seemed to be an aging surfer type, hair bleached almost white from the sun mixed with strands of real gray, all tied into a pony tail. He saw what Ramón was looking at. "You from St. Michael's?"

"Yeah, I was just down sailing, and Mr. Brandt told me where I could find these."

"Yes, he's really quite good, isn't he? I wish he could spend more time painting, instead of fooling around fixing boats and things—but I guess he does what he wants to do. Anyway, we've managed to sell quite a few of his paintings, for such a little place—some to tourists passing through, but some to residents, too."

Ramón studied the wall of paintings a little longer. He wished he could afford the one of the apostle John, but the price was far beyond his reach. "Well, thanks for letting me see them."

"Sure, any time."

As Ramón trudged up St. Michael's road to the top of the bluff, he found that some of his muscles had started to stiffen from the extraordinary workout of the afternoon. He picked up his pace a little, hoping to have time for a hot shower before Vespers and dinner.

The refectory seemed almost noisy after the quiet singing of Vespers. Brother Thomas, face redder than ever from the heat of the steam table, served Ramón's tray and slid it across to him with a smile. Ramón looked around for Mark, but he was surrounded by two other brothers and a number of guests. Gerhard Brandt was also eating with the brothers tonight, listening to some guests without ever breaching the aura of stillness which he seemed to wear like a cloak. Ramón found a place by himself at the end of another of the long tables. Shortly, however, he found himself among a group of monastery visitors. Beside him was a comfortable looking black woman with thick, graying hair and glasses suspended from a cord around her neck. She introduced herself as Yvonne Jackson, up from the city like Ramón. "Where do you work?" she asked. "You look kind of familiar."

"I'm a unit manager at the county hospital," Ramón answered a little unwillingly.

"No, no, that's not it." She shook her head. "Don't get over there too often. I'm a hospice nurse. Group of us started coming out here, oh, a couple of years ago, to get, you know, re-focused. This time Brother Mark and Brother Damian are our retreat masters—have you met them?"

"I've met Mark."

"Oh, he's a wonderful man. So insightful." Her mouth quirked. "So pretty, too. Pity he's a monk! But I guess you wouldn't have the same reaction…"

Ramón hated assumptions. "Then again, maybe I would. I'm also with the AIDS Project."

"What? Oh…" She snapped her fingers. "*That's* where I've seen you—you spoke in the cathedral at the AIDS Memorial last summer. That was a beautiful speech—such restrained passion. Do you suppose you could come and talk to the Hospice Association sometime?"

Ramón looked down. "Don't know what I'd have to say. Anyway, I'm kind of… burned out, right now."

"Hey, we've all been there—that's part of the experience, too. At least let me have your phone number, so I can convince you later." And in spite of his protests, Ramón was not allowed to escape the dining room until he had written his phone number on a scrap of napkin for Yvonne.

Ramón stopped in the arcade outside his room and looked out across the courtyard to the eucalyptus grove on the bluff. What had he gotten himself into this time? He hated giving speeches. He was self-conscious about his accent, for one thing, and he never knew quite what he should be saying. He had spent days working on his short talk for the AIDS Memorial. The ceremonies had been carried on the local cable, and when he went by afterwards to take care of Anthony, he had found the boy in tears. "I felt like you said it for me," Anthony had said, and Ramón had answered, "I did." It was the first time he realized that Anthony was falling in love with him. It had been stupid to return those feelings—but he had.

Now he took a deep breath, feeling the pungent odor of the eucalyptus leaves in his nostrils. There were bird sounds in the distance, and the colors of early evening brightened the sky. And there was no one to share it with.

Well, at least he'd be meeting Mark later. He went into his room, picked up one of the books Anthony had left him, and threw himself on the bed to read.

Ramón slipped into the chapel for Compline a little late. The monks were already in their places on either side of the chancel intoning the opening song—he could see Mark's blond hair among the others. Quickly he slid into a back pew and knelt for a brief prayer, and then tried to find his place in the prayer book.

When it came time for the Gospel, Prior Damian got up to read. He finished with, "And if anyone would come after me, let him deny himself, and take up his cross, and follow me."

He closed the book reverently, looked out over his little congregation, and added a commentary of his own. "But do not feel that this sacrifice has no compensation. My brothers and I have given up personal possessions and many worldly possibilities, but we are allowed to live here or at least come home to this beautiful place, and have the joy of meeting and sometimes helping people like you, who have made your way here for a time of spiritual refreshment. And I know that many of you have important work and grave responsibilities in the world, and many of you have given up much for that work. But I believe that for you, as for us, the reward is great—that the sacrifice will increase the abundance of our lives, and that each of us will one day hear our Lord say, 'Well done, thou good and faithful servant.' Amen."

As the monks began chanting the response, Ramón turned over the old prior's words in his mind. Sometimes the promised abundant life seemed very far away—but surely, he had had his rewards too? Perhaps Mark would have something to say about that... he felt an edge of tense excitement at the thought.

And now the bell was ringing to announce the beginning of the Hours of Silence. The monks filed from the chapel, and with no sound but the occasional scrape of a shoe on the Spanish tile floor, the monastery guests dispersed to pray or study or sleep. Ramón stopped by his room, put on his favorite heavy lumberjack shirt, tucked it into his jeans, and walked quietly across the courtyard into the eucalyptus grove.

It was dark under the trees, but a little light from the young moon filtered through the leaves. Ramón made his way to the shoreward edge of the grove where they had talked before and stood looking out over the ocean, glittering in the silvery moonlight. A gentle breeze brought him the smells of seaweed and salt spray from the narrow beach far below, and he could hear the restless surge of the waves against the rocks.

He had begun to fear that Mark would not come, when a twig snapped and he heard the sound of footsteps in the leaves on the forest floor. He turned with a welcoming smile for Mark—but instead it was Gerhard Brandt he saw by the pale moonlight. "Oh... hello," he said.

"Brother Mark asked me to tell you that he would not be able to meet you tonight."

Disappointment gripped Ramón's heart. "But... couldn't he have at least come to tell me himself?"

"No. No, he could not." Then, as Ramón continued to look bewildered, Brandt went on in a harsh whisper, "You still don't understand, do you? He was afraid that, if he walked into this grove, he wouldn't have come out with all of his vows intact."

Shaken, Ramón frowned in denial. "I wouldn't have done anything like that."

"Maybe not," the other replied quietly. "Maybe he was afraid *he* would."

Ramón fought back tears. "No, no, it wouldn't have been that way..."

"Listen," the other hissed. "You've known Mark for a day. I've known him for years, since he was a novice, even."

"And wanted him, too, no doubt," Ramón shot back.

There was a moment's hesitation. "Of course. And *never* touched him. Why do you think he trusted me enough to come to me with this?"

Ramón felt the whole fragile, unformed hope crumble away to dust. His eyes burned. "But won't there ever be anything for me?" he whispered. And then, aloud, "Okay, I've got the message. Thank you for at least telling me, I guess. Just... leave now, okay?"

Without waiting for an answer he spun away and stumbled back into the trees. His shoulder collided with a tree trunk. Unable to go further, he gripped the tree and leaned his head against the smooth bark, crying silently for Mark, for Anthony, for everything he had lost and never had.

He didn't notice the faint crunch of footsteps in the dead eucalyptus leaves until strong arms encircled his shaking shoulder. He stiffened, wondering just for an instant if... but it was Brandt's voice whispering softly, "Let it go, younger brother. Let it go."

Brandt kneaded his shoulders. Ramón relaxed and let him do it. Eventually he let go of the tree trunk and turned in Brandt's arms to lay his head on the other's breast. For a moment he thought of the picture of the beloved disciple which this man had painted with the same hands which were now gently stroking the tense muscles of his back. Ramón pulled him closer, into a true embrace.

For a while they stood like that, not moving. But at last, though his front was warm where they touched, Ramón's back and shoulders were chilled by the cool breeze off the ocean, and he started to shiver. "Would you… like to come back to my studio?" Brandt asked softly.

"Yeah. Yeah, I… okay."

They said nothing more, but somehow it seemed right that Brandt should take his hand as they slipped through the silence and darkness to the outbuilding which Brandt had converted into a studio. Inside, Brandt went around and lit a few candles, revealing a single large room with a friendly clutter of finished and partly finished canvases, some other kind of project occupying a workbench, and a collection of tools. In the far corner was a low bed covered with a handmade quilt. A faint odor of oil paint mingled with the candle smoke.

Brandt came back and stood in front of Ramón, gazing at him intently, his expression unreadable. The silence stretched.

It was Ramón who finally reached up and very deliberately unbuttoned his shirt, tossing it aside. "Oh, yes," Brandt breathed. He took Ramón in his arms, taking charge again, stroking Ramón's smooth brown flesh, undressing Ramón and himself. He said nothing, except for an awed whisper *Was hat Gott gemacht?* when he slid Ramón's shorts down to reveal what was beneath them.

Brandt laid him on the bed, knelt beside him for a moment to admire the glow of candlelight on his body, and then stretched out at his side. Ramón closed his eyes and let it happen, feeling himself held and surrounded by warmth, finally penetrated by a stronger warmth which spread from his very center. There was no pain at all, only heat which filled him as they rushed higher and higher. The heat was around him as well as in him, holding him firmly, bringing them to the edge of the cliff together—and together they leaped and soared, gliding downward in great spirals as the unbearable tension flowed out of them, and at last they landed softly in the bed.

For a while they floated there, rocked gently on the waves of the passion they'd shared, thoroughly entangled, still wrapped in unaccustomed warmth and lassitude. Ramón slept.

A clanging bell woke him from a deep sleep. The first light of morning filtered in through the windows, and he gradually made out the cheerful clutter of piled canvases and work tools. The studio, then. The events of the night slowly reordered themselves in his mind. He turned his head to look at the sleeping body warm against his side.

Brandt stirred and opened his eyes. "That's the bell for Matins," he said.

"Do you have to go?"

"Lord, I hope not. Why do you think I never became a monk?"

"Why *did* you never become a monk?"

Brandt grew serious. "There was some stuff in my life that needed to be left a long way behind. Maybe I'll tell you about that sometime. So this is a good place for me to be. But I don't have to be a brother. This way I can do my work, serve the Order in my own way—everyone has his own ministry."

Ramón looked at him. "And last night you were ministering to me."

"No. No, we were ministering to each other. Sometimes I think sex is sort of a sacrament—two people together celebrating God's gift of life." The smile lines at the corners of his eyes crinkled. "Prior Damian hates it when I say things like that."

Brandt stretched and changed position, and Ramón put an arm around his lightly freckled shoulders. "So why did you decide to minister to me?"

Brandt raised his head from Ramón's chest and looked at him. "Mark told me some things about you—the caring you pour out on other people—how you needed just a little bit for yourself. I think he was half hoping I'd tell him to go for it. It was hard to know what to say, because I think I was a little jealous."

"Because you wanted Mark."

"Yes, that… and because I wanted you."

"Me!?" Ramón laughed incredulously. "You'd hardly met me!"

"Some people just strike straight to the heart," Brandt murmured. Then, looking at Ramón's expression, "You don't believe me? Here, I want to show you something."

He jumped out of bed and padded across the room, Ramón following his naked body with his eyes, admiring the slender, well-shaped form and the firm round buttocks. Brandt came back carrying a sketch pad. He handed it to Ramón. "I did this yesterday afternoon."

Ramón stared at him for a second, and then looked down. It was a pencil sketch of Ramón in the sailboat, his body taut against the force of the wind in the tautly curved sails. Sunlight gleamed on the hard planes of his upraised face, and droplets of spray glistened on his naked torso. The tension and the exultation were all there. Ramón was stunned. "But... this is beautiful."

"Yes," Brandt agreed, "you are. This was before supper. So when Mark came to me after supper... you see why I didn't know what to say?"

He laid the sketch book aside and slipped back under the covers. "Then he made it worse. He asked me to... bring you here."

Ramón jerked away. "You mean, that's why..."

Brandt dragged him back with a surprisingly strong grip. "Don't be so quick to be offended. I told him no."

Ramón shook his head, confused. "But, then...?"

"But then, I met you in the grove, and... I guess in spite of my own noble intentions, God brought us here anyway."

Ramón shook his head again wonderingly. "Thou art God," he said.

"What?"

"Oh, it was something Mark said yesterday. I was being childish about how God hadn't been there for Anthony..." He looked up to see if Brandt knew about that, and the other nodded. "Anyway, he tried to show me that God *had* been there for him, in me. So, last night..."

"I see. Well, thou art God, too. An angel of God, anyway. A bright angel...." His voice dropped and his eyes focused on something far away. "Yes," he whispered. "Oh, Jesus and Mary, yes!"

He threw back the blanket and pulled Ramón to his feet. "Here, kneel down next to the bed." He grabbed his sketch pad. "You're looking at someone in the bed, your arm over him maybe—yes, just like that. Hold that. Oh, yes."

He sketched urgently, the pencil flying over the paper. Ramón tried not to move, though the position was awkward. It was easier when he visualized Anthony on the bed, in pain but trusting him, gripping his hand, needing him just to be there. Finally the vision faded, but the warmth of his hand was still there.

Behind him he heard Brandt's stool scrape on the floor boards. "Here, look."

Ramón got to his feet and took the outstretched sketch pad. He saw a young man kneeling by a sickbed, gazing with infinite compassion on a boy who lay there staring at him. The young man was strong, muscles in thighs and shoulders defined—and from his shoulders grew powerful wings with brilliant white feathers, partially extended as if to shelter the boy on the bed.

Brandt put his arm around Ramón's waist but said nothing as Ramón stared at the drawing. At last Ramón raised his eyes. "Is… is this what you see?"

Brandt nodded. "This is what I see, and feel, and touch." He drew Ramón, still in shock, into his arms.

And so they made love again in the early morning light, not stopping until both fell back drained and content against the pillows. "God, I don't want to leave!" Ramón said.

Brandt looked back at him very seriously. "And I don't want you to leave. But my work is here and your work is there, and people need you." He relented with a little smile. "You might consider coming back, though."

"Could I? I mean… sometime?"

Brandt shook his head. "You still don't understand, do you? This year I think I'll be painting nothing but you. Of course you can come back, any time… But now you have just enough time for breakfast and morning service before you go. You'd better get dressed."

"Aren't you coming?"

Brandt shook his head. "If I sit there next to you, the silly grin on my face will make very public what should be private for us and God. Anyway, we've already said goodbye in the best way we can."

"Yeah, we have, haven't we?" Ramón pulled on his clothes, tucked the work shirt into his jeans, and laced up his boots, while Brandt watched silently. Then he got up, still naked, and led Ramón to the door.

Ramón hugged him close. "Truly, thou art God," he murmured.

Brandt met his gaze. "You, too. A little of God will go away when you do. Come back soon."

Their lips met quickly, and the door closed behind him.

The chapel was nearly full. Some people from the town had come up to join the brothers and guests at Sunday morning service. Mark and Brother Vincent, flowing white surplices over their robes, flanked Prior Damian as they swept in and bowed before the altar. Ramón listened to the chants and prayers feeling sober, a little sad, but also happy, ready to go back to his work and his patients. He noticed Yvonne a couple of rows up—perhaps he would even go and speak to her hospice group. He kept his eyes on Mark as his young blond friend assisted Prior Damian at the Eucharist, and afterwards when Ramón carried his luggage to the van, Mark came out to say goodbye.

"I hope you're not mad at me," he whispered.

Ramón stared at him. "Of course not. Thou art God!"

Mark's luminous smile broke out. "But I seem to remember you've been angry at God!"

"Not today." His grin faded. "You're a good person, Mark. Pray for me?"

"If you'll pray for me. Come back soon." He hugged Ramón impulsively. "*Vaya con Dios, hermano mío.*"

As Ramón threw his bag into the van and climbed in beside Brother Thomas, the bell of St. Michael's clanged to call the people of God to their next tasks.

So What is the Charm?

Bert Herrman

A charmed life is a life of faith, though not necessarily one of religious faith. What matters is authenticity.

The authentic life appears to outsiders to be a charmed life and appears to carry some magic quotient. And it does. But to those inside the circle it is perfectly natural. The gifts of spirit (God, if you wish) are the natural path of those who endeavor to make themselves, in the here and now, more "Christ-like"—the term mystics in the Christian tradition have employed for fulfillment of the spiritual quest. But this concept transcends any particular religion. To be Christ-like, Buddha-like or G*d-like is to recognize the oneness of all things and hence to live as a fountain of love; to serve others rather than to serve oneself; to forgive others their trespasses; to let go of fear, anger and hatred before it collects; and not to judge others, but to accept them as they are, a natural part of the universe.

When one has cleared most of the negativity out of their person, one then is able to access soul, the inner programming of spirit that lies tapped or untapped in each of us. This is not magic; it just seems so because it's beyond access to people still blocked by negativity and greed. The one who has the most toys when he dies is not, by any means, the winner!

Walt Whitman's physician, Richard Maurice Bucke, published a landmark book in 1898, titled *Cosmic Consciousness: A Study in the Evolution of the Human Mind*. In this work he describes individuals through history who appear to have reached this state.

Illumination or Cosmic Consciousness, as Bucke called it, is a level of consciousness "which enables man to realize the oneness of the Universe, to sense the presence in it and throughout it of the Creator, to be free of all fears of evil, of disaster or death, to comprehend that Love is the rule and the basis of the Cosmos."

As Bucke observed, few individuals flower into Cosmic Consciousness before their 30's or 40's, but they have usually grown up with a strong parent or parents instilling in them solid ethical values. Compassion and ethics (not to be confused with morality) are the earmarks of spiritual consciousness. Interestingly, a number of the people that Bucke discusses in *Cosmic Consciousness* are now known to be homosexual, including Socrates, Walt Whitman and Edward Carpenter.

I would not suggest that being gay in itself automatically leads to such consciousness, but it does set one apart and gets one to thinking and exploring. It also allows one to diverge from society's standards of masculinity and femininity that keep individuals from personal balance. I would also suggest that following lock-step the standards of the general culture, marrying and raising a family, often side-steps one from the necessary introspection to reach such consciousness. Freeing oneself from the obsession of "normalcy" can be a key step in achieving Illumination.

Psychology, religion, philosophy and metaphysics, disciplines that have become more conjoined in recent years, provide explanations and clues to charmed, happy lives, but the true secrets are learned in silence as an individual delves into his or her personal underlying instructions, their soul if you wish, that offer the unique day to day path each individual must follow to find his or her authenticity and completeness. The psychologist Abraham Maslow termed this "self-actualization."

Our souls guide us to select which of the massive number of incoming thoughts we choose to focus upon. Metaphysicians of the 20th century explain how from the input we take in and how we select, analyze and shape it, "we create our own reality." Our lives follow our thoughts and what we allow into our reality shapes that reality. Gautama the Buddha, one of those people Bucke identified, explained centuries ago that most individuals travel in the stream of Samsara or suffering, but a few raise themselves out of Samsara into Nirvana, the stream of bliss. But Samsara and Nirvana are concomitant. They both exist at the same time. The difference is not in the historic world in which one exists, but where one's mind is. One's mind subsequently shapes one's personal history.

Living a charmed life does not mean one does not have crises, challenges or even good health. The presence of pain can "make one a pain" or it can challenge one to separate themselves from the pain so they can deal at a level of compassion and teach that compassion to those around them. Those gay men and lesbians who so magnificently cared for our dying during the plague years could clearly distinguish those who merely suffered from those who inspired by their example.

Socrates said, "The unexamined life is not worth living." Coming out requires such self-examination. Gay people who have learned to accept and rejoice in their gayness have taken the first step in accepting their uniqueness, and if they should continue to explore and accept their authenticity, they may be on the requisite path for true happiness.

Grace is not really magic, it is a natural state of being, but for those who reach it, it works like a charm.

...and, finally

In preparation for the Gay Spirituality Summit in 2004, Michael Sigmann invited the members of the Ritual Planning Committee to summarize their hopes and expectations for the Summit in a word or phrase that signified "gay spirit." Sigmann arranged these into a poetical and surprisingly meaningful statement about the charm of gay life.

Listen
Don't go back to sleep
Love
Represented by being
And the light that is free
Ride the wave
Follow the curve
Into the circle
Whole and open
Tell me your truth
In Solidarity
Respect
The threads of connection
Hand over hand over hand
Blue sky
Thank you for holding me
Now
In peace, we relax together
Like a still pool of water
Surrounded by the bushes and trees
Of all our ancestors
Smiling
Blessing
From that thin space between worlds
You are safe
To feel the fire
Where hope is challenged
We work to be present
Getting to know each other

The Authors

Mark Abramson is best known as a producer of Men Behind Bars and mega-dance parties Pier Pressure and High Tea. His work has appeared in Christopher Street Magazine and many of the gay periodicals of its era. More recently, he has written for the White Crane Journal and the Advocate on-line. He is currently finishing *Sustiva Dreams*, one of a series of novels set in the present day Castro district, while also editing copious volumes of his hand-written San Francisco diaries, unearthing stories since the days of such notorious friends as the late John Preston and Al Parker. He appears regularly in San Francisco at Smack Dab at Magnet, 4122 18th St. www.magnetsf.org

Eric Andrews-Katz has been writing since he could hold a pen. He studied journalism and creative writing at the University of South Florida and eventually moved back to Gainesville where he attended the Florida School of Massage. He has a successful Licensed Massage Practice and currently, with his partner, calls Seattle home. After three years of writing for a website (under the name Michael Young) Eric has finished his first book *Magdalene* and his second novel, a spy-parody called *The Jesus Injection*. His story, "Mr. Grimm's Faery Tale" will be published in the upcoming anthology, *So Fey: Queer Fairy Fiction* (Haworth Press, July 2007).

Victor J. Banis, a lecturer, writing instructor, and an early fighter for gay rights and freedom of the press, is the critically acclaimed author ("a master storyteller..." Publishers Weekly) of more than 140 books, fiction and non-fiction, and his verse and short pieces have appeared in numerous journals and reviews, including *Blithe House Quarterly* and several anthologies, among them *Cowboys: Gay Erotic Tales* (Cleis, 2006) and *Paws and Reflect* (Alyson, 2006). A native of Ohio, and longtime Californian, he lives and writes now in West Virginia's beautiful blue ridge.

Jeffery Beam is the author of nine books of poetry including *Midwinter Fires, The Fountain, An Elizabethan Bestiary: Retold, Jeffery Beam's Allnatural Heatsensitive Ganeshaapproved Zuppapoetica AlphabeatSpiritbodySoup*, two online books, and a spoken word audio collection, *What We Have Lost: New & Selected Poems 1977 – 2001*. Born and raised in Kannapolis, NC, Beam now lives in Hillsborough, NC and Austin, TX with his partner of 27 years, Stanley Finch. He serves as poetry editor for *Oyster Boy Review* and contributing editor to *Arabesques Review*. He works as the Assistant to the Biology Librarian in the Botany Library at the University of North Carolina at Chapel Hill. His website is www.unc.edu/~jeffbeam/index.html.

Bill Blackburn is the principal of Building Community with Heart. He works in community organizing, HIV prevention, integral diversity, and cultural change. He is a student of evolutionary consciousness, a teacher of consensus and circle processes, and a leader of intimacy, heart, and healing experiences for the gaybiqueer men's community. Bill has been active in the LGBT liberation movement since 1978 and the broader peace and social justice movement since 1983. He presented his story of visiting Harry at Harry Hay's memorial at Glide Church in 2002. He's wondering what personal survival means unless we turn this Titanic culture away from the frosty fate that's looming. He lives in Sonoma County, California, and can be reached at bheart@sonic.net.

Donald L. Boisvert (PhD, University of Ottawa) teaches in the Department of Religion at Concordia University in Montreal. He is the author of *Out On Holy Ground: Meditations On Gay Men's Spirituality* (The Pilgrim Press, 2000), and *Sanctity And Male Desire: A Gay Reading Of Saints* (The Pilgrim Press, 2004), which was a finalist for the Lambda Literary Award. He has also co-edited *Gay Catholic Priests And Clerical Sexual Misconduct: Breaking The Silence* with Robert E. Goss (Haworth Press, 2005). Dr. Boisvert has served for many years as Co-chair of the Gay Men's Issues in Religion Group of the American Academy of Religion.

Perry Brass co-edited New York's Gay Liberation Front newspaper *Come Out!* in the late 60s. In 1972 with with two friends he started the Gay Men's Health Project Clinic, the first clinic for gay men on the East Coast. He has published 14 books including *How to Survive Your Own Gay Life* and *The Substance of God, A Spiritual Thriller.* His newest title is *Carnal Sacraments, An Historical Novel of the Future.* www.perrybrass.com.

Don Clark, PhD lives in San Francisco, California with his husband of twenty years, Dr. Michael A. Graves. Dr. Clark is a Fellow and Lifetime Member of the American Psychological Association. Since 1966, he has published both fiction and non-fiction, including his classic *Loving Someone Gay,* in print continuously since 1977 and now in its fourth edition, *Living Gay,* and *As We Are.* His recently completed memoir is tentatively titled *Becoming Gay.* More information about him can be found at DonClarkPhD.com

Gary Craig was born and raised in California, taught sailing on San Francisco Bay, conducted an orchestra for a year in graduate school, piloted small planes all over Texas, and collected material along the way for a hundred stories. He lives with his partner in Texas and, when not doing cancer research or teaching or rehearsing, works on the eighty that haven't been written yet....

JRG deMarco lives and writes in Philadelphia and Montréal. A former columnist for The Advocate, In Touch, and Gaysweek (NY), his articles have appeared in the Philadelphia Gay News, The New York Native, Gay Community News, and others. His article, "Gay Racism," won the Gay Press Association's Best Feature Writing award and was anthologized in *We Are Everywhere, BlackMen WhiteMen,* and *Men's Lives.* His stories and essays appear in collections including the Quickies series (Arsenal Pulp Press), *Men Seeking Men* (Painted Leaf Press), *Gay Life* (Doubleday), *Hey Paisan!* (Guernica), *Paws and Reflect* (Alyson), *The International Encyclopedia of Marriage and Family* (Macmillan), the *Encyclopedia of Men and Masculinities* (ABC CLIO) and others. He is Editor-in-Chief of Mysterical-E (www.mystericale.com) and is writing a mystery series.

Lewis DeSimone is the author of the novel *Chemistry* (Harrington Park, 2006). Born and raised in the Boston area, he earned a bachelor's degree in English from Harvard University and a master's in Creative Writing from the University of California, Davis. His work has also appeared in *Christopher Street,* the *James White Review, Harrington Gay Men's Fiction Quarterly,* the *Gay and Lesbian Review Worldwide,* and the anthology *Beyond Definition: New Writing from Gay and Lesbian San Francisco.* He currently makes his home in San Francisco, where he is working on another novel. www.lewisdesimone.com

Bill Goodman was born and grew up in San Antonio, Texas. He is an estate planning and probate attorney, with a special outreach to the GLBTI community. Dealing with death and dying has been a part of Bill's practice for many years, but his partner's passing has given him a new perspective and heightened level of empathy. He's also taken up yoga, with all its benefits for mind, body and spirit.

Michael Gouda was born and raised in London, England. After a change of direction he left the world of commerce and entered that of education and is now a teacher at a Comprehensive school in Worcestershire, England, teaching English and Information Technology. He lives in a limestone cottage in the Cotswolds with a very neurotic Border Collie (like calling to like?).

Will Gray lives in upstate New York with his lover, Gregor Benko. They have raised two boys, Will's son Ed and his nephew Ryan. They are now "grandparents" to Ryan's daughter, Katherine. Gray has written about gay parenting and adoption, and was a founding member of Center Kids in New York City, an organization supporting lesbians and gay men who are parents or are interested in becoming parents. He describes himself as "father, poet, lover and friend." He has moderated a web site for poets and developed a class for gay men who don't consider themselves poets...yet. He can sometimes be found at Easton Mountain Retreat Center where he shares his love of the richness the world has brought him and, occasionally, his poetry.

Bert Herrman is author of three books, including *Being • Being Happy • Being Gay: Pathways to a Rewarding Life for Lesbians and Gay Men*. He is owner of Alamo Square Press, a leading publisher of gay/lesbian spirituality books and ASP Wholesale, distributors of books to gay/lesbian bookstores. Herrman is a graduate of the University of Pennsylvania Wharton School of Finance and holds a Masters Degree from the Ohio University School of Communication. He has been a student of Zen Buddhism and New Age metaphysics for over 20 years. Herrman and his partner own a bed and breakfast in the mountains outside of Albuquerque, New Mexico.

Steven A. Hoffman has lived in seventeen states and countries and has been very happy to call Sioux Falls, South Dakota, home since 1997. He oversees a seven gallery visual arts center, a science center with three floors of hands-on exhibits, a domed large format theater, and a performing arts center. He has curated performing arts series, festivals, events and individual performances for over 15 years and has worked and taught in Chicago, New York, Ann Arbor, and Madison. He has been published in trade and literary publications. Since living in South Dakota his appreciation for country music, hunting, and fishing has grown steadily. In 2005, he and his partner Jason were married in Winnipeg, Canada. Steve can be contacted at SH.writings@hotmail.com.

Mark Horn has taught the oral tradition of Jewish storytelling at Prozdor, the high school of the Jewish Theological Seminary in New York. He performs in cafes, schools, churches, synagogues and festivals telling stories from many traditions. His writings have appeared in The Washington Post, the Los Angeles Times, The Far East Traveler, and MetroSource Magazine. He has also written many plays, lasting no longer than 30 seconds each, for broadcast on television (you might call them commercials) in his capacity as a creative director at a Madison Avenue advertising agency. He is the author/editor of a Queer Jewish liturgy for Pride week, *The Stonewall Seder*. He lived in Japan from 1981-87. In the 70's, he was one of the original members of the Gay Activists Alliance.

Sterling Houston has been working in professional theater for more than forty years as a performer, playwright and composer. He has written 30 produced plays since 1989. His plays are known for their biting social commentary, burlesque humor, and intensive musical ideas. His first novel, *Le Griffon*, was published by Pecan Grove Press in 2000. An anthology of his work, *Myth Magic and Farce*, was published in 2006 by NTS Books, an imprint of Texas A&M Press. Houston is Artistic Director and writer-in-residence at Jump-Start Performance Co. in San Antonio.

John McFarland has had his work published everywhere from *Cricket Magazine* to *The BadBoy Book of Erotic Poetry*. He has contributed short fiction to the anthologies CONTRA/DICTION (Arsenal Pulp Press) and *Boy Meets Boy* (St. Martins Press), as well as non-fiction to *The Isherwood Century* (University of Wisconsin Press) and *The Queer Encyclopedia of Music, Dance and Musical Theater, The Queer Encyclopedia of the Visual Arts* and *The Queer Encyclopedia of Film and Television* (Cleis Press). He lives in Seattle with his partner of over thirty years.

Bryn Marlow, writer, artist and clown, father and grandfather, lives with his husband Dave at Old Winters Place, a farmhouse situated on 18 wooded acres in rural Indiana. There they tend chickens and flowers.

Jay Michaelson (www.metatronics.net) is the chief editor of *Zeek: A Jewish Journal of Thought and Culture* (www.zeek.net), and the director of Nehirim: A Spiritual Initiative for GLBT Jews (www.nehirim.org). An active member of New York's "Pride in the Pulpit" project and a contributor to *White Crane Journal*, Jay is a writer and teacher on issues of sexuality and religion. His publications include articles in *Tikkun, The Forward*, and *The Jerusalem Post*, as well as *Mentsh: On Being Jewish and Queer* (Alyson, 2004). He is a Ph.D candidate in Jewish Thought at Hebrew University, and also holds a J.D. from Yale and B.A. from Columbia. His most recent book is *God in Your Body: Kabbalah, Mindfulness, and Embodied Spiritual Practice* (Jewish Lights, 2006).

David Nimmons is founder of Manifest Love, a national project helping gay men find new ways to be with, and for, each other. The author of six books, he was for six years President of New York's Lesbian and Gay Community Services Center, and won a Revson fellowship at Columbia University for his work on values-based cultural change among gay men. His article here is based on material presented in expanded form in his groundbreaking and truly "consciousness-raising" book *The Soul Beneath the Skin: The Hidden Hearts and Habits of Gay Men* (St. Martin's Press). www.manifestlove.org

Neil Ellis Orts is a writer and performer, currently residing in Houston, Texas. He has previously published in Concho River Review and Langdon Review of the Arts in Texas as well as in other places. His story "Grandfather's Photograph" originally appeared in LoopHole, published by the Columbia College Chicago Pride student organization, 2002. Orts also creates short performance pieces, which he has shown in showcases in Houston, Chicago, and Atlanta. In July of 2006, he launched the small press, neoNuma Arts, with the publication of the short story anthology, *Able to...* www.neonuma.com

Andrew Ramer is the author of the underground gay classic, *Two Flutes Playing*. He writes a regular column, "Praxis," for the gay men's spirituality journal, White Crane. His next book, *Queering the Text: Biblical, Medieval, and Modern Jewish Stories*, will be published in November 2007 by Suspect Thoughts Press. Ramer lives in San Francisco.

Michael Sigmann is the founder and lead facilitator of The Gateway— Men's Inner Journey. He lives in San Francisco. He was one of the organizers of the May 2004 Gay Spirituality Summit, held at Garrison, NY in a former Franciscan monastery turned Buddhist Meditation Center, situated—meaningfully?—across the Hudson River from West Point Military Academy. Called by Patrick McNamara's Gay Spirit Culture Project, in partnership with White Crane Journal, Gay Spirit Visions, Easton Mountain Retreat Center, Manifest Love, Body Electric, Spirit Journeys, and other community service providers, the Summit gathered "leaders, luminaries, and change agents" in the gay men's spirituality movement together to envision the future and the direction of the movement. Michael Sigmann's website: www.tothegateway.org

Ruth Sims is a 67 year old, heterosexual woman, married to her high school boyfriend for 46 years, and a grandmother of three girls. In addition to an earlier novel and several short stories published many years ago, she recently published a novel, *The Phoenix*, that tells the story of gay lovers in the theater world of the late 1800s. She has four other novels in progress, three of which are gay and historic. She lives in the same small, very conservative Illinois city where she has always lived. Though she admits she is an unlikely person to be writing gay stories, her serious stories underscore her belief that being openly gay requires great inner strength and courage. www.ruthsims.com

Martin K. Smith was born in 1959 and grew up in the Washington, D.C. suburbs until '75, when his father changed careers and moved the family to Omaha, Nebraska. After college (for architecture) in Ohio, he moved to North Carolina. He married his husband last year at St. John's M.C.C. of Raleigh and lives quietly and happily in Durham. Smith has worked as an architects' draftsman, movie theatre projectionist, census clerk and hobby shop staff. He has written as a hobby all his life, and currently publishes a (very) nonprofit regional literary magazine, The Blotter (www.blotterrag.com).

Dan Stone supports his lifelong learning habit by working as an educator, freelance writer/editor, and coach. His work has appeared in *White Crane Journal, A&U Magazine, Astropoetica, Bay Windows, Chiron Review, Queer Poets Journal, Brave New Tick*, as well as *Gents, Badboys, and Barbarians: New Gay Male Poetry*, and *Rebel Yell: Stories by Contemporary Southern Gay Authors*. He lives in the Denver area and can be reached via e-mail at dan@dansville.net or at www.successalliances.com.

Mark Thompson is a writer, editor, and therapist. His books include *Gay Spirit, Gay Soul,* and *Gay Body.* He was for many years an editor at *The Advocate.* **The Rev. Canon Malcolm Boyd** is the author of the spiritual classic, *Are You Running With Me, Jesus?,* and 30 other books. He is the poet-writer in residence at Los Angeles' Episcopal Cathedral Center of St. Paul. They live in the Silver Lake area of Los Angeles.

Jim Toevs came out as a gay man at age 38. He was married to a woman he loved for seventeen years and is the father of two grown sons. Two core issues in his life have been accepting and celebrating his homosexuality and recovering from alcoholism. He recently celebrated twenty-three years of continuous sobriety, and lives as an open, happy, gay man in the village of Hot Springs, Montana. His passion in life is the reclaiming of the unity of sex, sexuality, and spirituality for all men and women on the Planet.

Tyler Tone lives in Vancouver. An avid reader, he has dabbled in writing short erotic fiction. He helped write, produce and perform a gay men's Vaudeville-style show in 1999. For the past 17 years he has worked as a costume designer for theatre and film. His story came out of an exercise undertaken by members of a book club he had belonged to for nine years to write about Pride Day experiences of the summer of 2005.

Christos Tsirbas lives and writes Toronto. His work has been featured in Fab Magazine, on CBC Radio and in anthologies such as *Island Dreams: Montreal Writers of the Fantastic* and *Darkfire IV: Bones of the World.* He holds a degree in philosophy from *Université de Montréal* and is currently enrolled in the Second City Writing Program. An avid photographer, he is partnered to visual artist John Hyslop, a fellow shutterbug.

Jim Van Buskirk's writinghas appeared in a variety of books, magazines, and newspapers. He is co-author of *Gay by the Bay* and *Celluloid San Francisco,* and co-editor of the forthcoming anthologies *Identity Envy: Wanting to be Who We're Not* and *Love, Castro Street: A Celebration of Queer San Francisco.* He is the program manager of the James C. Hormel Gay & Lesbian Center at the San Francisco Public Library. "Reversing Vandalism" appeared previously in the may 2004 issue of *Common Ground Magazine.*

$\sim\!\!\overset{\cdot}{\cdot}\!\!\supset$

Toby Johnson, PhD is a former psychotherapist and past editor of *White Crane Journal* (where his contribution here appeared in shorter form in Issue #37). He was a student and friend of the renowned comparative religions scholar Joseph Campbell. He is author of both fiction and non-fiction titles including *Gay Spirituality: The Role of Gay Identity in the Transformation of Human Consciousness* and *The Myth of the Great Secret: An Appreciation of Joseph Campbell.* Johnson's mystical gay-positive storytelling is exemplified in *Getting Life in Perspective, Two Spirits: A Story of Life With the Navajo* (with Walter L. Williams) and the Lammy-winning sci-fi romance *Secret Matter.* He and Kip Dollar, partners since 1984, ran Liberty Books, the lesbian and gay community bookstore in Austin, and gay B&Bs in Colorado and Texas. In 1993 Dollar and Johnson were the first male couple registered as Domestic Partners in Texas. Website: www.tobyjohnson.com

Steve Berman has been writing stories both queer and strange for many years. He has had more than 70 stories and articles published and his work has appeared in such books as *Best Gay Love Stories* and *The Faery Reel.* His debut novel, *Vintage: A Ghost Story* shows how dangerous coming out can be. Steve once worked as a professional bookbuyer to expand his personal library and he now lives in Boston, surrounded by many old and odd books. Why not dawdle online at his website www.steveberman.com.

From White Crane Institute
in association with
Lethe Press

The White Crane Wisdom Series
—Fine books of insight, discernment and spiritual discovery—

Charmed Lives: Gay Spirit in Storytelling
edited by Toby Johnson & Steve Berman

ALL: A James Broughton Reader
edited by Jack Foley

The White Crane Spirituality Series
—Keeping cultural classics available through state-of-the-art publishing—

Gay Spirituality: The Role of Gay Identity in the
Transformation of Human Consciousness
Toby Johnson

Two Flutes Playing
Andrew Ramer

Gay Spirit: Myth & Meaning
Mark Thompson

...and more to come

For other titles of gay interest, please visit
gaywisdom.org
lethepressbooks.com

Printed in the United States
65233LVS00005B/1-78